Dear Cath

Enjoy that romantic escape to the sunny/stormy shores of Maine!

Lots of love

Carrie

(AKA Victoria)

SIRENS BAY

By Cassie Bruce

Wide Eye Press

Wide Eye Press

First published in Great Britain in 2024.
Copyright © Cassie Bruce 2024.

The moral right of the author has been asserted.

A CIP catalogue record for this book is available at the British Library.

ISBN: 9781738564101

Editorial Coordinator: Victoria Robson
Editorial Consultant: James Robson
Cover design: Amy Cox
Book Design: James Warren
Author photo: Emma Croman

For Oriana and Sabina,
Beauties, I love you so much. Big squeeze.

Chapter One

Bang, bang, bang. A wave of noise crashed through Emma's brain. She tossed over, pulling the comforter over her head. Burrowing her face into her pillow, she tried to sink back into sleep. Another, louder, thump yanked her back to the surface.

Where was it coming from?

A weight landed on her back and made her gasp. Bloody cat. Was there no peace? She turned over, gently pushing at Tallulah's warm fur. The cat resisted and pedaled her claws in Emma's tangle of copper hair.

"Ouw." She flicked her paws away with the back of her hand.

Emma wished she'd never agreed to take the cat, but Ben had left her no choice. How could she refuse a dying old man, her dear friend, when he asked her to look after his treasured tabby?

She forced her eyes open. Daylight winked through the gap in the curtain. Her phone on the nightstand read 11:07. AM. Jesus. She'd crawled into bed yesterday afternoon for a nap. She'd been asleep for more than, what, eighteen hours?

She rubbed her face. In the field, she functioned on scraps of broken sleep, late nights followed by early starts, and still kept sharp and focused. She wrenched her body to sitting, blinking. She blamed the drugs. The guilty packet of Oleptro sat in her bedside drawer. She had argued hard against taking them, but Louise had insisted she get a prescription as a condition of her return to work.

"Our insurers require a full medical. Get straightened out then we can have a conversation about next steps," she had said with a cold smile as she closed her corner office door.

Dr. Daniels had assured her the pills would help with her nightmares. That was true. Sleep was a black hole; she couldn't remember any of her dreams.

"Miss James?" A male voice demanded from somewhere outside the apartment. "Is anyone home?"

"For Christ's sake," Emma muttered, placing the cat on the floor. "Give me a minute."

Wearing Doug's favorite Darwin Buffaloes t-shirt that had been on duty for days, she stumbled toward the door, Tallulah at her heels. In the corner, the TV streamed images of a hurricane making landfall in the Florida Keys. A valiant, rain-battered reporter in a bright blue windbreaker talked earnestly to camera. Emma squinted and then rolled her eyes. She recognized the journalist's face, his sapphire eyes, and his chiseled jaw. Kit Renick. She allowed herself a cynical half-smile. You're so brave.

She had met Renick at the bar of the Babylon Rotana in Baghdad that cruel summer almost a year ago. From the safety of the roof of the five-star hotel with its panoramic view of the city, he'd filmed his piece to camera on the fatal bombings at a crowded suburban market. The explosion was safely miles away. Then he'd screeched off to the airport in the backseat of a Chevrolet Tahoe with blacked-out windows. He was the type of celebrity reporter who flew in for the top news requiring his face recognition and specific brand of solemn delivery. Not for him the nitty-gritty, often hairy, day-to-day on-the-ground grind of collecting news from the field, which she endured, and loved. He was for the glory only.

Emma rested her hand on the latch. "Hello? Who is it?" Her voice caught in her throat.

Since Louise had demanded her security pass six weeks ago and told her to stay away from the office, the only people she'd spoken to were Dr. D, twice, and hi and goodbye to an anonymous stream of DoorDash delivery guys. And the cat.

"Who's there?"

"It's UPS. ma'am."

Emma glanced behind her. The debris of a Korean takeout and a dirty selection of mugs and glasses littered the surface of the coffee table. Usually, her place was pristine, like a hotel suite she'd barely slept in. Whoever was behind the door didn't need to see her mess. She loosened the chain and stuck her eye in the crack. The courier pushed a large brown envelope through the gap.

"Have a great day, ma'am," he sang as he retreated down the corridor.

Great day, Emma mumbled to herself as she held the packet out in front of her. Unlikely. She frowned. Who was sending her tracked mail? A pink slip from the Informer?

She'd done everything they'd asked since the episode in the office. She hadn't meant to scare her colleagues. It was unfortunate that an eighteen-wheeler backfired directly below her desk and sent her diving to the floor, trembling and fighting for breath. Later, she had sat with her head in her hands, her cheeks aflame, and tears of embarrassment stinging the backs of her eyes. Louise had to explain to her what had happened.

Emma turned over the envelope. She'd worked for the paper for almost a decade, most of her career, traveling to all corners of the Earth, no questions asked, risking her life at times to be the first to the story. If they were going to fire her, they'd better get ready for a fight. She'd resisted medical leave, pleading with Louise that she knew that she would recover faster if she was allowed back into the fray. Her boss, never one to sugar-coat a situation, said, not this time. She told her she was a liability. There were HR hoops and she, Emma, had to jump through them, just like anyone else. Emma had left Louise's office, rage washing away her shame, slamming the door behind her before her boss had a chance to make good on her threat and call security—although apparently that had been the last thing Louise wanted to do.

Emma opened the curtains and let the midday light stream into her living room. She perched on the edge of her distressed leather sofa, the most expensive thing she owned, clutching the courier pouch. She wasn't sure if she wanted to know what was inside. She didn't know if she could take another blow. Loss had already mined a pit so deep in her stomach that if she fell any further, she might never claw her way out.

She took a deep breath, reassured by the thought that Ben would be spitting feathers if he knew they had let her go. He'd tell her to contest it. He'd battled against retirement until the bitter end. If he were still alive and Editor Emeritus at the International Informer, she could count on him to have her back. He'd always protected her, in the field and the office, while teaching her to fight her corner. Tough love was his style, but he was consistent and honest, reliable. You couldn't say that about many people.

Emma tore at the package to reveal a second envelope. Swallowing her impatience, she gently tugged at the seal. This was like that annoying kids' game of pass-the-parcel, where wrapper after wrapper came off until all that was left was a tube of candy. She pulled out a sheaf of papers attached to a courtesy slip from Guttman, Phillips & Schwartz, attorneys at law. A note addressed to her, just her first name, blue ink pen on heavy-grain white paper, slid from the bundle onto her lap. Her breath caught in her chest. She knew that handwriting. It wasn't a severance notice from the office. This bold cursive covered Post-its and notepads all over Ben's office. She unfurled the letter on her knee.

Dearest Emma,

Please accept this gift from me. There's no one else I'd rather leave it to.

See you on the other side,

Ben

She traced a finger over the ink and gasped for breath to stem tears welling. Seeing the loops and strokes was like hearing his voice. She swallowed against a ball of heat in her throat. What gift? Underneath the attorney's slip, she read the words Property Deed. What the hell? She slid onto the sofa cushion, her eyes wide in disbelief.

The document mentioned a plot of real estate named The Pines in a town called Sirens Bay, somewhere in Maine. Every summer Ben had fled the humidity of the city for two weeks of fishing somewhere up the coast near his hometown. He kept his rods in the corner of his tiny office at the Informer, ready to go. The vacation was his annual ritual, his retreat. She had an open-ended invitation to join him at his cottage, but she'd always been too busy finishing up a story or gone on assignment. That was The Pines in Sirens Bay?

Emma's eyes pinballed down the first page again. Ben had left her a cottage. Was this some kind of joke from beyond the grave? No. The letter was legit. What did he think she would do with a cottage? He, of all people, knew how she lived, that she was never in one place for over five minutes. Her apartment in D.C. was barely furnished, its sand-colored walls and curtains identical landlord-regulation decor as when she moved in years ago. She'd never owned her own home, and she liked it that way—no ties, no responsibilities.

Tallulah jumped onto the paperwork, pushing sheaves across her knees and purred. Ben, what were you thinking, a cat and a house? Emma looked to the ceiling as if he would answer from his seat in heaven. There was no answer, of course.

She would call his lawyers and instruct them she couldn't accept. It was too much. Ben must have other relatives who would enjoy the place or might even need it. She was unmarried, thirty-six, no kids, no aging parents, and no other dependents. She still had the bulk of her inheritance locked up in investments, had always contributed to a 401K, and the Informer had certainly made her aware of the value of their health insurance. That was more than enough security for her. A house would be a millstone around her neck.

Emma marched into her bedroom, letter in hand, and grabbed her cell from the nightstand. No battery. Tallulah sprang, knocking over the bedside lamp and sending a framed photo crashing to the floor.

"Tallulah! What's with you? I can't take a step…" Emma bent to pick up the picture, the glass still intact. Two freckled and sunburned faces grinned at the phone camera, the blue of Doug's eyes hidden behind his beloved pair of Oakleys, a strand of her hair blown by the scorching desert wind across her face. They both looked exhausted from weeks on the road chasing fighting along the border. Their last assignment seemed like a lifetime ago. It was not even twelve months.

Emma reached down to the carpet for the short strip of paper Tallulah was batting between her paws. "Leave that!"

Holding the fortune cookie strip out in front of her, she read the familiar advice, *Don't Be Afraid to Take a Big Step.*

She smiled sadly as she tucked it back in the space between the glass and the wooden surround, where it belonged. Dinner at the Chinese on the corner of her street had been their last meal before their flight to Istanbul. Doug had broken open his cookie and read aloud in his Aussie slur, *Don't Take Any Unnecessary Risks.* He tore it up, tossing the dry, broken biscuit into his mouth before he took a long slug of his beer. Faces flushed with alcohol, they'd laughed at their contrasting fates. They should have cried.

Emma sat on her bed, her mind whirring as the cat settled

beside her. Work, roaming the world reporting, had been her life. That was how she'd liked it. That was how he liked it. Now that life had shrunk to the size of her one-bed apartment and her one feline friend. Out of the corner of her eye, her open closet stared at her, stuffed with boxes of books, shoes, and a backpack of Doug's stuff she couldn't face sorting through and throwing out. A trash bag of her sweaters that she'd not seen in years lived in the corner.

She was sick of the sight of this apartment. Her solution to feeling low had always been to keep moving, but somehow, she'd stopped, blocked by the thought that everyone she loved, she lost. So, what was the point, the point of anything?

The cat stretched and repositioned herself on the pillow. Emma lay down beside her. *Don't be afraid to take a big step.* The words trickled through her brain.

Right.

Her hand reached for the letter. She was reading it before she knew what she was doing. Sirens Bay. Maine. She imagined tall pines, rugged mountains, the cold Atlantic Ocean. Fresh air. Emma had lived in the US for most of her adult life and never ventured so much as a few miles beyond the city limits of D.C., New York, and LA. She saw herself as a city girl, but that was ridiculous. Emma had been brought up in the English countryside, climbing trees and building dams in the little stream at the bottom of their garden. That was before her childhood came to a screeching halt.

What was Ben thinking? Maybe she should at least see the place. It would be polite, at the very least, to pay a visit. Ben. Her buddy. He was showing her a last act of kindness. Her mentor. A newspaper titan with two Pulitzers and a string of other awards under his belt and hundreds if not thousands of front-page headlines to his name, who still had time to lend an ear and dispense invaluable advice. A Vietnam vet from a small town who'd found his home at the Informer as a globally renowned journalist reporting from the front lines, an encyclopedia of modern international politics. She couldn't imagine him holed up in some dinky fishing cabin. What did he do up there?

She could find out.

It would be an adventure, of sorts, a way to connect to him for one last time, perhaps. Ben had family up there, maybe a brother? If he was still alive, would he look like Ben? Ben had so many friends, a work family of colleagues, associates, and sources, that he didn't talk about his actual family, and she hadn't asked. And, to her relief, he hadn't asked too many questions about hers. There wasn't much to say. Her parents were dead, and she was an only child.

Emma turned to the cat. "What do you think? Road trip?"

Purrs vibrated from Tallulah's body.

"So, that's a yes?"

Emma had the time. All she had was time. She was drowning in time. A trip could be a lifeline. For Ben's sake, she should visit the cottage and pay her respects. She had nothing to lose.

Chapter Two

Standing in the middle of her bedroom, curtains open, the streetlights fading to orange as the sun came up, Emma shoved her toothbrush into her wash bag and bundled it into her duffel. Was a trip really a good idea? She could call the attorneys and say thank you, but no thanks and stay home. She threw the bag over her shoulder. Every time she packed, self-doubt came knocking—you won't be safe, don't venture out into the danger, you don't know what will happen, did you forget something? And then something of equal strength—curiosity—always pulled her through the door. Her world was shrinking by the day. She really needed to get out of here and make it big again.

The cat stared at her from the bed, her yellow eyes round like buttons. Tallulah never left the apartment. She seemed uninterested in exploring U-Street and its rushing traffic. Instead, she prowled across the carpet like she owned the place. "See you later, Kitty. I won't be gone long. Two days max. Your tray is clean and there's kibble in the bowl." The cat tipped her head in that unnerving way she had of seeming to read Emma's mind. "You'll be fine." She'd have to be. Emma wouldn't recognize a neighbor if she bumped into them in the hall, and she couldn't think of a colleague she knew well enough to take her. "Anyway, they eat cats in Maine." Tallulah didn't look convinced. "The bears, I mean."

The weight of the canvas sack on her back was familiar and comforting. She was on her way. Except this time, she wasn't headed for Baghdad, Damascus or Istanbul loaded with a single change of clothes, satellite phone, charger, batteries, laptop, first aid kit, protein bars and bath plug, eager to see for herself what was really happening on the ground. This time, she had unearthed a pair of denim shorts from the dresser and a handful of t-shirts, like a normal person going on vacation. When was the last time she'd taken one of those? Cabo on a bachelorette party after grad school. She'd almost lost her mind with boredom sitting on a sun lounger.

Emma grabbed her keys from the hook. Going to places she'd never been before was what she was good at. Maine would be a walk in the park. What did they say about nature? It was good for your mental health. Dr. Daniels would be delighted. The drive alone would do her good. She thrust open the apartment door. "Alrighty, let's go!" She announced to no one as the door clicked shut behind her.

She'd forgotten the attorney's letter. Dumping everything in the hall, she hurried back inside, snatched it from the table and strode out again.

No turning back.

At the wheel of the Dodge Avenger, she felt like a ten-year-old playing at driving daddy's car. The guy at the hire company had asked her what she wanted. "Maybe something red?"

There was a pause on the line before he asked, "Size and make?"

"Something that will make it to Maine and back," she'd clarified.

The leather armchair seat had a 20-ounce cup holder to match. Nothing was going to touch her in this beauty. It was as solid as a tank. She checked directions on her phone and slid it into the casing on the dash. Twelve hours, give or take. She was used to long excursions to strange, sometimes hostile destinations. On this drive, she would not have to worry about mortar fire or aerial bombing, just other drivers, who were perhaps as deadly. As she pulled away from the curb, the prospect of a mission hummed through her. What would she find there?

Ben's townhouse on the Hill, where he'd lived for decades, was an Aladdin's cave of artwork and souvenirs from his travels. What had happened to that pair of dark wooden Igbo figures that stood proudly on either side of the door to his high-ceilinged dining room? Sold, she guessed during the house clearance, along with the beaten silver box from Khan El-Khalili containing blobs of crystalized frankincense bought in Muscat, which she'd always opened and inhaled when she visited. A cabin on the Atlantic Coast didn't quite fit.

On the Beltway, she let her shoulders drop. The car kept in lane like it could drive itself. North of Philly, the road narrowed to two lanes for no reason she could immediately see. The Dodge rolled to a stop. A guy walked up between the stationary vehicles to get a better view. She turned off the engine.

At first, she thought something was caught in the AC, a leaf or perhaps a feather? She turned off the fan. As the car grew hotter, the scratching sound grew louder, like someone was scraping the tines of a fork across nylon carpet. The clawing rattle filled her head. She swallowed down the panic rising in her chest. She could change a tire, but she was no mechanic. Stranded on the turnpike was no place to wait out the recovery service. Sweat tickled her temples. In that moment, she realized how rare it was to be driving alone. Doug was usually beside her, his boots on the dash, giving her directions, fiddling with the radio, talking rubbish. She missed him.

The car in front inched forward, breaking her train of thought. She flicked the ignition and moved. Try to look forward, Dr. Daniels said.

At the first exit sign, dripping with relief the car hadn't stalled, she turned off. The scratching had become almost frantic. Trucks and SUVs jammed the service plaza parking lot. Safety. Parked, she yanked open the trunk, ready to inspect. A blur of brown and orange flashed past her. She stepped back. Realization made her giddy.

"Goddammit, Tallulah!"

The cat scrambled under a motorhome. Emma stared after her. How the hell? A six-wheeler rolled past throwing up choking dust. Ben would never forgive her if his precious pet ended up as roadkill.

Shading her eyes from the sun, she tiptoed down the row of vehicles, softly calling Tallulah's name. This was why she shouldn't be responsible for things: people, kids, cars, or property. She crouched by the wheel arch of a six-by-six still steaming from the road, squinting into the darkness.

"Here kitty, kitty." Car tires flashed. Hot fumes caught in her throat. Her patience was short at the best of times, and this was not one of them. "If you don't appear in …" she glanced at her watch, "sixty seconds I'm going to leave you here." She coughed. "I don't have time for this."

Unexpected and unwelcome tears brimmed and slid down her face.

"Are you OK?" A handsome face stared down at her. The man's kind brown eyes looked concerned. Her skin flushed. "Can I help?"

"No. I'm fine." Emma faked a tight smile. "Totally fine."

She stood up, feeling ridiculous. She never used to be a crier, not even when faced with the evidence of horrific conflict and violence. She might scream or pull at her hair. She sometimes vomited, wrung her hands. But never cried. Not until now. Now, she could dissolve into tears at any moment. Dr. D said that was progress. She didn't see how.

The guy waited for a beat, unsure, before he backed away. "OK then. Safe travels."

"You, too."

She hadn't meant to sound cold, but she could look after herself.

Emma glanced over toward the Dodge, where the trunk rested half open, her laptop and purse in plain sight. Tallulah sat on its roof, cleaning her paws.

"That bloody cat," she muttered under her breath, wiping sweat from her face.

Emma leaned against the steering wheel, blinking into the darkness, her eyes propped open by caffeine. Bloody endless drive. Poor phone signal had frozen her map hours ago when they crossed the state line greeted by a giant green and white sign announcing: "Welcome to Maine, the way life should be."

Really? She'd thought to herself. How did they know that? She swallowed down her grief and pressed her foot on the gas.

Apart from the rare sets of glaring headlights that made her squint, they were the only car on the road. Maine was bigger than Scotland, she remembered Ben saying. Sixteen hours on the road and her ass felt like it had merged with the seat padding, and her biceps ached. She was supposed to have arrived three hours ago. There were always delays, a roadblock you didn't expect, a sudden sandstorm, a diversion away from an IED explosion, construction. She should have planned for a delay.

She glanced enviously at the cat blissfully asleep on the passenger seat. "You're not much of a navigator, kitty." Tallulah opened her eyes. "Don't look at me like that. You want out of the car. Me too. But some of this is your fault, missus."

Tallulah casually licked her paw. Where was Emma going to buy cat food and a litter tray at this hour? She yawned. Surely there would be a grocery store close by.

More and more road. Her phone buzzed into life. Shuttered outlet stores and clusters of overly-lit strip malls gave her hope they were close to civilization. Welcome to Sirens Bay!

She thumped the steering wheel.

Darkened houses with tall gables and picket-fenced front yards graced tree-lined streets. Two. More. Miles. Almost. There. On Main Street, a strip of cozy stores selling everything you might need for a vacation spent fishing, sailing, and hiking, a couple wandered hand in hand under the streetlights. Not another soul in sight. And no grocery store. "We're in the country now, kitty."

The car rattled over a truss bridge, and they were back to driving through woods. At a hand-painted placard announcing The Pines, she cranked the wheel, tires crunching down the gravel driveway. At last. The houselights of the single-story clapboard A-frame glowed like a beacon in the night. Ben's niece Beth had waited up. God love her.

As she stepped out of the Dodge, a rush of blood dissolved the numbness in her limbs and the sharp tang of pine and salt hit her nose. Something brushed against her leg. Tallulah's shadow dashed into a wall of conifers. Emma shook her head. What was wrong with that animal? Racoons and coyotes probably roamed around here ready to make a snack of a small pet.

"Tallulah!" Nothing moved in the darkness. Damn that cat.

Emma grabbed her duffel. She was too tired, and the niece had waited far too long already. The salt-rusted knocker creaked. No one answered the front door. She picked her way around to the back and stopped dead at the sight of the inky blue ocean rippling gently against the shore, its surface glittering in the moonlight. In the far distance, what looked like the beam of a lighthouse flashed across the horizon. And far above, a sweep of stars cascaded across the night like heavenly glitter powder. She gasped. Chin lifted, her gaze stayed fixed on the sky as she moved toward the porch.

Warm firmness slammed into her, knocking her stumbling backward and onto her ass. The ground jolted her bones. "Jesus!"

"Nope." A male voice was abrupt and accusing.

Her sweatshirt lay heavy on her skin. She was wet from her collar to its hem. Emma held up her hands. Some sort of sticky liquid covered her from chest to waist. "What the…?"

A tall silhouette stared down at her, backlit by the porch light. A guy, well-built but lean, stood clutching, she soon realized as her eyes became accustomed to the moonlight, a dripping can of gloss in one hand and the cat in the crook of his other arm.

"Is this paint?" she asked, globs of white dripping from her fingers onto the ground.

"It'll come off." He jerked his head to a bottle of solvent on the porch step.

"You sure?" Exhaustion ate her manners.

In the silvery light, he looked like the quintessential handsome hero of a Hollywood rom-com. But he did not extend his hand to help her up. He wasn't a gentleman. She clambered to her feet, grit and sand caking her palms. She stank of gloss.

"You're late", he said with a frown. No names. No introductions. No apology. Asshole.

"Construction on I-95." She glanced at the cat purring away against his chest and decided against recounting their service station adventure. She wiped her hand on her cargoes and held it out. "I'm Emma. Nice to meet you. And that is Tallulah." He left it hanging in midair. Emma continued: "Is Beth here?"

"The kids needed her at home. I came instead." Before she could reply, he spoke again. "Usually, people say thank you."

She looked down at her sweatshirt, her favorite, faded pale

green in the laundry, its cuffs fraying. A wide splash of white obscured the letters spelling out Columbia University. Doug had bought this sweater as a souvenir of her alma mater. Now it was headed for the trash.

"For waiting," he clarified.

So, this was the famous small town welcome. "Thank you," she managed. "Are you Beth's husband?"

He chuckled in a humorless way. "Nope."

Not Jesus or her husband. Then who? She waited. Nothing. "You're here doing repairs?"

"Something like that." He turned and walked toward the porch. "Maybe you want to change before you go inside."

His officiousness grated. "Maybe."

Unfortunately, he was right.

She didn't want to tread paint through this quaint, homey-looking place; which she realized in a flash, now belonged to her.

Standing by the Dodge's open trunk, every muscle aching and her skin prickling as the cool sea breeze whipped her hair in her face, she heaved the sweatshirt over her head and let it drop to the ground. Ruined. For a second, she thought she might cry again. The burning in her eyelids passed. Idiot guy. She glanced at the curtains to check for movement. None. Relief. He was an ass, but not a creep, it seemed. She pulled on a button-up shirt and stepped into clean cut-offs.

What a way to arrive.

In the main room, the contractor stuffed tools into a bag. He was striking—close-cropped dark hair, blue eyes, deep tan, fine lips—and a jerk. He dug into his jeans pocket and handed her a set of keys. His long fingers brushed her palm.

"I am really very sorry I kept you," she tried to start again.

In rapid fire, he pointed around the room. "Kitchen." That

was obvious. The small, open plan set up housed a refrigerator, a large stove, and lots of cupboards. Their doors and handles had a sixties vibe, harking back to the time when the cottage must have been built. The interior was meticulously maintained, just as she'd expect of Ben.

"Living room." He jabbed his finger toward a plaid couch set before a wide stone fireplace and mantel. A pile of logs stood to one side of a wood-burning stove. On the coffee table she recognized a stack of old Life magazines. She smiled at Ben's desire to keep a record of his work. At the far end of the room, she noticed the front door bolted from the inside.

He continued, pointing in the other direction. "Through there is the bathroom. You turn on the immersion here." He cocked his head toward a switch by the refrigerator. "And there is the bedroom."

"Thank you. Noted." She resisted the urge to salute.

"Beth bought some milk and bread and stuff. It's all in the refrigerator." He held out the cat, who squirmed in his grip. "I guess she didn't know you'd be bringing a pet."

"Neither did I." Emma stepped forward, fumbling to grab Tallulah, willing her not to scratch with her flailing paws. The guy smelled clean, of cedar and soap. The muscles threading down his forearms twitched as he gently placed the wriggling fur ball in her arms. Tallulah meowed a complaint, making it clear who was her preferred person.

"Phone service isn't good here. But there's Wi-Fi." He nodded to the router.

Thank God for the internet. There was no TV either. Ben weaned himself off the intravenous drip feed of the 24-hour news cycle up here, it seemed. She guessed spending time on a fishing vacation was a rare moment of peace for him, a couple of weeks when the newsroom slid to the back of his mind. Perhaps the cottage could work that magic for her too over the next few days?

At the porch door, the guy looked back. "What ya gonna do with the place?"

His directness caught her off guard. She stuttered, her eyes wandering around the room, taking it in. "I don't know yet. I've only just learned of its existence." She paused. "Sell it I guess?"

He left without saying another word, letting the screen door slam behind him. She shook her head, bemused by his hostility.

Pulling back the blue plaid curtains, she watched his truck's high beams shrink down the track. The night washed against the windows. She was entirely alone, except for Tallulah purring in her arms, in a remote cottage in a place she'd yet to see in daylight.

Emma walked into the kitchen and switched on the immersion ready to shower off the day. She wasn't scared; she was relieved. Quiet. No people meant no interruptions and no aggravation. She could be here and please herself. Bliss.

"Welcome to Sirens Bay, kitty. I hope you enjoy your brief stay here," she mumbled into the cat's fur before she let her down onto the floor. "Don't get used to it."

Chapter Three

Jordan's headlights strafed the pitch black. He pressed his foot on the accelerator. He knew the bends and straights of this road like the back of hand. Emma James had a nerve, turning up at midnight. She even had to be prompted to apologize.

Her English accent rang in his head: "I am really very sorry I kept you."

Yeah, right, she was. She probably assumed he was the muscle, there to do her bidding. Didn't even seem happy about the place. She never even once mentioned Uncle Ben and his kindness. There wasn't a trace of gratitude in her voice. The special charm of the cottage was invisible to her, it seemed. Maybe she was even a little resentful that she'd had to come up and deal with it. He'd shown her around out of politeness—Ben would have wanted that—and Beth asked him too, but she didn't seem appreciative of that even. Uptight out-of-towner.

Still, she wasn't quite what he'd expected. Tall, in a sweatshirt and cargo pants, with long copper hair and ivory skin, she wasn't the fuddy-duddy red-faced English woman he had imagined. She was maybe mid-thirties, with freckles and green eyes and a tiny scar along her hairline. He was sorry about tipping paint on her, embarrassed, but she'd walked into him.

Jordan sped along Route One before cutting down to the Point. The truck rocked on the dirt road. Ahead sea rippled like black velvet as the beam of the lighthouse swept across. God, he loved this spot.

Why had his great uncle left his place, the setting for so many family celebrations and parties, to this stranger, who wasn't family and was going to flip it to the highest bidder, and wouldn't be seen for dust? What was he thinking? Ben should have bequeathed it to Beth's girls. Beth could have continued to manage it as a holiday rental and generated some income for their college fund. His sister was enterprising like that. Trading the ups and downs of the real estate market along their stretch of the coast on behalf of her clients was her bread and butter.

If he had the money to pay the exorbitant price that its new owner would probably ask for it, he'd buy The Pines. Real estate values had soared in recent years, propelled by flatlanders from Boston buying second homes. He got it. Sirens Bay was beautiful. Surrounded by miles and miles of unspoiled rocky coves and sandy beaches, the town sparkled in the clear air. And the locals had a reputation for being friendly. If you could afford a bolt-hole, buy here, sure. It was just that the boom was squeezing out the lobster and fisherman, the folks that worked in the hotels and restaurants, everyday people who called the town home. He was lucky Lily let him rent the lighthouse cottage for cheap. She was a good person. She'd really helped him out since he arrived back.

Jordan pulled up, shaking his head at the memory. He'd been in pieces and Lily and Beth had picked him up, dusted him off and set him gently back down again on his feet and watched him as he learned to walk through life again. He hadn't wanted to go on, but they never let him take that path. There was a safe distance now between that place and where he stood today. He was never going back. No more chaos, nights spent drinking, days sleeping it off or glaring at the TV. His life was on a narrow, straight track now. He worked construction jobs for clients he liked, bumped his income with the carpentry that he loved. He had his art. That was all he needed. And his family: his sister, mom and nieces, and Mason, they would always come first.

Chapter Four

Emma stretched, yawned, and blinked against the golden morning light pouring in through the kitchen window. Outside, a yellow shimmer spread across the water. She took a long inhale of first light air and pulled open the refrigerator. Beth had packed it with cheese, sausage, eggs, butter, fruit, bread, muffins, milk. So much. So kind. And she was starving. Perhaps the locals were going to be friendlier than the contractor guy had led her to believe. There was small-batch ground coffee in the cupboard and typed instructions about how to use the espresso machine. Emma made a cup and drifted out onto the back porch with a giant blueberry muffin that smelled like it was baked in Nana's kitchen in her palm.

The air was so fresh it burned her throat. Firs so green they were almost black cascaded down the slopes on either side of the cove. In the far distance, she could make out the red and white dot of a lighthouse tower—she'd been right—and a little building, maybe the lighthouse keeper's cottage at its base. The bluest sea she'd ever seen stretched toward the horizon from the strip of shingle beyond a shallow patch of grass. At the edge of the property, right up against the tree line, a thin-hulled fishing boat bobbed against a short wooden dock, its pale blue rim cracked in the sun. She imagined Ben standing in the shallows, tall in his waders, cigar jammed in his mouth, sunhat on, casting a line. She smiled.

Sitting on the porch bench, she stared, mesmerized by the serene beauty. Usually, for her, a long journey ended at the reception desk of a two-star hotel manned by staff that rarely encountered a foreign guest, never at a destination like this. Ben had said that Maine would surprise her. She'd been a fool not to take him up on his invitation while he was alive. She'd never imagined such glory.

Walking inside to top up her cup, she took a moment to notice the simple décor so at odds with Ben's D.C. place. It revealed perhaps an old-fashioned or nostalgic side to her friend, who she never realized liked cozy plaid and wood burning hominess. And yet, it felt essentially Ben in a way she couldn't quite understand. Away from the buzz of D.C., Ben had reverted to being a country boy, it seemed, which perhaps he'd always been underneath a cosmopolitan veneer.

At the fireplace, Emma lifted a tiny frame from the mantel. In the yellowing photo, a very skinny guy, on closer inspection a very young Ben, wearing army fatigues and a press badge pinned to his shirt, lent against the hood of a jeep with his arms folded over his chest and a cigarette clamped in the side of his grin. It was taken during one of his tours of Vietnam. She placed it back beside another photo, this time of an older Ben with thick, dark hair and wearing a brown suit with a wide-collared shirt. One of his hands rested on the shoulder of a child standing on each side of him. They all shared the same smile. Could the girl be Beth?

At the wooden sideboard next to the front door, she yanked at a drawer. It didn't open. She jerked backward as it came unstuck. Underneath an assortment of string, paperclips, a dried-up tube of adhesive, erasers, and lots and lots of biros, she found a high school yearbook. Class of 1961. She opened the stiff cover, scanning the glossy pages of faces. It didn't take her long. Under a gray scale image of a very wholesome-looking kid with a twinkle in his eye, trademark thick wavy hair parted to one side, ran the text: "Benjamin Allen. Most likely to travel the world and make a name for himself."

Emma clutched the book to her chest and dropped her chin.

That couldn't have been truer. She let a long exhale stream from her lips. It was going to be tough sorting out this place. There were memories of Ben everywhere. She had the feeling she was going to get to know him a whole lot better, and that, perhaps, that was his last gift to her?

Her phone buzzed on the counter and broke her train of thought. A WhatsApp from Beth: Sorry about yesterday. Kid got sick. Meet you at the cottage today at 6?

Emma texted back: Thank you for arranging the keys. Apologies for late arrival. See you at 6.

She was curious to meet any member of Ben's family. Ben was a unique person. What would his relations be like, the ones he left behind?

Tallulah rubbed the side of her face against Emma's leg. She looked down. "OK, OK, I'm on it. Give me a minute and I'll see what there is."

Cat fed with breakfast sausage, she needed to go into town to buy Tallulah some supplies. As she locked the porch door behind her, Tallulah sat inside on the mat, staring up at her. "I'm sorry, but no outdoors for you, young lady."

Emma wound down the car window and let the breeze tickle her face. To her left, the wide expanse of sea rippled, and to her right, the emerald-green mountains of the state park soared into a cloudless blue sky. It was like she was driving along the seam where heaven met earth. Last night, hidden by the dark, she'd hurried by all this beauty totally unaware.

Approaching downtown, she passed the flat-roofed police station. She imagined the local force sitting inside, feet up, scoffing donuts, waiting for the phone to ring. Locating lost tourists was probably as exciting as it got up here. An unmissable arrow pointed her to the 'Historic Center Parking' next to the quayside. White sailing boats, fishing vessels with blue or green hulls and a handful of modest-sized yachts bobbed against their moorings. Stepping out of the car, the crisp sea air smelled of salt and kerosene, of earning a living on the water. It invigorated her spirits. She strolled past a fancy-looking restaurant with a deck. A kid, college-age and probably bussing tables to earn cash over the summer, looked bored as he folded white linen napkins. She'd spent her college vacations driving through Mexico or hiking in Costa Rica. She'd been lucky, in some ways, that she had her inheritance.

At the warehouses, she turned away from the stench of fish and toward the main drag. She stopped outside The Scarlet Claw Est 1892. She bet the red brick corner building with etched glass windows filled up with fishermen and town gossip when the sun went down. At The Easterlies, a guesthouse with slate gables and a wide veranda that curved around a corner, she could go left or right. She chose left. She realized with surprise that she was enjoying wandering, taking in her surroundings with no pressure to make a detailed mental note of everything she saw, or urgent need to find any specific place or person.

The display in the window of The Book Nook featured the top ten titles on the New York Times bestseller list on one side, including a self-help book on mindfulness Dr. Daniels had suggested she buy, but she hadn't read—yet. On the other, stood a pile of Sirens Bay's Most Read, which included an antique fishing almanac, a dog-eared copy of a Michelin guide to Maine, and a 1978 edition of the Rules of the Road, and a stack of Murder She Wrote novels. Cute. Someone had a sense of humor.

A tiny bell rung above her head as Emma gently pushed the door. She could never resist a bookshop. Behind the counter, a baby-faced guy wearing a navy-blue crew neck and round wire-framed glasses looked up from the register. "Hi, welcome!" His voice was soft and friendly. "First time here?"

"Er, yes, just arrived."

"Please, look around."

For a second, his eager smile caught her off guard. She reminded herself that she was on vacation, not headed into hostile territory. "Oh, thank you."

Split over two levels, the store's wooden shelving heaved with books. In a basket marked 50¢ she spied a chewed copy of Dan Brown's The Da Vinci Code. Following a sign for 'Books on Maine', she climbed the oak staircase to the mezzanine level and wove her way through a treasure trove of pamphlets, mysterious cloth-wrapped hardbacks and stacks of well-thumbed magazines to the rare maps. Her eyes widened. Stuffed in a back alcove were boxes of geological surveys organized by date, the oldest marked 1756. A framed document hung on the wall announcing the incorporation of Allen Bay in 1791. Curly signatures danced across the bottom of the thick scroll. A small glass fronted wooden cabinet displayed a collection of knots, each with its own label: Clinch, Palomar, Turle, Dropper, Snell, a love letter to all things nautical.

Downstairs, she proclaimed to the guy's delighted face, "This place is incredible."

"We do our best! There's new fiction over there," he pointed to the far side of the store, "and contemporary non-fiction this side."

She picked up a book about the Obama Administration's foreign policy mistakes written by a guy she once worked with at The Times. She'd promised herself she would get around to reading it. He was an excellent writer, but he didn't understand the Middle East. But if not now, then when? She placed the book on the counter. The man held out his hand. "I'm Erik, by the way. Good to meet you."

She shook it. "Emma."

"Coffee? On the house?"

"Oh, thank you, that's kind."

"Please, my treat. Cappuccino?"

She smiled. Erik turned to the young woman standing near the espresso machine. "Riley, one cappuccino please."

"Comin' right up."

Emma had never quite got used to American levels of service. She always half expected to be met with a bored, blank face that didn't hide its disdain for her needs.

"British, huh?" The young woman was probably in her mid-twenties. Razor trimmed bangs framed her pretty pixie face and her thick black kohl liner highlighted her hazel eyes. She slid the coffee across the counter.

"Yes."

"Nice."

Emma was never sure how to respond to that. It was a fact, nothing she had chosen, earned, or could change. And she'd never worked out if Americans loved Brits for their quaintness and history, or, simply tolerated their weird eccentricities as relics from the old country. It didn't matter. She loved Americans' positivity.

The brass bell chimed as the door flew open. A tiny woman with a bright white bob and tanned lined face, wearing a fleece and jeans, heaved a trolley loaded with newspapers over the step. She stopped and gasped for breath.

Erik rushed forward. "I'll take it from here, Kirsty."

The older woman caught her gaze. "Emma, right?" she asked with a forty-a-day croak.

News traveled fast. "Yep."

"Whad'ya make of Sirens Bay?"

"From what I've seen, it's lovely."

"It is." She looked like she was about to say more about the town. Instead, her chin dropped, and she said, "Good to meet a friend of Ben's. He was a great guy."

"He was," Emma agreed, but Kirsty had already backed out of the door with the empty trolley.

"Wanna have a read?" Erik offered her a copy of The Siren newspaper.

"Sure."

She sat at one of the mismatched tables gathered close to the coffee counter. The front-page splashed on a legal dispute between elderly neighbors fighting over who had the right to trim a maple spreading over both their back yards. One said he'd sue the other for destruction of a native species if he continued to hack off its branches. The other said the tree stole light from his entire house and slashed the price of his property. He threatened to sue for loss of income. It pictured two men standing in front of said tree, growling at the camera. Such were the dramas driving news coverage in Sirens Bay.

The bell jingled. Riley chirped, "Hi, Jordan!"

Emma's eyes left the page to see who was next to visit this little social hub. They landed on the contractor from the night before. His gaze met hers. On either side, he held the hand of a little girl, one maybe eight and the other ten. His daughters, she guessed. They shared a likeness with their father, including their thick brown hair. She smiled and cleared her throat to say hello. The guy swung his head toward the counter before she could speak. His rudeness, while unnecessary, was a relief. Emma turned the page to news of a bake sale.

Riley, her voice a few notes higher, asked how Jordan was doing, how his week had been, and what he was planning to do with his weekend. Emma could hear gentle flirting in her tone. Jordan ignored it. "Is Erik around?"

"Here!" Erik appeared from the back carrying a brown paper parcel tied together with string. "They came in yesterday. Let me know what you think."

Jordan's face broke into a wide smile. He had no manners, but he looked extra handsome when he grinned. "Will do."

Riley pointed to the gateau stand. "Devil's food cake. You want? Freshly baked this morning. By yours truly."

Emma had to give it to the young woman, she didn't give up easily. Jordan shook his head. The older girl pulled on his arm, looking up with her blue eyes. "We could share it?"

"Kiddo, you've just had a snack. No cake," he said softly.

The girl's face crumpled. He tucked a strand of hair behind her ear. "Choose a book instead."

She ran with her sister to a wall of kids' story books. Without thinking, Emma's gaze fell to his ring finger. Unadorned. He was one of those men who felt emasculated by jewelry announcing his betrothal. Or he was a good-looking divorcee. Or perhaps he was a pitiful widower and loving single dad, which meant he was drowning in attention from every female in this town, regardless of age or intention. She bet on the first option. He seemed the thin-skinned type. Although the second was a possibility. As if he felt her eyes on him, he glanced over.

Her face prickled. She feigned a smile and kept her voice neutral. "Nice to see you again."

He frowned. Jesus, even a hello was too much for him.

"You've got…" He tapped his upper lip with his finger. "Foam mustache …."

She swiped a napkin across her mouth. Heat flashed up her cheeks. "Err, thanks," she stuttered. And then, added quickly, "Beautiful girls."

"Thanks."

He paid for the kids' books and picked up his package. Niceties over, it seemed. Some locals were more friendly than others. And this one was just stone cold.

Chapter Five

Emma swayed in the hammock, watching the low sun torch the horizon. End of Day One in Sirens Bay. The town was charming and steeped in history; the people she'd met were lovely, bar one, and the bookshop was a fabulous surprise. Her eyes followed the curve of the bay. The scenery reminded her of the Lake District in England, where her parents used to take her on holiday. As a child, she'd scramble on the granite crags and paddle in the freezing streams. Happy memories. She could see why Ben loved it here.

The moan of a car engine put a full-stop on her reveries.

A woman around her age, with a heart-shaped face and a big smile, blond hair pulled into a high ponytail, met her at the porch steps.

"Beth?" Emma smiled and held out her hand.

Beth had a firm grip. "Emma, hey, good to meet you. I'm so sorry about yesterday."

"No, it's me who should apologize. Thank you for arranging for someone to be here so late. And for filling the refrigerator. Tea?"

Inside, Beth pulled a manila packet from her red leather laptop bag and laid it on the kitchen counter. "Everything's in here."

As Emma filled the kettle, it occurred to her that Beth was more familiar with this kitchen and this house than she would ever be. Guilt that Ben had left the place to her and not one of his blood relatives stabbed again at her sense of fairness. Ben was a thoughtful, decisive man, but his thinking this time made little sense. Why had he overlooked his family? She hadn't got a whiff of any kind of rift. There was no trace of hostility or resentment in Beth's voice or body language. So, why not give this place to her?

As Emma sifted through the stack of recent bills, an aged land survey, a copy of the deed, and a fishing license, gratitude-coated sadness sloshed at her insides and threatened to leak out as tears. The kettle squealed. She slammed the drawers, searching for a dishcloth or tea towel to lift it off the heat.

"Let me," said Beth, using a cloth from under the sink. "It's a lot to take in, I get it," she said, resting her palm lightly on Emma's shoulder. Her hand felt warm, kind. It was welcome human touch. The last person to place their fingers on her body was the paramedic who levered her out from under her desk in the Informer's newsroom. She'd been so gentle and patient. Emma had clung to her as the room swirled and then turned to black.

"It's just…" A scratch caught in Emma's throat. "It's just so generous of him."

The papers were evidence that it wasn't some fever dream. The cottage was bricks and mortar that she now owned. Beth pulled two mugs from the shelf and opened a box of tea bags. "That's Ben. Heart of gold."

Emma cringed with embarrassment at her upset. "I'm sorry, you must miss him so much."

"We do."

Outside, they sipped on their chamomile tea, watching Tallulah lay on the deck in the last rays of sun. She seemed entirely content to pad around the cottage and watch birds from the porch without venturing further. Perhaps it was Ben's imperceptible presence that soothed her and kept her close. Emma could feel it, too.

"So, you really want to sell?" Beth asked, her eyes fixed on the water.

"You want to buy?" It was a joke. Immediately Emma realized its poor taste.

"Noo," Beth brushed it aside. "Our place is enough house for us to handle. We live on Elm Drive, a big ol' Cape with five bedrooms and a shingle roof that creaks and groans. Upkeep costs a fortune. But we love it. It's been in the family five generations."

"It sounds wonderful." A breeze tickled through the trees. "It's so beautiful here. But I don't see how I can keep this place." Emma's eyes stayed fixed on the ocean. Water the color of mercury lapped the shore. "I travel so much for work. I'm never in D.C. for long, and certainly not long enough to come up here on vacation." Around the cove, lights popped on as the last of the sun shrank behind the horizon. "This place deserves to be loved and cherished."

She didn't say it, but the thought ran through her mind: By someone who deserves it.

"He'd be disappointed, you know," Beth looked at her with a resigned smile, "if you didn't at least enjoy it for one season."

It was true. Selling immediately would feel like committing a cold betrayal of Ben's kindness, but she'd seen the place; she had the paperwork; and it was time to return to D.C. Mission accomplished. Passing it on now would mean it wouldn't stand empty, wasted for a summer, and come fall, be difficult to off-load.

Beth continued: "Speaking professionally, the structure is solid and well-maintained, but you'd get more for it if you did a few tiny renovations — patched the storm damage to the roof and repainted the porch and replaced the screen. Easy fixes."

Emma took a deep breath. Hiring contractors meant hassle and cost.

"It wouldn't take long," Beth persisted.

"How long?"

"Couple of days, maybe a week, max. It would really boost your valuation. And, I think it would do Uncle Ben proud."

Ben abhorred shoddy: rushed prep, poor sourcing, loose story structure, inaccurate quoting. His D.C. apartment was eclectic, but everything had its exact spot. Beth was right: he'd want the cottage to look its best when its new owner arrived. "Can you recommend someone?"

"There are quite a few contractors in town, but to be honest, Jordan's the best."

That guy. Emma raised her eyebrows. "Man of few words."

"Yep, that's my brother. The strong, silent type." Beth laughed.

Emma's face stretched in surprise. "He's your brother?" That grumpy asshole was family. Wait, Ben's nephew? Wow. Wasn't he the grit in the family oyster? Beth and Ben shared a sense of kindness and charm. Not that guy. Emma shook her head.

Beth nodded. "And there isn't anyone who can compete with him for timber-work. You should see what he's done to his place, the lighthouse cottage. Total renovation. It is beautiful."

"He lives there?" Her eyes swung to the beam strobing the darkening water.

"Yup. And I'm not just saying all this because he's my brother."

The thought of having him around for even a few days prickled her skin with irritation. She clenched her jaw. This was supposed to be simple. Then make it so, she told herself. Stop being a baby. On assignment, she had spent days holed up in a bombed-out building, sharing water and energy bars with rival reporters she couldn't stand the sight or smell of. She could cope with a surly contractor for a week. She'd keep out of his way. The work would get done. It would only be a week. And then she'd be gone.

Chapter Six

Jordan heaved a bag of cement from the flatbed onto his shoulder and strode around to the back of the cottage. The sun shone high in the sky. A stream of sweat raced down the side of his face, down his neck, and over his chest. From her seat on the porch, Emma didn't utter a word as he passed by; didn't deign to speak to the hired help. She kept her eyes on the water like she was some sort of English princess or something. She hadn't offered him so much as a coffee. He didn't like to judge, but honestly, she seemed like a snob.

Jordan dumped the bag at the base of the ladder and reached for the bucket. He hadn't wanted to take this job. At all. He liked to help his little sister; it made him feel good to be of service, if he could be. But this was a tough ask. Beth understood how he felt about the cottage's change of ownership. Technically, they could still contest Ben's will if they wanted to. As his brother, Mason was his next of kin and with Jordan, Beth and the girls, they were Ben's only surviving blood relatives. Beth rejected that idea flat out and threatened to find someone else to do the work. She knew he wouldn't stand for another contractor touching the place, and that he'd want to do right by Ben and have it looking spick and span before they lost it forever. So, he'd agreed.

The cat, prim and upright, watched him from her spot at Her Royal Highness' feet. That woman made him feel like the dumb yokel paid for his muscle. He had a bachelor's in criminal psychology from the University of Texas, for God's sake. It hadn't been easy to keep on top of his classes while he was working at the department, but he was no slouch when it had come to studying. The Drug Enforcement Administration taught him the value of an excellent education, something his father had badgered him about for years as a kid.

Jordan poured cement powder into the bucket and started mixing. The cotton of his damp t-shirt pulled against his skin. He yanked it over his head and immediately felt relieved. One boot on the bottom rung. He glanced at his client. He knew the value of an honest day's work, and he was pretty sure she didn't.

Jordan blinked at the sun bouncing off the roof tiles. He'd really miss this place when it was gone. Sophie loved it up here. She'd swing in the hammock and read. They spent every weekend in the months before his father's death in this very house. He'd always be grateful to Ben for that. It was a precious time. He was glad he'd patched things up with his father.

By then, he understood the cruelty of addiction that had trapped his dad and had dropped the blame. He simply felt sorry. It meant that when he passed, Jordan was there and had no regrets. If he knew he was going to lose Soph too a few years later, he wouldn't have wasted a minute of their time together. Not one second. No one understood him like she did. No one laughed with him like she did; no one supported him like she did; and no one held his heart as tenderly and generously as she did, or ever would. They had all loved her, his family, but he loved her the most and more.

But he'd had no idea.

Jordan sighed and ran a trowel of cement around the base of the chimney. Those days were over, well and truly. And they weren't coming back. This was his new life. Work, keep sober, and keep going. Soph would want that. Never again would he be the guy she left behind: broken, desperate, sad, and looking for answers in the wrong places, back home in Sirens Bay, ragged and lost. Soph would have despised that guy; she wouldn't have recognized him.

Stradling the roof ridge, he pulled at a loose tile. This was his life. It wasn't what he'd planned or worked for, but he had become grateful for it.

A gull swooped low, hovered for a moment, and dived. It resurfaced, a fish flapping in its mouth, water spraying from its wings. Emma sipped her tea. If you paid attention, watching the bay was like sitting in a front-row seat at a play. Characters arrived on stage, like that mob of brown seabirds who skidded across the rippling water scaring off the gulls, played their part, and retreated to the wings before returning later for an encore, like those black headed geese back again to cruise the water's edge. She wished Doug was here to see it all. They never spent a moment together in a place like this, away from the urgency, the heat and dust of an assignment.

The sight of Jordan descending the ladder with Tallulah tucked under his arm tugged at her gaze. The cat looked utterly comfortable, resting against the cushion of his tanned bicep. His chest glistened in the sun. She wasn't a prude, but couldn't the guy keep his shirt on in front of a stranger? Her eyes darted back to the water as he strode passed again carrying the bucket in one hand and a half full bag of cement on his shoulder, Tallulah trotting behind him. That cat couldn't leave him alone. Traitor. Emma shook her head.

Jordan's truck engine gunned. The flock of geese snapped into the air, flapping low over the cottage, screaming their alarm. Emma ducked, raising her hands over her head. She squeezed her eyes shut, trying to put a brake on the images unspooling through her head.

A lorry backfired. It was midday and the desert sun was vicious. Soldiers smoked and laughed as they leaned against the breeze block gatepost supporting the barrier holding back a line of agitated traffic. Their hire car pulsed with heat and sweat. The temperature had sucked them dry of any conversation. Doug's fingers tapped the wheel, his tired, dry face twitching with annoyance. Exhaustion had drained them both of patience. She ached to be moving, heading to their next stop for a shower and sleep. She heard the rumble before she saw the truck roar toward them down the road on the other side. The soldiers primed their weapons, but it didn't seem to slow down. Dust spumed from its heavy tires. A guard turned his Russian-made machine gun on the driver: a boy, maybe nine or ten, bent over the wheel, his face a picture of determination.

In that moment, she had looked at Doug, and they'd grabbed for each other. They knew what was going to happen. The truck smashed through the checkpoint. Before she could speak, a blast threw her back and emptied her head. The car leaped into the air. Her seat belt cut into her neck. The explosion sucked Doug out the open door to be consumed by thunderous charcoal smoke. She remembered coming round, hearing her voice chastising him for never wearing his bloody seatbelt. He wasn't there. How stupid.

On the porch, Emma gasped for breath. Her palm pressed to her chest as she took a long inhale, counting to four, held it for four, exhaled for four, and stopped for four counts. Her eyes stung as her hand rubbed gently on her sternum. Tears of shock streamed down her face. She inhaled again. Why was she so fragile? Why couldn't she make these memories stop?

Slowly, the panic raging through her body ebbed and she could focus on the tide lapping the shingle with an even rhythm. Now, five things she could see: ocean, birds, sky, trees, cat. Five things she could touch: her arms, the bench, her feet on the floor, her mug, her hair. Her fingers trembled, but she was landing. Five things she could hear: the whisper of the breeze through the trees, a boat motor somewhere far off, the gentle creek of the screen door, her breath steadying, and the sound of Jordan's truck radio. Him. She didn't want him here. She could feel the resentment fizzing off him. He couldn't see her like this.

She walked inside, her anxiety switching to irritation. He was doing his best to make her feel like an unwelcome outsider—and he was good at it—but this was her place, whether or not he liked it. Why didn't he tell her he was Ben's nephew? He'd lied by omission, or at the very least misled her. Why hadn't he simply introduced himself?

She lay on the bed, watching the sunlight dance across the ceiling; her eyelids relaxing as she watched leaf-shaped shadows flutter across the blanket as the breeze moved through the blueberry shrub outside her window.

There was a silver-lining to the delay. A few more days here might help. That was the first flashback she'd had since she'd arrived. In D.C., she had at least one a day, sometimes more. They came from nowhere, triggered by the doorbell or an overheard conversation in the hallway, or a sound from the street. They differed in intensity, but always flattened her. Here there was space to breathe fresh air. As her eyes closed, she considered that right here might not be an awful place to spend some time regrouping, trying to shift some of the loss clogging her system and short-circuiting her sanity. Here, among Ben's things and his furniture, was not the worst place to cross off some days on the calendar of her enforced medical leave.

Jordan washed his hands under the tap at the front of the house and splashed water over his face and hair. It was gloriously cool on his skin. He'd have loved to have gone for a swim, let the ocean wash off the sweat and grit, but the cottage's little beach was now off limits—forever. Her Highness wouldn't have liked it, he was sure, if she caught him walking across her property in his swim shorts.

He saw that look on her face when he, working up a sweat, removed his shirt. Yanking it back on, his shoulder muscles stiff with hauling and yanking, he shook his head. But it had been a good day's work. He'd fixed the new tiles on the roof and secured the chimney and gable, which should all stay put through the worst of any winter storm. Ben would be pleased, and that's what mattered.

Jordan walked back around to the porch to tell her he was done for the day and would be back at nine to finish up in the bathroom. Emma wasn't in her usual spot. He knocked on the porch door. No answer. Her bedroom door was closed. Figured. She'd gone for a nap without as much as a thanks.

He tickled the cat's head and opened the screen door to let her inside. "Thanks for your company, Tallulah."

The sooner he was out of here, the better. Being at the cottage was making him sad.

Chapter Seven

As Emma strode back and forth on the little beach trying to catch signal, she just about managed to catch Beth inviting her to Mason's 80th birthday party. She said it would be a wonderful opportunity to meet him and other local folks. Emma stalled, taking advantage of a sudden break in connection. She was not in the mood to be with people she didn't know and wasn't sure if she could plug herself into the social energy to hide it. But Mason intrigued her. What would the brother of her wise, well-traveled, adventurous, intellectually curious friend be like? A man who had never left this small town. Her curiosity wouldn't let her decline.

"I'd love to," she exaggerated when Beth's voice stuttered back on the line.

"Wicked good. See you at The Claw."

Emma swallowed and pushed against the wooden door. The twang of guitar rock and chatter hit her before she'd stepped inside. The bar, with its bare brick walls, elegant sweep of polished counter, and warm lighting was everything she'd imagined. A group of men in denims and caps, local lobstermen she supposed, sat at the bar talking loudly at each other although they were leaning in close, and laughing, while a busy team of waitstaff bussed bottles and pitchers of beer to tables jammed with people drinking and eating—what else?—what looked like lobster rolls and fries.

A hand shot up, and she spotted Beth standing among the crowd beside two gold helium balloons, an eight and zero, bobbing in the air. A skinny old man in a short-sleeved golfing shirt, knitted vest, pale slacks and cap, perched on the stool they were tied to, talking with an unlit cigar clenched between his teeth. He looked like he was just about to tee-off. With his square jaw, thick gray hair and a familiar twinkle in his eyes, she could clearly recognize the resemblance. Her heart skittered, and she smiled. Ben's brother, Beth's grandfather: Mason.

The guy standing behind him talking to someone in the group turned around. Jordan. The warmth in her chest dissipated. She couldn't get away from the guy. Be positive, she told herself. The evening was about Mason. And getting to know more about Ben.

She stepped forward with a smile fixed on her face. "Hi Beth. Jordan. Mason? Happy Birthday."

"So glad you could make it." Beth beamed. Jordan dipped his head and informed no one in particular that he was going to the bathroom.

Beth turned to the old man. "Grandpa, this is Emma."

Mason's blue eyes bore into her. "So, you are my brother's friend? How do you like the place?"

"It's lovely." She remembered the bottle of whiskey clutched under her arm. It was an unopened eighteen-year Glenlivet she'd found under the kitchen sink. Ben would have turned in his grave if she'd poured it away. She handed it to him. "Happy birthday."

"Thank you. Scotch?" the old man asked over the noise.

"No, thanks." She never drank spirits and whisky caused even more trouble.

"No, I asked, are you Scotch? You look Scotch." He examined her face.

"Ah, no." That old chestnut. It was the red hair and freckles. "English."

Mason looked disappointed. Having attended more than one of Ben's Burns Night dinners, where a raucous group of wannabe Scots ate neeps and tatties as they took turns reading eighteenth century verse aloud, she was well aware of the Allens' proud Highland roots, and their adopted antipathy toward the English.

Emma pulled a conciliatory face.

"Sorry."

"Never mind." Mason sighed. "I won't hold it against you if he didn't."

Emma grinned.

"Let's get you a drink." Beth waved to a woman with relaxed black curls streaked with gray, glowing skin, and a broad grin, who arrived carrying a tray of beer. The woman stuck out her hand. "I'm Lily, and this is my place. And you must be Emma. Welcome."

Lily's shake was warm and firm and soothed some of her nerves. "Thank you. It's a popular spot."

"Even when it's not peak season, we pull a good crowd." She handed Emma a bottle of local craft.

"Thank you." It was freezing in her hand. Its malty fizz slid down nicely.

"You up from D.C.?"

Emma nodded. "Just for a few days."

"My husband Earl and I, God rest his soul, moved up here twenty years ago from Baltimore. It's a beautiful place. And now it's home." She turned and made her way back to the bar, stopping to catch Jordan stepping through the crowd the other way, presumably back to the party. They talked for a second. She patted him on the arm. He nodded. They both smiled. Friends. He had one.

"Cheers!" Mason bellowed. He clinked his glass against her bottle. "How did you know I like a good Scotch?"

"Just a hunch." The more she looked at him, the more layers of Ben revealed themselves in the crinkles around his eyes, the pinch of his lips.

Emma stood to one side, trying to be as inconspicuous as a

city-living single woman from out of town could be, sipping her
beer.

"Hi, I'm Dave," a middle-aged man arrived next to her. His
navy blue tie matched the tones of the stripy dress shirt stretched
over his paunch and cinched into his tightly belted pants.
"Reporter at The Siren. Heard you work for the Informer?"

Of course he had. She nodded. "That's right." Although she
wasn't entirely sure how long that would be the case.

"How's that? I worked at The Globe, back in the day. I miss it
sometimes though. The noise of the newsroom, the rush. What'd
you cover?"

"Middle East affairs."

He raised his eyebrows, apparently impressed. Emma flicked
her eyes to locate another source of incoming attention. Jordan
glanced away.

"Where was your last assignment?"

A molten unease stirred in her gut. It was a trip she didn't even
want to think about, let alone discuss with a stranger. Since the
explosion, running from her grief, she'd worked stories back-to-
back, returning only to D.C. when Louise insisted she needed to
spend some downtime in the office. The irony. Wired and
exhausted, edging toward burnout, she hadn't noticed in those
short weeks that Ben has lost weight, wasn't quite his ferocious
self at work. Emma should have asked questions; she shouldn't
have left that last time. She'd squandered the time she could have
spent with him, being there for him. Saying goodbye.

She switched topic. "How do you know Mason?"

"I work at The Siren." Dave seemed confused. "He's my boss."

Her eyebrows shot up in surprise. "He's the editor?"

Ben, who spent his luminous career traveling the globe,
reporting from the front lines, interviewing presidents and prime

ministers, explaining a complex world to the Informer's readership, had never mentioned his brother toiling away at the town rag.

"Yup. He owns it. He writes my paycheck."

How on earth did it make any money?

Stunned, it took a moment for Emma to realize that Beth had put her hand on her shoulder and was steering her toward a delicate-looking older woman in a wheelchair, who seemed way out of place in the crowded bar. "Here, meet my mom, Abigail. She didn't want to miss the party."

"No reason she should," Jordan appeared, standing beside his mother, his hands jammed in his jeans pocket. Protective.

"And she wanted to meet you." Beth beamed.

"Have you met Nora and Piper?" Abigail asked. Her gaze drifted up to Jordan, a slow sadness dropping over her face. Jordan's stern expression didn't move.

The kids from the bookshop? Emma frowned, unsure.

"They're my girls," Beth clarified. "Eight and ten. They're at home, tucked up in bed. I hope. Where maybe you should be, Mom?"

"You saw them at Book Nook," Jordan mumbled.

They were Beth's kids, not his. Figured. Nothing about this guy was as it seemed.

"Do you have children?" The woman's voice wavered as she spoke, but her question landed with a thud directly from leftfield.

"Mom!" Beth whispered.

"No." Emma replied, looking from Abigail to Beth and back, wondering in which excruciating direction this conversation was headed. Children had never been part of the plan.

Emma stifled a yawn. She'd met more new people tonight than she had in the past few months. Social energy drained, she had little left in the tank to field unwanted questions about her private life.

"Excuse me," she fixed a smile. "I've had a long day. And I should probably check on the cat. She's not used to being alone." Jordan raised his eyebrows in a question. She stared back. That last part was true. "Where can I get a cab?"

Beth, Jordan, and Abigail exchanged inquiring glances.

"Taxi'll take a while," Mason returned to his stool, his skin flushed. "McGrudy's taken his family upta camp. Twins' birthday."

"There's only one taxi in town?" Emma swallowed her dismay.

"Other's 'll be flat out." Abigail mused.

"Jordan?" Beth tipped her head.

"What?" he replied, his mouth set flat.

Beth turned toward the door to the deck and jerked her head in its direction. "Please give us a minute."

Outside on the deck, the air was several glorious degrees cooler on Jordan's sunburnt skin.

"What?" He knew what Beth was about to ask, but he wanted to hear her say it.

"Be a gentleman and give her a ride."

"I am a gentleman, Beth, not a taxi service." He folded his arms across his chest. His back muscles stretched and throbbed, aching from a day's work on the roof.

"C'mon Jordy. Don't be an ass." His sister stared at him. "She's new in town."

"Exactly. She's a stranger. Why are you acting like we owe her something? We owe her nothing. In fact. She owes us." His sister was infuriating when she turned on the do-gooder charm. "Beth, she's gonna flip that cottage the second it's ready and be outta here. I don't know why you invited her to Mason's party. We are not going to be friends with her. And. If she can make it through a war-zone, as she claims, she can make it home from The Claw by herself."

He couldn't seem to get away from the woman.

"Are you gonna head off soon?"

"Yes."

"All I'm asking is for you to drive her home. It's on your way. Please."

"And all I'm asking is for you to stop asking me to do things for her."

His little sister cocked her head just like she used to do when she was a kid and wanted something. "You literally drive past the entrance to The Pines. This is the last thing I'll ask. And as you said, soon she'll be gone."

Jordan sighed. "This is it. One ride. And she better be ready to leave."

He sat in the truck, engine running. Typical, she was making him wait.

Emma ran to the passenger door. "Sorry, I lost my wallet," she panted as she climbed in. "It must have fallen out of my bag. That's never happened to me before." She shook her head in apparent disbelief. "Someone handed it in at the bar."

He shoved the truck into gear. "Yup. People are nice around here."

The route out of town was clear of traffic. They coasted along, the radio on low. There was no need for small talk. But. Something had bothered him since she'd arrived, and now was his chance to ask.

"I don't remember seeing you at the memorial."

"What? Sorry?" In the moonlight, her skin glowed like white marble.

"I don't remember seeing you at Uncle Ben's memorial service." He repeated, speaking louder this time.

"Oh." Emma fiddled with the bag strap in her lap. "I wasn't there."

Figured. Supposedly such a close friend and she couldn't even be bothered to turn up to Ben's last farewell?

"Lots of other folks were there, in the cathedral. Hundreds of people. Including your colleagues from the Informer."

"Yes, I heard." She turned her head to look out the window. She should be embarrassed. It was the least Ben deserved.

Jordan pressed the accelerator. The darkness outside raced by. He waited for her to explain, or at the very least offer an excuse, but she said nothing. Just stared out the window. The sooner this woman was out of his truck and out of their lives, the better.

Tallulah landed softly beside her on the bed. The cat stared in her almost supernatural way. Emma tickled her head. The sound of her purring softened the jagged shame cutting her insides.

Why did Jordan have to ask about the memorial service? Her friend had died and all the loss she'd tried to bury had exploded to the surface. Grief had flattened her. She couldn't get out of bed to honor his memory. She hadn't even known until the very end that Ben had cancer. When she'd got home from assignment to find him in hospital, he'd finally told her he'd been having treatment for six months. He said he hadn't wanted to burden her with it. Emma had been furious and then unbearably sad as she sat by his bedside, wiping dribble from his chin, wires snaking from his arms. She wouldn't leave his side, couldn't. She'd held his hand as he rasped his last breath.

Where were they, his family?

47

She wasn't being fair. The oncologist, a young guy eager to please, said Ben might have months if he made it through this dip. He'd given them false hope. She knew he wouldn't want to stick around.

He had whispered in her ear, a strained grin stretching across his face, that he'd been everywhere he'd ever wanted to go and met everyone he'd wanted to. He wasn't afraid.

Emma wiped away a tear and then another. She was so sorry she'd failed him at the memorial. In her despair, she'd missed the moment to tell everyone how great, brave, and honest he was. But he had to know how much he meant to her. Didn't he? Is that why he left her this place? She didn't deserve it.

Chapter Eight

As Jordan lifted his hand to knock on the back door, he glanced down at the porch bench. His great uncle would sit there chewing on a cigar as he told stories of hiking through the jungles of Vietnam. He was there at Khe Sanh, La Drang, Tet, the Easter Offensive and more, battles Ben could recall in exacting detail. As a kid, Jordan would sit on the deck, listening in silence, drinking in every word: every act of heroism, every failure and mistake, and the astonishing bravery and comradery of the troops, guys thrown together to fight for a cause thousands of miles from home that the people at home had begun to question, and then outright reject. Their brotherhood and commitment to serving their country, right or wrong, was why he'd signed up for the Marines. People said Mason was lucky to have escaped the draft. A genetic heart defect discovered during his Army medical meant he stayed home. But Jordan disagreed. It was a challenge and an honor to serve. Being a Marine had made him the man he was, for better or worse.

Who would sit here once the place sold? What idiot would give up this view? Behind him, the sea stretched out like a bolt of blue satin. Who wouldn't want to stay here forever?

He knocked. No answer. He got out his key. There was just the lock on the bathroom window to check and he was done. He could be proud of his work on the cottage. He hoped Ben would be too.

A stack of old magazines stood on the kitchen counter. She was about to throw them in the trash, he guessed. He lifted the top copy, an edition of Life dated August 1969. Pages of close-set font described pride and astonishment at the moon landing, accompanied by the yellowing image of Apollo 11 about to blast off. He wished he'd been alive to see it. His thumb flicked to a page of black and white headshots, all young men staring straight at the camera like faces in a high school yearbook. He read the title and gulped. One Week's Dead.

He looked closer, holding the magazine gently in his hands. They were soldiers and airmen who'd died fighting in Vietnam over the course of just seven days. Pages of them. His heart dropped. What a sacrifice. He had lost buddies during tours of Afghanistan and Iraq, good men and women. There was no getting away from death, and it hurt. But here were so many.

In a piece about plummeting troop morale, he spotted Ben's byline. He must have written it after the Army discharged him from active duty and he returned to the conflict as a reporter for the Informer. It was a brave, honest assessment. People didn't want to know how hard it was to be a soldier in the field: the fear, the physical discomfort, the killing. He'd left the Marines after a bullet seared through his left thigh during an ambush in Ramadi. If their platoon's medic hadn't been crouched beside him, he'd have lost his leg. Simple as that. As it was, his military career was over.

He placed the magazine back on the pile. Had she even looked at them? He would ask her for that edition to keep as a memento. Save it for the girls. Spending time in the cottage was making him nostalgic, melancholy. One more task and he'd be out of here.

Tallulah watched him as he opened and closed the small bathroom window, checking the fit of the new lock against the frame. The cat was like his work buddy. She was always around and she purred like a starboard motor when you tickled her head or chin. He pulled the window open once more, adjusting the hinge. This one wouldn't rattle. As he jiggled the screw, the cat dashed for the ledge. He caught her in his palm. He would not be responsible for letting her out. Emma resented him enough already.

Tallulah wriggled and swiped her claws. He stepped back, dropping her in the bath. She skittered over the enamel, up onto the sink and out the door, back legs flying. Emma's wash bag crashed to the floor in her wake. Jordan sucked a cut on his wrist, murmuring.

"Dammit!"

After a quick search of the cottage, the cat was nowhere to be found. She was hiding. He knew to let her be. She'd come out when she was ready. He kneeled to gather Emma's toiletries scattered over the tiles. An eyeshadow pallet cracked open in his hand, showering glittery dust everywhere.

"Jesus," Jordan wiped the shimmering pigment onto his shorts. "Goddamn."

He dipped low, straining underneath the claw-foot bath to reach a brown plastic bottle. The typed label read: Demerol. He froze. The tub of fifty milligram pills was small in his palm. And so evil. He squeezed it as if it would crumble. Prescribed by doctors who had sworn an oath to do no harm, and marketed as a medicine, they were pure narcotic. Legal heroin. They had seduced his father away from everything he held dear, including his family. A mild-mannered man more suited to being a high school teacher than a local newspaper editor, he was not your typical candidate for life-ending addiction. This poison had quelled the agony of a cracked vertebra. Then gripped his dad so hard, he chased it down a dark tunnel right to his grave.

Jordan shoved the little bottle back into the bag and tidied around the sink. Why was she taking them? Only a fool who never watched the evening news didn't know how dangerous opioids were.

"Hi, have you got five minutes? I wanted to ask for your advice." Emma approached the Book Nook register.

"Sure." Erik cocked an eyebrow with faux earnestness. "But I don't do relationship, financial or medical." He was a sweet guy, funny.

She smiled. "No need for any of the above."

Since Doug's death, any type of romantic liaison was way off her agenda. She couldn't see one ever happening again. She couldn't trust herself to bear the pain. Her finances were stable. And she'd had more health advice over the past months than she could almost take.

"Good. But just so you know, there are no secrets around here." He swung his head around to look at Riley. "Walls have ears."

"Hey, what'ya tryin' to imply?" Riley asked, wide-eyed, mock affronted.

Erik ushered Emma to a table and said under his breath. "So, what do you need?"

His air of secrecy was cute. She drew a piece of paper from her purse. "I'm clearing out the cottage, and I found these."

Through his round glasses, she could see his eyes narrow as he scanned her list of titles and publication dates. "If these are in good condition…"

"Most of them are mint. The magazines are in number order, and some books are still in their original paper bags. Ben was meticulous."

Erik looked up. "They could be valuable."

"Can you find a new home for them? I've got nowhere to keep them once I sell the cottage. My apartment in D.C. is too small. I want to make sure they end up in the right place."

"You want to sell them?"

"Yes." She'd donate the proceeds to the Vets Association. Ben would like that.

"Let me speak to some brokers I know. In the meantime, I could keep them in the storeroom out back. It's climate controlled for the rare stuff."

"Thank you."

"So, you're leaving?" His face flattened. That news hadn't reached as far as the Book Nook. "That's a shame."

"I've got to get back."

He rested back in the chair. "You know, once you're in, you're in."

"In?"

"Once you make this place your home, the community really embraces you."

She nodded; she could see that might be the case. "How did you wind up here?"

"It's a long story, but let's just say academia wasn't right for me. My dreams of making tenure exploded in my face. But!" He raised a finger in the air, beaming. "I got my happy ending. I turned my passion for collecting old books into a business."

Riley chipped in. "The place was a total wreck before he arrived."

Emma took in the varnished oak bookcases and the sweep of the staircase. "Really?"

"An old couple ran it as a kind of flea market. Then I bought it. Jordan did the refit. He built all of it, down to the doorknobs." Erik pointed to the post at the bottom of the banister carved with a delicate maple leaf design twisting around the turned oak. "He's a very talented craftsman."

Emma nodded, surprised. "Is that right?"

Erik folded the list and slid it into his back pocket as he stood up. "Let me get back to you with a price."

"Thank you."

As Emma opened the door, a teenager walked in with a satchel slung across his lanky body.

"Hi Nerd," Riley called out.

"When I'm a start-up billionaire with his own algorithm and helicopter and you're still here frothing milk, you can make my Nitro lattes." The kid slid into a spot in the corner.

"They are always like this." Erik shook his head.

"Don't worry," Riley said directly to Emma. "He's like a little brother to me. But smart."

"God, no!" the boy announced. "We do not share DNA."

"They love each other, really," Erik said.

"We do not!" Riley and Han chimed.

"Anyway. This is Emma," Riley said it like she was showing her off. "She's British. She lives in D.C. Han's from out of town, too. Arrived from San Francisco a year ago."

"She doesn't need my bio." He blushed as he opened his laptop. In his polo shirt and square glasses, he looked like a geek, but he had a glint of something determined about him.

"Just trying to be friendly." Riley said like she was making a point. "Unlike some people."

"How long have you lived here?" Emma asked, curious. She let the door close again.

"Here? A year." The kid shrugged.

"You like it?"

"It's OK." He didn't sound sure.

Riley spoke again. "His parents are from Vietnam. Refugees from the war. They came over as kids in the seventies."

Han shot Riley a sideways glare.

"What? She's a war reporter," Riley thew up her hands, as if that justified divulging details of his background to a stranger. "You guys have loads in common."

"Really, you're a journalist?" His face softened as she nodded. "Cool."

A box of yellowing reporter notebooks she'd found in the sideboard detailing Ben's time in the Mekong Delta stood on the kitchen counter while she wondered what to do with it. It was funny how strangers' lives could loop around each other's, and you'd never know unless you started asking questions. "Are you writing something?"

"Just code." Han's eyes fell to his screen.

"Nice to meet you, Han. See you later, Riley. Erik." Emma opened the door and stepped toward the afternoon sun.

"See you later!" A chorus followed her out.

An unfamiliar feeling swept her insides. It was something like being welcomed.

—————— **Chapter Nine** ——————

The late afternoon sunlight rippled through the canopy of spruce and maple arching over the drive. It was the perfect evening for a picnic on the porch, watching the sun dissolve into the water. She had groceries and a baguette from the artisanal section of the store. She turned into the driveway and frowned.

"Dammit!" ground out her mouth.

His truck stood on the gravel. How long could it take to fix a window? When was he going to leave her in peace?

As she circled round to the back of the cottage, arms laden, Jordan appeared on the porch, his white tank rippling with pink glitter and a streak of peach across his cheekbone. In his hand he held a cracked eyeshadow pallet.

"Sorry," he grimaced. "There was an accident."

Emma's eyebrows flew up. Never mind the makeup had cost a fortune, and she had never even used it. It was a gift, and she had never had any occasion to wear it. What was he doing going through her stuff? "What…?"

He rushed out: "Tallulah knocked your wash bag onto the bathroom floor, and everything tipped out. This broke. I'll buy you a new one."

She shook her head, icy irritation catching in my throat. He was blaming the cat. She shoved out her hand, ready to receive the crumbling shadow pallet. "Please. Don't touch my things."

"She's inside somewhere." He jerked his head back. "I spooked her. She ran. I'm sorry." His cobalt blue eyes, the same color as the ocean, remained fixed on her as he waited for absolution. He looked kind of ridiculous in his work clothes, smothered with sparkles.

She softened.

"Never mind." She walked past him. "You're done, right?"

He followed her inside. "Yup."

Her eyes scanned the room looking for a furry body. When she didn't hear the door close, she turned. "Was there something else?"

"There is one thing."

Emma almost groaned aloud. Please, no more repairs.

Jordan pulled a small brown bottle from the pocket of his pants and offered it to her. "These are real addictive."

Emma jolted to her full height and snatched the bottle from his hand. What the hell had he been doing while she was out?

"Give them to me. It's time for you to leave."

"Wait, hear me out…"

"I asked you to leave." Her face drained of color and set like stone. He had violated her privacy and had the audacity to remain standing there.

"It's just that …" He stepped toward her. "Listen, those drugs, my dad…"

It seemed he was about to deliver a lecture. Who did this guy think he was? Fury burst from her. "Get out of my house…"

The little bottle of Demerol had sat unopened in her wash bag since she left the hospital. She hadn't taken even one. In truth, she was scared. The pain in her arm had been real, but it was something to cling to when her mind seemed to swim in circles.

He shot back: "Ben's house."

"My house." Her voice was low and measured. Tallulah appeared from the bedroom and sat at her feet. At last, that cat picked the right team. Boiling with anger, she stood staring at Jordan, unblinking, daring him to speak. He turned in silence, picked up his bag, and left.

57

Jordan's truck swerved around the bend a little too fast. He gripped the wheel. Wow, she'd overreacted. He was only trying to help; to look out for her and he didn't even like her. But he'd seen firsthand what damage those drugs could do.

At the cottage, on the step, he yanked off his boots and jammed them into the rack. She wasn't prepared to hear him out. He stalked inside, stripping off his work shirt and pants and threw them into the laundry room. Goddammit. He was just trying to be a good guy.

At the kitchen faucet, he drew a large glass of water and gulped it back. Her face had been of alive with rage, her green eyes burning into his face. She'd stood her ground; he'd give her that. She'd even scared him a little with her fury; she was kind of magnificent when she was angry. He shook his head and ran his fingers through his hair. He needed to stop thinking about Emma. She was taking up too much of his brain.

Through the kitchen window, the ocean rolled and dipped. The sight of this vast body of water always calmed him, reminded him of the mightiness of nature and that he was just a speck bumbling through a huge universe about which he knew very little. His gaze drifted toward the cottage on the other side of the cove. He could just about make out the slope of the roof. The little house seemed so far away; it wasn't a good feeling. It was no longer theirs.

She'd asked him to leave. And he was never going back. His last link to great uncle Ben was severed.

He took a deep breath. He hadn't meant to sound judgmental. He'd just been trying to warn her. There was something about her, her manner, the way she held herself and looked at him, that agitated him. He wasn't himself around her. He felt brittle. She got right under his skin. And that annoyed him.

Soaped and shampooed, with a towel wrapped around his

waist, Jordan opened the refrigerator door. Deliciously cool air brushed over his damp skin. Bottles of soda rattled in on the shelf. Two eggs, half a lemon, an avocado and a bottle of Tabasco. He sighed and rubbed his palm over his stomach as it gnawed with hunger. Working his butt off on The Pines, he'd forgotten to go to the store. He let the door swing closed as he walked into his bedroom, dropped his towel, and pulled on a pair of jeans. Work on his carving would wait. He needed Lily's cooking to put him straight.

The Claw was still quiet. A scattering of lobstermen sat in their usual spots at the bar downing a cold one after a long day on the water. Lily finished chalking a list of specials on the board.

"Hi stranger, what brings you in so early?" she asked.

Jordan claimed his regular barstool. "Hunger."

"Eddie!" Lily poked her head through the hatch and called into the kitchen. "One fried-chicken medium spicy, extra fries."

Jordan smiled. She knew him so well.

"So. What's been happening?" Lily leaned against the bar.

"Not much." He shrugged. "Working."

Lily waited a beat with a have-you-been-causing-trouble look on her face. "Really?"

Jordan sighed. "It's Ben's cottage."

Lily raised her eyebrows as if to say, "More."

"I've been working there, and…and…" Trying to sound in charge of his feelings about Emma's presence at The Pines, he reverted to therapy speak. "I am struggling to come to terms with its transfer to a new owner."

Lily held his gaze. "I see."

Reluctantly he added: "We kinda had a fight." He told her about the cat, the toiletry bag, the eyeshadow, and the Demerol.

She gave him a stern look. "You know you overstepped. You got into her business."

He nodded. "Yup."

He shouldn't have said anything; he understood that now. He paused. "But it really pisses me off he left that place to someone we don't know and who really doesn't appreciate it."

"And how do you know that?" Lily stopped arranging tickets on the counter.

"She clearly doesn't." It was so obvious Emma didn't give a damn. "She's selling."

"And you know this woman, how she thinks?" She tipped her head to one side.

"No." He gave her a half-shrug. "Not really. But…"

"I suggest you don't know her at all. People are not always what they seem, Jordan. Your Uncle Ben made a choice, and you need to have faith in his judgement and accept it. Do you trust him?"

"Lily, of course, I do."

Ben was a wise, upright, honest guy. That's what Jordan loved about him.

"Sounds like he had a special relationship with this young lady, one that he cherished."

"Maybe." Jordan wasn't convinced. He had seen nothing to admire in Emma yet.

Lily placed two hands on the bar and leaned forward. "Do you want The Pines for yourself?"

His words rushed out. "No, no!" He didn't mind that Ben left the cottage to someone else. He just wanted the property to stay in the family. "I'm not jealous. It just feels wrong, weird that she's there."

"She makes you uncomfortable."

"I guess." He frowned.

A mischievous smile spread across Lily's face. "Interesting."

"What's that supposed to mean?"

Lily placed a plate of chicken and a basket of fries on the counter and smiled again. "Nothing."

Chapter Ten

At the intersection of Bayview and Allen, the signal turned red, and Emma crossed the street. Ahead, a three-story flatiron edifice occupied the entire block, a grand old lady of a building constructed of redbrick with tall windows and a heavy black front door. The smoked-glass panel spelled out in gold nineteenth century font: The Siren Newspaper. Printing since 1867. This is who recorded the neighborhood disputes and bake sales.

A circular antique clockface still kept time above the entrance, its pointed second hand clicking around its roman numerals, marking the march of time. Time had not been kind to local papers. There were so few survivors left to keep up the battle against the onslaught of digitization, social media and the twenty-four-hour news cycle.

Standing on the sidewalk, taking in the building's grandeur, Emma understood that back in the day, The Allens had been a big deal; they were almost Maine royalty. And Ben had left this all behind.

She startled as the door swung open.

"Morning, young lady." Mason looked chipper in his mint green sweater and cap. "You come to pay us a visit?"

"Ahh," she hadn't, but she wanted to be polite. "Just admiring your beautiful building," she smiled. "I'm on my way to the Book Nook." She patted the bag hanging from her shoulder. "I've got some of Ben's books from the cottage for Erik to look at."

"What are they?"

Instantly, she realized that she'd assumed the family had removed everything from the cottage that they wanted. But perhaps that wasn't the case. "Would you like to look first?"

"Sure," he said, ushering her forward. "Come in, have a look around."

Framed, yellowing front pages covered the wall behind the deserted reception desk. In one, under the headline Beached!, a black-and-white photo showed a team of men in dungarees and cloth caps standing behind a bloated mink whale lying on the sand. One guy, his arms crossed and grinning, a pipe dangling from his lip, looked proud to be photographed for the local paper. Another page ran the stark black headline, President Slain, above a picture of JFK's motorcade. November, 1963. She shivered as if the paper had landed in her lap in real time.

In the newsroom, dust motes danced in the buttery sunlight streaming in through the windows and streaking across the dark wooden desks, all empty except for one. She waved at Dave, jabbing at his laptop with his index fingers, phone sandwiched under his ear. With its high ceiling and gothic beams, the room was more regal than any newsroom she'd ever worked in. And way more untidy, if that was possible. Stacks of paper, newspapers, and cardboard boxes crammed any available shelf. Digital archiving had yet to catalogue this treasure trove, it seemed.

At the Informer, news TV, desktops and open laptops, mobile phones and cables plastered every surface in the newsroom. The low hum of people hurrying, talking on the phone, ordering coffee, gathering for meetings, and catching up over the back of their seats filled the space. In this room, you could hear a pin drop.

Emma reached into her tote to retrieve the four books she'd found about the history of Maine. Mason dismissed them with a wave of his hand and a frown. "You want to see something really special?"

"Always," she replied as he led her past an ancient Telex machine serving as a plant stand. The Informer kept one of those in a glass case in the lobby, a souvenir of the glory days of

Bernstein and Woodward. As Mason showed her into a dim stairwell, he noticed her spot three defunct fax machines of various vintages piled on top of each other in the corner.

"You never know when you might need 'em."

Emma raised her eyebrows. "Sure." They were so old they were probably worth something on eBay. "Where are we going?"

"You'll see." He gripped the banister as he stepped gingerly down the staircase. She followed behind, wondering if she'd be able to catch him if he showed any sign of tumbling.

At the bottom, they both breathed a sigh of relief. Mason reached into his pocket and pulled out a large brass keyring. He was enjoying the theater of this little tour. The long skeleton key clicked in the lock, and he pushed gently at the heavy steel door. Two strip lights flickered.

Emma's eyes widened. "Wow."

"Beautiful, isn't she?" Mason motioned for her to take a better look.

In the middle of the windowless room, like a glorious ocean liner consigned to dry dock, stood a nineteenth century printing press, complete with huge steel rollers, brass wheels, cogs, and rods.

"She's more than one hundred and fifty years old. Manufactured before the Civil War. She'd take a bit of grease to get going, but isn't she gorgeous?" Mason beamed like a proud father.

"It's wonderful."

Once upon a time, this small town would have relied on The Siren to keep up to date with the outside world. This bit of kit would have been the height of tech innovation. She ran her hand over the polished metal railing protecting the gears, gliding around the machine, taking in the detail of its handles and levers, imaging the noise it must have made when the print was rolling, the smell of the ink and fresh newsprint. She touched a tray of metal type arranged in alphabetical order shelved neatly on the wall behind ready to be placed onto printing plates.

"Totally incredible. This is the actual press that printed The Siren?" she asked. No reply. "Mason?"

She peered around the machine. Her eyes popped. He lay on the floor just inside the door, not moving. Emma crouched down. "Mason? Can you hear me?"

His face was ashen and beaded with sweat. She bent her ear to his mouth. A shallow breath scraped through his throat. His neck pulse was almost imperceptible. She reached for her cell to call an ambulance. No signal. She ran to the stairwell and shouted for Dave.

"Hello?" His voice boomed down the stairs.

"Call an ambulance. Mason's collapsed."

She skidded back to him and let her field training kick in. Gently placing Mason's hands by his side, she blew into his mouth and started pushing on his narrow chest. "One, two, three, four," she whispered to herself. At ten, she stopped. "Mason?"

No response. He wasn't breathing. She began again. Rest and repeat. Rest and repeat. At last, a cacophony of feet scuffed down the stairs and a hand landed on her shoulder. A male paramedic in green overalls bent down beside her, concerned, but calm. "What happened?"

"I don't know, he just fell."

"How long for CPR?" he asked.

Emma checked her phone. "Seven minutes. Thereabouts." It had seemed like an age.

"Good job. We can take it from here."

His female colleague stepped forward and placed a yellow box on the floor.

Emma stood up, her focus twisting. Dave arrived breathless and murmured, "Jesus."

"One, two, three."

Mason's torso lurched, charged by the defibrillator. Dave winced and turned his face away, but Emma's eyes stayed stuck on Mason's pallid face. Ben's death mask slid over it. Bile rose in her mouth. She couldn't see another person take their last breath, not so soon. Not ever. She started counting her breath in and out, urging herself to stay present. They might need her. With an oxygen mask secured over Mason's empty face, they lifted him onto the padded gurney and moved toward the stairs.

"Who can ride with us?" the female medic asked.

Emma glanced at Dave.

"You go. I'll lock up and get his things," Dave offered, his skin drained of color. "And call Beth."

Ashen-faced, she stepped up into the ambulance, relieved that she would see for herself that he made it there.

Jordan zigzagged through the crowded emergency room. He spotted Beth standing in a quiet spot in a corridor off the reception area. Emma stood beside her, arms by her sides, staring into space.

Catching his breath, he asked: "What the hell happened?" He looked from one woman to the other.

Beth wrapped him in a hug. "Mason's had a kind of mini-heart attack. He's stable now. They are getting ready to move him to the cardiac unit for more tests."

Jordan ran his fingers through his hair. "But is he OK?"

"We'll know more after the tests." Beth shrugged, calm but unsure.

Jordan let out a long, worried breath. "You were there, right?" He looked at Emma, who hadn't acknowledged his arrival. She didn't reply. His first instinct was to think she was ignoring him, but there was something odd about her demeanor, something not fully present, like she'd iced over. He glanced at Beth and back. "Hey, Emma, are you OK?"

Emma's eyes swiveled to meet his. Pools of black had swallowed her irises. She slowly shook her head, eyes cast down, and spoke as if she was talking to herself. "I shouldn't have let him take me down there. I didn't realize."

Beth placed her hand on Emma's shoulder. "It wasn't your fault. She performed CPR. She saved his life. Thank God you were there."

"It must have been too much," Emma whispered. "The stairs."

Jordan understood. His grandpa loved to show visitors the old printing press, his pride and joy. "What can I do?"

Beth shook her head slowly. "All we can do is wait."

They stood silent for what felt like eternity. A ghostly paleness shrouded Emma's skin. Standing in the air-conned corridor, she looked cold in her t-shirt.

"Take my jacket," he offered, shrugging it off. She shook her head. "OK. You want a drink, water, Coke? A coffee?" Both women wordlessly declined. There had to be something he could do. "I'll get you both a chair."

As Emma sat down, her gaze hovered over a spot on the floor. As a marine, he'd seen people in shock many times, first during training when, pushed beyond their physical and psychological limits, guys crashed. And later, on active duty. People froze, trembled, gasped for breath, sometimes passed out. And sometimes they simply zoned out. One time, at the agency, after a brutal arrest and seizure, his partner had seemed absolutely fine, even high on achievement. Then he had vomited profusely in the car as they pulled into the office. Shock was a strange, unpredictable beast.

"Have you seen a doctor?" Jordan looked directly into Emma's face.

"I'm fine." Emma said, low and flat.

"She won't. I tried." Beth whispered. "Listen." He recognized the change in the tone of his sister's voice. Getting organized was her way of coping with uncertainty. "Let's take shifts. I'll stay. Troy is on his way. No point us all being here. Jordy, you give Emma a ride home and then swing by Grandpa's and grab his overnight things?"

"Good plan," he nodded. "Shall we go?"

"I'll wait with Beth," Emma said. "For news."

He guessed she didn't want to be in his company. She didn't trust him after the incident at the cottage. Shame bit his pride.

"I'm sorry," he blurted, "about the Demerol." Beth frowned at him as if to ask, what the hell? "I shouldn't have said anything. I stuck my nose in where it didn't belong. I am really sorry."

He expected to see a flare of anger. Instead, Emma said, "Sure. No worries." It was like she was speaking from the bottom of a deep pit.

"She needs to see a doctor, Beth," he told his sister.

Emma looked his way, but it was as if she didn't see him. "I'm fine," she announced. "No doctors."

Jordan spoke to Beth. "Make sure she does."

Chapter Eleven

Emma tapped her fingers on the steering wheel of the Dodge and inched forward. Trucks, RVs, and cars with trailers piled high with camping and fishing gear chugged along Route 1 heading south. Temperatures of ninety-six degrees and a cloudless cobalt sky had drawn weekend visitors to the water, and now everyone had decided at the same time to head home, it seemed. The delicate bell-shaped petals of the Harebells she'd picked from the yard for Beth were browning.

At first, she'd turned down Beth's invitation. But Beth had insisted she go over so she could thank her properly for being with Mason in his hour of need. She insisted Emma had saved his life. Like she'd insisted Emma see a medic at the hospital and then she and Troy take her home. The doctor confirmed Emma was having a panic attack, nothing more, and prescribed Xanax and rest. She refused the drugs but had spent the last two days hanging out at the cottage alone. She was grateful Mason was recuperating in his hospital bed.

To her surprise, she looked forward to some company and home cooking. It had been an age since anyone had made her a decent meal. The kitchen was Doug's domain. She could unpick the intricacies of a foreign war from her spot in an urban battlefield. But drop her next to an oven with a recipe and a collection of ingredients and she came undone.

The Allen family home was easy to find. The pale pink, clapboarded Cape stood proudly on a corner plot, substantial, just like the Allen family's roots in this place.

At the door, Beth stepped forward for a hug. "So good to see you."

Her husband, Troy, a dark-haired man with a stubbled chin, wearing jeans and a Portland Seadogs t-shirt, appeared beside her.

69

"How ya feelin'?" His calloused hand took hers in a forceful grip.

"Fine. Good," she blushed. "Much better now."

"Good. We were worried about you."

Emma's cheeks flushed.

"Come in." Beth beamed.

Emma handed her the flowers as she took in the hall's dark wooden floors and white walls covered in framed photos. Light streamed in from the porthole window above the turn of a wide staircase.

"You have a beautiful home."

Two chattering girls peered over the top banister before clattering down.

Beth put one arm around the taller girl. "This is Nora." And her other arm around the smaller child. "And this is Piper."

"Hi," they chorused. Their shy eagerness made Emma smile.

Nora had her mother's delicate heart-shaped face and narrow build, while Piper, blessed with her father's dimples, looked like a cute pixie.

"Wanna see our tree house?" Nora looked hopeful.

Emma was powerless to resist as the girls swept her through the kitchen and out into the yard.

"Dinner will be five minutes," Beth called after them.

Standing in the shade of an enormous maple, Piper tugged at a nylon cord and a rope ladder dropped against its wide trunk.

"This is how we get up," Nora told Emma as she hauled her body upwards, followed by Piper.

They arrived on a wooden platform resting over several thick branches. The girls were carefree and agile, unafraid. Emma longed to feel that childlike freedom again.

"You coming?" Nora's face peered out from among the branches.

Before she could tell them she was too old, Beth's voice called them for dinner.

Hands washed, Emma, the two girls, and Troy took their seats at the table. There were three empty spots: one for Beth and two others. Her host hadn't mentioned inviting anyone else. Beth placed a steaming lasagna on the mat. The aroma of melted cheese and ground beef made Emma's stomach rumble. From the hallway, Abigail appeared, pushing a walker. From behind, Jordan guided her, his hand on her back, making sure she didn't fall. Emma's heart sank. Any hopes she had were dashed of a breezy evening of good-natured conversation. They exchanged polite smiles as Jordan settled his mom toward the end of the table and pulled out the last empty chair. Next to Emma.

"Let's eat!" Troy announced. "Honey?"

Beth dished out the food. Within touching distance of Jordan, Emma felt stiff and self-conscious. "How long has the house been in the family?" she managed.

"It's one of the first built in the area," Beth said. "Our ancestor Angus Allen arrived from Scotland in the 1740s and made the bay his home. The house was built much later in 1867."

Perhaps bored by a topic she'd surely heard discussed hundreds of times, Piper pulled a face at Jordan who, in reply, scrunched up his nose and stuck out his tongue. The girls collapsed into peals of laughter.

Beth continued, reaching for Troy's hand, "We moved in here shortly after we were married. We're very lucky."

Beth and Troy were one of those couples who seemed an unlikely match but fitted together precisely. She was neat, organized and bubbly, while he appeared to be a little rough around the edges, but was warm and direct. By the way they looked at each other, it was clear they loved each other very much.

"How did you meet?" Emma asked.

"They were high school sweethearts," Nora grinned like she was sharing a secret. "Mom was homecoming queen and Dad asked her to prom. He'd liked her since middle school, but he didn't think he had a chance."

"Yeah, thank you, young lady," Troy interrupted. "We don't need all the details. So, Emma, where are your folks from?"

"A little town just north of London, St Albans."

"They still live there?"

Emma had a choice to make about how much to tell them. She knew an awkward pause would follow. "Erm, I was an only child and my parents died in a car accident when I was eleven."

Silence, as usual.

"I'm so sorry," Beth said.

"Me too," said Troy. "That must have been hard."

"It was a long time ago." Emma said lightly, trying to lift the mood.

The girls stared at her. Jordan said nothing and turned to help his mom wipe her face with a napkin. Downplaying the impact of her parents' death always felt like a betrayal of how much she loved them, but she didn't want to answer any more questions. Her loss had always been private. Time to change the topic.

"How's Mason?"

"He's doing fine, great," Beth said. "He'll be in there for a few more weeks. They want to do more tests."

Abigail mumbled something to Jordan, who nodded.

"Thank God he's got great insurance!" Troy added.

"More?" Beth spooned another slice of lasagna onto Emma's plate.

Emma reached for the salt grinder. Still looking at his mom, Jordan extended his arm in the same direction. Their fingers brushed. She dropped her fist to her lap as if he'd burned her. He startled before he appeared to recover his manners. "You first."

"No, you first."

"No, you." He nodded.

"Thanks." Her skin was about to peel off with embarrassment. She did not know why, but Jordan could make her feel like she was in the wrong place, out of time and exposed.

"Do you live in Great Uncle Ben's cottage?" Piper asked.

Emma tightened. From questions about her parents' death, they'd segued into another sensitive topic. Jordan had made it crystal clear that her presence there offended him.

"For now." Emma hoped that was enough to satisfy the little girl's curiosity.

"Was he your uncle?" she asked.

Emma smiled. "No, but he was a very, very good friend of mine."

"How did you know him?" Nora's sapphire blue eyes fixed on her.

Emma relaxed a notch. Ben was easy to talk about. "We worked together at the International Informer, the newspaper."

Nora nodded. "He was a famous reporter." She stuffed a fork of pasta in her mouth.

"Yes. And a very good one. He taught me, showed me who to talk to, and how to ask the right questions. And how to keep safe in dangerous places."

Nora's gaze didn't waver. "He traveled everywhere."

"That's right."

"Where did you meet?"

"In a place called Syria."

"That is in the Middle East. It's a long way from here." Nora's tone was serious. Her obvious interest in her uncle's work reminded Emma of herself at that age. She would be a natural in the newsroom.

"That's right."

That first assignment when they met had been rough. She was new in the field. The demand from the office for stories was relentless and working out what was going on, where she needed to be, and how to get there exhausted her mind and body. The paper had dropped her in at the deep end, and she was just about keeping her head above water. Ben kept her afloat.

"You didn't have your mom and dad with you, so Uncle Ben looked after you?" Piper asked quietly.

Emma felt tears prick the back of her eyes. They got it. "We looked after each other."

Emma looked from Piper to Beth. She didn't wish to sound presumptuous in front of Ben's blood relatives, but what she was going to say was the truth. "He was family to me."

Jordan stood up. "That's enough with the questions, kiddos," he said. "Let's clear the table."

The clanking of cutlery and dishes and pushing back of chairs cleared the air.

While his wife and kids walked into the kitchen, Troy turned to her. "Emma, you sail or fish?"

"No," she smiled, grateful for the small talk. "Not unless you count a holiday cruising round the Greek islands when I finished college." It sounded idyllic, but she'd spent most of it lying on her mattress, swallowing down the urge to puke and wishing she was back in New York on dry land.

"Blueberry Slump." Nora walked in slowly, carefully holding a wide dessert dish in between oven gloves. "Uncle Jordan and I made it."

The girls' innocence and lack of cynicism was a welcome break from the persistent whir of thoughts and memories that had been spinning through her head for months. Who knew the company of kids could be so soothing?

"Family recipe." Troy's eyes widened.

The pudding was delicious. The mix of stewed blueberries and sweet dumplings reminded Emma of school crumble. Jordan could bake and he cooked with his nieces. She couldn't make him out. He was apparently sweet and kind with Beth, his mother, and the girls, but also ice cold with an edge of bitterness.

Around the table, the conversation had moved on to fishing.

"It's going to wipe out the lobster beds if someone doesn't do something." Troy pushed his empty bowl away, his heavy brow creased.

"What proof do you have?" Jordan asked.

"The beds are dying, man. It's obvious. And contamination from the plant is doin' it. Have you been to Sharpe's Rock recently? The sea grass is rotting on the beach. It's like Jell-O. It's covered in foam, and it stinks. We went out looking for birds, didn't we kids?" The girls nodded. "None. No gulls, cormorants, terns, razorbills. Nothing. What more proof do you need?" He threw his napkin into his bowl. "Ed says there're signs of pollution as far south as Cornwell's Lighthouse."

"That's miles away," Jordan sounded doubtful. His blue eyes twinkled like a faceted sapphire as focused on his brother-in-law. Emma shifted her attention away from his face and the unwelcome twang in her body to Piper licking her bowl cupped to her face. "You are certain it's because of the plant?"

"Where else could it be from?" Troy threw up his hands. "That cleanup three years ago. Has it happened? As we all know. No. Meanwhile, the catch is down. We're talking about our livelihoods, man, my girls' college funds, the future of this town."

"Has the Association raised it?"

"Of course we have." Troy's voice rose with frustration. "At city and state level," he continued. "Actual harm is going to come to this town, and no one is listening. It's devastation. It's corruption." Emma straightened up, her reporter's brain clicking into gear. "Ask yourself, where is the money, our taxpayer dollars, earmarked for the cleanup? Where has it gone? I'll tell you." Troy rammed his index finger into the tablecloth. "Into the pockets of those Boston fat cats, I betcha." He shook his head, exasperated. "You know, I read on the internet that Maine lobstering totals about half a billion dollars a year. There's a lot at stake that someone somewhere doesn't give a shit about. Excuse me, ladies."

Emma had heard much worse. "Has anyone reported any of this? The contamination. I mean, in the media?"

"She's interested!" Troy pointed at Emma. "She understands the seriousness. And she's been here five minutes! No offence."

"None taken," Emma replied.

"No one is on this. And why is that? And The Siren, what can Dave do all by himself?" His voice dropped. "No one reads that piece of ..."

"Troy." Beth shot him a warning look.

"Honey, it's the truth, and you know it. The paper's days are numbered. Only Mace's money keeps it going."

Historic Maine fishing town under threat from corporate contamination. "There is a story there," Emma said. "Perhaps you should go national?"

"How?" Troy sighed. "Fat chance."

"I know people."

After dinner, Beth washed the pots while Emma dried, both watching Jordan and the girls through the window as they horsed around in the yard. He grabbed Nora, who squealed with delight as he tucked her under one powerful arm and Piper under the other and swirled them around like they were bags of feathers. Whenever he stopped, panting, and lowered them to the ground, the girls begged him to chase them and begin the game again, and he obliged.

"He's so great with the kids." Beth rested her hands on the sink edge and said quietly, "He'd have made a great dad."

Jordan was probably in his mid-thirties. He had years ahead of him. "He is still a young guy."

"I don't think he's interested anymore."

"In having kids?" He seemed to love them. "Why not?"

"He was married. Didn't he mention it?"

He hadn't told her much of anything. She'd been wrong on all counts; he was a divorcee with no kids. Lucky escape for the wife. "No."

Jordan stood in the middle of the lawn with his hands over his face, apparently counting while the girls ran to hide. Beth placed the lasagna dish on the draining board. "I thought he'd have a tribe of kids, but Sophie passed before they had the chance."

"His wife died?" Emma said, surprised, and suddenly guilty that she'd judged him.

Beth appeared to catch herself. "You know, he's always telling me to mind my own business. I'll leave it to him to tell you about it."

Jordan lay on his sofa, his hands behind his head, watching the game, feeling as if a rock had lodged in his gut. He'd eaten too much pasta and pie, but it was more than that. It had been an all-round uncomfortable meal. He was sitting next to her and was pretty sure that wasn't by accident. He was grateful Emma was there for Mason, but that didn't mean they needed to have her in their family home. He knew from bitter experience that Beth couldn't resist a set up. He cringed at the memory of that teacher from the high school—what was her name?—Kiera. Beth had invited her to a 4th July barbecue, hoping they'd hit it off. She was sweet, but boring as hell. And then there was the vet. Beth made him take their dog because she had a 'sore paw'. And the waitress at The Claw, Lily's niece, Meesha. Beth and Lily had worked in cahoots on that one. Meesha was gorgeous, but same story. He chose not to get involved.

On September 1, it would be six years since Sophie's death. He was sober, steady, and earning a living. He had his art, his home, and his sanity. That was more than enough. It was priceless. He would allow nothing, not anyone, to rock his boat. Beth should give it a break with the matchmaker routine. Particularly with this woman, who seemed to despise him. She didn't speak to him the entire meal, except when they both went for the salt. For some explicable reason, when their fingers brushed, he felt a kindling in blood. Primal reflex, he guessed. She had just told them about a cruise around the Aegean. The image of her in a bikini, her long legs stretched out, tanning on the deck, still lingered in his imagination.

Emma was probably still sore about their fight. He'd meant to apologize again, but there wasn't an opportunity without humiliating himself and her. When he came in from playing with the kids, she'd gone.

He hit mute on the control as the game switched to commercials. He'd never met anyone quite like her. His female Marine friends were tough, fearless, particularly the officers who took no shit from anyone. They'd had to claw their way up a greasy pole. They were physically strong, too. DEA female agents were built of similar stuff. They'd scaled the ranks of an organization dominated by men, and macho guys at that. Emma was intrepid, independent, operated in a man's world apparently, but she didn't give off the same vibe. She was a mix of super-bright, obviously, like Ben, and but also vulnerable, somehow, to cracking. There was something delicate about her. And beautiful, he had to admit. He was a sucker for red hair, and her freckles were adorable.

He'd enjoyed listening to her talk about work. Troy had asked a million questions over coffee. He could have shared his own stories, if he'd wanted to. What she'd seen in Syria wasn't so different from the things he'd witnessed on active duty in Afghanistan and Iraq; they just saw it from different angles. She was one of only a few people in this town who could understand what it was like out there. And, he would admit, it seemed she really loved Uncle Ben. Admiration coated every word she said about him. She'd been beside him when he died, Beth said. He hadn't known that. It should have been one of the family but Mason, it seemed, got confused by Ben's doctor's medical speak. They didn't realize how serious it was and time was short. He was glad Emma was there.

Jordan shifted on the sofa. Perhaps he'd misjudged her and should cut her some slack. She had her own problems to deal with. He could not imagine what it would be like to lose your folks so young and be so alone. His parents had their issues, but they'd given him and his sister a solid childhood. They were loved. Abigail was fading, but they knew she'd given them her all. He'd been twenty-five and married, an adult, when his father passed. Beth was twenty-three and with Troy. She was a pain in the ass, but God, he appreciated having her around.

The game resumed. He clicked on the sound. What did it matter? Emma would be gone in a heartbeat, anyway.

Chapter Twelve

Standing on the little jetty, Emma untethered the skiff bobbing in the water and stepped one foot in. A wave lifted the hull, and she toppled inside like a sack of potatoes.

A horizontal pole pointed at her. It must be the rudder thing. The cord dangling off the motor, she was almost certain, was the way to get it started. She grabbed and yanked. Nothing. She pulled again. Nothing. The motor appeared well maintained but ancient; perhaps it was out of gas. Her heart sank. She looked at it as if it would tell her what was wrong. Third time lucky, it stuttered and spat. The little craft leaped forward, and she scrambled for the pole. The boat swerved right and then she over-corrected sharp left before pointing it straight out to sea.

The sea breeze whipped her hair across her face. She breathed out and forced her shoulders to relax as the cottage shrank behind her. The ocean stretched before her like blue silk. Achievement spread a smile across her face. Google Maps showed Sharpe's Rock was maybe two miles away? It couldn't be far; Troy had taken the girls there on one of their birdwatching trips. She should know it when she saw it. He had insisted that the impact of the pollution was obvious: dead birds and grass.

If the damage was as extensive as Troy suggested, she'd take photos and call the Informer. She reached into her back pocket for her phone to check her course. No phone. Dammit. With one eye on the water, she reached into her camera bag. Not there either. She could see it resting on the kitchen counter. For a split second, she considered turning back. No. She didn't want to waste fuel. She had no idea how much she had. But the route was simple to remember: head for the lighthouse—easy to spot—curve round the promontory, obvious, and the island should be in sight. She wasn't a sailor, but how difficult could it be?

The lighthouse was further away than she imagined. Motoring in the little boat was a bit like walking in the desert. You could be out there for hours and still barely seem to move forward.

Swells dragged at the boat as she approached the rocks. Spray hit her face. She gripped the rudder. If she made it past the lighthouse, she was sure the current would subside. It took all of her strength to keep on course. A stiffening wind buffeted the water. Salt stung her face, bare arms and legs. Wearing a t-shirt and shorts, she'd slathered on sunscreen, worried about UV rays, not windburn. The tide switched and yanked the boat sideways.

Droplets of rain landed on her face. She gunned the motor, trying to resist the momentum dragging her east into a wide expanse of limitless sea.

It didn't matter if she swung the pole left or right, the little skiff didn't respond. Panic raced up her spine. The prow lurched into the air and smashed back down into the rolling surf. Her brain stuttered. Bombarded by a shower of ocean, hair plastered to her skull, water cascading down her face, she gasped for breath.

Her wet fingers turned white clamped around the edge of the little bench. The tiny boat flew upward and suddenly she was there, gripping the plastic door handle, black smoke rushing at her as she catapulted out of a tumbling car. Freezing water tipping into the hull brought her back. As the boat bounced from crest to crest, she huddled low clutching her camera bag, her clothes stuck to her skin, terrified she was about to capsize. She wasn't a great swimmer, the water was ice cold, and there was no life vest.

Jordan picked up his phone from his kitchen counter and walked out onto the step. A sharp wind raced up over the gravel. A metallic zing hit his nose. Electricity in the air.

A text from Ramon: Rain check?

The sky darkened. It was going to be a big one. This was only the first act. Not a day to take the boat out collecting driftwood, that was for sure. He tapped a reply: Yup. Good call.

As he turned, the breeze beginning to bite, he thought he heard the faint splutter of a motor. He scanned the bay. What idiot would be out on the water? His weather app promised 89 percent thunder and lightning. The fishing crews had hunkered down in The Claw, boats lashed to the quay. Troy was complaining about missing a day's catch. Same for the tourist skippers. You'd be a jerk to take anyone out there today.

The motor puttered on and off like a bumble bee bashing against glass. He stared at the blackening water, his eyes narrowing. The prow of a boat peaked into his line of vision. Was it a flash of red hair? No. Seriously? The little craft caught another wave and reared up. If it capsized and she wasn't wearing a lifejacket, that was her done. Game over. The skiff shrank as it rushed toward open water. What was she thinking? She would get smashed out there.

He ran down to the beach, waving his arms and making a circling motion with his hand. "Emma!" he shouted. "Emma, about turn, get to shore!" The little boat had almost disappeared. He hoped to God she wasn't in Ben's old fishing rig. That was only just about safe enough to sail in the shallows of the cove. She either hadn't heard him or was ignoring him. That would be a dumbass tourist move. Which wasn't unlikely.

"Emma!" he screamed.

Jordan ran inside, grabbed his kitbag, distress flares, marine radio, and two lifejackets. He pulled on his waterproof pants and jacket and slid the keys to the dinghy into his pocket. In the minutes it took him to haul the trailer down to the little dock, she had disappeared. Crazy woman. Clipping on his life jacket, he revved the motor, and the dinghy pitched forward. Rain stung his face, then stabbed at it with hail pellets. Where the hell was she?

A flash of electricity tore open the sky, followed by a thunderous boom that seemed to echo off the mountains. Wincing, he pushed the dinghy hard into the wind, steering clear of the rocks.

Through the deluge, he spotted her. Where was she going? Why didn't she turn ashore? Then he realized the boat was out of control.

Thunder rolled overhead like a Challenger tank storming through the desert. He hunched forward. In just a few minutes it would be too dangerous, and he would have to turn back. The little boat soared into view on a rolling wave. He pushed the dinghy hard to reach it. The tiny vessel rocked precariously, revealing Emma, soaked through, curled up into a ball in the hull. She was taking on water, and she wasn't moving.

"Emma!" he shouted, the wind swallowing her name. "Emma!" The dinghy rose and fell with the push and pull of the waves. "Emma!" His voice was hoarse. She lifted her head. Her face was white with fear. "It's Jordan," he bellowed above the howling wind. "Do exactly what I tell you. Grab this ring."

She nodded, crawling on all fours to face him. He tossed the lifebuoy directly at her, hoping it would land inside the boat. He hit his mark. "Hold on to it and whatever you do," he hollered as loud as he could, "don't let go!"

Blank-eyed, she gripped the ring with both arms. He slowly reeled the little boat toward him, rain streaming down his face. As soon as she was close enough to touch, he strained forward, grabbed her cold forearm and the strap of her camera bag and yanked her aboard. The waves sucked the empty skiff under the surface. He grimaced.

Emma slumped on the bottom of the dinghy, her entire body shaking, trying to catch her breath. He let the boat surf the current north toward a sliver of blue sky, all the way to Sharpe's Rock. They could wait out the storm there.

Jordan rammed the dinghy up onto the shingle and hauled it out of the water. Panting, he collapsed onto his ass. Thunder rumbled over the distant mountains. The storm was racing inland, taking the worst of the rain with it.

Emma swayed on her feet, her hair, t-shirt, shorts, and sneakers soaked through, her camera bag slung across her chest.

"Have you got a death wish?" he yelled at her.

"No," she shook her head. "Have you?"

Her response rocketed his adrenaline. It was so bizarre, for a second, he didn't know what to say. "I just saved your life."

She blinked as if he was speaking a foreign language.

"Take your shirt off," he said as calmly as he could as he removed his jacket.

"What?" Her eyes rolled left and right, trying, it seemed, to make sense of where they were.

"Take your shirt off." He lifted his t-shirt over his head. She was in shock and needed to warm up fast if she wasn't going to get hypothermia.

"What? Why?" She seemed affronted. He was trying to do her a favor by offering her his dry clothes and she was being awkward. If the stakes weren't so high, he'd leave her here to fend for herself.

"You'll get sick if you don't." He handed her his shirt. "Put it on."

"Do I have to?"

"Yes." It was like arguing with Nora and Piper.

She turned away as she stripped off her top. He tried not to look, but her smooth back was ivory white against the purple sea beyond. His shirt swamped her.

"Sit next to me and we can share my jacket."

She eyed him suspiciously, her arms clasped around her slim, shivering body.

"You can sit here or not. I don't care." He was trying to be kind, but she made it so difficult. "But I recommend you keep as warm as possible."

Emma carefully placed herself next to him on the damp sand. He draped his Gore-Tex across their shoulders. "I won't bite."

She didn't even crack a smile. Her skin was ice cold against his.

"We gotta wait here until the sea calms. Then I'll take you home."

She dropped her forehead to her knees, breathing hard, apparently exhausted.

He could have explained to her the dangers of not taking the sea seriously, but she'd probably learned that the hard way. All he said was, "You're welcome."

Sand prickled her body, burning her skin. Ash floated above her face. The stench of charred metal clogged her nose. A siren wailed. Heat and fire.

Her toes burrowed into the cold sand. Caustic wind slapped her face. Her thoughts began to line up in a logical order. Warmth flooded against one side of her body. Another human. A living one. She lifted her head. A familiar face. Jordan.

"Where are we?" The sky looked wrung out and gray.

"Sharpe's Rock."

"Seriously?" Her gaze swept across the beach. It seemed to sway beneath her. "How did we get here?"

"You don't remember?" His voice was flat.

"I was on my way here," she marveled. Somehow, she'd made it through the storm and arrived at exactly the place she'd intended to.

He raised his eyebrows. "You sure chose a dramatic way to get here."

His face was just inches from hers. Water dripped from his short, wet hair over his tanned skin. His eyes were a storm of anger and concern.

"Where's the boat?"

"Matchsticks at the bottom of the ocean, I expect."

She shivered, her eyes resting on the dinghy. "You found me?"

He nodded. "Just in time."

Crashing waves; water in the hull; a streak of lightning. She'd been stupid. She had put her life, and maybe his, at risk. She'd broken her own rule to be prepared for any eventuality. How had he known she was out there? It didn't matter. She was lucky. She had that knack. With relief and regret, a tear slipped down her face, and then another.

Embarrassed by the enormity of her mistake and that he, of all people, was her rescuer, she wiped them away. She owed him, now. He didn't say a word, though, and she was grateful.

They stared out at the sea as the wind retreated. Soaked, with no idea how long they would have to wait huddled together, his muscled arm resting against hers, she felt an unfamiliar feeling that took her a minute to identify: she felt safe.

She turned to him. "It could have been bad, right?"

"Yup."

"I'm so sorry, Jordan." She swallowed hard. "I'm so, so sorry."

He nodded, apparently understanding the sincerity of her apology. He didn't claim the moral high-ground and lecture her on how dumb she'd been, like she deserved. "Thank you. Really.

From the bottom of my heart." It sounded cheesy, but she meant every word.

"No problem."

Streaks of sun cut through the cloud, lighting up the sky in glorious shimmers of gold and silver as they sat in silence, staring out.

"Listen," he looked directly at her, speaking fast. "I want to explain about the Demerol thing. My dad was an addict and I just know it's not a good scene to get into. But I shouldn't have said anything. I overstepped. I interfered. And I'm sorry." He sighed, apparently glad to get that off his chest. "Really sorry."

His apology took her by surprise. The incident seemed silly now.

"Oh, no worries," she said. She didn't owe him an explanation, but she wanted to give him one. "Full disclosure. I don't take them. The bottle is still sealed."

"Good call." He nodded emphatically.

A tiny bird with black feathers landed on the beach three feet away, pecked the sand and took off again.

"Weather's improving," he stated, looking at the blue cutting through the sky.

Before he could move, she asked: "Your dad overdosed?"

"Yup."

"I'm sorry, that's really sad."

He shrugged. "I wasn't a kid. I was twenty-six and married—just." He was matter of fact, like the event drained of emotion years ago, but his behavior at her place told her that wasn't the case.

People always thought that because she lost her mum and dad when she was so young, her pain must be greater than their grief, like it was a competition. She knew it wasn't. "Still. It hurts."

"It was brutal." He said almost to himself.

She paused. "Did your dad teach you to handle a dinghy like that?"

He smiled and shook his head. Apparently, it was a silly question. "Marines."

Emma could have guessed he was a military veteran. He had the build for one thing, and that physical confidence. "How long were you in?"

"Five years."

A gentle breeze brushed over them. "Where were you deployed?"

"Afghanistan and Iraq. Four tours. Two and two."

"Wow." She nodded, impressed. "No scars or broken bones to show for it?"

"A bullet wound in my left thigh that almost cost me my life."

He stood up. She understood he didn't want to talk anymore. "Shall we?" He offered his hand and pulled her to her feet. Together, they pushed the dinghy back into the water.

"Why were you headed out here anyway?" he asked.

"Curious about the pollution." She clambered onto the boat as he held it level. Hot anxiety fired through her veins. Boats, it seemed, were not her thing. She clenched her fists against it. She tried to sound unfazed as he passed her a life jacket and started the motor.

"Can we take a quick look, as we're here?"

She'd never make it back here.

"At what? The pollution?"

She nodded.

"We need to get you back and in warm clothes."

"Aren't you curious to see what Troy was talking about?"

"Sure, I am." He steered the dinghy along the shallows. "But now?"

"Why not? Make it worth it."

"Two minutes and we're gone."

She smiled.

Leaning against the edge of the dinghy her camera out of its case and resting in her freezing fingers, Emma scanned the water. "There!"

Jordan cut the engine and let the boat drift closer to a band of rotting sea grass. Among the matted blades lay a dead baby seal blanketed in white foam. Emma lifted the lens, let it focus, and then gagged. The stench was incredible. Jordan looked aghast.

"There's more." She pointed ahead at two dead herons floating in a shallow yellow puddle. She raised her camera again.

The pictures were grim but could never convey the full horror of the scene. It was horrific, even to her, and she'd seen her share of death and wanton destruction. Jordan shook his head. She thought maybe she saw tears in his eyes.

"Someone has to tell people about this," he announced, dumbstruck. He trained his topaz eyes on her. "You're a reporter, you gotta write something. You have pictures now. People need to see what's going on here."

Chapter Thirteen

In The Claw, sitting at a table in the corner, Emma sipped her coffee. Lily, dressed in denim overalls, her hair spiralling out of her wide headband, appeared from the kitchen and strolled over to top up her mug.

"How are you doing?"

Emma's face flushed. Word had already got round about the city-girl who'd taken out an ancient rowboat in a summer storm and had to be rescued. Lily placed a hand on her shoulder. "I'm glad you're safe. The weather up here is fickle. Unpredictable. It's something I've gotten used to. Now I love it. But you need to respect it."

Emma nodded. "I've taken that lesson totally onboard."

"Good."

"Hi," Jordan's voice floated up from behind Lily. He locked eyes with hers. She blushed, surprised. "I didn't expect to see you around town today," he continued. "You need to rest."

"I'm waiting for Beth," Emma said, and coughed. "She wants to talk about the cottage." Her text suggested the news might not be great. Whatever it was, she needed to know where she stood.

Lily returned to the bar.

Jordan peered at her. "How are you feeling? Did you see a doctor?"

Another one. Jordan was being nice, but it was unnecessary. And she was certainly not going to visit a doctor. She'd seen too many of those.

Once the wind had dropped to a slight breeze, they'd glided back to the mainland in the dinghy, and Jordan had driven her home. He'd been so kind. Huddled in his jacket, she couldn't stop shivering. He had walked her all the way to the porch door and left her there, insisting she take a hot shower and call if she felt at all unwell. She did exactly as she was told and went to bed. That he'd seen her like that was mortifying. She wanted to tell him that this wasn't the person she was. Before the bomb shattered her brain and bits of her body, she didn't flinch, she didn't scare, she never blacked out in panic.

"Really, I'm fine. I've had a fantastic night's sleep and have just eaten a huge breakfast," she said lightly, looking at Lily at the bar for confirmation.

"I wouldn't say huge."

"Not by your standards. Big," Emma conceded.

"No nausea, headache, or fever?" He wouldn't stop.

She shook her head. Saltwater still burned in her nose. But she'd get over it, eventually. No permanent harm done, but she would never live this down. "Just a massive dose of humiliation and self-recrimination."

Lily called over. "Isn't he a great guy? Quite the hero."

Jordan's eyes dropped to the floor.

"I was really lucky, so lucky you were there," Emma said, and she meant it. "You were amazing, and so kind. Again, thank you."

And now she wished they'd let it go.

Lily winked at her. What did that mean?

"You want to sit?" She asked politely, knowing he would decline. He must have seen enough of her over the past twenty-four hours to last the rest of her stay.

To her surprise, he pulled out a chair. He really must be worried about her health.

Emma tried breezy small talk. "What are you doing in here on a sunny day?"

"Meeting Beth and Troy for an early lunch while the girls are at ballet. Burgers on Saturday. Family tradition. Of sorts."

"Nice," she nodded, her head emptying of anything to say.

Taylor Swift filtered through the sound system, singing about faded love and longing. Emma sipped her coffee.

Jordan coughed. "This place is like my second home." His words landed awkwardly.

"But you don't drink?" Her question rolled out like an unintended challenge.

"Long story." He paused, looked at his hands and then into her face, and appeared to reconsider his answer. He took a breath. "I was married. To Sophie." He swallowed. "After my wife died, I sort of, well, I really, went off the rails."

Emma's mind filled with questions: how, when, and why did Sophie die? She was so young. Was it illness? Instead of asking, she listened. She was tired of talking about Doug, of reliving the moment, recounting the story of the explosion for the benefit of others' curiosity when it didn't benefit her. She suspected he might feel the same.

Jordan continued. "I thought alcohol was my friend. It wasn't. And now I'm sober, I don't want to go back there again. But I like it here. And Lily. She is a good, good friend."

Emma understood the value of those.

"I'm so sorry about your wife," was all she said before Beth appeared, panting for breath.

"Hi Emma!" she exclaimed, adding "Jordy." She looked from one to the other. "Am I late, again?"

Emma checked her phone. Half an hour. "Only a little."

Beth shook her head, talking a mile a minute. "Traffic is insane. I had a viewing in Rockcliff and then dropped by the hospital. Mason says hi. He's doing fine before anyone asks. He's got the nurses running round after our 'sweet old grandpa'." Beth rolled her eyes. "Troy will be another twenty minutes dropping the girls off. He couldn't find their tights." Emma smiled at the image of Troy chauffeuring a pair of little ballerinas. "Anyway… How are you?" Beth touched Emma's shoulder.

"Fine." Emma smiled and quickly deflected. "When'll Mason be out?"

"They are keeping him in for a few more days for more tests, which he is not happy about. God knows he's got good insurance! He's fretting about the paper," she sat down and glanced at the copy on the table, "which isn't helping his blood pressure."

"Sure." Emma blinked away the image of Mason on the tiled floor.

"To be honest, Troy and I think The Siren should close for the summer. Give Mason a break, time to convalesce. And when was the last time Dave took a vacation?"

"The paper has never missed an issue, not in its entire one hundred-and-fifty-six-year history," Jordan cut in. He seemed unusually dismayed.

"Well, we can't run it." A note of irritation lit Beth's voice. She seemed tired. Tiny lines crinkled around her eyes. She had a full-time job, two kids, an ill mom and her grandfather was in hospital. And it didn't sound like Troy's lobster business was raking it in.

"I'm booked solid. Back-to-back with viewings. It's high season, Jordy."

Jordan's mouth set in a firm line. He stood up. "I'll give you two some privacy."

Beth shook her head as Jordan retreated to the bar. "Let's get down to business. I have a potential buyer."

"Really?" Emma said, startled by the good news.

Beth didn't return her smile. "However." Here came the but. "Probate is taking a long time. It's complicated because the house is here, but the rest of the estate is in another state." She let out a long, frustrated sigh. "It could take a month or more to transfer the deed to you before we can embark on the sale. I've chased, but the DC probate office says they're buckling under a heavy caseload and the team is short-staffed over the summer. Everyone's on vacation."

Emma's heart sank. Sirens Bay was a beautiful place to take a quick break, but not somewhere to spend weeks and weeks whiling away time. She'd go stir-crazy. "Isn't there anything we can do?"

"I'll keep on it," Beth assured her. "Don't worry, it'll get done. But bear with me."

Emma nodded slowly. "Thanks, Beth."

Troy pulled out a chair. "No one is as determined as my wife."

"Hey, honey." Beth kissed him on the cheek. Even after the wear and tear of years of married life, they were still cute together.

Jordan sat down beside Emma.

"Hey dude." Troy smiled.

Jordan ignored him. "You could do it," he turned to Emma.

"Do what?" She had no idea what he was talking about.

"Run the paper while Mason is in hospital."

Emma leaned back, slowly shaking her head. "I'm a reporter, not a publisher. And I don't know anything about local papers. Or this town."

Beth's face came alive. "But you could learn? You've worked for papers for most of your career, right? You could run that itty-bitty newsletter with your eyes closed." She said it with such certainty. "It would only be a for a few weeks, maybe a month."

"A month?" It was a ridiculous suggestion right out of leftfield. And there was no way she was going to stick around for a month.

"We can pay. I'll waive my commission."

"It's not the money…"

"It would mean a lot to Mason." Troy added, warming to the idea.

"See it as a challenge?" Jordan said it like an instruction. He seemed to have grasped that a test was something she'd find hard to resist. "What else are you going to do with your time here?"

It was a good question, and the answer was none of his business. "I'm only staying a few more days."

"But you could, until the sale goes through." Beth's face glowed with hope. "Enjoy the property while you have it."

The Siren reported stories about lost cats and high school football scores. Emma shook her head.

Jordan's gaze fixed on her. He didn't blink. "Someone's got to write that story. Why not you, at The Siren?"

Three expectant faces waited for her to respond. It was time to leave. She raised her hands in a gesture of surrender meant to temporarily appease them before she came back later with a definitive, no thank you. "I'll think about it," she said vaguely.

Jordan watched as Emma strolled toward the door. Her long copper hair, brushed smooth, glowed in the light of the bar. The image of her, rain-drenched and scared, cowering in the bottom of the boat, flashed through his brain. A strange tightness gathered in his chest. He breathed out. Everything was fine. No one got hurt. She was fine.

"What do you really think about her taking over the paper for a little while?" Beth asked Troy as Jordan waved to Lily to take their order. His was the same every week: quarter-pounder cheeseburger, no pickle, extra fries, lots of ketchup.

"I'm all for it if it means she'll write that story." Troy poured himself a glass of water. "Think she'll do it?"

"I hope so." Jordan had no idea. Emma was hard to figure out. She wasn't the princess he had imagined. Perhaps he'd mistaken that thousand-yard stare for arrogance, when it was really something else: shyness? Grief? Trauma? It was hard to tell. She didn't spill. He had told her about his dad and Sophie, and he still knew next to nothing about her, except that her parents were gone. She was curious and resilient, that was clear, and she didn't display any self-pity. She had a thirst for adventure, for sure. He admired that, although hers verged on suicidal. If she could hold the fort at the paper for a while, she'd be doing them all a favor. Mason would be crushed if The Siren closed, even for a short while. He'd invested his heart and soul in that place. "If it helps Pops, and he's OK with it, it's a win-win."

Beth wriggled her nose.

"What?" He knew his sister was plotting something.

"If she says yes, I don't think we'll tell him. Not just yet."

"You sure that's a good idea?" Mason would hit the roof if he thought they'd gone behind his back. The paper was his baby, his pride and joy. He'd poured so much money and time into it over the years.

Before Beth could answer, Lily placed their burgers on the table. She looked at Jordan with concern. "How bad was it?"

"At Sharpe's Rock? Pretty bad."

"That's my brother, always ready to rescue a damsel in distress," Beth grinned.

"I was talking about the pollution," he said, irritated. "There's yellow foam everywhere, dead birds, a dead seal. And it stinks."

"Told you." Troy stuffed a fry into his mouth.

"What was she thinking heading out alone?" Lily asked.

"God knows." Jordan shook his head. "She doesn't have any friends up here, I guess, to accompany her." It sounded sad as he said it. "She could have come to real harm out there." Beth and Lily shared a look. "What?"

"Nothing," Beth said, patting her napkin against her lip.

"What?" he insisted.

"About what?" Beth smiled and caught Lily's eye.

He got it. Lily, it seemed, had joined his sister in playing cupid. He shook his head. "Don't even think about it."

"Enjoy your meals." Lily spun on her heel. As she walked away, she glanced over her shoulder and winked at Beth.

—————————— **Chapter Fourteen** ——————————

Emma stirred her cappuccino, watching the chocolate powder swirl and dissolve into the froth. Should she? The question had tumbled around in her brain since yesterday. It was a great story, an important story, and it needed to be told, for the sake of the town but also for anyone who cared about corporate accountability and the environment. She'd been aching to get back into the field. Perhaps this could baby-steps, a way to prove to Louise in D.C. that she was ready and that her news nose was still keen, that she could deliver. Getting to the bottom of what was happening at Sharpe's Rock would hone her rusty reporting skills and boost her confidence. Or should she leave well alone, head out as planned?

Erik appeared from out back, carrying a box of what looked like school supplies.

"Hey Emma, how are you? No news about Ben's stuff, yet." He rested his load on her table.

"Oh, no, I wasn't expecting you would." She paused. She needed a sounding board. Erik was half local, half outsider, and he seemed nice, down to earth. "Have you got a minute?"

"Sure. What's up?" He pulled out a chair.

Emma glanced at Riley, cleaning the spout on the coffee machine just within earshot. It was crazy that she was even thinking of taking Beth and Jordan's suggestion seriously. But her current options were to stay in Sirens Bay, twiddling her thumbs until the sale completed, or return to her stuffy apartment and do the same there until her medical leave ended and Louise called her in to discuss her future.

"Did you find more magazines?" He looked excited.

"Oh, no." Emma shook her head. "It's that ... you know

Mason is still in the hospital?" Erik nodded. "Well, Beth's asked me to run The Siren until he's well enough to return to work."

Erik's eyebrows rose above his glasses frame. He said nothing.

"Is it nuts?"

Erik appeared to consider the idea, then shook his head. "You're a journalist, right?"

"Yeah, but…"

"Too small-time for you?" He wasn't being sarcastic, just real.

"Umm, no." He'd touched a nerve. Maybe her hesitation about taking on the paper for just a few weeks was her reporter ego telling her she, Emma James, foreign correspondent for the Informer, was above writing local news. News was news, after all, as Ben would say.

Erik continued. "The paper needs some—what's the word—direction?" He paused and seemed to change tack. "That said, maybe you're just the one Mason needs to set it back on course?"

If she got involved, she would have to run it differently and print different stories; her professional integrity wouldn't let her churn out the guff Mason allowed to go to print. Her focus would be Sharpe's Rock and the pollution.

Riley spoke up: "I'd start with the website and take off all those annoying pop-up ads so you can actually read the news."

Han lifted his head from his laptop. "That's an easy fix. Super simple."

Emma turned to look at him. "Really?"

Han nodded. "And there are way better ways to generate ad-revenue."

"He is a genius." Riley stated.

"You could do that?"

He nodded and resumed typing.

The bell jingled.

"Traffic is a bitch today," Kirsty announced in her forty-a-day rasp, pushing an empty trolley. "Don't people know it's a day of rest?"

Erik piled the previous week's unread copies of The Siren onto her wheels. "Let's ask Kirsty."

"Ask me what, Bub?"

"What do you think about The Siren?"

Kirsty rolled her eyes. "Don't get me wrong, Mason is an old friend of mine; we go way back. I love the guy. But it's way past the time for him to retire and a new broom to sweep that place clean from top to bottom. We need a solid local paper. I help him out because I believe in a local press; I don't want the paper to die. I believe in our community, transparency, accountability. We deserve better." Erik looked at Emma as if to say, there's your answer. "And," Kirsty continued with a note of sadness in her voice, "I remember what the paper used to be."

The front pages hanging on the wall of The Siren's reception flicked through Emma's mind. They screamed the biggest stories, steering the lives of the people of this town. She'd bet her paycheck there was more than negligence killing the wildlife at Sharpe's Rock, that there was some more sinister reason nothing had been done to stop the contamination. Somebody somewhere had something to gain at the town's cost. It would be a huge story for a little paper and a team of two to cover. But with her field experience and Dave's local knowledge, they could pull it off. She was sure they could. He'd know the backstory, the sources, and where to start. She'd bring tenacity, the ability to navigate complex terrain, and an outside perspective.

A sense of eagerness she'd not felt in a good while gathered in her chest. The psychiatrist had warned her not to isolate, told her to keep busy. Stepping in would make Dr. Daniels happy.

Emma looked over to Han. "Monday. Tomorrow. 9:00am. The Siren's offices?"

Chapter Fifteen

Wearing a threadbare bikini she'd owned since college, Emma tiptoed over the shingle and paddled into the water up to her knees, shivering as the freezing ocean lapped against the warm skin of her legs. Behind her on the little beach lay a neat pile of dusty wooden planks, lengths of rope of various widths strung with cobwebs, and a collection of old gardening tools, all of which she'd hauled out of the tiny outbuilding buried in the trees a few yards from the cottage. Fine grit and silky threads of spider web stuck to her sweaty skin. A few more steps, she willed herself, waggling her palms under the surface. Thigh-deep, she stopped again to look down. The water was crystal clear. There was only one thing that would kill gathering anxiety about the ocean and that was to dive straight back in. She counted to three and threw herself forward.

The ice-water slipped over her, rinsing off an afternoon of hard work. Her body fizzed with cold. Floating on her back, she coached her muscles to relax as she let herself drift. The sky stretched above a gorgeous baby blue. She glanced toward the cottage. Still swimming distance.

A shape moved near the house. She righted herself, her toes finding soft sand. A man knocked on the porch door. Tallulah scampered toward him. In a tank and board shorts, she recognized the man's toned physique as Jordan's. He'd come by to drop off her key, as promised. She waded ashore. She understood his possessiveness about the cottage; he clearly held a lot of fond memories of the place. And he had done a good job with the repairs. And she owed him for Sharpe's Rock. And he was a nicer guy than she'd first thought. But she was glad he wouldn't be coming round anymore. The place was beginning to feel like hers;

somewhere she could relax, alone. She didn't want frequent visitors.

"Hi," she called as she rose from the ocean, squeezing water from her hair.

He turned. "Oh, hey. Good swim?" He seemed surprised to see her near the sea.

"Getting right back on that horse." She grabbed for her towel. "Water's amazing."

"I bet. Good for you."

Emma smiled.

He pointed to the pile on the lawn. "What's all this?"

"Stuff from the boathouse." She pulled her towel tight around her body, suddenly feeling conspicuously bare skinned as his eyes landed back on her. "Must have been in there for years. Any thoughts on what to do with it?" It needed to be disposed of before the cottage went on sale.

He bent down and turned over a plank of wood. "I'll take it."

"Really?" Her voice lit with surprise. "Everything?"

"Sure. I can use it."

She was glad she'd asked. Still wrapped in her towel, Emma watched him from the porch bench as he hoisted a stack of planks onto his shoulder with ease. What had taken her hours to move took him minutes. He coiled the ropes around his thick forearms and marched them around to the truck. The tools disappeared, tucked under his arms.

"Done." He reappeared, lifting his tank to wipe the sweat from his face, revealing ridged abs. Emma looked away, suddenly bashful, and then embarrassed at her schoolgirl prudishness. It had been a while, but she had seen a man's bare torso before, she reminded herself.

"Oh, and don't forget this." He stepped onto the porch and dropped the yale key into her palm.

Her mind jumped back to the night they first met; the sour set of his face, how tired and prickly she'd been, and the mutual awkwardness that had lingered while he worked on the place. Despite all that, he'd followed her into a storm. Maybe they could be friends. She needed a friend.

"I'll do it," she said just as he seemed about to turn and go. "The paper. Just for a couple of weeks."

His face cracked into an enormous grin that made her smile, too. "That's fantastic!"

"No worries. Will you tell Dave I'll be in tomorrow?"

He brushed a cobweb off his neck and nodded. "And I'll tell Beth to leave a key under the mat."

Emma smiled. That would only ever happen here, never in D.C.

"You should go in." Emma nodded her head at the ocean. It might be the last time he'd have the chance. "Beth said you used to swim here as kids."

"All the time." He smiled. "You don't mind?"

"Not at all. Be my guest."

Jordan jogged down to the beach, pulling off his shirt. He lifted his arms and dove forward, his traps heaving as he hit the water and powered on. Soon he was a speck in the distance. He turned and swam back. She tried not to look as he stepped onto the shingle, water dripping from his skin, the fabric of his shorts stuck to the roped muscles of his thighs. She turned to Tallulah purring beside her and whispered, "Not bad."

The water was beautiful, sparkling, and salty on his lips. He pulled himself through with one long stroke and then another, alternating arms, breathing hard, feeling the cool rush over him.

His father had taught him to swim at this beach. His dad had stood knee-deep in the water, holding out his arms, slowly stepping backwards into the shallows as he urged Jordan forward. With his water wings on, Jordan had splashed toward him, fully trusting that if he went under, Dad would catch him. It was a hazy memory. What would he have been, three years old, maybe younger?

There were multiple times in junior high, when Abigail would stand on that shoreline, one hand shielding her eyes against the glare of the setting sun, shouting for him to come in immediately or he'd have to walk home. As a teenager, they'd built campfires on the beach, gone midnight skinny-dipping, the guys and the girls daring each other to remove their bathing suits. And spent many an afternoon exploring where they shouldn't: the properties on either side of Ben's plot, and each other. Good times.

The cottage looked tiny from out here. Different. The longer she stayed, the less it felt like Uncle Ben's fishing hangout and the more like her place, even though she hadn't changed much, except clear out some old books and magazines. Her body occupied the space differently and filled it with a new light.

He turned when the current tugged and slowly front-crawled back, enjoying the stretch and pull. Somewhere on the porch, Emma was watching him, he was sure. Wearing a red and white polka dot two-piece, she looked amazing emerging from the water; smooth curves and long limbs, all in proportion, water dripping from her pale skin, freckles scattered over her shoulders and down her arms. She seemed more at home, like her British reserve had thawed just a little. They'd reached a new level of polite friendliness. What was she like when she let her guard down? His palms pushed against the water. Where were her friends? There was stuff going on there. It was obvious to everyone, even if she didn't want to talk about it.

The muscles in his arms and legs sang as stepped onto the beach. He shook the water from his hair and ran his hands over his face. He felt energized and strong.

"God, that was good," he announced, meeting Emma as she passed him a towel. She'd changed into a t-shirt and shorts, her hair scraped up into a bun on her head, revealing the line of her neck.

"Thanks." He wrapped the cloth around his waist, recognizing it as one of the ancient beach sheets Ben kept on the lowest shelf in the closet in the bathroom. To his surprise, he didn't feel any possessiveness. "And thanks for the swim."

Chapter Sixteen

Dust motes glittered in the air as Emma cleared the last stack of yellowing newspapers into a box and heaved it onto the pile at the back of the newsroom. Hands on hips, she admired her handiwork. What she couldn't pack away, she'd arranged neatly into batches of similar material: old notebooks she'd placed on consecutive shelves, ancient letterhead and rolls of unused Telex paper she'd put aside to be recycled; and she'd filled a box with old batteries, pens, two calculators, typewriter ribbon, and random cables.

Old tech, including an electric typewriter she'd found under a desk, she'd placed next to the Telex machine, ready for someone stronger to move them downstairs at some later date. She'd poked her head around Mason's office door, took in the large desk, paraphernalia-lined walls and bookcases, and backed away, leaving it well alone. It wasn't her place to intrude.

She'd work downstairs in the newsroom.

The main door opened, letting the sound of traffic spill in.

Dave stood with his hands planted on his hips. "Holy Moly!"

"Morning," Emma mopped sweat from her brow with the back of her hand. "I hope you don't mind, I just wanted to create some space," she took a dep breath, "so we can work."

Dave's eyes swiveled from corner to corner, amazed and apparently delighted.

Emma added quickly: "I didn't touch your desk."

"Jeez, you've done a good job."

Relief rushed through her. She didn't want to get off on the wrong foot.

"How did you get in?" Dave placed his satchel on his chair.

"Beth left the key. She told you I'd be here?"

Dave nodded.

A tentative voice called, "Hello?"

"Come in," Dave and Emma called back. Emma smiled awkwardly. She was going to be in charge, but she didn't want to bulldoze her way onto his patch. She needed Dave.

"Dave this is Han, Han, Dave." The two nodded at each other. "Han's going to help us with the website."

Emma waited for Dave to question his presence or raise an objection. Instead, he stuck out his hand. "Welcome on board, son. You're a braver man than I."

Han stepped forward with his laptop bag slung over his shoulder and shook it. "This place is like a museum," he gasped, looking around.

"Sure is," Dave chuckled. "Bar Mason, I'm the oldest exhibit in it."

Han sneezed, raising a Kleenex to his face. "Dust allergies." He blew his nose. "Do you even have Wi-Fi?"

"We have inched into the twenty-first century," Dave grinned. "The router is around here somewhere."

Han stared at the Telex machine. "You should sell this stuff. People really dig vintage tech."

Emma smiled to herself. Dave shook his head and glanced at her as if he was thinking, Millennials, they're a different breed. He handed Han a Post-it with the network password written on it in biro.

"When you're both ready, I thought we'd start as we mean to go on with a 9:00am editorial meeting, chat through some ideas for the paper," Emma suggested. "Han, you'll join us so you can understand how everything works. Sound good?"

"Sounds great!" Dave rubbed his hands together. He was more enthusiastic about Emma and Han's presence than she could ever have imagined. She guessed he was glad of the company and perhaps tired of lonely days at his desk churning out enough copy week after week to fill an entire paper largely all by himself. "Just like the old days at The Globe."

Han seemed startled to be included.

"You'll pick it up in no time," Dave assured him.

Emma had an inkling that the two guys were going to get along. "Meanwhile, I'll wash up."

Fifteen minutes later, the three of them pulled chairs around a table.

"Dave, what's in the diary?" Emma asked. It was like she'd never missed a day of work. The newsroom was her territory, its rhythms and tempo as familiar to her as her heartbeat. Her shoulders dropped as her attention focused on his reply.

Dave flipped open his notebook. "The town council is announcing changes to its affordable housing proposals at three. There've been objections. I've got calls in. And the Sparks—that's the high school cheerleading team—are performing at Mountain Mall on Route 1 tonight. One mom said she'll take photos."

Emma cringed inwardly at the mention of the mall performance. She wanted to print news that meant something to the lives of the people of this town, not fluffy filler. "I'd focus on the council. What are the objections and who are they from? Do they have legs?"

"Sure."

"Han, if you could get cracking on a review of the site, what's there, what shouldn't be, etc. If we're going to write stories, they need to be read."

"It's done. I've already prepared a task list of things I think will improve performance."

"Brilliant!" Of course he had. "And finally. I have a lead. It might take some time to explore, but Dave, what do you know about the pollution from the Maynland Chemical plant?"

Dave shook his head. "There've been rumors for a while. Some folks say it's reached the beaches. It's something I've wanted to get into, but..."

"No need to explain. You haven't had the resources, I get it." Emma nodded. "But I think we should. We must."

Dave looked at her. "You heard something?"

"I've seen it up close. It's bad. The contamination has spread as far as Sharpe's Rock."

"The Rock?" Dave seemed aghast. "Jeez. So, it's real? How'd you get out there?"

"Jordan Allen." She flushed saying his name. She hated to admit it—God, she'd been reckless—but he was the reason she was sitting here, alive and well. He was the reason she had this story.

Dave paused, thinking. "If it's moving south, it's headed for the lobster beds."

"Exactly."

Han tapped on his phone. "Look." He passed the screen to Dave, whose eyes widened as he took in the images on Google Earth.

Dave sat up straighter, energized. "I had no idea. This is huge. The plant closed years ago. It was big news. Hundreds of jobs lost. They got millions of dollars from the state to clean up the site."

"How much?" Emma took the phone Han offered her. He'd switch to show her an Instagram feed belonging to @bugbayEd. Troy's weathered face was in some images. Was Ed Troy's business partner? They'd been trying to get the news out for a while.

"Something like $180 million, which, if I remember correctly, the county contributed about $60 million or thereabouts."

Emma handed the phone back to Han. "Where have those taxpayers' dollars gone?"

Dave shrugged. Han looked blank. It was one of many questions they needed to answer.

"We'll all work together on this," she said. "Dave. You focus on the money trail, and I'll look into the plant itself and its owners, see what's going on there. That work?"

He nodded. "Sure does." He rubbed his hands together.

"And Han, you monitor socials for any associated leads, comment, or pics."

"Sure." Han seemed surprised that his role has expanded to include some actual journalism. Immediately, he began tapping on his laptop.

"Let's do it!" Dave clapped his palms.

The guys' enthusiasm was heartening.

Emma sat at her new desk, close to the window. According to Google Earth, dense forest surrounded the vacated plant, and a double razor wire fence sealed it off from an access road. She could pick out security gates, lights, and a guard's hut. There would be cameras, too. She needed to look around unmonitored. How she might get in to do that wasn't obvious. A river formed the boundary on the other side of the site. That looked a more promising route in but involved a trek uphill through the forest. She would need a guide. She would never underestimate Mother Nature again.

Who? She chewed her pen and glanced at Dave and Han. Neither would work.

Could she ask him? Jordan. He would know the lie of the land. And be prepared for anything they might encounter.

Would that be weird? She tapped her pen lightly against her teeth, not completely understanding her hesitation. He'd seen the destruction. His brother-in-law's business was at stake. The story was for his grandfather's paper.

Emma reached for her phone.

—————————— **Chapter Seventeen** ——————————

Jordan held the length of wood in both hands. It was heavy, solid, with a fine, straight grain that would carve beautifully. He couldn't be sure, but it probably came from the old maple that stood on the drive at Ben's cottage before the storm that whipped across the state a few years back toppled it. It had taken a crew of six of them with chainsaws to clear it off the road. It was a tower of a tree.

He turned the length over, grateful that he'd spotted the pile of planks on the lawn before Emma could give them away, or worse, dump them. He appreciated the opportunity to create something out of material that had grown on his great uncle's land. That was special.

He placed the maple back on the stack for another day, and reached for a wide piece of driftwood, hollow at the core, that he'd shaped upwards like a flame, the flow of grain forming tendrils of fire. The piece was close to finished and ready for the show. He glided the chisel over its surface one last time, refining its contours, careful not to overwork it. Holding its base in the palm of his hand, he smoothed out one more nick with a worn piece of sandpaper and placed it on his workbench. Of the pieces he selected to exhibit at Felix's gallery, this one was his favorite. It was optimistic, alive.

With his latest work, he'd let his imagination rip, responding to the wood as it asked to be held, honing its beauty, encouraging new life out of it. And he'd gone big, bigger than he'd ever done. Bookends and place mats were a thing of the past. There was no going back. Looking at his new work lined up on the bench ready to be packed and taken to the gallery, it seemed obvious to him he was working with a different energy and these latest carvings revealed that change in him, although he didn't know what it was exactly. Showing them in public stirred a feeling akin to walking naked into a firefight without body armor strapped to his chest, a feeling he disliked.

Felix and Ramon insisted he shouldn't be nervous and that they would be there with him all the way. They were a great couple. Their move to Sirens Bay from the city to open the gallery had changed his life. Their interest in his work had encouraged him to take his talent seriously, to see it as more than a hobby, more than just whittling, as Mason still referred to it. They were the first to see his carvings as art.

Traffic into town was slow moving and ground to a halt at the signal at Main and Allen. Golden sunlight rippled off the tall windows of The Siren building. He rested his hands on the wheel. He'd never been interested in the paper, never held so much as a summer job there. He'd seen the toll it took on his dad, who had neither the talent nor the commitment to be a successful editor, but who struggled on running the thing to keep Mason happy. Exactly what happened inside the red brick building to ensure a new edition came out every week was a mystery.

Jordan was tempted to drop by to check how Emma's first day had gone. He was curious to see how she worked, what she was like with Dave, how different she might be in the office. He'd suggested so much to Beth and she'd told him on no circumstances to go. She was probably right. He didn't know a brief from a feature and wouldn't spot a spelling mistake if Emma highlighted it in yellow and circled it with a red pen.

His phone rang. He looked down at the tiny screen and jolted his chin up in surprise. It was her. He was about to answer when the signal changed. He pressed his foot on the gas. He'd call back later.

Chapter Eighteen

The paper's press deadline, the hard stop by which everything needed to be submitted, edited, laid out, proofed, and signed off, was just three days and four hours and thirty-two minutes away and Emma still had no idea how they were going to fill a whole edition and chase the Maynland Chemical scoop. She tried to keep the rising waves of panic turning her stomach in check.

Landing in the middle of a conflict zone was scary, but putting a local paper together in a town you didn't know well for a readership who did, and who you might bump into at the store, was terrifying. She didn't want to fail and make a mess of it and let Mason down. She reminded herself that everything was always last minute in journalism. An interview confirmation, putting the final touches on a story, meeting and deadline, never happened until the very last second. She must keep her nerve. It was going to be OK. And all the while in the back of her mind, she was thinking about Sharpe's Rock and getting up to the plant. She'd left a voicemail for Jordan, but he'd not called back.

The mainline rang. Emma answered the extension. In her new role as editor, she was also the receptionist, office manager, picture editor, and sales associate. The Siren badly needed resources, and that included people.

"Who was that?" Dave asked.

"Advertizer. Addison someone." She checked the name scrawled on her pad. "McCraw. They're dropping their ad for this week."

Dave's brow furrowed. "Dang-it. They're one of our biggest clients. Did they say why?"

"Costs."

Dave nodded. "Everyone's feeling it this year."

CASSIE BRUCE

He had showed her the paper's balance sheet. It wasn't pretty. Mason had been propping up the paper for years with his own money. It wasn't a viable standalone enterprise, more a privately sponsored community non-profit. If the paper could stand on its own two feet, Mason could hire more staff and eventually retire. If he sold, that would eliminate the question of who would take over when the time came for him to step back for good.

"You ever had anyone selling spots?" Emma asked.

"Not for years." Dave shook his head. "Mason oversees display."

Made sense. "We need ad income," Emma whispered to herself.

"Riley could do it." Han piped up.

Emma lifted her head. "Riley?" She seemed an unlikely candidate.

"From the bookstore. She's always looking for extra cash, and she can talk her way in and out of anything. Trust me. We got stopped once by the trooper and he ripped up the speeding ticket. It happens a lot." Han rolled his eyes.

Emma was far from convinced by his example.

"I think she'd be great," a gruff voice chimed as Kirsty walked in. She couldn't resist, it seemed, dropping by to see how the new editor was getting on. "She's a single mom and a hard worker."

Emma was surprised Riley had a kid. "But does she have a head for numbers?"

"She does the books at Erik's," Kirsty said.

"Really?" Emma hadn't expected that.

"What about asking her on a commission only basis?" Dave suggested. "Nothing to lose and everything to gain."

"Mmm." Emma wavered. If she was going to take a hiring risk, she needed to be one hundred percent clear about about why, should it all go wrong and she had some explaining to do.

116

"Trial her, Bub," Kirsty insisted.

Emma let the idea percolate. It would mean one less thing on her plate.

After chatting to Dave, the older woman came and perched on the edge of Emma's desk as if she wanted to chat.

"What can we do for you, Kirsty?" Emma looked up at her tanned face. She liked the woman, but she didn't have time right now to gossip.

"Things are changing around here," Kirsty said, looking approvingly at the tidy room.

"Yes, a little."

"I'm offering my services."

"Yes, of course. We'll still need you for deliveries. Nothing's changed there!" Emma was quick to reassure her. Mason was lucky Kirsty volunteered to do the rounds.

"No. I was thinking as a designer."

"A designer?"

The layout of the paper was boxy and didn't do the stories justice. The publishing software was a decade old and the design template badly needed an overhaul. Working with those restrictions, Dave and Mason laid out the copy themselves, which explained the glitches and weird formatting.

Emma wasn't sure what to say. This was an offer she didn't see coming.

"Well, don't just stare. Waddya think?" Kirsty threw up her hands.

"Do you have experience?" Emma asked.

Kirsty seemed aggrieved. "Of course, I do. I wouldn't offer otherwise, would I? I worked for Condé Nast for twenty years." Her chin lifted with pride. "I'm no stranger to InDesign."

Emma looked at Dave. He nodded gently.

"Well, yes then. Absolutely. Welcome aboard," Emma said. These people were full of hidden talents. She added quickly, "We can't pay you…Yet."

"Call it a favor for an old friend. As I said, I believe in a strong local press. We need it." Kirsty plonked her purse down. "Where shall I start?"

Chapter Nineteen

Parents, kids, and other townsfolk streamed across the grass, making their way from the high school parking lot to the baseball field. For a Wednesday evening, it was a good home crowd. Beth unfolded camping chairs and set the cooler close to the chain-link fence running down one side of the diamond. Jordan leaned against the barrier, watching to see if Emma had arrived yet. No sign. He was surprised but kind of glad that Beth had invited her to join them to watch the game, and equally surprised that she'd accepted.

Troy's twin fourteen-year-old nephews waved as they jogged onto the field with their teammates, all wearing oversized blue shirts and white pants, orange caps planted on their heads. The guys seemed pumped.

"Go Hawks," Beth cried out.

"Go get 'em!" Troy shouted as Nora and Piper, both dressed in team colors, burst into applause. The rest of the crowd murmured its approval, although nobody had done anything yet. On the other side of the field, the visiting team stood in a huddle. Coach Brady got the Hawks doing sprints. Someone blew a whistle. The guys took their position on the field. The hitter, a tall kid from the other school with a reputation for being a slugger, marched up to home plate, swinging his bat. Troy bent over the fence, screaming directions at an outfielder. Jordan smiled. The game hadn't even begun.

Jordan turned as he heard Beth exclaim, "Just in time!"

The girls' faces lit up.

"Sit next to me?" Piper grabbed Emma's hand.

Emma lifted her palm in a wave. "Hi."

Something pleasantly sweet but unnerving flitted through his stomach. "Hi."

Before he caught himself, his eyes scanned the curve of her neck, the spot where it slid into her shoulder. He blinked and turned back to the game. He didn't want her to think he was a creep. He corrected himself; it didn't matter what she thought. It wasn't as if they were going to hook up. First, because he'd never want to, and second, he'd promised himself no more summer flings; they weren't worth it. When the relationship fizzled, he was reminded that the high wasn't worth the low. It took weeks to climb out of that self-hating hole where all he could see was Sophie's face asking him what the hell he was doing.

The umpire shouted, "Play ball!"

The crowd hushed. On the mound, Troy's nephew Ryan glanced at the runner at second, clasped the ball between his palms, turned his gaze to the catcher, took a breath, and let it fly. The batter swung. The ball landed smack in the catcher's mitt. Ryan was talented. He and the catcher had a good rapport. Jordan remembered his days on the high school sports field. Football was his passion, but he could play a good shortstop. He loved being in the center of the action, and exercising the agility and speed required to out a base runner. If he was honest, he basked a little too much in adulation. Folks in Sirens Bay took high school baseball extremely seriously.

After the first inning, Beth excused herself to go to the bathroom, followed by the girls, who whined they didn't need to go. Troy argued the pros and cons of Coach Brady's strategy with another dad.

Jordan turned to Emma sitting the chair, her long legs crossed at the knee. She seemed tired. He hadn't heard back from her and didn't know why. He couldn't help himself. "How's it going with the paper?"

"Good," she nodded. He waited, but she didn't elaborate.

"You enjoying it?"

"Yes."

They fell into silence. He tried a different tack. "You a baseball fan?"

"Not really."

They'd parted on friendly terms at the cottage, and he'd replied to her message with a yes, but now it seemed she was being cool toward him. He didn't understand this woman at all.

She asked, "Did you play at high school?"

"Some. Football mostly."

"He was a total jock." Beth had returned with his nieces in tow. "Quarterback. He ranks among North Harbor High's top ten-point scorers. And he was very popular with the cheerleading team."

"Beth…" His face flushed.

"What? It's true."

"I enjoyed playing sports." He turned back to the field, bringing the conversation to an end. He loved high school. He was a popular kid, not super-smart, but he could hold his own in class and he was athletic. And girls liked him. It was true, and that had been fun.

"Our parents thought he'd go to college on a football scholarship, study journalism," Beth continued.

"Really?" Emma sounded surprised.

He had no idea why his sister would bring that up. He looked directly at her. "Instead, Elisabeth, as we know, I served my country in the Marines."

He spoke in a tone that insisted that the topic was closed. But he heard Beth whisper: "He and Dad didn't speak for years."

Jordan's hands gripped the railing in frustration, but he said nothing. Beth couldn't keep her nose out of other people's business if her life depended on it.

The runner reached the home plate and the crowd on their side of the boundary fence groaned with disappointment. Jordan shook his head. The anticipation of a fun evening out at the game with his family soured.

"Anyone want a hotdog?" Jordan asked.

His nieces shot up their hands.

Troy held up two fingers without his gaze leaving the field. "Mustard and ketchup, please Bud." His regular order ran off his tongue.

Beth shook her head. No thanks.

Emma stood up. "I'll come with you. Stretch my legs."

Astonished, Jordan led the way to the food truck.

They joined the end of the line. It seemed to Emma that the whole town had turned out to watch the game. A carnival atmosphere spread over the playing fields. Why hadn't Jordan given her an answer? This was her chance to ask.

It bothered her that he thought her request wasn't worthy of a response. After all, she was helping them out at the paper. Wasn't he at all interested in what they were up to? He was the one who had told her she needed to write the story; he'd insisted. Instead of blanking her, he could have simply said he wasn't available. She'd find someone else to take her to the plant; it wasn't that. But she had thought they'd finally reached some sort of mutual regard, maybe even friendship. But he appeared to resent her presence at the game and was back to being virtually monosyllabic. She realized she was disappointed.

Doug had been a moody guy, too. His sudden grumpiness, like Jordan's, had driven her insane. Her tactic with him had been to carry on, regardless. She would treat Jordan the same.

The evening sun beat on her face. She scrabbled around in her bag for a tube of sunscreen. Once she'd smothered on the SPF 50, she offered it to Jordan as an icebreaker. He shook his head.

"Tough guys don't wear sunscreen?" she asked. "I know for a fact that isn't true." Soldiers she'd met in the field knew sunburn could be a killer.

He smiled and nodded. His face relaxed, revealing a whiff of a sense of humor, which he appeared to expend some energy keeping well hidden.

The line inched closer to the grease and onions. "Can I ask you something?"

His blue eyes stared straight at her. "Sure."

"Why didn't you reply to my message?" she asked. He looked confused. "About hiking to the plant."

His voice was insistent. "I did."

She paused, scrutinizing his face, trying to tell if he was being truthful or a jerk.

He continued: "I left a voicemail on your cell. Your D.C. number. You didn't get it?"

Emma pulled her phone from her purse and rechecked her missed calls, baffled. "Nope."

"Reception isn't the greatest in some spots around here. I said yes. It's rough terrain up there. Don't go alone." He gave her a sideways look that appeared to say, and we all know what happens when you strike out alone.

"Huh." Suddenly she felt silly. She'd been quick to judge him and a little prickly. "Fabulous. Saturday?"

"Done."

They stepped forward.

She was curious: "You have a grandfather who owns a newspaper and a great-uncle who was a prizewinning reporter and you never wanted to be a journalist?"

"Nah, not my bag." He shook his head. "Writing is not my thing. At all. I'm dyslexic." He turned away to look at something on the far side of the field.

Emma knew several talented dyslexic journalists, but he seemed reluctant to discuss it any further, and it was none of her business.

Poor Mason. No one in his family wished to assume the burden of a paper he strived to keep publishing. She hoped the minor changes she was making to the website and hard copy design would make his life easier when he returned to the office.

"Hey bro!" They'd arrived at the hatch. A large man with a big friendly face running with sweat greeted Jordan. "How's it going?" he asked as he sliced through a bun and yanked a frankfurter out from the steamer.

"Hey, Marshall. Good thanks. You?"

"Hey Jordan!" Riley, wearing an apron, turned around to face them, her eyes rimmed red from prepping onions. She leaned against the counter with the kitchen knife in her hand, as if she was taking a break for a chat.

"Hi," Jordan appeared to stiffen. "Moonlighting?"

"Brodie's playing Little League," she nodded to the far field. "I might as well make the most of it while I'm here."

Riley seemed far too young to have a boy old enough to play baseball. Emma guessed Han and Kirsty were right: she was a grafter and she needed cash. Selling advertising for The Siren might be the break both women needed.

As Marshall loaded the hotdogs, Emma spoke up, hauling Riley's attention away from Jordan. "Will you be in the bookshop tomorrow?"

"Uhuh." Riley looked over, puzzled.

"Great, there's something I want to ask you."

Jordan handed Emma two dogs in paper wrappers and then another two for her other hand. He balanced three in his palm as he dug in his back pocket for his wallet. His face burned. Riley had embarrassed him. The attention she paid him was totally inappropriate. He could be her uncle. Her mom was just a few years older than himself.

He could remember the morning Riley was born, for God's sake. Everyone in senior year was talking about the recent ex-student with the Hell's Angel boyfriend having a kid. He watched Riley once or twice when her mom started night school. He remembered bouncing her on his knee. And somehow it was worse when Riley flirted in front of Emma. He never wanted Emma to think he'd encouraged Riley's crush one iota.

A welcome breeze brushed over his cheeks as they walked back to the game. He tried to explain to Emma why ketchup with mustard was against the rules. As she laughed, a strand of hair fell over her face. Without thinking, he reached across with his free hand and gently hooked it behind her ear.

"Thanks," she said softly, her cheeks flushing the palest pink.

Emma was like a diamond. Depending on the light, a different facet reflected of her. She could be sharp, flinty, but also beautiful and bright. She was probably shyer than he had first imagined. She was, after all, a stranger finding her way around a small town where everyone knew everyone. He was glad she'd asked him to take her up to the plant. He hadn't hesitated to say yes. He hated she thought he'd blanked her. Sailing out after her in the storm, landing safely on Sharpe's Rock and making sure they returned home in one piece, had made him feel strong in a way he hadn't felt for a long time. He felt useful. He wanted her to know that she could rely on him.

Chapter Twenty

Press day. Emma, Dave, Kirsty, and Han peered at the pages of The Siren spread across her desk. She had dissected the entire edition for errors more times than she could remember.

The clocks on the wall showed the time in Los Angeles, Chicago, New York, and Sirens Bay. Four fifty-two.

Emma chewed her lip. There was still lots to do to update the layout, but for her first edition to land on its readers' doormats in time for their Saturday morning coffee, the commercial printer in Portland needed a digital file by five.

Her new team had given the edition everything. All week they'd come in early, put their heads down and got on with the job. Riley had even booked two last-minute slots just that morning, before she flew off for her shift at the bookshop. She was going to work out as an ace saleswoman. Emma could feel it. She was tenacious and had something to prove.

Dave nodded his head slowly. "It's gonna make people sit up and take notice."

"I damn hope so," Kirsty replied.

Above the fold, Emma had splashed a huge picture of a dead seal. Below it, she had placed her story describing the devastation at Sharpe's Rock. The headline simply demanded: Why? It was a question they were going to answer in time. It was enough for now to flag the issue as serious. No one was talking on record yet about the cause. The article should jog memories, kick-start the conversation. The Siren was only just beginning to get their teeth into this one.

Her tummy fluttered. "All agreed we're ready? Han?"

"Ready when you are."

Dave patted him on the back. "Nice work, son."

Emma beamed. The kid was a find. Days of debugging and coming up with fixes and the website was clear of clutter and delays. She took a deep breath. "OK. Upload."

Han tapped the enter key on his laptop. "Done."

Emma's shoulders dropped. They'd sent the issue to the printer. It was live on the website. She felt suddenly unburdened. There was no more they could do.

It had been a good week. And tomorrow, Jordan would take her to Maynland Chemical.

"Drink at The Claw?" Dave looked hopeful. "To celebrate?"

"Sure." Kirsty grabbed her bag. She poked Han in the ribs. "Kiddo, I'll buy you a coke."

"No way!" Emma shut her laptop. Three faces dropped. "Drinks are on me."

─────────────── **Chapter Twenty-One** ───────────────

Jordan pushed open the door to the bookstore to find Emma sitting alone at a table, nursing a coffee. He was surprised to see her. He thought she'd be getting ready. Saturday burgers with Beth and Troy were off. Instead, he had prepared his kit and mapped out the route up to the plant. He was kind of excited about it. He loved a physical challenge, but there was more to the buzz than simply the chance to explore the Maynland site. Since the baseball game, Emma had been walking through his thoughts. He was looking forward to spending the day with her.

Emma looked up and smiled. He walked toward her. "What are you doing here?"

A cringe tangled up his insides. He sounded dumb. She was obviously just hanging out having a coffee.

"Waiting for Kirsty to deliver the latest edition of The Siren." She seemed tense.

"Of course." He was grateful for Mason's sake that they hadn't missed one. Writing about scout meets and local land disputes was probably quite a change in pace for her, but she hadn't complained. "Your first issue."

She nodded. "Should be here any minute now."

As if on cue, Kirsty pushed through the door, hauling her trolley stacked with papers. The two women stood side by side, scanning the front page. They beamed at one another.

There was still no sign of Erik, so Jordan picked up a copy and sat down. It was noticeably thinner. He expected Emma had done her best at short notice. He flipped it over to read the front page. He gasped.

A gruesome picture of a poor dead seal filled the top half under an accusing headline. And she had ditched the usual avuncular tone the community expected from Mason's news sheet. The story was hard-edged and disturbing.

He scanned the inside page. Gone were the cartoons and the recipes, replaced by an editorial raising questions about the pollution. It was a fair piece for a daily like the Informer, but entirely out of character for his grandpa's paper. His eyes flicked to the contributor's panel. Mason was listed as proprietor and editor, Dave as chief reporter, and Emma as acting editor. Someone called Han appeared as 'digital editor', whatever that meant, and Kirsty, the woman who did the paper round, was named as the designer. What the hell? And worse–what was this?– Riley was the head of advertising sales. Did Mason know about it? Did Beth? Because he certainly didn't.

Emma and Kirsty high-fived. She was supposed to step in, not stage a coup. She'd completely overhauled the paper and filled the place with a bunch of random people. Were they even allowed to be on the premises?

"Did Mason give you permission to make these changes?" He tossed the paper onto the table, shaken by how angry he felt. This was an intrusion into something his family had held precious for generations at a time when his grandfather was in hospital in a critical condition. It was like she was criticizing everything he'd created.

Emma and Kirsty immediately stopped smiling.

"For what?" she asked. Her tone was cool.

"This." He jammed his finger onto the front page.

She looked confused. "You knew we were going to run a piece on Sharpe's Rock. You asked me to. You were there, remember?"

"Yeah, but not a horror story that's gonna scare everyone. This is brutal."

"It's news." Her eyes glinted with anger. "And sometimes it's scary."

Jordan shook his head. When he'd told her she needed to write the story, he wasn't sure what he had in mind, but it was not this. She didn't get it; the paper was a neighborly friend sharing gossip and information, not a tabloid. "And Riley. She is selling advertising?"

He had nothing against her as a person, but he wasn't even sure that she'd finished high school. Mason was literally going to have another heart attack.

Emma visibly bristled. "She booked two slots on her first day. That's two more than anyone else has in a long time. It's all money in the pot."

"She's good, Bub," Kirsty chipped in.

Jordan shook his head. Who did Emma think she was? And she'd involved Kirsty in this charade. What did Dave make of all this? Poor guy, he must be stuck between a rock and a hard place, trying to make nice while he waited for Mason to return.

Jordan blinked back his fury. "We asked you to help, not be a wrecking ball. The paper has been in our family for generations… There's gonna be uproar." She'd crossed a line into territory where she didn't belong, and she had to know it. She was unpicking more than a hundred years of history. The town was gonna be mad about this.

"Yes," Emma answered slowly. "You asked me to help, and I've given you my time and the benefit of my experience. The story's got huge local significance and needs profile. It needs attention. Where did you think we were going to run it? And, while I've been doing that, I've been making some improvements, little ones, all long overdue, that will strengthen the paper ready for when Mason is back."

It was a mistake to invite her in. It had been his idea; he'd been stupid. He couldn't support it any longer. Why couldn't she see she was out of line?

"Hike's off. Find someone else to show you the way up there."

Emma's face stretched in disbelief. With an incredulous laugh, she said, "Fine." She paused for a beat. "If you don't want me to continue busting a gut on your behalf, I have other places to be."

Kirsty stared at him as Emma swept out the door.

"What?" An angry pulse beat behind his eyes. He rubbed his face.

"You're an idiot." She left her trolley and marched out.

Jordan stood alone in the bookshop. Was he missing something? He was trying to protect his family and the things they loved, the paper the town loved. He pulled his cell from his back pocket and called Beth. "Have you seen The Siren?"

She was on speaker, driving. "Yeah, looks good."

"You think? Did she ask you about making changes first?" It would be just like his sister to agree to something and not mention it.

"No, but what does it matter?"

"It's not her place, Beth. Of course, it matters. The paper's Mason's life."

"It's only for a few weeks." His sister sounded tired. Perhaps that was why she was being so unusually relaxed about this. "Troy's stoked that story is on the front page."

"She could do a lot of damage in a few weeks."

She sighed. "I don't have time to run the paper. Do you? And would you even want to?"

He wouldn't have a clue where to start. "No."

"Then drop it, hothead. She's doing us a favor. Someone with her background, be grateful she's around until Mason comes back.

131

Let him deal with it. Because you know if he's not happy, he will let her know. Until then, The Siren lives."

Jordan took a deep breath. "I guess," he mumbled. This wasn't an argument he was going to win. Deflated, he hunched in a chair and ran his hand through his hair. Beth might not have the hours in the day or the energy to keep a close eye on what was going on at The Siren, but he would make it his business. It was his duty to his family.

Erik burst in, struggling to carry a large cardboard box. "Sorry I'm late. Huge line at book depository," he puffed as he set his load down and pulled out a leather-bound volume.

"Here."

Jordan's eyes widened with anticipation. He couldn't believe that Erik had tracked down a first edition of The Annals of Sirens Bay, published in 1877. He was holding history in his hands.

Erik picked up the copy of The Siren from the table. "This the latest?" His eyes scanned the front page. "She's done a great job. Wow."

Jordan clenched his teeth, kept his eyes fixed on the book, and didn't reply.

Chapter Twenty-Two

It was five to nine on a Monday morning and everyone was already at the office, ready for the week ahead. Emma picked up a copy of The Siren. "Any other feedback?"

"Certainly got folks' attention," Dave said.

Riley added: "My mom, who ne-e-v-er reads the paper, she cried. The seal really upset her. Something's got to be done."

That was the point. People were resistant to change, and no more so than a small town community, and they needed stirring up if they were going to take action. She was counting on their readers' latent appetite for genuine news to overcome any precious attachment to the paper's usual content. Beth had called to say thank you for all their hard work. Apparently, Troy had punched the air when he saw the frontpage story. It was the vote of confidence she needed after Jordan's outburst.

"What did you find up there at the plant?" Han asked.

"Didn't go." Emma flushed with annoyance. "Couldn't find anyone to take me."

"Jordan didn't come to his senses?" Kirsty asked.

"Nope." The guy was an idiot calling off the hike. She couldn't believe he had been so petulant and childish, and so ungrateful.

"Damn." Dave sighed.

"I'll find another way."

Exploring the facility was the key to moving the story forward. Her eyes moved around the table looking at colleagues who were laser focused on putting together a newspaper that would have impact. They got it from the start. While Jordan entirely misunderstood what she was trying to do.

"I'm having a beer with a coastguard buddy in The Claw later," Dave continued. "I'll see if he's got any ideas."

Emma nodded. "Or any insights on the course of the pollution itself. Where's it headed? The more detail, the better. Obviously."

She had to remember Dave knew what he was doing. He was a born newshound who had been distracted by too many demands on his time, so many he hadn't had a minute to get his teeth into a good story. She got the sense he was relishing the new tempo. Diary discussed and tasks assigned, they broke huddle and got to work.

Chapter Twenty-Three

The streetlamps flickered on, lighting his route as Jordan drove his truck down Bayview, headed home. His mom was doing well. Mason was in a bossy mood, which Jordan took to be a good sign that he was returning to his old self. He hadn't shown him the paper, although he'd asked. He'd pretended that he'd forgotten to bring in the latest issue. His expected explosion would only set him back. Jordan shook his head at Emma's arrogance.

Through the gallery window, he saw Felix and Ramon putting the finishing touches to the show. They'd loved his pieces and chosen three to exhibit. Ramon was confident they would sell. It was an amazing feeling to know they valued his work, that someone else saw anything in it.

The Easterlies' veranda buzzed with tourists returning from days out on the water and those already settled in for an early evening drink. He remembered Soph sitting in that spot in the corner, looking beautiful in a white dress, her blonde hair falling over her tanned shoulders. He'd emerged from the bar clutching their drinks and stopped in the doorway to watch his wife as the last of the day's sun lit up her skin. It was the evening of Beth and Troy's rehearsal dinner. It had been a glorious, sun-blessed weekend full of family and old friends. He'd never felt happier, except on his own wedding day.

He drove on. The hotel slid into his rearview mirror. Those days were long gone.

Ahead, the fluorescent lights of the Siren's newsroom spilled over the pavement. They were working late. Mason would have been sitting in the lounge bar at the golf club by now, sneaking a cigar he would deny, which everyone could smell on his clothes. He stopped to let a family cross the road. Emma was the new arrival, but she made him feel like he was the one out of the loop. He should have learned by now that things never stayed the same, even if you clung on with both hands.

A black SUV roared up behind, swerved in front of his truck and veered across the street to stop by The Siren.

"What the..." Jordan hissed under his breath.

The tinted glass of the passenger seat window slid down. An arm launched what looked like a brick that crashed through the newspaper's window. The SUV lurched into the middle of the road, jumped the signal, and accelerated into the distance.

Riley ran out of The Siren's main door, shoving her two middle fingers into the air, although the vehicle was almost out of sight. The kid from the bookshop, Han, he guessed, arrived beside her, trying to film the vehicle on his phone.

Blood beat in his ears as he screeched to a halt and sprinted across the street to join them.

"Some jerk just through a brick through the window," Riley announced, incredulous.

"Is anyone hurt?" Jordan panted.

"Dave got smacked on the head," she said.

Jordan burst into the newsroom to find the older man sitting in the middle of the floor beside a toppled chair. Emma tended to an abrasion on his head while Kirsty held him upright. Blood stained his shirt collar and spotted his pants. A shattered brick lay in pieces on the floor beside him.

"Jesus. What the... Can I help?" Jordan's eyes skipped from Dave to Kirsty to Emma.

"Dave says there's a first aid kit in Mason's office upstairs. Please get it for me," Emma said calmly without looking look up. She remained totally focused on staunching the blood flow with what looked like an old dishcloth.

"Sure."

Jordan took the stairs in twos. Mason's office appeared to be exactly as the old guy had left it, with papers strewn across his desk and a set of golf clubs propped up in the corner, ready for his next round. Jordan marched straight to the cupboard where he knew his grandpa used to keep a green tin with a white cross on it. It was a source of fascination for him and Beth when they were little kids. To his surprise and relief, he still kept the kit there, albeit a newer one.

"Here." Out of breath, he offered the box to Emma.

"If there's any iodine, please soak a gauze or bandage with it and pass it to me." She issued the instructions without looking at him. It was exactly what any battlefield medic would have requested.

"Sure, of course."

He kneeled beside her, a square of dripping yellow cotton in his hand. He was ready to do whatever else she asked.

"Dave, do you feel dizzy or sick?" Emma asked.

"I'm not feeling my best." He tried to smile. "A brick just landed on my head."

"Just as well you have a thick skull." Kirsty patted his arm. "You should see the brick!"

"Hilarious."

Emma remained deadly serious. "Do you feel you're going to pass out?"

"No."

"Let's get you something to drink, something sweet. Han, Riley, one or both of you, could you run out and grab a soda from The Claw?" Emma turned back to Dave. "It'll be good for the shock." She knew the drill and was entirely in command. She was just the sort of person you'd want with you on patrol: steady, unflappable. She must have been just like this with Mason. Thank God.

Emma turned to Jordan. "Call an ambulance, please."

"Of course." He pulled out his cell.

"Don't tell my wife," Dave looked at Kirsty.

"About what, the soda?" she replied with mischief in her voice. "Still on that diet?" He nodded. "Don't worry, I gotcha." Kirsty patted his shoulder.

Riley dropped to her knees to join them. "Sprite."

As they waited for the medics to arrive, Dave sipped at the bottle while Kirsty appeared to use all her weight to keep him upright. Emma sustained the pressure on his cut with her hand, and Han and Riley kept him talking. Jordan stood out of the way and watched. Empty takeout boxes, open laptops and notepads covered each surface. The place looked busy and full of purpose. He hadn't seen it like this in years.

Emma turned to Riley and Han. "Guys, if you need to get home, we can take it from here."

"No," Riley was adamant. "I'm staying."

"And Brodie?" Emma asked.

"Mom's got Brodie."

"And my mom knows I'll be late. I texted her already," Han added. "Riley will give me a ride home later."

No one was going anywhere until Dave was taken care of. This group of individuals had formed a squad, Jordan realized.

When the paramedics arrived, the woman looked at Emma and asked: "You planning on making a habit of this? You know we're hiring."

It was a joke, but Emma's face didn't register the humor. "Trouble seems to follow me around," she replied, her voice flat, as if she was retreating inside herself. "Can't shake it."

Kirsty offered to accompany Dave in the ambulance. Once they were gone, the police sergeant arrived and took witness statements. He was a new guy Jordan didn't recognize. Once Han showed him his video, Emma said that in no uncertain terms, he and Riley should go home.

"We'll try to get the plates," the officer suggested, looking doubtful. He scooped fragments of brick into an evidence bag. "It was probably some prankster."

"It didn't look like a prank," Jordan interrupted before Emma could respond. "Dave could have been really, really hurt. Any of them could." Including Emma. The guy was incompetent or lazy, or near the end of his shift. "They meant business."

Emma looked deadly serious. "Please let me know what you find out. We will press charges."

The officer nodded, closed his notebook, took one last look around. "What about the window?" The three of them looked at the frame rimmed with ragged glass. The hole was big enough for a small child to climb through. "I wouldn't leave it like that."

No shit. "I'll board it up." Jordan offered.

When he returned from the truck with his toolbox and a width of plyboard, Emma had swept the shattered glass into a trash bag. In all the years his family had owned the paper, he had never heard of anything like this. Angry letters from readers, threats to sue, canceled subscriptions, and criticism voiced loudly in The Claw, but never violence. "Who was it, do you think?"

She shrugged. "You tell me. We're a little paper that writes about ninth grade baseball." Her tone was almost sarcastic, but he could tell by the frown on her face that she was concerned and churning through the possibilities.

"And dead seals killed by a chemical leak." He hammered a nail into the frame.

"Yes." She nodded. It seemed she had considered the idea that their front page story had provoked this response. "We reported what anyone with a boat could get out and see for themselves. We haven't even really got started."

He spiked with shame. He didn't like what she'd done to the paper, but his response, he could see now, had been juvenile and his cancellation of the hike a punitive attempt to rein her in. Except, it hadn't. On a whiteboard on the back wall, under the heading 'Maynland Chem', someone had written a list of 'Knowns' and another of 'Unknowns'. The list of unknowns was extensive: Who—question mark; why—question mark, when, the same. There was just one known written in red sharpie: what—wildlife is dying.

She was trying to do a good thing. "I will take you," he stated.

Emma looked at him, doubt troubling her face. She didn't believe him.

"Seriously. I promise. And I won't back out," he added quickly. "I'm sorry. I was thrown off-guard … by the changes and … worried about how Mason would take it."

She still didn't speak, apparently weighing up if she could trust him. He couldn't blame her for her indecision, but that his reliability was in question flooded him with disappointment.

Then she asked, "Are you free tomorrow?"

"Can be." Relieved, he swept sawdust off the ledge with his palm and tossed it into the trash.

"Good. The sooner the better."

He could sense the urgency. "I'll make sure I am." He hammered a nail into the ply board. "If I let you go by yourself and you got lost and eaten by bears, it'll be on my conscience forever." He was only half joking.

"There are bears up there?" She looked up from shoving a pizza box in the trash.

"There are bears everywhere." And they needed to be treated with due respect and necessary caution.

"Oh." Beneath her quiet reply, she appeared genuinely unnerved.

That sealed it. She couldn't go alone. "When shall we leave?"

Chapter Twenty-Four

Emma craned over the steering wheel, scanning the dense forest for any sign of Jordan's truck. He said to meet a quarter of a mile north of Scatton's Bridge on Route One. She would see him parked off the road.

She pressed her foot gently on the brake, her fingers tapping on the wheel, apprehensive. She didn't want to have to reschedule, but more than that, she was nervous, uneasy in her gut. She'd headed off to places unknown plenty of times; she always felt a pang of trepidation around who she would encounter and what she would find. It was part of the process; adrenaline was necessary. It kept her focused and moving. But on this assignment, she was way out of her comfort zone. Rural Maine, with its shadowy forests and fast-flowing, ice-cold rivers, and expanses of ocean, was totally unfamiliar territory. The near-miss of the storm clouded the edges of her confidence. The only way to conquer self-doubt was to move through it.

Jordan's tall shape waved at her from the grass verge. She swung across the road and parked her car beside his truck. She had to admit, he looked handsome in his black cap, t-shirt and dark combat trousers, a bandana looped around his neck. Sinews stretched and curved up his arms as he pulled a green tarp over his vehicle.

"Don't want to draw any attention," he said.

"Right." His seriousness twanged at her unease. Who or what did he think they were going to encounter up there? "I've been meaning to say it since we met, but I didn't have you pegged as a muscle car driver." A smile flittered across his lips as he threw a second tarp over her car.

"What, you thought I drove a Rolls Royce?"

"Don't all English people?"

She smiled.

He turned serious. "It's about fifteen minutes on foot to the river through the woods, and another hour upstream to the old dock, if we keep at a moderate pace. There the track turns steep, and we'll be on it for the best part of two hours," he told her. "You up for that?"

"Of course." She was tense, but she wasn't backing out. She needed to see for herself the source of the stink and foam. And this time, she was prepared. In her pack she carried water, snacks, bug spray, and a travel first aid kit, as well as a phone battery pack and a torch. He was her guide, but this was her assignment, and she could look after herself.

"From the dock to the fence encircling the perimeter of the plant is all private property. If we get caught, we say we are hikers who got lost. OK?"

She nodded. He'd thought of a cover story. That was reassuring. That they might need one wasn't.

He continued, "According to my calculations, we should get there while it's still light, have time to regroup, and decide when to breach the fence."

"Let's do it."

Emma fixed her gaze on Jordan's back as he trod a narrow path through the thicket and into the shade of the forest. The air chilled her bare arms. He walked ahead with easy self-assurance, setting a swift pace. They were about to work up a sweat.

"You've been up there before?" she asked, flapping tiny bugs from her eyes.

"Not for years." He kept walking without turning his head. "And never to the plant. But I remember the terrain. We used to camp on the mountain all the time as kids."

Following the riverbank, they marched upstream. Her apprehension turned to curiosity. The plant should be deserted. Would anyone be up there? Google Earth showed concrete barricades and a barbed wire fence meant to deter trespassers. Or did they have something to hide?

Jordan waited for her at a bend in the path. His blue eyes shone in the afternoon light. "You OK?"

"Yep," she replied breathless but eager to keep moving.

Further on, a lace of white foam swamped a bank of tangled reeds. The stench caught in her throat and stung her eyes. She blinked and lifted her scarf to her face as Jordan did the same.

"Good Lord," she said, horrified, leaning forward against a tree trunk to get a better look at the water.

"Careful," Jordan warned, reaching for her arm. His grip was firm. "It's deep. They dredged the river for the tankers." He suddenly withdrew his hand as if he should never have touched her, and started moving. "We've still got a good mile to go until we reach the dock."

At a wide glade, they emerged into the sunlight.

"There it is," Jordan pointed at the abandoned loading platform. One end of the rusting metal structure had entirely collapsed into the river. Careless owners, who clearly had no regard for the impact on fish or plant life, had left it to decay. They were in the right spot.

Jordan pointed to a broad-gauge pipe emerging from the reinforced strip of concrete. "That has got to be it."

Emma pulled out her camera and started taking pictures. Edging forward, she switched to video, scanning the scum floating on the surface, and zoomed across for a closeup of the mouth of the pipe dripping foam.

"What the hell is that?" She tiptoed down a set of partially corroded steps and hooked out a piece of red plastic caught in the grill. It was a Maynland Chemical security pass displaying a grainy image of a guy in a suit.

Jordan arrived beside her. "Probably from when the plant was operational."

She turned it over. "No, there's an expiry date. Not valid after December this year." She looked at him. "Whoever that is, he's been at the plant recently."

Her eyes swept the patch of overgrown riverbank and landed on two blue plastic barrels left standing by a gap in the trees where the cracked concrete road began. Among the dilapidation and wildness, the tubs looked conspicuously clean.

"What is going on here?" she asked.

Sweat smarted in his eyes as he took a long swig from his water bottle. He'd expected the trail to be matted with regrowth and for them to have to fight their way through, but the track up from the river to the plant was clear. The shrubs on either side were dense, but it was as if someone had cut them back to maintain the route.

Jordan bent down and picked up a cigarette butt, its filter bright white and untouched by weather.

Emma frowned, her emerald eyes glinting with questions. "Fresh. What do you think?"

"I think we need to be extra vigilant."

Emma nodded.

His eyes swiveled around the forest, flicking to any crackle, creak, or bird call. As they kept pace, the sun dipped behind the mountain peak. Cresting the top of the long slope, he slowed as the fence encircling the plant came into view. A yellow, single leaf swing gate blocked the access road. A heavy-set guy in a navy-blue security uniform sat in the shade of the guardhouse beside it, reading the paper and holding what looked like a lit cigarette between his fingers. Striding toward the thicket, Jordan beckoned with his hand for her to follow.

As she caught up, he took her hand without speaking. Pushing away branches that scratched at his face and arms, he led them further out of sight. The forest closed around them. He winced as twigs snapped underfoot; his ears pricked for the hostile sound of boots trampling the undergrowth. Emma was head-down, thrusting through, just a few feet behind. At a fallen tree, he motioned to sit. The shade was welcome after the heat of the afternoon sun.

"Why would a decommissioned chemical plant halfway up a mountain need a security guard on site?" Emma whispered. "How many teenagers are they expecting to bother to hike up here and create mischief? Expensive for a defunct facility in the middle of literally nowhere."

He shrugged, his mind ticking through their options. "We're gonna have to wait till it's dark and he goes off duty." He wiped his brow and took a deep gulp of water, his heart banging in his chest, his body stiff. Their breath was the only sound.

After a while, Emma asked quietly, "What exactly do kids do out here on the mountain?" She looked around at the tangled plants and trees.

"Drink, hangout, fool around, have fun, of course, far away from the watchful eyes of our parents," he replied softly. It seemed obvious. "You never skipped out with your friends away from adult supervision?"

"Not really."

Immediately, he realized his blunder. Teenage Emma had no parents to evade. "I'm so sorry. I didn't mean to be insensitive."

"No," she smiled, "I get it. My aunt was strict as hell. I could have had some fun avoiding her watchful gaze, but I was a straight-A student who spent her evenings doing homework and her weekends playing county netball or running track."

"Figures," he said.

She seemed amused. "What does that mean? You think I'm a nerd?"

Nothing was further from the truth. He bet she was a popular, top-of-the-class, athletic student who had her pick of guys to date.

"Over-achiever, is what I meant."

"Huh." Leaves rustled in the breeze. "Nothing wrong with nerds, though." A bird of prey whistled as it passed overhead. "How long til sunset?"

He checked his watch. "Two hours, twenty-seven minutes. We made good time getting here."

He felt at home in the woods. She hadn't annoyed him by challenging his navigation skills, insist on her chosen route, or stop every five minutes to rest, like he'd expected. He had been churlish to make such a fuss about coming up here. He'd thought he was the one doing her a favor when, in fact, she'd given him the gift of an afternoon in the wild, where he belonged.

Slowly, the light faded. Jordan pulled on his hoody.

"Are there really bears out here?" Emma asked, offering him a cereal bar.

"Thank you." He opened the packet slowly. "Only one or two tourists get eaten by bears every year," he replied, and bit into the snack.

"Really?" Her eyes widened, the whites catching the last of the light.

He nodded earnestly before he broke into a chuckle.

She slapped him lightly on the shoulder, an embarrassed grin on her face. "Don't mess with me because I'm a stupid 'flatlander'."

"Ah, you're picking up the dialect!" His eyes twinkled. "No one has ever got eaten by a bear in my company. I promise."

"Good news." She nodded. "The best news."

Emma trod carefully as Jordan led her slowly through the pitch black of the forest toward the bright white floodlight mounted over the access gate. Their NorthStar. They stopped at the edge of the trees. Emboldened by his confidence, she was ready to find out what was inside the boundary fence. They crept closer. No one appeared to be in the guard hut. The windows were dark. The swing gate, meant to bar vehicle admittance, was padlocked but easy to climb over.

Moonlight polished the outline of a warren of iron-clad factory buildings riddled with staircases, metal walkways, and piping.

"Bloody hell," she whispered under her breath. "It's huge." She turned to look at Jordan, who was staring at his phone.

"I downloaded a blueprint of the plant. It's the original scheme submitted for zoning regs." He looked up. "And as far as I can tell, the actual build looks pretty much the same."

She should have thought about doing that. You could count on an ex-military guy to bring a map. His fingers widened to zoom in on the detail. She leaned in close, their faces inches apart and their breaths mingling together.

"We're here." He moved the floor plan with one finger.

"Where's the main office?"

"Here." He pointed to a building right in the heart of the complex, and a room on the second floor above some kind of workshop.

"Let's go."

Together, they jogged across an area that was once a loading bay into a dark corridor of industrial buildings.

He tapped her on the arm and pointed left, then straight. He knew where they were. She could trust him. He was safe hands. In the dimness of a desolate chemical plant where they shouldn't be, it was a welcome feeling.

Emma winced as their feet clanged on the exterior metal staircase. Jordan's head snapped round to scan for signs of movement. At the door, the metal handle wouldn't give no matter how hard she tugged. Standing close behind her, could feel Jordan's breath on the back of her neck.

"Step back." He reached into his pocket. With one quick movement, he shoved a slim metal tool similar to a screwdriver into the keyhole and the door opened.

"I'm impressed. Fruits of a misspent youth?" she asked under her breath.

"The DEA teaches you all kinds of things."

"As in the Drug Enforcement Administration?"

"Tell you about it later."

The room was ice cold, as if someone had left the AC running. Her phone torch lit up a clutch of empty desks and a laptop cable plugged into the socket. Someone was working here. Doing what?

A filing cabinet squealed as the drawer opened. "Nothing in here," Jordan announced.

The beam of her torch swept over a delicate model of an old sailing boat. "Mason has one of those in his office."

Jordan moved next to her. "Yeah, the city gave one to every local business to celebrate the two-hundred and fiftieth anniversary of the first European settlement in the area." He tenderly lifted the souvenir from its stand. "It's supposed to be a replica of the original USS Siren. Got a USB on the mast." His voice dipped into gentle sarcasm. "Nice touch, hey."

"Really?" Emma gently pulled at the flag, releasing the memory stick. "No shit."

She slipped it into her pocket.

A siren screamed. Emma clasped her ears against the noise circling her skull. Through the blinds, she could see florescent lights flashing outside. Busted.

"Time to go," Jordan hissed.

They crashed down the outside steps as a truck with roof-mounted hunting lights swung around the corner. Emma's stomach lurched with adrenaline.

"This way." Jordan took a sharp right down a narrow alley between two buildings, the bright light still burning her retinas. She tripped over a low pipe and crumpled to her knees. Jordan hauled her to her feet, and they were running again, heading across a vast turning circle toward the swing gate.

The truck roared up behind them. A furious male voice boomed through a bullhorn, "Stop and desist! You are trespassing in violation of State Law …."

Her pulse bashed in her eardrums. Following Jordan, she carted over the metal barrier and dived into the cover of the trees. A dog barked. The alarm continued to howl as she stumbled after him through the undergrowth, gasping for breath.

"Jordan?" All her eyes could see was darkness.

"I'm here." His palm grabbed hers. "Keep moving."

He moved fast. She felt like her lungs would burst, but she kept a tight grip on his hand. The USB in her pocket pressed against her thigh.

The adrenaline flooding Jordan's veins made him feel like he was flying a foot above the ground. He clutched Emma's hand and wouldn't let it go. He wasn't about to lose her out here. Behind them, the sharp beam of the hunting lights strobed the forest. The guy would have to follow on foot in the dark through dense thicket to catch them. He probably wasn't paid enough to bother. But he might have buddies. They needed to keep moving fast, heading down toward the river where he would make another plan. His breath evened out as they hit a steady rhythm.

"You OK?" he whispered.

"Yes, you?" She squeezed his fingers, shooting a pulse up his arm.

"This is my idea of a perfect Saturday night." He said it as a joke, but somewhere in his heart, he knew there was more than an element of truth in his words. This was the most fun he'd had with a woman in a long time.

Deep in the trees, his eyes took a while to adjust to the lack of any sort of light. Suddenly, teeth grabbed at his ankle, tearing the skin. Heat soared up his leg like a missile. It was all he could do to stop crying out. He clenched his jaw. "Jesus Christ! What the hell?" Before he knew it, he hit the ground cradling his knee.

"Jordan?" He felt her hands on his arm.

"Holy shit!" His fingers traced over a thick band of metal biting into his flesh. Her phone torch flicked on. His face twisted in agony. "Trap. Be careful."

Emma seemed incredulous. "Aren't those illegal?"

"Not here…" He sucked air through his teeth and gasped, "Got to get it off."

"What do I do?" She kneeled beside him, her hand on his shoulder, trying to calm him or hold him still.

He shook his head as if that would ease the throbbing. "At the side… two levers… above the springs?" She nodded. "Get them down…with your foot."

She bit her lip as she gently positioned his boot on the ground. He yelped. "Sorry."

"Just do it," he begged.

She stood on the lever with all her body weight. The snare sprung open. He yanked his leg clear, trying not to scream. The trap snapped shut.

"Jesus," he moaned, pain drumming through muscle into his shin bone.

"Let me see." Emma rolled up his pant leg to reveal two deep gashes. "Mmm."

She pulled out her first aid kit.

"You've missed your calling," he tried to joke, hoping to distract himself. A smile flickered across her face. "As a paramedic."

"I know what you meant," she mumbled, focused on applying the antiseptic wipe. She positioned a gauze and wrapped a bandage tightly around his calf. His face stretched into a wince. "OK?" He nodded through the pain. "There's quite a lot of blood. This won't hold for long. Can you walk?"

Using Emma as a support, Jordan pulled himself to standing and tried to put pressure on his foot. The wound pounded, melting his determination. His knee buckled.

"Lean on me?" She threw her arm around his waist. "We need to get you to a hospital. You need shots. Fast."

"Hospital." He wrapped his arm around her shoulder and hopped forward. "Where Dave and Mason will throw us a welcome party."

"Indeed. You Sirens Bay guys are really something."

"Only since you arrived."

Her laugh hit a strange chord. "It's me, is it?"

They carved a clumsy path through the trees for maybe five minutes before his good foot caught on a root and he found himself on the forest floor again. She landed beside him.

"Can we wait for a moment?" he gasped. His ankle pulsed against the dressing. He could feel his heartbeat in the gash.

They sat with their backs against a wide tree trunk. He couldn't see her face in the darkness. "Please, if you want, go on without me. Just continue to head down. At the river, call Frank at Search and Rescue. They'll come with the boat and get you and then me."

She shifted. "I'm not leaving you alone out here. And. I have absolutely no idea where we are. And." He heard an attempt at a joke in her voice. "I'm not getting lost where there are bears."

Relief dropped through him. It was selfish, but he didn't want her to go. The forest was entirely black, except for the moon cracking through the canopy and glinting off a scattering of leaves. He fidgeted, trying to ease the pain. His thoughts drifted and collided. He needed to think.

Emma spoke, her voice clear in the silence. "Tell me. When were you at the DEA?"

Good idea. Keep talking; keep awake. He took a moment to straighten his head. He seldom talked about that life, except to Lily and his family. No one else in Sirens Bay would understand his choices; they would judge him for his mistakes. There would be questions, millions of them, and more gossip and rumor than there already was. God knows he already condemned himself. It was so long ago; and also felt like yesterday.

Emma, though, might understand the necessary calculation of risk that came with the job, and how sometimes you could get it so wrong. He took a deep breath. The night surrounded them as if they were the only people alive. He had nothing to lose.

"I left the Marines and joined the DEA when Sophie, my wife, and I decided to try for a baby. When I got shot in the leg in Iraq. Almost lost it. Lying in my hospital bed in Germany, waiting to be flown home, that's when I finally quit. The DEA seemed a better fit for family life."

"Makes sense." She paused. "I think."

"I could never do a desk job. Soph knew that. When I left the service, I got an offer from the DEA and we settled in Houston. We loved it there." His voice trailed off.

"How long were you an agent?"

"Five years." They were exceptional years. He was away more than they liked, but the job was challenging and rewarding in equal measure, and he felt like he was doing good.

She asked quietly, "And you chose the DEA because? No coincidence that your dad had a habit?"

"I guess." If anyone else had made that connection before, they'd never said it out loud. He was touched it had occurred to her.

Perhaps it was the shock and light-headedness, but words poured from him. "Soph and I had a beautiful house close to the office. Single story, huge yard, trees all around. I did a lot of work on the place; learned a lot about carpentry. Sophie had a great job working for a law firm downtown, making decent money. And I thought I was making a contribution to a better world." His voice faltered. "And then…"

"And then what?"

He considered whether to continue. Be honest. "I messed up. Big time."

"It can't have been that bad?"

In the dark, his leg throbbing, a cloak of failure settled over his shoulders. The urge to confide in Emma rose from a deep, lonely place. He wanted her to know who he truly was. She would probably think differently, probably poorly, of him, not want to associate with him any further, but the past was the past. There was no denying it. Or getting away from it. It was set. It was who he was.

He took a deep breath. "I was working on assignment.

Undercover. I was good. But I got crossed by a contact, who tried to turn me by threatening my wife. In the heat of the moment, I rushed back to Houston to check if she was OK. Call it my savior complex." He let out a wry laugh. "They tailed me. I should have known. I didn't think it through. Didn't follow protocol. There was gunfire. And my wife got shot. She died then and there, right on our driveway." He lifted his eyes to the starlit sky. "It was… awful."

Jordan heard Emma inhale with what might have been a mix of shock and compassion. His eyes swelled with tears. He dropped his head and couldn't speak. How could he be the one to live? After all the places he'd been and everything he'd been through, how could it be his lovely wife that took a bullet?

After a stretch of silence, her fingers found his, and she squeezed them. She whispered, "It wasn't your fault."

He coughed away a sob. Life had a way of reminding you that you weren't the person you hoped you would be.

"Yeah. Easy to say. Reality is, I put her directly in harm's way." His voice wavered, then strengthened to something he hoped approached normal. "Two of the cartel also died at the scene, and my efforts took out a section of the supply chain. The DEA gave me an honorable discharge." He grunted with self-disgust. "But there was nothing honorable about it."

The sting of shame coursed through him for the umpteenth time. There wasn't a day when the thought didn't cross his mind that if he could go back, he would change places with Sophie in a heartbeat. Emma's hand continued to hold his, radiating comfort. Hiding in the darkness, her presence was soothing, in an unexpected way.

"In dangerous jobs—in life—stuff happens that we can't control," Emma said gently.

He wiped a tear from his face, glad she couldn't see him. "Thanks. That's kind."

Emma lifted her head, rubbing her neck as the first rays of morning sun cracked through the canopy. She couldn't tell how long she'd been asleep on Jordan's shoulder. Her companion, his arms crossed firmly on his chest, appeared to be dozing. Blood had oozed through the bandage on his shin, forming a ruddy brown contour map of his injury. He needed to see a doctor. She wondered whether to wake him or let him continue to rest.

An early morning breeze brushed over her face. How many times had she and Doug waited out the night in a foxhole dug in the sand, or huddled against the only wall still standing in a blasted building, or rested against the concrete floor of a bomb shelter, wearing yesterday's clothes, grit under her fingernails, teeth furry and unbrushed, hungry, tired and unsure from which direction the next shot of danger was going to come? So many.

Doug was like her twin. She could read his thoughts even before he had them. They were a team. She glanced at Jordan; in sleep, his strong face was set like a mask. He was unknown, opaque. He wasn't just the muscled carpenter, or small-town jock she'd thought he was. He carried the burden of regret at the choices he'd made. She understood the weight of that responsibility.

If she hadn't begged Doug to accompany her on that one last interview before they left the country, he'd be alive. He went because she'd persuaded a local militia chief who never talked to journalists to give her five minutes, and she'd dangled the opportunity to get an exclusive picture in front of his face. She had pushed their joint luck and Doug paid the price. She was a jinx. Whatever man she encountered got hurt. Doug, Mason, even Dave, and now Jordan. She never set out to put anyone in danger, but somehow, it happened.

Jordan stirred and turned to her, his irises deep blue in the morning light and his voice low. "You get any sleep?"

"Some. I think." She brushed the dirt off her pants. "How are you feeling? Ready to walk?"

"Grumpy, aching, and out of water. We gotta move. We got a lot of ground to cover." He winced. "Help me up?"

With his arm around Emma's shoulder and his lips pursed, she could tell Jordan was trying not to place too much weight on her, but his ankle buckled when he put any kind of load on it. Sweat ran down her face. He was heavy, a solid guy built for manual work and in more pain, she was sure, than he let on. They walked in short bursts, stopping to catch their breath.

"It's a good job you're tall. You're just the right height for a crutch," he tried to joke.

"Glad to be useful. Take as much time as you need."

He smiled. "You sound like my mom supervising my homework." He steadied himself. "Although, if I'd been chased and threatened with arrest back then, perhaps I'd have been a better student."

The forest was dense, and their progress was slow, but there was no sign of anyone else close by. It was just the two of them gripping onto each other as they made their way downhill.

Hobbling into the daylight, they collapsed on the long grass at the water's edge. Her whole body burned with effort. It had taken them hours to make the descent. Her water bottle was empty and the last thing she'd eaten was a cereal bar yesterday afternoon. Jordan's face had turned ashen and gleamed with sweat. He passed her his phone. "Call Frank."

A long hour later, the reassuring throb of a starboard motor echoed up the valley. It took Emma and Frank to lift Jordan into the boat. His limbs seemed to have drained of strength and his face had turned an alarming white. He lay across the hull, his mouth clamped shut with pain. He hadn't complained once. Doug was like that. Tough.

When they met the rescue team at the base of the bridge, she felt an unexpected wrench as they maneuvered Jordan onto the back of the skid unit and sped him off to the hospital. The guys in the second truck gave her a ride to her car.

Home, showered, relieved and buzzing with adrenaline that offset the empty feeling dragging at her energy, she found herself driving straight to work.

Chapter Twenty-Five

The corners of the USB cut into her palm. She placed her laptop on the desk, impatient for it to boot up. She slid in the memory stick, her heels bouncing on the newsroom's wooden floor. Wednesday morning. Fifty-six hours at the most until deadline.

Encrypted. The screen demanded a username and password. Damn. The USB was significant; she was sure. Why else would it still be at the plant, hidden in the boat? Out of sheer frustration, she typed in a grab bag of random words she had little hope would work. The page screamed back: Access Denied.

"Are you OK?" Han placed his satchel on the desk.

"Oh, thank God." She sat up straighter. "I need you." She pointed to the screen. "Can you get in?"

"Have you slept?" He peered at her.

"Not really. Can you do it?"

"I'll give it my best shot."

Han took over. Emma examined her hands, picking at a thin rim of what must have been Jordan's blood that stubbornly remained under her little fingernail. She hoped he was getting the care he needed. She'd done her best, but his wound was vicious. It could easily have got infected. They'd been out there so long with limited medical supplies.

"Any luck?" she asked.

Han remained bent toward the screen. "Mmm."

She couldn't wait and watch. "I need coffee, you want?"

"Er, no, thanks."

Walking to The Claw, a brew of adrenaline, over-exertion, and fatigue laced with anticipation percolated through her system. She was back in action. Only the uncertainty about Jordan dampened her excitement.

Coffee drunk and spiking with caffeine, Emma paced as Han continued to work on the USB. "C'mon, show me the backdoor," he instructed the screen. And then to her, "What's actually on here?"

"We'll find out."

She texted Jordan: How are you?

No reply. Was he having surgery? Had they let him go home? So many questions that needed answers.

Dave appeared in the doorway with a Band-Aid stuck to his forehead.

"Dave!" she cried. "Should you be here?"

"I had the best two night's sleep I've had in years in that hospital bed. My wife snores. A little bird told me you got something?" He walked toward his desk.

"You saw Jordan?"

"Briefly."

"And?"

"He's gonna be fine."

Gratefulness flooded through her.

"We're in!" Han announced.

The three of them hunched around the screen, peering at a catalogue of folders and files. It was good. They were looking at a cache of documents dating back years. She pointed to a folder named 'Birdwatching'.

"Open that one, please, Han."

A kaleidoscope of thumbnail images filled the display: dead seagulls, decaying, lifeless geese, and a nest in rotting reeds.

"Holy Moly," Dave exclaimed. "They know all about it."

"Yup." Emma shook her head and reached for her phone to show them the picture of the waste pipe at the dock. "It looks like they are actively dumping chemical runoff into the water. It's not a failed cleanup; it's no cleanup. This is big."

Kirsty arrived, her handbag over her shoulder and her hands on hips. "Morning folks. What did I miss?"

Chapter Twenty-Six

Jordan sat on his deck, his foot resting on a stool, watching the early evening light play on the water. The bay was so beautiful at this time of day, swept with more hues of blue than he could ever paint. He glanced at the bandage around his ankle. A tetanus shot and a course of antibiotics and the wound would heal in no time if he kept the dressing clean.

Tires crunched on the gravel. The Dodge. He grinned.

Emma stepped out of the vehicle. "Hi," she waved.

"Hey," he lifted his hand, pleased by her unexpected visit.

"I've been texting you?" It was a question, not a rebuke.

"Phone's inside." She looked beautiful in her t-shirt and jeans as she strode toward him, her hair rippling in the breeze. "Did you go straight to work?" He asked with a mix of concern and admiration for her commitment to the assignment. They'd had a tough night; they both needed to rest.

"More or less. I got into the USB. I came to tell you, we've stumbled on to something huge."

"Stumbled being the word."

She smiled as she sat on the bench beside him. "Listen, I came by to say thank you for taking me up there. I really appreciate it. I would never have found my way to the plant, or back, alone. Never."

"No problem."

"Are you feeling OK?"

"Yup. Twelve stitches. I've been through worse."

She nodded. "And I also wanted to apologize."

"What for?" It was he who felt churlish. He was supposed to be intimate with the terrain and know the perils to avoid. He'd literally made a misstep and put them at risk of getting caught.

"Things seem to happen wherever I am, or more accurately, to people who I'm with, and I'm sorry you got hurt."

"It wasn't your fault!" He was aghast she would take responsibility for his mistake. "I'm sorry I wasn't more careful, and that I held us up and we had a spend a night in the woods."

"You're sounding like an English person now," she grinned. "All the apologizing."

"Sorry."

"See what I mean."

He laughed. The truth was, wherever Emma was, it was exciting. She was alive, curious, and undeterred by the unknown. She brought an energy with her that was captivating. "No need for you to apologize, either. We're even."

"Good." She clapped her hands on her thighs as if she was about to stand up and leave.

He didn't want her to. "Can I ask you something?"

"Sure."

"What brought a nice English lady to the US?"

Emma grinned and frowned. Her face could do that: look offended and amused at the same time. "You make me sound like Miss Marple. OK. Short or long version?"

"Whichever you wish to share."

"Abbreviated. I studied Russian at Dartmouth. Then I did a master's in journalism at Columbia, and then I got my first reporting job in New York, and then another one, and I just stayed."

"Just like that." She seemed to underplay how smart and ambitious she clearly was.

"I love it here. I love the sense of possibility. It feels like there is space for me. No one judging me for being too this or too that. And I've got a great job."

"You don't miss home?" He could never leave Sirens Bay again. He hadn't realized how homesick he'd been for the bay until he returned after Sophie's death: the clean air, the fresh, cool water, the sturdiness of the forest, even the snowdrifts in winter grounded him, made him feel part of something real.

"D.C.?"

"No, England."

She paused for long enough for him to wonder if he should've asked. "I don't have anyone left there to miss."

He couldn't imagine having no family at all. Beth and Abigail could be a pain in the ass sometimes, and Nora and Piper, but he wouldn't be without them, any of them. They were his foundation.

"You don't miss fish and chips?" he teased, trying to shift the tone.

She turned to him, her green eyes smiling directly into his face, and said earnestly, "No. I hate to disappoint you. But I hate fish and chips." She stifled a yawn.

"You need to get some sleep."

Emma nodded. "Tallulah will think I've gone back to D.C. without her."

"Right," he nodded. "You can't leave that cat wondering."

Emma touched his shoulder, sending a warm ripple through his skin. "Thank you again. I'm so grateful."

"Sure thing," he shrugged, his pride kindling.

Chapter Twenty-Seven

Working her way through the list of folders cramming her screen, Emma found old invoices for equipment and products, wage dockets, employee lists, even historical weather reports and news clippings, a variety of intell that may or may not hold a clue to decisions made at the plant. She clicked on an Excel file. Columns of names, dates, bank account numbers and dollar sums spread across her laptop.

"What the hell is this?" she whispered, bending her face toward the screen. "Dave," she waved him over. "Dave, look. Who are these people?"

Dave landed on the chair beside her. "Jeez." He pointed to a row. "There's the ex-mayor Bucky Pelletier, and here's Pete Anderson, who used to run the police service. He's just retired. And here's Senator McDermott. And what's that—$2.57 million?"

Emma and Dave exchanged glances. Could it be what she thought it was?

"You mean our current State Senator Harmond McDermott?" Kirsty stood behind them.

"Yup," Dave sounded amazed.

"What are you looking at?" Riley asked.

"It seems to be a list of payments," Emma said. Dave nodded gravely in agreement.

"Bribes?" Riley's eyes opened wide.

"Yup. It appears so." Dave's voice wavered with shock.

"Whoa," Han exclaimed. "The senator's taking bribes?"

Their story about environmental mismanagement had just turned into a scoop about corruption and some sort of coverup. Emma looked at her team. Bar Dave, they weren't seasoned journalists. She needed to think about how to proceed. She needed to be cautious. They couldn't make any mistakes and she wouldn't put any of them in danger.

"Well, that explains the broken window," Kirsty said. "They wouldn't want folks poking around. They think they can scare us."

"Indeed," Emma paused. "This information will put some very influential people in a tough spot. They won't like it." She looked at her assembled team. "This is not a straightforward story; it's dangerous. There are risks." She jerked her head toward the boarded-up window. She hoped she was clear. "There's no obligation for anyone to continue working on this. We can stop at any time. We're a small local paper, after all." It would pain her to pass on what they had to a national, but she would. "What do you want to do?"

"Nail 'em to the wall!" Kirsty rasped. "They deserve it."

Emma suppressed a smile. She admired the older woman's zest for justice. She looked at Han and Riley for a response. They were new to this. She'd brought them in. He was a kid, and it was her responsibility to keep them safe.

"I'm in." Riley was definite. "Those suckers are creaming off millions while us working people struggle to make a buck. It's not right."

Kirsty nodded vigorously. "Someone has to take a stand."

"This could be the most important story The Siren's published in years. We can't not report it," Dave added. His eyes twinkled. "And. It could be fun."

He was right. She turned to Han. "Han?"

"We need to strengthen the site's cyber security, that's for sure." He didn't seem to understand what she was asking. "Will your parents be OK with you working on this story? Do they understand what you are doing here, the risks?"

"Please don't send me home." His eyes met hers.

Her heart sank. She loved having him in the office and they needed him, but he was sixteen. She had to remember that. "Please ask them."

Jordan hadn't hesitated when Emma called, asking him for some advice. He felt needed. He stood in the newsroom at the whiteboard, a Sharpie in his hand and his ankle throbbing.

"New security protocol," he announced.

The team fixed their gaze on him. The boy should be at home, but apparently his parents were glad he was accumulating college credits.

He didn't want to freak them all out, but the Maynland thugs, whoever they were, would have no compunction messing with them: three women, a middle-aged man and a kid. The plant owners surely had the resources and motivation. As grandson of the owner of the paper, it was his duty to protect this little band of journos.

"The lock on the front door is less than adequate and needs to be replaced," he continued. With his good leg, he could kick the door in. What was Mason thinking, leaving the business so vulnerable? Didn't he worry about his insurance? "My guy will install a new intercom, new window locks, a security camera, and an alarm system this afternoon. No one, and I mean no one, is to open the door without confirming who is trying to gain entry. Got it?"

"Yes, sir," Dave confirmed.

"Emma?"

Her face tipped up as her eyes locked on his. "Yes, got it."

His chest swelled a little. "The new security camera will monitor the door 24-7. He held up a hardback ledger he'd bought on his own account. "Even so, everyone who enters the building must sign in and out."

"Old school," the kid mumbled.

"It's basic fire regs. And, finally, no one works here alone. Agreed."

"Agreed." The team replied in unison.

"Will you be dropping by more often?" Riley asked, her head tipped to one side. "To check on us?"

Sometimes he thought she did it just to make him blush. Han rolled his eyes. Emma appeared to swallow a smile. Riley just didn't get it; he was way too old for her and too tarnished by life. He wasn't interested.

"Thanks, Jordan, for coming in." Emma brought the meeting to a close.

It felt good to be out of the quiet of his workshop and in the company of others. He missed being on a team, interacting with buddies, and being accountable. His eyes drifted to Emma as she sat at her desk, her head buried in her laptop, a look of stern concentration across her face. She looked cute like that.

These people, they trusted her; she led with natural authority. His shoulders softened as he continued to appreciate the way the light glowed on her skin. She looked up. He jerked his gaze away. Out of the corner of his eye, he thought he caught her smile.

Chapter Twenty-Eight

The evening sky outside turned a deep navy blue. Emma swelled with admiration for her colleagues and their commitment to the story. They were brave and undaunted, working hard. Ben, she realized with a jolt, would be proud.

The new intercom system buzzed. She startled and looked at Dave, who frowned in reply.

"A visitor at this hour?" Kirsty asked.

A fist hammered on the door.

Dave got up. A gust of evening air blast through the newsroom as he opened the main door.

"What the hell is going on?" Mason's voice chafed in his throat. He stood in the doorway to the newsroom, leaning against his cane, his golfing vest and trousers hanging off his reduced frame and what looked like a folded copy of The Siren under his arm. "What the hell is going on here?!" he repeated, his pale lips quivering with rage. "I couldn't get into my own building!"

"Hi Mason…" Emma said calmly, ready to explain.

"What are you doing here?" Mason seemed genuinely baffled. "And who is he?" He pointed at Han with a bony finger.

"Mason, take a seat." Kirsty pulled out a chair.

Emma moved toward Han, ready to shield him from further interrogation. "This is Han. He is providing some technical support."

"Technical what?"

"Support. For the paper." She realized in a stunned moment that Beth and Jordan hadn't told him. "Mason. Beth and Jordan asked me to take the helm while you were recuperating. To keep things going." She paused to check he was following. "For things to work, I had to make a few changes."

"Changes?" His frail body looked like it might combust with a mix of incomprehension and indignation. "I didn't give anyone permission to interfere with my paper."

"Mason," Kirsty put her hand on his shoulder. "We're just ..."

"Just what?" His rheumy eyes circled the office. "What have you done in here?" He gasped for breath. Emma tensed, anticipating another collapse. Instead, he thrust his finger at her. "You better get out before I call the cops!" He pointed at Han and then Riley. "And you too, and you!"

Emma clamped her lips shut. The old man was fresh out of hospital and probably in pain, but his viciousness was breathtaking. They'd been working so he'd have something to return to when he was fit. His grandchildren hadn't informed him because, she realized, they knew he'd react like this. She shouldn't have let them talk her into stepping into this muddle. There was no way she would stay to be spoken to like this.

Mason scowled at Kirsty. "You too. You've always wanted to meddle in my business." He turned to Dave. "You stay and tell me exactly what you've let happen here!"

Emma grabbed her laptop. As the three of them walked toward the door, she stopped. "We have been working long hours to keep The Siren alive." His blue eyes stared at her, flickering with rage. "I think, a thank you might have been more appropriate."

Emma stormed out onto the sidewalk, swerving a group of sunburnt and happy tourists. Behind her, Kirsty offered to give Han and Riley a ride. Mason wasn't even curious to see what they'd achieved. He didn't even want to know what they had been working on or recognize the goodwill and talent they'd contributed. He hadn't even asked what stories were in the pipeline. He should have been excited, delighted they'd put their time and energy into improving his sorry excuse for a paper. His small-town mindset was going to lead the thing he loved through a slow death.

Emma swung the Dodge into the driveway and parked in front of the cottage. If the paper didn't need her, she had nothing to do here but wait. She might as well be in D.C. where she could start her campaign to get her real job back.

Jordan stepped out of the shower with a towel around his waist and checked his phone. Beth had left him a voicemail: "Hey, something's happened at The Siren. Mason called. Can you get down there? Mom having a terrible night, she needs me here. Call me when you know what's going on."

He hit the highway expecting to find another smashed window or worse. But when Dave buzzed him in, The Siren was totally quiet. Dave led him into the newsroom where Mason sat on a chair, looking as if he was chewing a wasp.

"Where is everyone?" Jordan asked. Usually, the guys were here late into the evening.

"Everyone is here," Mason announced, gruffly.

"Where's Emma?"

Mason shook his head in disgust. "You handed our family's inheritance over to a total stranger!"

Jordan understood what had happened—there'd been some sort of fight and Emma had left. He had some explaining to do. "We asked Emma to…"

"Why didn't you ask me first?" His grandfather's face trembled with a mix of what appeared to be rage and distress. Jordan regretted his upset.

"Pops, you were really sick. We didn't want to bother you. You needed to rest. And someone had to run the paper."

"Look what they've done." Mason's eyes scanned the room.

"Seems like they cleared a few things away and tidied up," Jordan said softly, then asked: "What do you think of the new look of the paper? I think it looks good."

Mason picked up the edition on his lap and mumbled, "It's OK."

Jordan and Dave exchanged glances. Jordan continued. "I think it's better than that."

"We ran an awesome story," Dave said. "Everyone in town is talking about it."

"I heard," Mason grunted.

Dave continued quietly, "To be honest, having extra bodies really helped, Mason. Carrying on without you would have been a lot to do by myself."

Mason sighed, and a tear ran down his face. "I feel ancient."

Jordan kneeled beside him and put his arm around his grandfather's shoulder. His was as delicate as porcelain.

"I'm sorry, Pops. No one meant to undermine you or hurt your feelings."

Mason shook his head, bewildered. A sharp pang of remorse cut through Jordan. By asking Emma to help, they'd made their grandfather feel obsolete. That was never the aim. "We need you!"

"Of course we do," Dave said.

Mason dropped his gaze, re-reading the front page. Finally, he said, "It is a good story."

"Thanks Chief." Dave paused. "We've been working on a follow up. It's going to raise hell."

"Really?" Mason's voice lit a note of curiosity.

Dave described what they'd found on the USB stick.

"Well, I'll be. That sonofabitch," the old man swore.

"We can't do it alone," Dave stated. "It's way too big. And Emma found it. We need her."

"Work with Emma, Pops." Jordan stood up. "She'll need you, your connections. Let The Siren be the paper to tell everyone about these creeps messing up our beaches and killing our wildlife."

Mason's eyes circled the room as he appeared to consider the idea. "She's gone."

In the short time Emma had been in town, she'd turned up the dimmer switch on his life, reigniting it with adventure: the storm at Sharpe's Rock, the brick through the window, the hike to the plant. She reminded him of the man he had been and could be again: capable, strong, necessary. He couldn't imagine her not being around.

"Well, get her back," Jordan said. "Or I will."

Chapter Twenty-nine

Jordan strode around to the back of the cottage and pounded on the screen door. Emma appeared and stood aside to let him in. "So, you heard."

Jordan shook his head as he walked inside. "He's really upset."

She nodded. "You should have told him."

Jordan stood in the middle of the living room. "I know. It was a mistake." He sounded lame, even to himself. His gaze landed on rucksack and piles of clothes and books stacked on the sofa. "What are you doing?"

"I'm packing."

"Why?" He tried to keep the alarm out of his voice.

"I'm going home."

He blinked, stunned. "You're leaving, just like that?"

"I need to go back. These weeks at The Siren have shown me I need to work. That's not happening here. I can sort out the cottage by phone and email and come up as and when."

He stepped toward her, fueled by urgency. "I'm here to ask you to come back to the paper," he blurted. "Mason wants you back."

She shook her head. "I don't care what Mason wants." He was failing. "I'm a senior reporter at the International Informer with years of experience in the field. I was trying to help, and my team—I—don't deserve to be shouted at. I won't tolerate it. Plenty of other, frankly better, news organizations would be grateful to have me on board."

"He is grateful."

Emma snorted, "Really?"

"I'm so sorry he exploded. It wasn't cool." How could he convince her? "Mason is an old, irascible guy who's feeling like his life is slipping out of his control."

"He was unfair, rude." She picked up a book from the counter and tossed it onto the pile. "And I've seen too much of that in my career."

His brain raced to find something that would give her better reason to reconsider. "Mace and Dave can't get the story without you. The news won't get out without you. Those guys from the plant they won't be stopped if you're not there to shine the light."

She shrugged. "You do it."

"I can't."

Emma was clearheaded, determined, and observant. She had good instincts; she was the one who'd reached for the USB hidden in the model's mast. She could put together a story. And she had nerves of steel. He didn't possess that combination of qualities.

Jordan walked toward her, unsure of his next move. He took her hand expecting her to pull away, but she let him gently hold her fingers. "I am asking you to stay." He looked into her eyes; she glanced away, avoiding his gaze. For the first time, he noticed little flecks of gold glistening in her irises. He reached for her other hand. "Please."

Agitation busy on her face, she still looked beautiful. He squeezed her hands and stepped closer. Her arms felt heavy, like her bones were tired.

"At least until the cottage has a buyer." She blinked slowly, as if she was reluctantly considering what he was asking. If he had to beg, he would. "Emma. Please. Mason needs you. The paper needs you. Stay. Please."

Jordan pushed a strand of hair from her face. He tipped her chin and, before he thought twice about it, placed his lips on hers. Her mouth parted slightly. He gently deepened his kiss, waiting for her to jerk away. She tasted sweet of fire and hope. The fresh scent of her was new and familiar at the same time.

She stepped back. A void gaped between them. His brain

caught up with his body. He'd gone too far.

"I shouldn't have done that. Sorry," he said, flushed with embarrassment. He hadn't planned for their conversation to go like this. "I should go."

She didn't say a word to stop him. At the door, he turned, an unwelcome ache rising from the pit of his stomach. "Goodbye, then, Emma."

Chapter Thirty

Emma wrapped her shawl around her shoulders and watched the dawn open the sky into a glorious powder blue. Tallulah purred and rubbed her head against her thigh. The sun revealed layers of beauty, from the dark rugged line of the mountain tops to the subtle topaz shading of the ocean.

Yesterday evening, in those seconds she'd let herself melt into Jordan's embrace, she felt like she was quenching a long thirst. She felt seen and held, secure.

And then she couldn't sleep.

It couldn't happen again. However much she might want it to. Jordan was a good, genuine guy, but she wasn't in a place to reciprocate any feelings he might have. The kiss alone was reason to leave. But then there was the story. She hated the idea that they wouldn't hold the officials on the USB to account, or perhaps worse, that someone else would publish their exclusive. She wasn't a quitter. The team had worked so hard. Would Mason keep Han, Riley, and Kirsty on if she wasn't there? She doubted it.

She sipped her coffee and rubbed Tallulah's tummy. The sun climbed fast. It was going to be a scorcher. She needed to decide. It was Friday morning, press day. She either let Dave and Mason struggle to do the best they could, or she jumped back in and continued where she had left off.

Laptop under her arm, hoping she was doing the right thing, Emma buzzed the intercom.

"Hullo?"

"Dave, it's me."

"Sweet Mary, Joseph and the blessed donkey, I'm so glad you're here." The catch released, and she stepped into the reception area.

He met her at the entrance to the newsroom.

"He's upstairs."

"How is he?" Emma braced herself for a spikey welcome.

"In a much better mood."

"He'd have to be." She raised an eyebrow.

Dave gave her a sad smile. "I'm so sorry about yesterday."

She followed him in. "Not your fault."

Dave turned. "I believe in what we're doing here, what you're trying to do; it must happen. I think he sees that, too."

"I hope so."

Emma knocked on the heavy wooden door of Mason's office.

"Come," Mason croaked from his desk. As she entered, he put down his nine iron and the towel he was using to polish it and straightened up in his chair. Behind him on the bookshelf stood his model of The Siren. "I'm glad to see you, young lady," he announced, gesturing for her to sit. She opened her mouth to reply, but he interrupted. "Before you say anything, I wanted to thank you for your assistance on the day I collapsed. I surely wouldn't be here if you hadn't been there." His eyes seemed to glisten. "I'm truly grateful."

It wasn't what she had expected to hear. "I was glad to help."

"It seems you're quite the medic. Dave is a big fan. And my nephew, particularly," he cackled.

His mirth forced her face to thaw. "I just seem to have the knack of being in the right place at the right time."

He nodded. "And second. I wish to apologize for my outburst yesterday. I've not been well, and I was ... surprised by your presence." He broke into a dry cough. "I meant no offense. Beth is right, as always, I should thank you for putting so much energy and thought into the paper while I was gone." Ah, Beth had given him a talking to. Mason continued: "I am grateful. And I can see why my brother Ben liked you. You have tenacity and intelligence."

"Thank you. That is quite the compliment." She took a deep breath, realizing he was an old man struggling to adapt to even the slightest change. "And I'm sorry if I caused any upset. That was never my intention. I was just trying to do a good job."

"I know, I understand." Mason nodded. "Dave has enjoyed having you here. So, I want to ask you, will you be my editor?"

They needed to set terms. "Am I free to run the newsroom as I see fit?"

"Of course."

Emma scanned his face. Mason seemed sincere. She grinned. "There's a lot to get done before five. Shall I get started?"

"You bet."

Emma pulled a can of Coke from the refrigerator, walked out to the porch, and handed it to Jordan, sitting on the porch step. He seemed relaxed, at home. His ease reminded her he had spent a lot of time at this place.

"How did it go today?" he asked, his tanned face expectant.

"The edition went to press on time. We published the images from the loading dock across the center spread."

"I meant with Mason."

"Oh, he had a great time." Mason had spun a complete one-eighty and had followed her around all day asking question after question about story angles and layout choices, eager to learn. He seemed delighted to have people around to fire ideas off and a lifetime of local paper experience to share. He'd been useful. By lunchtime, Kirsty and Han were back, and they were on a roll.

"He's got quite a sly sense of humor, hasn't he?"

"That sounds like Mason." Jordan smiled, his face boyishly handsome. "Thank you,"

They settled into an easy silence, letting the warmth of the evening envelop them.

"What was it like growing up here?" Emma held her mug to her lips. What she really wanted to know was why hadn't some nice local girl snapped him up before he left this town.

"Fun, safe. Free. Always something to do." He looked at her. "Beautiful."

Her stomach glitched. "Listen, Jordan…" She swallowed, awkwardness staining her skin pink. She didn't want to embarrass him, but it seemed she needed to make one thing clear. "I can't…I don't…want a…relationship."

He held up his palm. He appeared alarmed. "Neither do I. I apologize for yesterday, for the kiss. I was out of line. Let's pretend it never happened." Her shoulders dropped with relief. He looked at her earnestly. "We're good?"

"Good," she nodded firmly. He wasn't looking for more; they could be friends. "Your childhood sounds idyllic. So why leave this place?"

"My father and I argued about my path in life. To be honest, from a little kid, I never wanted to go into the paper and couldn't handle his disappointment. When he began his journey into opioids when I was a teenager, the disappointment turned mutual. By my senior year of high school, he was a total embarrassment—I'm ashamed to say now. Around that time Lily and Earl arrived and renovated The Claw. I worked there washing dishes, doing whatever. They were full of stories about being the Navy. Ben had served in Vietnam. I guess I always knew it, but they confirmed a feeling in me that there was an entire world beyond Sirens Bay, one I needed to see. And I signed up for the Marines."

His story was edged with melancholy, but it made sense. She needed to fact check one thing. "Lily was in the Navy?"

"Yup. That's where she met Earl. Great guy."

"And where is Earl now?" Lily wore a gold band on her ring finger, but Emma had never seen him.

"Died of cancer maybe two years after they moved here. Heartbreaking. Right out of the blue."

"That's so sad."

He lowered his head. "When I came crawling back to Sirens Bay after Sophie passed, Lily knew exactly what I was going through. She was amazing. She was my rock. Still is."

"Good friends are precious," Emma said.

Ben was irreplaceable. And no one was as insane or funny or loyal as Doug. When people described their partner as their other half, she cringed, but she understood. She and Doug were a team. If he was here, he'd tell her she needed to man up, stop moping, and that life was bloody short, and she should get on with it. She smiled as her eyes smoothed over the tiny cresting waves lapping on her little shingle beach.

Jordan nodded. "What about you? Ever been married?"

The question landed from nowhere. "No."

Tallulah sashayed across the porch with her tail held high toward Jordan, ready to be stroked. Jordan tickled her head. "You never wanted to have a family?"

"Yeah, but…" she trailed off, tongue-tied. What could she tell him—that she held a lonely fear that her life was not meant to include family Christmases, kids' birthday parties, trips to the zoo, a husband to share the journey with. That the drive to keep moving was a blessing and a curse. Travel kept her sane; but it was also exhausting. And alienating. But most of all, that anyone who ever meant anything to her was taken away, and she couldn't take that risk. Instead, she tried to laugh off the question: "There's still time! I'm not that old!"

"So." He paused for a beat. "What's happening with the sale of the cottage?" He apparently understood that he might have stepped on sensitive ground and changed tack.

Emma sipped her tea, grateful. "I'm waiting for Ben's probate attorneys to send over yet more paperwork. I didn't realize it would all take this long."

"Yup." He nodded sadly, as if he knew exactly what she was talking about.

She flinched. She couldn't imagine having to go through the pain of winding up the estate of someone you thought you'd spend the rest of your life with, contact all your friends and theirs, sort through all their possessions, turn off their email. It would be the little details that derailed you, she was sure. Doug's sister was his next of kin, it turned out. Those chores fell to her.

Emma made sure she held Jordan's gaze. She wanted to be clear, to make sure that he understood she was sincere. "Ben meant an awful lot to me, you know."

His eyes sparkled blue like the ocean. "I know."

He placed his empty can on the floor and removed the cat from his thighs. "I've got to get going." He seemed about to say something more, appeared to change his mind, paused again and then changed it back. "Listen, you know Felix Fine Arts on Bayview? It's up the street from The Siren."

"Yeah, I've seen it." The gallery with white walls.

He jumped off the step. "I'm in a show there. Opens tomorrow. If you're not doing anything else, and you probably are, but if you're not, do you want to come?" He added quickly,

"Not a date. As friends."

"You're an artist?" There were layers and layers to his man. Now she looked, she could see that with his long fingers, he had the hands of a painter.

"Don't look so astonished. I'm a sculptor."

"Sorry, I didn't mean it like that. I'm impressed by anyone who can do anything creative." And she was curious to see his work. "I'd love to come!"

He grinned. "Tomorrow at 6pm. See you there."

Chapter Thirty-One

Jordan took a seat at the bar just as Lily emerged from the kitchen, pulling a striped cotton apron over her head. It was smeared with fish entrails.

"The chef's called in sick, the dishwasher's gone apeshit, and the cooking oil delivery hasn't come." She sighed. "On a Saturday!" Lily rested her hip against the bar. She seemed exhausted. She gave him a closer look. "Anyways. How are you doing?"

"Fine." He tried to sound calm, easy.

"The show is tonight." She said it like there was more to say on the topic.

"Are you coming?" It was his first proper exhibition, and he wanted everyone he cared about to be there.

"Of course. When I can get away from here. Nervous?"

"Nah." It was a little white lie.

"What's bothering you then?" Lily's head tipped to one side.

"Well…" Jordan swung gently on the bar stool.

"I know that look." She grabbed her purse. "Come with me to Costco?"

"Sure." He hopped off the stool and followed her out back. Accompanying Lily on her errands was a sure-fire way to get her full attention, a little routine they established when he was a teenager and fighting with his dad and needed her advice.

Lily headed south, the cloudless blue sky above signaling a hot one. Jordan glanced at the gallery as they passed. Brown paper covered its windows. Felix, no doubt, was busy inside, perfecting the final touches.

"You pleased with the work you're showing?" Lily glanced over.

He was proud of his pieces. He knew that should have been enough. Even so, he felt a low-grade hum of anxiety about how they would be received. He wasn't a trained sculptor with a degree in fine art from some prestigious college. He was just himself. But the show wasn't what was occupying his thoughts.

"Yup."

"Oh, My Good Lord!" Lily braked at the lights and turned to him. "I'm a busy woman. Do I have to beat it out of you?"

"It's Emma."

"Ohhhh." Lily stretched out the word.

"Don't sound like that."

"Like what? I said nothing."

He got to the point. "I kissed her."

Her eyes fixed on the road; he couldn't tell what she was thinking. Would she scold him for making a move, or congratulate him for being bold?

Lily took a right, heading for the highway. "And?"

"And what? Did I mess up?"

"I don't know. I wasn't there. What do you think?"

"Why don't you sound surprised?"

Lily shrugged.

Jordan sighed. "I think I messed up. I'm firmly in the friendzone."

"She said that?" Lily squinted against the sun streaming in through the windshield.

"She doesn't want a relationship. But neither do I."

"Huh." Lily overtook a car ambling along in the slow lane. "You sure?"

"I don't know, Lily," he said, exasperated at his own inability to put his feelings into words. "I told her I didn't want one either, and I don't, but maybe…"

She nodded and grinned. "You're confused."

"Don't make fun of me."

"I'm not." She reached for his hand and gave it a quick squeeze. "I'm proud of you, really. This is a big step."

Jordan was glad of her support. "Not one I planned. She's smart, she's funny, she's interesting to talk to…."

"She has the longest legs I've ever seen on a woman…."

"That doesn't hurt." Jordan grinned. "I guess… I like her."

Lily pulled into the Costco parking lot, searching for a space. It was packed with shoppers getting in supplies for the weekend. A truck reversed and she swerved into a spot.

"Good!" Lily seemed genuinely pleased. "That's progress."

"I'm not sure it is. I feel stupid and conflicted and glad and devastated all at the same time. And I wish I'd never said we were good as friends." Jordan shook his head at the muddle of emotions swirling through his blood. "But that's what she wants."

"Umm." Lily killed the ignition.

"Lily, put me out of my misery. Tell me what to do." He turned to her, his eyes pleading, like he was a hapless teenager.

She looked at him, a sympathetic smile on her face. "I can't."

"Dammit." His hands clapped his thighs. He'd have to be a grownup and decide for himself.

Chapter Thirty-Two

The gallery whirred with chattering people, many more than Jordan expected, including well-heeled folk from Rockcliff and some New York and Boston accents. He must have missed the memo to dress in black. He sipped his club soda although he wasn't thirsty, searching the crowd for a familiar face. Beth and Troy were on their way. Lily said she'd come later, once the dinner rush was over. Emma hadn't shown. Yet.

He felt a slap on the shoulder. Felix beamed up at him while a kid decked out in a white shirt and black pants passed by with a tray of shrimp canapes. He shook his head; he couldn't stomach a bite.

"Good turnout, eh?" Felix looked elated.

"Yeah." Jordan nodded.

"Don't let it make you nervous. People should see your art and appreciate it. Enjoy it!"

Not at all likely.

Jordan stared at one of his pieces mounted on a small plinth. It looked incredible up there on the wall, like a flame catching light, twisting, and pulling as gathered strength. The tasteful white card beneath stated his name and a ludicrous $700 price tag. The work was eye catching, but no one would ever pay that.

A gray-haired couple in identical square-framed tortoiseshell glasses scrutinized another of his carvings. He'd let his chisel follow the grain of the wood to reveal a wide-eyed face with full lips. Felix had written some blurb about the future of humanity emerging from the castoffs from the past and priced it at a whopping $1,250. Jordan was just waiting for someone to laugh out loud. Unbelievably, an orange dot already adorned his third piece. Sold. It was one of his earlier, more literal works, where he'd shaped a branch found on the beach outside the cottage to resemble a horse in full gallop and polished the curves of the grain to a high shine. It always amazed him what you could find on the shore. Someone who remained unknown to him had paid $400 for it.

A woman with a blonde box-cut bob wearing bright red lipstick held out her hand. "Lisa."

"Jordan."

"I know," she said, leaning close. Seeming a little tipsy from the free champagne, she informed him of the erotic appeal of wood knots. He nodded silently, looking for an escape. He felt her breath on his face as she told him about the sublime sexual power of sinew and muscle, or something like that. Panic gripped his stomach.

Emma appeared in the doorway wearing a white halter neck maxi-dress that flowed over her body down to the floor. Her soft rust-colored hair hung loose. She looked incredible.

"Excuse me," Jordan unhitched himself. "There's someone I need to talk to."

Lisa frowned and wobbled away.

"Hi," he tried to sound casual, like a friend would. "So good you could come."

She smiled, her green eyes iridescent. "Sports jacket. Nice."

"Felix insisted. Apparently, t-shirt and boards weren't appropriate. Nice dress."

"Well, I thought I should make an effort."

"You look lovely." That was an understatement. A spray of freckles decorated her nose and decolletage. And she smelled fantastic, a mix of something good like vanilla cookies, jasmine, and musk. "Here, let me get you a drink."

As he handed her a flute of champagne, Felix took his arm. "You've got to meet the Bergdorfs."

Jordan rolled his eyes. Emma grinned. "Good luck!"

"Beth will be here any minute," he called over his shoulder as Felix steered him away.

Felix introduced him to one collector after another. Every time he turned to see where Emma was, she appeared to be happily chatting to someone new magnetized to her presence. He wished he had her gift for small talk. He wanted to be with her, not talking to people he didn't know who seemed desperate to understand what he was trying to achieve with his carvings and stick intellectual labels on it. The art spoke for itself. They were wood carvings, after all. He feigned another smile and shook another hand, forcing himself to remember that Felix, his friend, was working hard in his best interest.

From across the room, Jordan caught sight of Emma talking to Beth and Troy. He relaxed. She sipped her drink, her eyes bright with laughter. A guy probably his age or older, wearing a black business suit, joined them. Even from a distance, he appeared keen to get Emma's attention. He stood facing Emma with his back to Beth and Troy, who seemed to get the hint, and melted away.

Jordan realized with surprise that the feeling heating his veins was jealousy. Not cool, he reprimanded himself. Be a stand-up guy. She's not yours. You're just friends. She doesn't know anyone; she's having fun. Still, the guy's possessiveness bothered him.

By eleven the crowd had thinned, finally. Jordan helped Ramon collect glasses while Emma, Lily and Erik perched on the step out front. Beth and Troy had stayed long enough to let him know they cared, but it wasn't Troy's scene and they'd headed home early to let the babysitter go. Mason, too, had come and gone. They were proud of him, and that's all that mattered.

Erik rested his hand on a spot on the floor behind Emma to

steady himself and leaned in close. They'd all had too much to drink and were giggling like sorority girls. Was Erik making a move? Maybe she liked nice, gentle guys. Jordan shook his head, frustrated with himself. It wasn't his business. Friends, he reminded himself. That's what she wants.

He took the tray of glasses out to the tiny galley kitchen and loaded the dishwasher.

Ramon arrived in the narrow doorway. "They are waiting for you," he said, making a shoeing motion. "Go. Leave. Your job here is done. We'll get the rest."

Felix stepped forward and gave him a huge, exhausted hug. "You sold everything."

"Everything?" He took a disbelieving breath. "Even The Flame?"

"Yes. Look happy!"

"I am. Thanks, guys. For everything."

Jordan found his jacket on a hook in the bathroom. As he walked through the gallery, Erik, Lily, and Emma stood up.

Erik hiccupped. "I gotta go. It's late. I gotta work tomorrow. I'm drunk." Lily and Beth giggled. "Congratulations!" Erik blinked behind his thick lenses and gave Jordan a sloppy cuddle. "It was a great night."

Erik kissed Jordan on the cheek, then each of the women, and strolled off.

Lily slid her arm through Jordan's and Emma did the same on the other side.

"I have also had a few glasses of champagne," Lily announced. "It's been a long day."

"No shit." He squeezed her arm under his elbow. He really loved this woman. Deep purple circles under her eyes told him she was beat, but she still came to celebrate the opening of a new chapter in his life. She understood how much it meant. "Thank you so much for being here. It means the world to me." He kissed her lightly on the cheek before he turned to Emma. Her face shone ivory white in the moonlight. "You too."

"You are a man of hidden talents, Jordan Allen." Emma swayed slightly.

Before he could answer, Lily cackled, "That's what all the ladies say!"

"Lily!" He could feel the heat crawling up his face. "Jesus."

They strolled down Bayview toward The Claw, the cool night air on their faces. At the bar, Lily waved goodbye.

Jordan and Emma walked on toward the parking lot, still arm in arm. He turned to face her. "Shall I drive you home?"

She picked a speck of lint off his lapel. "No worries, I'll get a taxi."

"I'm literally going your way."

In his mind, he reached forward and held his finger under her chin, tipped up her face and touched his lips to hers with a long, lingering kiss. He blinked the picture from his head and instead reached into his pocket for his keys. His imagination was driving him nuts.

"C'mon, I'll give you a ride."

A headache gathering in her skull, Emma scrutinized her reflection in the bathroom mirror for any traces of makeup. She'd felt beautiful and confident in that dress, which now lay in a pool of fabric on the floor. She hadn't laughed so much in a very long time. Erik, sweet Erik, a silly drunk after just two flutes of champagne. And Lily, what a lovely woman. They had rescued her from the guy in the suit. He'd asked a million questions about being a journalist: who she worked for, for how long, did she like it, could he get her number? She'd tried to move away from him several times, first politely, then abruptly, but he didn't take the hint and trailed her around the gallery. She shivered at the memory. Creep.

Emma brushed her teeth. Jordan truly was a revelation. His work was sensitive, tactile, and earthy. The grainy forms reminded her of windy, rainy holidays at the coast with her parents spent scouring the shingle beach for wood whittled by the crashing current, and spiral shells that caught her eye. And he looked great, carefully casual in his jacket and chinos. Former marine, ex-DEA, carpenter, builder, and sculptor, all wrapped up in a six-foot bundle of muscle.

She'd insisted he drop her on the drive, that it wasn't necessary for him to see her to her door. He'd waited anyway, his high beams lighting her path to the cottage. Only after she stumbled inside and turned on the kitchen light did she hear his engine rev as the truck reversed. He was a gentleman. As she'd drawn the curtains, she'd watched his vehicle lights move through the trees, heading home. And now she felt oddly alone.

Chapter Thirty-Three

The team stared at Han as he booted up his laptop. He turned the machine around so they could see the screen. The new-look website was simple and clear, professional. Emma loved it. A new start for a new week. All eyes planted on Mason, waiting for him to respond.

"Well, I'll be," Mason cracked a smile. "I like it!"

A wave of relief swept the table.

"It's genius," Riley smiled.

"We need images, ideally something like an aerial shot of the pollution spreading across the bay, more from Sharpe's Rock and the dock, and the plant itself," Emma listed targets off on her fingers.

"We need high-res, recent and specific, Bub," Kirsty added.

"Any ideas how to get them?" Emma asked.

"Drone?" Dave chipped in. It was a good idea. Remotely piloted aerial systems conducted re-con ops along front lines all the time.

"My dad's got one," Han offered. "He built it himself. It's a hobby."

"Nerd." Riley teased, "Like father like son,"

Han ignored her. "I'll ask him if we can use it. It's got a great camera."

"Bald Eagle Peak would be your best vantage point," Dave suggested.

"Han, Riley, you know where that is?" Among all of them, they were the most likely to get her up there.

"Not really." Han didn't sound keen. Riley shrugged. She didn't seem like the outdoorsy type.

There was someone else tried and tested. Could she ask

another favor of him? Emma wasn't sure. And would his ankle even make it? Should she give the guy a break and stop taking up his time? Or would it be rude not to ask him, given their history? Would he take offense if she didn't? The muddle in her head was annoying. Usually, she was clear-sighted and resolute in pursuit of a story. She was making this complicated.

"Ask Jordan." Kirsty gave her an answer. It was as if she had read her mind.

Grateful for the older woman's instruction, Emma turned to Dave. "OK, so where are we? What do you have?"

"There is a lot of fear out there. People are being tightlipped."

Mason's eyes gleamed. "I had drinks yesterday at the club with a friend." He paused for effect. "This goes much further than Maynland Chem."

"How far?" Emma asked.

"Who's paying all these bribes?" Mason baited.

"Maynland Chem." Dave sounded confused.

"My source says it's a particular Maynland shareholder who plans to buy the land."

"That site is worth millions," Dave replied.

"More," Kirsty interjected.

"It's worthless with all those chemicals running all over it and out into the water," Mason stated. "And it would be in this investor's interest to buy the land cheap."

"So not just a failed cleanup, but deliberately poisoning the environment?" Emma asked.

"That's what they suggested."

"Jesus Christ," Dave murmured under his breath.

"And who is this shareholder?" Emma asked. "Do we know them?"

"The Lorenzo Family." Mason almost whispered the words.

Kirsty and Dave drew loud breaths.

Emma frowned. "Who are they?"

"North End Boston gangsters," Dave said, rubbing his forehead. "To recap. The mob is polluting the land and sea, by extension, so they can buy it for nothing? And they are paying people to turn a blind eye?"

"Yes," Mason said.

Emma interjected. "And this source is reliable?"

"Gold plated." The old man beamed from ear to ear.

"Great work Mason."

The overspill of big city criminality could shatter a small town like this. Dead seals were the tip of the iceberg. The goons were counting on the power of money and of intimidation, that no one with any regard for their own safety or that of their family would lift the lid on their shenanigans.

"What do they want the land for?" Emma asked.

"Imagine a Las Vegas-style resort with a five-star hotel, casino, and a water park. A wicked money-laundering opportunity."

"Jesus," Dave said, aghast.

"That spot on the way up, opposite the nature preserve, where they used to have the warehouses, has partially rewilded already. It's almost lovely again." Kirsty frowned at the prospect of it being lost.

Emma's career was built on reporting black-market paramilitary financing, militia networks, and weapons smuggling, but she had never investigated US organized crime. The destruction of stunning landscapes and ancient ecosystems in the pursuit of profit had to stop. But. Worried, she looked around her team. Were they up to it?

"Han, I think we need to call your parents again," she smiled at him, knowing she ran the risk that this time, they'd say no.

God only knew what they already thought about the hours he spent at The Siren. The boy looked stricken.

"I'll talk to 'em," Mason piped up.

"Are you sure?" Emma said, surprised and glad Mason seemed to have warmed to their tech guy.

"Of course. I'm the publisher after all," he said, winking at Han.

The intercom buzzed. They all froze.

"Anyone expecting anyone?" Emma asked. Shaking heads all round. She slowly approached the door. Through the glass, standing on the step, wearing a denim shirt and jeans and backlit by blue sky, Jordan looked like a Calvin Klein model, the angles of his chiseled face defined by shadow.

"Hi," he smiled, as she let him in.

Something tickled her insides. It was her good luck she could ask him about Bald Eagle Peak in person. "Hi."

"Mason here?" He walked through. "I just wanted to check on him."

From the other end of the room, Kirsty said loudly. "Mason's very lucky to have such an attentive nephew."

Emma wasn't sure what Kirsty's cheeky grin implied. It was good of Jordan to keep an eye on his grandfather. Drinks at the club didn't sound like he was sticking to his physician's advice.

Riley beamed as Emma led him through the newsroom. "He's in his office. Shall I take you up?"

"No need. I know my way."

Jordan reappeared after about ten minutes. He stopped at Emma's desk. "How's it going?"

"Good, thanks." She could feel eyes on her, watching. "I've got another favor to ask. I need to get up to Bald Eagle Peak."

"OK," he looked interested. "What's up there?"

"Drone footage."

"I can fly a drone."

Emma lifted her face. "More crucially, is your ankle up to it?"

"Almost good as new."

"So, last question—do you know where the bear traps are?"

He gazed down at her, grinning. "I. Will. Watch. My. Step," he said carefully.

Chapter Thirty-Four

Looking up at the mountain from the foot of the trail, Jordan felt like he was about to explore the path for the first time, even though he'd been up more times than he could remember.

Emma, wearing a hooded sweatshirt, shorts and what were possibly brand-new hiking boots, raised her face to the morning sun like a sunflower. She looked beautiful. A smile spread through his body.

He slipped on his cap and reached for the pack carrying the drone and started walking.

"What is this, our third adventure?" he said as she kept pace beside him.

"Adventure is a broad term."

He grinned. "Well, let's hope this scenic tour is less dramatic than previous ones." He nodded at her boots. "The only danger I see out here is bad blisters."

Emma sucked doubtfully on her lips. "I've broken them in a bit wearing them around the cottage this morning," she said, apparently unsure whether that was sufficient. It wasn't. He walked into the woods smiling and shaking his head.

Since the night she arrived, he'd thought about Emma every day. First it was with irritation. There was that week doing repairs at the cottage when he'd misunderstood her distance as superiority. His confusion as she sat in shock at the hospital as they waited to hear about Mason. Then there was the awkward dinner at Beth's, from which he could still feel his arm burn from her touch. And that unforgettable afternoon of the storm when she could have drowned shivering in the skiff. He shuddered.

So many moments.

That evening on the shore, when, as she sat on the deck and he swam, he felt his worries slip away. Their stupid fight over the paper. Her calm focus after the brick through The Siren's window, perpetrator still unconfirmed. And their hike to the plant when her resilience and dependability surprised him. She'd looked stunning at his show, when he wanted to make a move and didn't, or couldn't. When he'd kissed her, she'd kissed him back.

So much history had passed between them in such a brief space of time. It was as if she'd always been in the heart of his world. It was an odd, disorientating sensation.

The heat of the sun sliced through the trees. "Watch out." He took a giant stride around a patch of poison ivy.

"You think I'm an uptight city girl, don't you?"

"You said it, not me." He turned to catch her eye, checking she understood he was teasing. He grinned. She pulled a face. She could have reminded him again about the forest and the bear trap, how she'd helped him down the mountain, but she apparently decided not to. He was grateful she did not hold that over him.

Jordan mopped sweat from his face with his hands. He felt energized by the fresh air and alive, working up a sweat. He hoped she was enjoying this hike as much as he was.

About halfway to the peak, and an hour or more into their walk, they stopped so he could check his dressing. All good. The stitches were out and the skin was healing fast.

Emma sat on a tree stump and peeled off a blood-soaked sock. "Don't say a word," she instructed him as she produced a pack of Band-Aids from her pocket.

"Ouch. Blisters?"

"I said not a word."

He mimed pulling a zip across his mouth.

Boot back on, she stood up. "How is your ankle?"

He smiled. "Just fine."

Despite her raw feet, Emma kept up with him as the path grew rockier and steeper, until eventually they stepped through the tree line and out onto an escarpment of gray granite that reared up to meet the bluest sky. Her face glowed from exertion. Radiant.

"Incredible, isn't it?" He took a draw from his flask and passed it over as they began walking, slower this time. "The slope flattens out in about a quarter of a mile into a wide plateau. It's a great place to camp."

"Unless it's a burned-out building or foxhole under fire, I don't do camping," she joked.

"You've never camped with me."

He'd love to take her on a proper trip with a tent and equipment, show her the wild spots around the bay. She'd love it, he was sure. They could spend the night by a fire under the stars, listening to the breeze through the trees. She really wasn't the bougie madam he had first assumed her to be. Not at all. He was embarrassed he'd rushed to pigeonhole her. He hadn't thought he was that narrow-minded.

They marched on for another forty-five minutes in shared determination to reach the peak. He arrived first at the sign declaring: Elevation 1527 Feet. The sky shone vivid blue as the pair of them looked around, catching their breath. The three-hundred-and-sixty-degree view across the range and down to the ocean never failed to awe him. Beneath them, conifer forests spread for miles in all directions, like a dark green velvet blanket, cut through in the east by the meander of a narrow river that merged, ultimately with the misty blue of the ocean.

Emma turned slowly on the spot, her hand shading her eyes. "It is so beautiful. And so quiet, except for the wind. It makes you feel tiny. In a good way."

"Yeah, I feel that." He pointed in a northeasterly direction. "The plant is over there."

Emma inched closer to follow the line of his finger, the breeze whipping through her hair. Her mobile buzzed. She glanced at the screen and slid it back into her pocket.

"The team checking in?"

"No. Erik."

What was Erik calling for? Again, he reminded himself, it was none of his concern.

He glimpsed at her face in profile. He wasn't one to give up at the first hurdle. Perhaps he should make Erik his business? Or was he being an oaf? This ping-pong of should-he, shouldn't-he about Emma had him in a spin. He swallowed an exasperated sigh at his indecisiveness.

Focus on the task.

The drone was more sophisticated than the toys he'd played with before. "Nice bit of kit. What do they use it for?"

"Han's dad built it just for fun, apparently."

Jordan set the machine on the ground and examined the remote. "Han's a smart kid, isn't he?"

"Very."

He prickled with self-consciousness as Emma watched him set the machine up.

"He's a great kid," she continued. "Doesn't say much, just gets on with things. I think he's a little lonely, to be honest, and he's looking for his tribe."

Jordan knew that feeling. "He seems to have found one with you and The Siren."

"For the team, he's a blessing. To him, we are old," she laughed. "He needs friends his own age. I think his parents are just glad he's got some people to hang out with and isn't in his bedroom staring at his laptop, pining for California."

Jordan repositioned the machine's wings, ready for take-off. "Riley's not old."

"She is to him." Emma paused. "She has a soft spot for you, you know."

Jordan could feel Emma's eyes fix on him, looking for a reaction. He blushed. "I would never…She's too… oh, never mind." He didn't want to talk about Riley. He offered Emma the handset. "Shall we try it?"

Standing beside her, he explained where to place her fingers on the controls and how to move the drone. As she lifted the machine from the ground, she beamed. Her face tipped up toward the sky, following it as it soared.

"Fast learner." His eyes dropped to the line of her collar bone. He stepped away, putting some distance between them, suddenly mistrustful of his intensions. "All yours."

"Don't go anywhere." She instructed, her eyes still fixed skyward.

"I'm right here." He stood, his arms folded across his chest, holding in the desire to touch her. "We've got lots of time, thirty minutes of battery." He smiled encouragement. She guided the machine across the valley.

"Are you getting what you need?" He edged closer to view the tiny monitor. The image quality was impressive. "You're a natural."

Their faces hovered close as they watched a seam of white chemical foam thread its way through the watercourse, spilling out like a stain. He felt sick with disgust.

"And there it is," she murmured under her breath and glanced up at him, sending a charge of recognition through him.

Sitting cross-legged on the ground, Emma replayed the footage. She still couldn't quite believe what she'd captured on video. A vein of poison bled directly from the dock all the way downstream toward the ocean, where they knew it bubbled across the surf. This was ecological vandalism on a grand scale.

Standing beside her as she operated the drone, Jordan had been silent as his face registered horror at the images playing on the screen. From this height, the scope of the damage was even clearer. Countryside he knew well was being trashed not even by negligence but with deliberate intent. Her heart tore a little for him.

With his face inches from hers, she had felt a pull, like they were being cinched together, fast and secure on the mountaintop. She had twinged with disappointment when the battery drained and they had to bring in the craft or lose it in the valley. He'd reached across and placed his fingers over hers, gently guiding her to land the thing, the skin of his arms brushing hers. He smelled of eucalyptus.

"We should eat," Jordan said as he spread out a blanket. She watched as he produced from his pack two separately wrapped sandwiches, two cartons of juice, and what smelled like homemade banana bread in a Tupperware. "It'll make me feel better. Mozzarella and tomato, and that one's chicken mayo." He held them out to her.

"You made all this yourself?" Emma said, impressed, as she took one.

"Of course."

Reddening, Emma tossed in two cereal bars and two apples. "My contribution."

They ate in silence. A sharp breeze rolled through the valley, taking the edge off the building heat. A panorama of rugged, green-carpeted mountains rose toward the bluest sky. It felt like they were sitting on top of the world.

Jordan was an easy guy to hang out with. She actually enjoyed his company. That was a thought she never thought she'd have. He was kind and thoughtful. And she would never have got up here without him. He was game. And she liked that.

"That is the best cheese and tomato sandwich I have ever eaten," she said as she balled up her napkin. "Really."

He nodded. "High praise."

Her phone rang. "Hi Erik, yeah, see you later. Around six?"

Jordan couldn't help himself. "Hot date on a Tuesday?"

"With Erik? No, he's got a buyer for Ben's magazines."

Jordan's stomach unclenched.

Emma continued: "I've also shown him some stamps."

Jordan's memory snagged on an image. As a kid, it was a treat to be allowed to leaf through Ben's collection. "Are the albums leather bound, blue and red?"

"That's right. Do you want to look?" she added quickly, concern racing across her face.

"Nah, sell them to someone who appreciates them." He'd outgrown stamps years ago.

"If I sell them, I thought I'd give the proceeds to the coastguard." She seemed keen that he understood she wasn't money grabbing.

"Ben would like that," Jordan reassured her. He lay back, his stomach nicely full, and pointed up as a bird of prey swooped low. "Bald Eagle."

Emma leaned back onto her elbows, her long legs spread out in front of her, her head tilted to the sky. They watched the bird twist, dive, and rise. "So majestic."

"Almost went extinct sixty-odd years ago. DDT poisoning down the food chain."

"DDT? Here? They used that in Vietnam to control malaria."

"Yep. Ben told me that, too. Banned in Maine in the seventies and, surprise, surprise, the bird population came back."

"Huh." She was working something out. "So chemical contamination is nothing new round here." It was more a statement than a question. She shook her head, loose strands shining copper and gold in the sun.

"Yup, we've been here before."

Emma lay down on the blanket beside him. He could hear her breathing. She turned her head, her eyes glinting like malachite. "Thank you for being my tour guide, caterer, and tech support."

"No problem. It's always fun on assignment with you."

"That's one way of putting it," Emma laughed.

He couldn't stop himself. He reached to stroke her cheek with the knuckle of his index finger. She smiled. He gently rolled toward her, paused, and when she didn't move away, he cupped her face, searching for permission. Her smile widened, light dancing in her eyes. He kissed her lightly on the mouth. She hesitated for a moment that seemed to stretch for too long, and then, to his relief, kissed him back with soft lips.

He wrapped his arms around her, ready to let go if she pushed him away, but she didn't. Her fingers ran through his hair, sending shockwaves down his spine. His kiss grew more rapid and deep as he drew her on top of him. He could feel her hip bones press into his stomach as her body moved against his. Her hand moved down his torso to the waistband of his jeans. Now she was initiating their touch. His body lit on fire for her. His fingers glided under her top and over the smooth skin of her back. She lifted her head, panting gently. Still lying on him, propped up on her elbows, her palms cupping his face, something dark slid across her gaze. Maybe doubt or confusion.

"I can't give you anything," she said.

It was his turn to be perplexed. "What do you mean?"

She shifted off him, wiping her hand across her mouth. "I don't have the bandwidth to invest in a relationship. I can't…"

He lay on his back, disappointment pinning him to the ground. Why couldn't she enjoy the moment? Wanting to extinguish whatever was bothering her and make her feel better, he reached for her hand and squeezed it.

Emma spoke again. "I'm so sorry. I just… you don't deserve… I should tell you now, I'm not in a place to be with anyone right now."

Immaculate blue sky still hung above them, but the air pressure had changed.

"Emma, I'm not asking you to marry me."

"Thank God."

The force of her relief made him laugh. "Thanks!"

"Sorry, I didn't mean it like that," she frowned and clutched his hand. She turned her head, her eyes wide with sincerity. "I'm sure you are great husband material."

He knew he was not. "Listen. I like you." He waited for her reply.

"I like you too."

It was exactly what he wanted to hear. "Seriously. I think you're great. I know we got off to a bad start, but I think we could have some real fun together while you're here." He paused, hoping she would say she felt the same. She didn't speak. He continued. "No promises, no guarantees. Nothing serious. Casual. A kiss? Spend some time together? What do you think?"

"No expectations?"

He nodded.

"Can I think about it?" She rolled onto her back and rested her head on his shoulder. "I don't want to hurt anyone. Me or you."

He wanted to wrap her in his arms, kiss her furiously on the lips, and to tell her it was all going to be OK; that they were grownups, they could make it right. Instead, he stroked her hair, his heart sinking, and said simply, "Take all the time you need."

Chapter Thirty-Five

Emma strolled down Bayview toward the bookshop, enjoying the gentle warmth of the evening sun on her skin. Her brain ached from hours spent cutting and splicing the drone footage into a two-minute narrative. Her blisters throbbed from the hike, but it had been a good day's work.

"Emma!" a man's voice bellowed.

She stopped and looked. Ahead, on the other side of the road, Felix, wearing a jungle-patterned pink and blue shirt, waved to her from the gallery doorway. "Emma! Your piece is ready to take home!"

She followed him as he dipped inside. The gallery walls were almost bare.

"Wow, you sold almost everything?"

"It was an amazing night. Best of the season so far. Almost everything found a buyer." Felix beamed as he lifted a cardboard box into her arms. "Now, be careful when you open it. I know the carving seems quite robust, but in fact, it's a very delicate piece."

She nodded. She loved the sculpture's energy, the tooled tendrils of fire unspooling from the wood. She couldn't wait to place it on the mantel in the cottage. Ben would have loved it, she was sure. He'd be so proud. "Thank you."

Felix touched his finger to his lip. "Can I ask you something?"

"Sure." She hoped it wasn't why she bought one of Jordan's pieces. That would feel oddly personal.

"Who was that guy you were talking to at the show? Dark suit, expensive watch, super-deep tan. You talked for a while. He seemed to like you."

"That guy?" She suppressed a shudder. "His name was Vinnie something, I think, up from Boston. Why?"

"I hadn't seen him before. He wasn't on the guest list, and he's not an existing client. Kinda weird. But if he's a buyer, I should reach out to him. He only spoke to you."

"He only spoke to me?" It got worse. People had packed out the space; you couldn't move for people to talk to.

"Yup." Felix poked around in a fishbowl full of business cards and pulled one out. "This him?" He passed it to Emma.

Emma examined the card. Vincent Carretta, managing partner at Murphy & Khan LLP in Boston. "Must be. He said he headed up a law firm."

Uneasiness wobbled through her. Who was this guy who had singled her out and wouldn't leave her alone?

"Mind if I take a photograph of it?"

Felix shrugged. "Be my guest."

Emma pulled a slice of pizza from its box and held the tip of the triangle to her mouth. As she bit into the warm cheese, her eyes floated to the carving of the flame standing proud above the fireplace. It looked like it had always lived here. Jordan had a gift. He had hewn something quite ordinary, a chunk of found wood, into something magical, a spark of life, a new beginning maybe. There was high-reaching hope in his piece. She would never have thought he could craft something with such meaning and beauty out of something as mundane as driftwood.

When he had touched her face on the mountain, it was as if he had run his hand over her entire body. She had ignited. Her skin prickled with anticipation. She had fallen into his kiss hard and fast, and wanted more. As she lay on him, he had felt solid and sure beneath her, like he could hold her and not let her go. She felt protected. It was a new and unexpected sensation. His heart had beaten against her chest and filled her with reassuring warmth and desire. She had thirsted for him. But she'd pulled away.

On the descent, she'd watched the line of his shoulders as he'd moved along the path ahead of her, his t-shirt clinging to his biceps, the nape of his neck browned by the sun. The urge to be close to him tugged at her. For hours after they parted, as she sat tapping away at her desk, his scent wafted around her.

This want was driving her insane.

If she let herself surrender to it, it would be a disaster. He would expect more than she could give, she was sure. Or she might slip and become too invested, too attached. When she inevitably left, the tear would rip through them both. She wasn't strong enough to endure the pain of yet another wrenching goodbye.

And yet, the thought of his arms wrapped around her made her smile.

Tallulah jumped on the sofa and gave her a hard stare.

"You're right. I should step back from the ledge."

The cat settled beside her. With her eyes closed and purring loudly, she looked as if she held the answers to life's interminable questions in her feline brain.

"You like him, right?"

Tallulah yawned and scratched her ear.

Emma needed a friend, someone to talk to. Doug would tell her to lighten up. Life was for living. She could hear him now, instructing her with his New South Wales bluntness: "Take the stick out of your arse. Have some fun, why don't you."

He was brilliant like that, always on her side.

She scratched the cat's head. "But I can't," she whispered.

Chapter Thirty-Six

Jordan wiped sweat from his forehead with the back of his hand and flipped the burgers one last time. In the shade of the cherry tree, Abigail sat in her wheelchair, fanning her face. Lounging on a recliner beside her, Mason sipped a scotch, watching Nora and Piper as they bounced on the trampoline, squealing. Jordan smiled. He loved it when his family was all together.

He turned to Beth and Lily, setting the picnic table behind him. "I think being back at work is fantastic for him," he jerked his head toward his grandfather. "He's really enjoying being part of a new team."

Beth nodded. "I was real worried he'd do too much, but you're right, it's given him a boost."

"Where is Emma?" Lily asked. "Didn't you say she was coming?"

Jordan turned back to the grill, trying to look disinterested.

"She's having an early night," Beth said. "Troy's taking her out on the boat tomorrow."

Jordan prickled. She hadn't told him about going out on the boat. He reminded himself again that her business wasn't his business and added another patty to the fire. One minute he was hopeful she'd call, a second later he was telling himself to forget it and stop being juvenile. It was like walking on eggshells around himself.

"That woman is a breath of fresh air," Lily stated, a touch too loudly.

Jordan reached for the hotdogs.

Mason ambled to the grill. "Good job, yesterday," he whispered in Jordan's ear. "You got good stuff."

"Emma did. But thanks Pops." An unexpected wash of pride lifted his spirits.

"What happened yesterday?" Beth piped up.

Jordan let his grandfather explain. It was their exclusive, after all. "We filmed the pollution all the way from its source right down to the ocean. Amazing footage."

"You did?" Beth looked at him, concerned.

"Jordan and Emma. From Bald Eagle Peak." Mason sat at the table.

Jordan lifted burgers onto a plate, hoping to dodge any further questions. He knew it wouldn't work.

"You and Emma went on another hike?" his sister asked. As he turned to answer, he caught her winking at Lily.

"Yes. For work. For The Siren." He placed the plate of charcoal grilled patties on the table. "For Pops."

"What did you do up there?" Lily asked with a playful lilt in her voice.

The two women exchanged glances. He shook his head, irritated by their high school innuendo. "We walked up, took amazing video, as Pops said, and walked back down again."

"That's all?" Beth grinned. "You know, you look good together."

"Beth." He tried to keep his annoyance out of his voice. "That is all." He didn't enjoy lying to his sister, but if the two of them were going to continue to tease him, they didn't deserve to know. "It's time to eat."

Jordan's appetite was through the roof. He consumed two burgers, two dogs, two roasted corns, a baked potato, and a lot of salad, because Abigail insisted. Beth cleared some plates and hurried inside to get the cheesecake from the fridge and the ice cream. Abigail and Mason snoozed quietly in their seats. It was almost dark and time to take his mom to bed.

"So," Lily looked at him, her brown eyes expectant. "What happened?"

He knew what she was asking and stalled. "When?"

"With Emma. Of course. You seem a little sensitive about it."

Jordan shrugged, trying to sound casual. "I don't want to talk about her in front of the two of you together. Beth takes things too far." Lily waited. The urge to confide in someone overtook him. "I kissed her. She kissed me back." The words rushed from his mouth. "I could have kissed her for longer, but then she seemed to freak out a bit."

"Why?" Lily asked, gently frowning.

"She said something about not being able to make any promises or commitment. And I made a bad joke about not asking her to marry me." Not his smoothest move.

Lily nodded, encouraging him to continue.

"I said, we could do a no strings attached kinda thing, have fun, and she said she'd think it over." As he told her, he realized how off-hand he sounded.

"Like a summer fling?"

"I think I made a mistake." He had been trying to meet her where she was, but instead, he sounded like a player. "I feel good around her, Lily. It's new. And I messed up."

Immediately, he expected her judgement. It was enough that his conversation with Emma played on repeat in his head; he didn't need to feel worse.

But she asked: "Have you spoken since?"

"Nah, I was hoping she'd come today."

"Give her some space." Lily said. "You don't know what she's thinking. And go easy on yourself. As you said, it's new."

Lily gave advice knowing his strengths and his vulnerabilities. He was grateful. And still exasperated.

"Easy enough to say. I feel stupid."

213

He needed to know what Emma wanted, whether he was in with a chance or whether he'd blown it for good. He was churning. "I'm so out of practice with this. And this…this is different."

Lily looked from the table at him with such affection he felt his shoulders drop and his insides warm. She smiled. "Want some advice?"

"Sure." He paused. "Of course. Always."

"If it was me, and a guy I liked said he just wanted to have fun, I might take a minute to think it over."

That Emma might feel something for him lit him with surprise. "I thought that's what she wanted. I was trying to…give her options."

"I see that. But why pretend your feelings are casual if they're not? In the end, it's only you who will get hurt taking that approach." Lily was right, of course. "Wanna know what I think?"

He nodded, bracing himself for her unvarnished assessment.

"Bottom line, you weren't straight with her, and that's why you feel bad. You're not take it or leave it about her. You're not that guy. You gave her incorrect information and now you've got to wait and see what she says about it. Or. You could correct it."

On the mountain, he had thought kissing Emma was a bold move. Now he saw he made a half-assed effort. He'd not been honest. If she rebuffed him, it would be for a kind of relationship he hadn't wanted in the first place. But the thought of telling her how he really felt filled him with icy dread. She'd run for the hills, he was sure. She'd told him as much. He clenched his fists in his lap. She was the first woman for a very long time who stirred a want in him, and he couldn't win.

Beth marched out from the kitchen holding the cheesecake. The girls followed behind, one carrying bowls and the other the ice cream.

"Troy's back from laying the traps. Jordy, could you make him a plate?" his sister asked.

Jordan stood up and sighed. "Sure."

Chapter Thirty-Seven

Thirty-six hours until they went to press. In the beam of the quay light, Emma spotted Troy and Ed, the boat's co-owner, securing wire traps with nylon rope. She stifled an involuntary yawn. Troy smiled as she approached and tossed her a pair of yellow oilers.

"We're not expecting bad weather, but it can get wet out there."

Emma pulled on the waterproofs, reminding herself for the umpteenth time that the forecast predicted calm seas, that Troy and Ed were old sea dogs, that nothing would happen. They wouldn't be headed out if a huge storm was rolling in; and if it did, they would know exactly what to do.

These repeated statements hadn't stopped her from tossing and turning in the night. And when she slept, dreams of swirling oceans and crashing waves and the howl of lashing rain tormented her. She had considered asking Jordan if he'd like to come along; there was something soothing about the idea of having him aboard. He was her new partner in crime for exploring. But she hadn't. She could handle this. She was a big girl. She could deal with her anxieties herself. After all, no one was going to fix them for her. And seeing him would be awkward. She didn't know what she would say.

The engine puttered as Troy gently steered the fishing boat out into the channel. A seam of blue light cut across the horizon as the dawn drew upward like a blind. Out of the sharp breeze, Emma perched on a low step, squeezed in between two wire cages.

"Where are we headed?" she shouted above the motor.

"Due south, to the beds near Cornwell's Island," Troy yelled back to her as they gathered speed. She peered across the cove, trying to locate the cottage. The lighthouse swung its beam through the dawn. She thought of Jordan asleep in the little lodge beside it, what he might look lying peacefully without the weight of the world on his shoulders.

The sun inched higher. Troy cut the motor as the green slopes of the island came into focus. She could make out several white squares, buildings, she supposed, above the shoreline.

"We have a license to haul from here," Troy pointed at a yellow buoy some distance away, "to here." His finger passed across the water to another marker. "When I was a kid, you'd pull up a trap, and it'd be bouncing with lobster. Took two of us to land the thing. Now, it's slim pickings. Most don't come up to size. We toss those back, as well as any eggers or v-notches." Troy must have seen the look of confusion on her face. "Females either carrying eggs or able to breed. We throw them back for obvious reasons. Don't see many of those anymore."

"Or pollock, shad, crabs or any other bonus fish that get caught in there," Ed added, winding a rope around his thick forearm. "Sometimes we haul scrid."

"Nothin'," Troy translated.

"Where is everyone else, the other fishermen?" Emma asked. It was high season. She'd expected to see the area crowded with boats.

Ed dumped the rope in a corner. "We're the only ones left."

"Here we go." Troy pulled on a pair of heavy-duty gloves as both men set to work heaving the fleet of traps in, Ed turning the cable reel and Troy guiding the line. Emma pulled out her camera to capture the men at their grueling task. One by one, they landed the pots aboard and sorted through their catch. The stench of rotting, uneaten bait made her eyes water.

"Too small, too small, too small," Ed repeated as he chucked purple shellfish back into the ocean.

"That one's OK," Troy interrupted.

"Nah, Dude." Ed held up the disputed lobster. "It's not worth the risk. And Maggie only wants select." He threw it into the water.

Emma continued taking pictures, trying to keep out of the way. When they finished, the men stacked three plastic crates of angry lobsters, their claws snapping as they crawled over each other, inside the half-cabin.

Troy started the engine, bobbing his head at the boxes. "Is not a living anymore."

Without the lobster haul, Emma wondered what a man like Troy would do to make ends meet. What would any of these lobstermen, who had grown up here with few expectations other than to be a fisherman, do? Jordan was lucky. Or wise. He'd left once, seen life beyond the bay and had options his brother-in-law didn't. Troy seemed rooted in Sirens Bay.

"Why don't you fish somewhere else?" she asked.

Troy and Ed exchanged weary glances.

"Everyone's moving down the coast away from the pollution," Ed said. "But those spots are already claimed. Some guys hauling down there have held permits for generations. Moving in on that isn't right, never mind illegal."

"And big trouble," Troy added.

"What kind of trouble?"

"There's been fighting over rights to haul," said Troy. "Boats have been sabotaged; gear stolen. Then there's the retaliation. Threats. Physical violence. It's not good. It's moved onshore with people not speaking to one another. Guys, families, who've been friends for years, generations, are now at war. We're staying way out of it."

Ed stacked the last of the traps, lines, and buoys against the side of the boat. "If you wanna to speak to some of the others, maybe come to The Claw later?"

"Good idea," Troy agreed. "You'll get the full picture."

"Thanks," Emma said, the threads of the story already tying together in her head. "It'll be my round."

Huddled in the corner of the bar, their weathered, bristled faces hidden by faded baseball caps, Troy and the other lobstermen were easy to spot.

"Hi, I'm Emma." She shook each of their hands, trying to remember their names. Ruben, Hank, Saul, Mike, Pauly and Steve. There were more than she expected, and they seemed eager to talk.

"It's a war out there," Hank, one of the older guys, said. "I've never seen it like this."

Emma took notes, jotting down dwindling stock numbers, dates, stolen traps, fights between fishermen, and alleged permit violations. The pitchers of beer kept coming. In among the detail was a solid story the paper should have picked up on months ago, if only Dave had the time. Each man had something to say and was vehement: the pollution was the catalyst. Dave would know who on the town board they could approach for comment.

At some point, someone ordered a round of shots. The waitress handed out tiny glasses filled to the brim with amber fluid. The beer was already buzzing through Emma's veins. The scotch would send her flying. She shoved hers toward Troy.

"C'mon," he chided. "If you're buying, then at least join us."

His appeal to her sense of comradery was tempting, but she held back. "I won't. But thank you."

"Just one. For the guys." Ed spoke like she was letting them down.

These were good men, and she was grateful for their time and felt bad for their plight. She didn't wish to come off as standoffish. Against her better judgement, she folded. "Just one."

The alcohol scorched the back of her throat. A fire lit in her stomach. Someone made a joke, and the group laughed. She glowed, softening, looking at them with affection. These were hardworking, straightforward people who just wanted to make an honest living. The bar felt cozy and warm. Another man told a story they'd all clearly heard before about a pulling in their fleet of traps during a brutal storm. Someone else reminded the group of the time the sea froze over. Someone ordered another round of shots.

Emma tipped her head back and downed the liquor. One more couldn't hurt. She was among friends. Her vision blurred at the edges. She told a story about wild carp fishing in the Atlas Mountains in Morocco, how her line lay floating in the water for hours, until Doug finally cast-off and caught a twenty-three-kilo monster in minutes. The group roared. Tales of their biggest catch followed. Someone ordered another round. The whiskey slipped down like nectar.

The country music pumping through the speaker vibrated in her bones. A group of women, full of margaritas, got up to dance. Rolling her shoulders in time to the beat, Emma took another long draft of her beer, watching them spin and sway their hips. The young guy next to her—is name was Pauly, she thought—asked, "Dance?"

Chairs moved, the table got pushed back and suddenly a crowd was twirling and rocking, even Hank. Her head spun. Pauly reeled her in and threw her out. She careered into the table, sending a pitcher and tumblers crashing to the floor. She froze, breathing fast, wisps of hair stuck to her face, not sure what had just happened. Broken glass crunched under her feet.

"What's going on?" A puzzled male voice asked above the din, as the waitress pushed through with a broom.

"Bro!" Troy bellowed.

Emma turned to see who was there. Jordan. Her body swayed to the beat. "Oh, hi!"

"Hey, Emma." His face squashed into a strange expression. "Are you OK?"

"Just hot." She peeled off her shirt to reveal her tank underneath. He took her hand. His grip was firm but friendly. His skin was softer than she expected. She leaned into him to hold her balance.

"Hey Bud," Troy called across. "We're having a few drinks."

"I see."

Emma's arms slipped around his waist. "C'mon, dance."

Jordan's brow knitted. "Shall I take you home?"

"No, we're having a good time." She couldn't understand why he was being so grumpy. "Aren't we, guys?"

Her new friends cheered.

"I think maybe I should take you home?" Jordan insisted with something like concern.

She'd never seen eyes so very blue. She gripped his biceps and stared directly into his face, trying to focus.

His features aligned in perfect proportion. Where his plaid shirt opened at the neck, she could just see a sprinkling of coarse hairs. She resisted the urge to run her fingertip over them. Instead, she dropped her cheek to his chest. He held her steady. She blinked slowly, her gaze shifting. So comfortable. Perhaps she should let him take her home. Those lips were very kissable. She would enjoy exploring that body. She could have a little fun with him, a little romance. What had she got to lose?

Emma placed her palm on his chest to stop his face blurring. "I'll get my bag."

Jordan helped Emma into the truck. She collapsed into the seat while trying to tie her hair up. She was wasted. Troy would pay for it tomorrow with a thick head—he might pay for it tonight when it got home. The other guys didn't look so good either. He didn't blame them for cutting loose, though. It was tough times for all lobstermen.

"Ready?" He watched his passenger. She might vomit any minute. "Put your seatbelt on."

Emma grappled with the buckle before it eventually clicked into place. "Yep, ready when you are." She placed her hand on his thigh and squeezed. He gently lifted it off as he pulled out of the lot and onto Bayview.

The sky was velvet black, lit up by a spray of stars. "How much did you drink?"

"Not so much." She opened the window and stuck her face into the breeze. Even smashed, she looked beautiful, drinking in the fresh air.

"Right."

She swung her attention to him. "Can we put some music on?"

"Sure."

She grabbed for the stereo dial and turned up the volume, swinging in her seat to Garth Brooks, rolling her head back and forth on the rest.

"Easy." He adjusted the volume. "I didn't have you for a country girl."

"Every girl's a country girl, underneath," she slurred. "Are we going to your place?" She looked at him, her green eyes wide and expectant.

"No, I'm taking you home."

"Oh." She hiccupped. "I thought we were going to your place."

Jordan glanced across. He could keep an eye on her if she stayed the night. He could sleep on the sofa and if she needed anything, he'd be on hand. He'd worry less than if she was at the cottage alone. "Fine."

She leaned across and kissed him on the cheek. Her lips were warm on his skin and sent a fizz through his body. "What was that for?"

"Nothing." She clicked her fingers to the music.

He shook his head. "You are so drunk."

He had barely parked the truck when she jumped out, leaving her bag in the footwell, and ran to the shore. "I'm going for a swim," she announced, pulling off one sneaker, then another, and then her jeans and tank. In just her underwear, her skin shone like white marble in the moonlight.

"No, no, no." He jogged to catch up with her. "It's way too cold. And the swell is strong tonight."

Before he could reach her, she waded into the shallow water, announcing, "It's good for you!"

He stood at the water's edge with his arms outstretched. "Come back. Please," he beckoned. He picked up her clothes. They smelled of laundry detergent and perfume. She took a step further in, wobbled, and splashed under the surface. He was in the water, wading toward her when she resurfaced, half crying, half laughing, staggering toward him like a drenched zombie.

"I'm really wet." She held her arms out like a frozen child wanting to be picked up.

"No shit." He held her close, guiding her up to the beach, her long, slender arms looped around his neck. Her breath brushed across his neck. When her bare feet stumbled on the rocks, he picked her up and cradled her in his arms.

"You're so handsome," she murmured, water from her hair cascading down his shirt. "Like a model."

"You're drunk."

"Why don't you have a girlfriend?" she demanded, her face staring into his.

He wished she were sober.

"Sit here." He placed her gently on the porch bench and passed her a towel. "I'll put on some coffee."

By the time he returned with two steaming mugs, she'd fallen asleep wrapped in the bath sheet.

"Oh Emma," he said under his breath. In one movement, he lifted her and walked inside, swallowing down the desire swelling deep within. As he kicked open the door to his bedroom and laid her on his bed, arranging her head carefully on his pillow, she muttered something he didn't understand.

"You're a total mystery to me," he said as he spread a blanket over her.

Her eyelids closed; she was out for the count.

Jordan left the door open ajar and returned to the living room to make up the couch. He had the woman he wanted in his bed, and he wasn't in it with her.

Emma slowly pulled her eyes open. Sunlight streaked into the room through an unfamiliar gap in the curtains. Her fingertips felt a wool blanket. Not hers. She pulled herself up onto her elbows. A bookshelf containing rows of hardback books, the type that displayed artfully taken photographs of landscapes and naturally occurring textures, lined the wall. A series of three small paintings on the other wall depicted the darkening progress of a storm. On the battered brown leather trunk at the foot of the bed rested a framed photo of a young blond woman smiling directly at her. Pretty. Her eyes moved to the door. A long, dark plaid robe hung from a hook. A man's bedroom. The woman was somebody's wife?

Her head pounded. Her mouth felt like she'd been chewing on gravel. Her breath tasted of beer and whisky. And her hair was damp. Images from the bar flashed through her mind: shot glasses, ruddy faces, shattered glass. A guy called Pauly twirling her around and around. Dread sank through her insides.

She glanced under the blanket. She was wearing only her bra and underpants. Where the hell were her clothes? She fell back on the pillow, pulling the throw up to her chin, and stared at the copper and glass light fixture hanging from the ceiling like a ship's lantern. A lobsterman's bedroom? Glittery stars and the moon's reflection on the sea sparkled across her vision.

She sat up. She couldn't hide in here all day.

She found her jeans and shirt folded neatly on the chest. Dressed in yesterday's clothes, she took a deep breath and opened the bedroom door. Walking into what appeared to be a living room, its panoramic window revealed broad daylight outside. The ocean heaved over a rocky shingle beach. Beyond, she could see the line of the cove. As she passed, she ran her finger over the back of a cozy gray couch and admired the wood-burning stove. This home belonged to someone with great taste for simple, beautiful things. Probably not Pauly.

She knew who.

Quietly, and with a rising sense of foreboding, she followed the scent of coffee and stepped into the kitchen.

Jordan turned from the range. "Morning."

Of course. She had a vague memory of pulling him to dance.

Placing her hand on his thigh and squeezing his firm flesh. She winced. "Morning."

His muscles shimmied under the cotton of his t-shirt as he moved from the stove to the table, and back again, rearranging pots and plates.

A surprising thought: at least she wouldn't have the embarrassment of explaining to him she spent the night with one of Troy's buddies. And then a counter thought: I don't have to explain anything to him. He's not mine and I'm not his. A third astonishing thought dropped through her: she didn't want him to feel rejected because she'd chosen another.

She pulled out a chair and sat down. It was too many notions at once for her struggling brain to process.

Jordan's blue eyes twinkled. "How are you feeling?"

"Not great." She hooked a tangled strand of hair behind her ear. She must look a mess.

"Ah, that Great British understatement."

"I feel like a wreck."

He nodded in a way that conveyed, that's more like it. "You want eggs?"

She felt both ravenously hungry and as if she was about to throw up. "Maybe a little." He passed her a mug of coffee. "Listen. Did we…?"

He rested the spatula on a plate and said nothing for a moment. "No, Emma, we did not."

"I'm sorry. I know." She shook her head. He was a gentleman. "I just needed…to check."

"I slept in there." He pointed toward the living room with the utensil. "You were pretty gone. Remember stripping off at the beach and running into the sea?"

She frowned and closed her eyes. Her cheeks burned. The water had been freezing. "Thank you…for being there… for looking after me." Remorse clouded her face.

"No problem," he smiled. "I've been there. I'm the last to judge."

What had she been thinking? She hadn't been thinking. When she consumed spirits, craziness ensued. She shook her head gently. "I should never ever, ever, drink whisky."

"The guys are a bad influence."

"That's very kind."

He placed a dish of scrambled eggs and buttered toast in front of her. "You'll need this. It's Friday." Her mind stalled. "Press day? Right?"

Her eyes widened. She had a fast-paced day of decisions ahead and her brain was thumping a slow beat against her skull. She took several gulps of ice water from the tall glass he'd put beside her plate.

But, she reminded herself, I've got a story that's worth the hangover.

Chapter Thirty-Eight

Jordan hammered a run of new plastic guttering into place. Mason shouldn't have to worry anymore about overspill at the back of his house damaging the paintwork.

His phone bleeped in his back pocket.

Emma: Dinner tomorrow at Maggie's? To say thank u.

He stared at the screen. There was no need. That morning, sitting at his kitchen table wearing yesterday's clothes, pale, tired and clearly very hungover, her hair hanging in thick dark strands against the white of her skin, she was the loveliest thing he'd seen in a long while. He had wanted then to ask her about his suggestion they spend more time together, but he had guessed that it wasn't the moment. Of course, he was going to meet her. He tapped his reply: Yes! See you there. 7?

Emma: Done.

Was it a date? Nah, she was being polite. Gracious. Or had he missed something? He didn't know.

He hammered in another nail.

God, he was overthinking this.

Saturday night and the town parking lot it was a mess. It was the same every summer: cars, vans and trailers jammed in back-to-back. There were always people blocked in who wanted to leave, scrapes and bumps, angry altercations. He continued to The Claw where Lily let him park round the back if her truck wasn't there. He walked inside to let her know he'd taken her spot.

Lily placed her palms on the bar and leaned forward, beaming. "Well, don't you look nice!"

All day he'd gone back and forth on what he was going to wear.

It was ridiculous. Showered, clean-shaven, and wearing new jeans, he'd changed shirts twice before he settled on the light-blue linen long-sleeved number Beth had bought him for his birthday one time and he'd never had occasion to wear.

"All this for us?" Her eyebrows flew up.

"Nah, I'm meeting Emma at Maggie's. Here are the keys to the truck if you need to move it."

"Your idea?"

"Nope. Hers."

She took the keys, looking him right in the eye. "If she's important to you, speak your truth. Don't hold back."

He nodded. "I'll try."

"And remember," she said over her shoulder as she replaced a bottle of scotch on the rack. "Have a great time."

At the door to the restaurant, Jordan took a deep breath. The waitress, a college kid he'd known since she was in kindergarten, greeted him sporting a fitted white button-down shirt and a black tie.

"Your table is right on the water," she announced as she led him across the deck, festooned with fairy lights, their reflection rippling golden threads across the pitch-black ocean.

If it had been a date, this would have been a romantic place to pick. He took a seat and waited. He smoothed his palm over the crisp white linen tablecloth and straightened the two knives and then the two forks set on either side of his plate. He was nervous and felt stupid about it, but he was going to be himself. Who else could he be? If she didn't want to be more than friends, or just friends, then so be it. He felt like his high school senior self, waiting nervously at lunch to ask Becky McCall to prom. To his relief, Becky had said yes.

The restaurant, the priciest in town, buzzed with diners. The last time he'd eaten here was for Abigail's fiftieth birthday. That was the first time Sophie met all his family. Back then, he'd been on edge, terrified his dad would be loaded, that his mom would get upset, and Mason would explode in a tirade of paternal disappointment. His dad had behaved and Soph had taken their unabashed scrutiny all in her stride.

Emma walked toward him, looking amazing in a pale blue sleeveless cotton dress with a cinched waist and full skirt. The color matched his shirt.

"Am I late?"

"Nope, I'm early." He stood to kiss her lightly on the cheek. Her peach-pink lips set off her almost translucent skin.

"Drinks?" The waitress appeared as they settle back down, her eyes flicking from him to Emma as she seemed to appraise them as a couple.

"Just soda water for me, please." Emma picked up the menu. From behind it, she said: "I think I've drunk enough for this week, no month, or maybe a year, already."

It was cute that she was still embarrassed, but unnecessary. God knows he'd done far worse when under the influence. Once, he'd even driven home from The Claw absolutely slammed, parked the truck in the drive and fallen asleep at the wheel. He'd woken up horrified and ashamed. He could have seriously hurt someone. From that moment on, he got sober.

"Coke, please."

Emma looked directly into his face. "I'm so sorry about the other night." The glow of the candle in the glass lamp twinkled against the gold specks in her eyes. "I hope I didn't do anything… rash." She grimaced.

Would kissing him be so bad?

"Nah, you were drunk, that's all. I've done worse."

"That is probably not true."

He put down the menu. It was time she knew who he really was. "I drank a lot after my wife died. A lot. I got angry; I broke stuff. My things, never anyone else's. I was sad and didn't know what to do with it, so I crashed around, tossing my grief all over other people. I was irresponsible and lucky that no one else got physically injured, although I'm sure I hurt many people's feelings."

"You were in pain. That's understandable."

"No. It isn't." He owed Beth and Lily more than he could ever repay them for withstanding his rage and misery and never giving up on him. "I wasn't a nice guy to be around. I was hurting, bad, and I couldn't see past it."

"Are you…" She paused, seeming to consider if she wanted to continue with her question, "… still in recovery?"

"Yes. Always will be."

She nodded, but she didn't follow up with another question. He asked one for her. "Am I still sad and angry? Sometimes. Do I still miss my wife? Always. But life does somehow go on. And there's no need to be an asshole about it."

The waitress returned with their beverages and took their meal order. He took her lead: green salad with fancy herbs and grilled bass.

Jordan spoke again. He wanted Emma to understand. "My wife has been gone for five years. I have a new life now, a different one, with friends, some of whom are people she never knew. And Sophie will always be a part of my life."

Emma looked at him for a long time.

He continued: "It gets better." He said it for her sake as much as his own. That you can surface from rough waters seemed like something she needed to know. And then he'd talked enough about the past. He changed topic. "Listen, on the hike, I didn't mean to sound flippant about being…"

She interrupted. "I know. It's just," she stared down as she fiddled with her napkin in her lap, "I can't."

An unwelcome sense of desperation gripped him. He needed clarity. "Can't what?"

"I just feel this…" She glanced up and then away, her eyes drifting out over the ocean. He waited. "I feel this…"

He couldn't wait for her thoughts to form. He interrupted. "What? I like you, Emma. I really do." He hoped he sounded as sincere as he felt and not like a jackass trying to make up for lost time. Maybe he shouldn't have spoken about Sophie. Maybe he'd confused her by talking about another woman.

"I like you too." She clasped hands on the table, as if to steady herself.

Her admission gave him courage. It was time to be direct. "Listen," he said, "I'm not a casual guy. I want to spend proper time with you." There, he'd said it. She looked surprised but didn't speak. "I want to get to know you. It's not every day…"

Her face was inscrutable. Was she following along? Did she feel the same? He couldn't tell. His confidence wobbled. He looked at her, willing her to respond, to give him some encouragement to continue.

Emma opened her mouth to speak, but nothing came out. Her throat had sealed shut while her mind scrambled for something to say.

"What do you think?" he asked after a long silence, his blue eyes like lasers. "Talk to me."

She'd heard him say he liked her. She hadn't heard those words in such a long time. Part of her wanted to laugh. She'd come up to Sirens Bay to sell a property, not to find a love interest. She'd certainly never expected to discover a stunning man who hiked and swam and carved beautiful sculptures with powerful hands, someone who understood her life of travel and risk better than most people, never in this little corner of the world. That would have been an absurd fantasy.

But she could never sustain a relationship with anyone, Jordan included, however lighthearted, without worrying about how it would all end. Doug's and Ben's deaths had almost capsized her. Endings were so painful. It was better not to start in the first place, however achingly lonely she felt.

There was no way she could guarantee she wouldn't get attached to him; buried in her heart was the knowledge that she would. She didn't have the emotional bandwidth to weather another loss, another goodbye. She couldn't take that chance. She wasn't being dramatic; she was being practical. Protecting herself. And him. She had a life, and it was not in Sirens Bay. She wouldn't lead him on. He deserved better. There was a woman out there who would sink with easy delight into a relationship with Jordan, bask in his attention, and rightfully shower him with love and care, in return. It wasn't her.

"I just can't." She shook her head.

He seemed to retreat inside for a long moment, before he regrouped, forced a smile, and announced, "Can't fault a guy for tryin'."

Her shoulders relaxed at his attempt to lower the intensity. "Friends?" She suggested as she held up her water glass for a toast.

"Sure. Friends." He clinked his tumbler with hers.

Emma picked at her salad, asking questions about Jordan's family. He gamely chatted about Nora and Piper, their current likes and dislikes, seeming to understand that this was as far as their connection was going to go. When the waitress brought the check, he also seemed relieved that the effort at small talk was over. She filled with sadness that she'd broken something between them. But it had to be done.

"Thank you for dinner," he said, as they left Maggie's.

Jordan was such a nice guy. He wouldn't remain alone forever. "My pleasure," she replied.

"I'll walk you to your car."

The hum of the restaurant receded behind them. Her heart sank at his sweetness. She didn't want to separate from him, but the urge to curl up at home, alone, and lick her wounds in private was almost overwhelming.

"I had to park miles away."

She pulled her cardigan over her shoulders. He stuffed his hands in his pockets. As they strolled up Bayview, past the gallery and the bookshop, they were like magnets holding each other in place just beyond touching distance.

"You really did park quite far away." He smiled as they reached the dodge standing outside a corner store at the end of the main road.

"Parking here on the weekend is a nightmare."

"Spoken like a local."

She laughed.

"What was it like coming back here to live after you'd been away for so long?" How had he adjusted to the nearness of everything, the lack of anonymity and privacy?

"After Sophie passed, I didn't know what I was going to do. But I didn't plan to stay. I just landed here in a heap. But then I realized how great this town is, the ocean, folks, mountains. Everything is here. Honestly, I wouldn't want to live anywhere else."

"Really?"

"Really." He stopped. "But you seem like the type who likes to keep moving."

She was surprised her restlessness was that obvious. "I'm curious, that's all. I like to see new things."

"Sometimes, it's equally exciting to really get to know a place."

"Maybe." She needed convincing.

His words hung in her brain, ready to be examined again. He bent to kiss her on the check. His stubble brushed her skin before he stepped back, restoring the space between them. A force swept her body, telling her to bridge the gap. She opened the driver's door, determined not to give into the yearning. Her skin, lips, eyes, and arms wanted him, but she had to listen to her head.

"Goodnight," she raised her hand in a little wave.

"Goodnight, Emma." Jordan turned and walked away.

Chapter Thirty-Nine

Jordan's face wouldn't leave her mind. Emma even dreamed of him, his strong arms heavy around her waist, his lips planted on hers, her fingers searching his hair, pulling him closer, their bodies pressing together. The cozy warmth that swamped her when she thought of him was intoxicating.

But it couldn't happen.

She threw off the covers, walked into the kitchen, and filled the coffeepot. She couldn't spend all Sunday ruminating on their conversation, wondering if she'd done the right thing. Reason said they should be friends and no more. She needed a distraction from the ache lodged in her chest and expanding through her body like a fever. Work never failed to provide one.

"Hey!" Han greeted her as she walked into the newsroom. "What are you doing here?"

"I could ask the same of you." She placed her coffee and laptop on her desk. She wasn't the only one using The Siren as a refuge.

"Mom and Dad have taken my sister and her friend to Splash World. I'd rather eat my vomit than spend the day hanging out with them." Han could be discerningly direct sometimes.

"Oh. Right." She blinked. "What are you working on?"

"This website fix won't stick." He frowned. "Don't understand why. Traffic's way, way up on the site, so we need it to do what it's supposed to do."

Emma's lobster wars story had hit a nerve. Circulation was through the roof, according to Kirsty, who'd just about wheedled a second hard copy print run.

Footsteps echoed on the floorboards above. "Mason's here?"

"Yeah, he let me in."

The old man shuffled down the stairs. "Well done, young lady," he announced, catching his breath. He patted Emma on the arm as he passed by on his way to the front desk. "You should be proud of yourself."

"Thank you." High praise indeed. To her surprise, she felt a flare of pride and affection for him.

He returned, clutching a bunch of the latest editions under his arm. "Everyone in town is talking about the story. It's a scandal no one's been offered any compensation. Troy, Ed, they should sue!" He tapped the copies with his index finger. "You know, I think this just might work."

Emma and Han exchanged convert glances. Wow. Perhaps they'd won Mason over?

Jordan tossed a piece of driftwood from palm to palm. The grain of the branch curved and dipped round a knot the size of his fist. Was it possible to shape it into something more beautiful than it already was? He turned it over. How could he accentuate its wildness? He stared out of the window of his studio, a former bedroom now crammed with his workbench and tools shelved around his lathe.

Outside, there wasn't a cloud in the sky. It was going to be a scorcher. Later, the shore would be choc-a-block with yachts, jet skis, lobster cruises and paddle boarders. It was a day to keep far, far away from town and let the tourists do their thing.

He pulled a chisel from its pouch, and his mind drifted back to the night before. He should have kissed her on the lips when he had the chance. Underneath the chitchat blanketing their dinner, he knew she felt something for him, too. She'd said so. She liked him.

She didn't have to know right now what she wanted. He didn't know either. She said she couldn't make promises; he wasn't asking her to. He couldn't either. He had no idea how it would go with the first woman he'd had feelings for since Sophie. It was a risk for him, too. He just knew this woman was different, and he wanted to be around her. That was enough. It was ample.

His eyes settled on the contours of wood in his hands. There were layers and layers to Emma, and he wanted to see them all. She could give more than she knew. If she was scared, he would show her he could be trusted. Jordan pulled his phone from his pocket. His fingers tapped: You said you wanted to see more of SB. Pick you up at 1730 to take you to the secret cove?

He placed his phone on his worktable, hoping he'd stirred her curiosity. He tried not to look at it. He picked it up again and added: Good for research.

The opportunity to further the story might seal the deal.

Jordan ran his hand over the length of wood, trying not to think about her. He looked at the grain, searching for an invitation, a starting point that would guide the chisel. He would not give up on Emma. She might be wary or unsure, but he could shoulder some ambivalence for a while. Then he saw it, a nick in the wood that opened into a deep vein. A beginning. He was not a patient man, but he was learning to take his time finding his way into his work; he would try to apply the same lesson to Emma, although he knew it would not be easy. Gently, he touched the tip of the tool to the wood and began pressing.

After lunch, finally, he received her reply: That would be lovely. E

He let go a deep sigh of relief. She hadn't rejected him. He had another opportunity to prove he was a reliable and honorable guy. A hum of excitement moved him around the kitchen as he packed a Tupperware of strawberries, a quart of ice cream and two bottles of peach iced tea into the cooler. He grabbed a blanket, a ground mat, and camping light.

Emma appeared around the side of the cottage wearing a t-shirt, cut-offs and a sweater tied around her waist, with her camera bag hooked over her shoulder. As she walked toward the truck, he recognized the small brown leather case round her neck.

"Are those binoculars?" he asked as she climbed in. He landed a soft kiss on her cheek.

She nodded. "Found them in the sideboard."

"Ben used to take us birding and Beth and I would argue over who got to use them."

She laughed.

"Ready?" He smiled back.

"Always ready for an adventure."

"It's a broad term." He grinned. He hoped, eventually, her readiness might encompass him.

Route One was thick with holiday traffic, which he knew from a lifetime of experience should thin by the time they reached the other side of town. He glanced at the clock. Thirty minutes till sunset. They would make it.

"What did you do today?" he asked, trying to sound casual, light, non-intrusive.

"I went to the office."

"On a Sunday? Pops will be impressed."

"Actually, he was there." She turned to look at him directly, seeming to expect his next question. "He looked fine, don't worry. I think he was just pottering and taking calls from friends quizzing him about the permit story. We lit a fire there."

"You sure did." Jordan beamed. His grandpops was at the center of it all. He'd love that.

She nodded. "You?"

"Trying to figure out how to approach a new piece."

"Also working on a Sunday."

"I guess so, although I don't really see my sculptures like that."

"You should. Your pieces seem like more than a hobby. They sell!"

That's what Felix and Ramon kept telling him. Somehow it sounded truer coming from Emma.

The truck glided down the highway before Jordan slowed at a gap in the trees signaling the start of a dirt track, and turned off. The pickup bumped and rocked as they cut through the pines.

"Where are we going?" Emma asked, clinging to the handgrip. She seemed delighted and confused at the same time.

"I told you, to my secret cove. Don't worry, I'll get you back at a decent hour. I know it's a school night." He wished that wasn't the case.

He parked up in a tiny clearing surrounded by shrubs, knotted and gnarled by the sea breeze. The golden sand was soft underfoot.

"This way," he reached for her hand and led her along a winding footpath bordered by dune grass. Her palm was slight and warm in his and she let him keep hold of it.

"This isn't where you implicate me in a federal crime, is it?"

He grinned. "You guessed it. There's a boat waiting for us laden with several million dollars' worth of cocaine. Nearly there."

"Somehow that sounds like that's a situation you've encountered." She squeezed his hand.

"Yes. In fact." Underfoot, the sand transformed into something like fine sugar. "Close your eyes."

Doubt flashed across her face. "I like to see where I'm going."

"You don't have to, but it might be fun?"

"OK." She didn't seem entirely convinced, but she squeezed her lids shut.

With one arm around her waist, he gripped her other hand and guided her slowly over the crest of the dune and down the other side.

He stopped. "OK, now, look."

She opened her eyes and gasped. Ribbons of yellow, orange and rose pink streaked the sky. The sunset tinted peach the entire beach, while the sea glittered fairy-tale blue.

"Welcome to my secret beach."

"Wow." She turned, looking in every direction.

To the east, a high rocky cliff enclosed the cove, shielding them from most of the incoming wind. The granite twinkled in the fast approaching twilight. To the west, a cluster of boulders, like a giant's building blocks, toppled into the waves, creating a series of sharp-edged rock pools that filled and emptied as the ocean swept back and forth.

"This is incredible." An amazed smile spread across her face. The orange sun lit up the flecks of gold in her eyes and hair. She was ablaze.

"Isn't it?" He glowed with satisfaction that he'd surprised and pleased her.

"Very, very beautiful." She shook her head in disbelief.

"Yep." He glanced at her. That was right.

Jordan laid out his blanket and dropped his bag on it. He led her to the water's edge, where they took off their sneakers and let the ocean lap their toes. "Wanna swim?"

She blushed. "No, not this time. I may have just about spent enough time in the ocean recently."

He hadn't meant to embarrass her by reminding her of her drunken dip. Thinking back now, she had been lucky the current hadn't swept her out into deeper water. They both had. He shuddered and glanced at Emma's face, shining in the soft evening light. This woman was a mystery, a mix of physically reckless, intellectually inquisitive, and emotionally cautious. He yearned to know why.

Still standing at the shoreline, Emma lifted the binoculars to her face while he pointed out spots along the coast: local landmarks, his favorite places, and the approximate sweep of the pollution.

"Who would put all this at risk? She dropped the binoculars and stared at him with the question burning in her eyes. "And for what? For money?"

He had told himself he wouldn't, but before he knew it, he had taken her hands and pulled her gently toward him, holding her gaze. She didn't shake him off or speak. She lifted her chin, the hint of a smile on her lips as if she knew what was coming. Her irises sparkled.

He stepped closer and murmured, "I really want to kiss you."

She nodded. He touched his lips to hers as delicately as he could. She kissed him back gently. His mouth hovered over hers.

Emma whispered, "Don't stop."

Her arms reached up around his neck. He could feel her heartbeat quicken against his chest. His entire attention focused on sending her pleasure as his mouth moved across her collarbone and up to her earlobe. Her response gathered pace. Her fingers raked through his hair. She pulled his face closer. He kissed her deeper, his hands moving under her t-shirt, stroking the smooth skin of her back. She gnawed his lip, sending shivers of delight across his body. He cupped her face in his hands and drew back a fraction so he could see her eyes. This woman was so beautiful. He wanted to do everything to please her.

His voice low and rasping, he said, "Shall we?"

He looked at the blanket laid out on the beach.

"Yes."

They walked together hand in hand and dropped to their knees. Their mouths locked. He kissed her lips, her face, and her neck, gently sucking at the cord of muscle running down into her shoulder. She murmured his name. Heat soared through him. His hands smoothed around her waist. She pulled her t-shirt over her head and unhooked her bra. Her bare skin was almost too much to look at. He took one of her nipples in his mouth and she let out a long sigh and dropped her head back.

The saltiness of her skin was delicious. His mouth moved up to her throat. He could feel her breath in his hair. Her hand undid the button of his jeans. He was so ready for her; the ache in his groin was almost painful. He wanted her, all of her. But he had promised himself that they would take it slowly. He should stop. He didn't want to. Her fingers traced the elastic of his boxers. Her touch was moments away.

A ringtone burst from his bag.

"Stop," he whispered against her cheek. "Don't stop."

Her fingers slid inside his shorts, and he groaned with delight. Pleasure soared through him.

His phone sang out a second time.

"Do you need to get it?" Emma murmured into his ear.

His desire for her raged. "Nope."

He pulled off his shirt and grabbed for her, longing to feel her skin on his. Her face flushed. Her lips stung berry red. His tongue wanted to taste every inch of her mouth.

She wriggled out of her cutoffs. He slipped free of his jeans. He hugged her close so she could feel the full extent of his hardness. She wriggled against him. He moaned softly.

The ringtone blasted. He breathed heavily against her neck. His fingers slid into the back of her panties and, still kissing her mouth, he moved his hand around to the front, stroking and searching. This was more than he'd planned, way more. They were moving faster and faster, but he couldn't stop. His want for her had overtaken any other impulse. Her breathing wobbled as his index found her wetness. The tip of his finger moved against her velvet skin in a slow rhythm. She jerked with pleasure. He would not rush her. He would make her cry out with delight. She arched back as his finger entered, moving back and forth. She felt gorgeous. She clasped him and kissed him with a fury he hadn't expected. She reached for his groin, but he held her hand away. If she touched him now, it would be seconds.

His phone blasted again. Stopped. And began again.

She pulled away, a longing-filled gap between them. "It sounds urgent?"

Annoyed and panting, desire swirling around his body and looking for a release, he tipped his bag out, ready to turn the damn thing off. His phone dropped on the sand. Beth. A text: Call me. Now. It's Mom.

"Shit." He fell back, breathing hard like someone who'd been punched in the gut.

Emma's body still pulsed to the touch of his fingers. She tried to make it stop by clasping her hands together tightly in her lap and focusing on the highway ahead. It didn't work. She remembered his hand reaching into her underwear and could feel the heat of his palm. She chewed her lip, deliciously sore from the rough skin of his chin. She had needed his touch, to taste him and to feel his desire for her, to know it matched hers. He had given it so freely. She couldn't resist him. Her body had betrayed her mind, and she'd let it. He had surprised her with his gentleness and quiet determination. It made her want him more. She blinked hard, trying to focus on the clock. "How long will it take to get there?"

"Thirty minutes if we're lucky with the traffic." He placed his hand on her thigh and the pounding in her limbs struck up again.

At Beth's house, an ambulance blocked the driveway. Emma recognized the crew. Beth and Troy stood by its open doors with an arm around each other. At the end of a gurney, Abigail's socked feet poked out of a blanket.

Jordan flew from the truck. "Mom!"

Emma followed slowly behind.

"She couldn't breathe," Beth said through tears. "But she's still with us."

Jordan ran his fingers through his hair. "What are they waiting for; why are they still here?"

"Apparently, ER is savage," Troy said. "Sunstroke and broken limbs. The wait is horrific. They wanted to stabilize her first."

"They've given her oxygen and intravenous antibiotics," Beth said. "They reckon it's a severe chest infection. Will you sit with her and we'll follow behind?"

Jordan nodded and stepped up into the vehicle, giving Emma a short wave. She waved back, concerned. She could hear him quizzing the paramedic inside.

Beth turned to Emma. "Would you watch the girls?"

"Sure, of course."

The house was silent as she walked in. Nora and Piper huddled together on the living room couch, watching something on an iPad. Worried eyes looked up at her.

"Your mom and dad have gone to the hospital with your grandma. I'll stay with you until they come back."

Nora looked at her, her eyebrows knitted into a frown. "Is Grandma going to die?"

Emma's mind emptied. She had no experience with helping

children understand illness. She hoped for their sake, and Beth and Jordan's, that Abigail simply had an infection they could treat and nothing more complicated.

She lowered herself to the sofa cushion, deciding honesty was the best policy. "She seems pretty sick, but the doctors will know exactly what to do to help her when she gets to the hospital. Unfortunately, until then, we'll have to wait."

Piper looked earnestly into her face. Her lip quivered. Emma waited for the grave question that was obviously coming. "Can we have ice-cream?" the little girl asked.

Emma's shoulders dropped, relieved. "Why not?"

The girls' mood appeared to lighten as Emma pulled cartons out of the freezer. "Maple walnut, Coffee Oreo, Strawberry Shortcake, or Chocolate Sundae?"

"Chocolate Sundae!" they chimed.

"Bowls?"

Nora pointed to a cupboard next to the sink. "Down there."

The girls sat at the granite kitchen island as Emma spooned ice cream in exactly equal amounts. "Mommy says you need to stick around for as long as possible," Nora said.

"I won't go until they're back." She hoped one of the three would return before it got too late. The team had a big week ahead and she wanted to start it fresh.

"No." Nora continued, matter of fact. "For always."

"Oh." Emma's eyes widened.

Piper shook sprinkles onto her dessert. "She says you and Uncle Jordy could have a super solid relationship." She said like she was repeating an adult conversation she'd heard but didn't fully understand. "Isn't he already your friend?"

Emma blushed. "Of course." What was Beth getting at?

"Is he your boyfriend?" Nora said, as she stuck a huge spoonful of chocolate ice cream into her mouth. Her eyes closed with pleasure.

Emma turned toward the freezer, slotting the tubs back onto the shelf. She didn't even know how to describe Jordan to herself. Her friend-with-possible-benefits? Her potential new lover? Her seaside romance? The hottest guy she'd ever met?

"No." Emma shook her head. "Shall we watch TV?"

The girls didn't budge.

Nora carefully squirted more chocolate sauce around the edge of her dish. "Why not?"

"What?"

"Isn't he your boyfriend?" she persisted.

"Well …" Emma's face was aflame.

"Don't you like him?" Nora looked at her as if she was making a serious accusation that needed to be met with an honest answer. These girls were more rigorous than some journalists she'd worked with.

"Oh yes, of course I like him, your uncle. He is a great guy." She hedged and cringed. She sounded like she was telling a colleague about a mundane mutual acquaintance.

"Then he should be your boyfriend," Nora said, licking her spoon before dropping it into her empty bowl.

"He should be your boyfriend," Piper echoed her sister, sounding as if it was the most obvious conclusion in the world.

Emma's heart pounded. "Let's see what's on TV, shall we?"

Jordan inched open the front door. The house was silent and dark except for the glow of a standing lamp in the hallway. As he walked into the living room, he saw the shape of her body lying under a blanket on the couch. He crouched down beside her and gently lifted a strand of hair off her face. Emma looked so peaceful, her skin as smooth as marble. Her eyelids fluttered.

"Hi." She shuffled onto her elbow. "What time is it?"

"Two-thirty," he whispered, his hand resting on her shoulder.

"In the morning?"

He smiled, "Of course."

"How's Abigail?"

"She's gonna be OK."

"And Beth?"

"They're gonna stay the night at the hospital." He sat on the couch. "May I?"

Half smiling, half puzzled, she nodded.

He lifted the edge of the plaid throw and squeezed in beside her.

"What are you doing?" she whispered, a smile in her voice.

"Getting on the couch with you." He looped his arm underneath her head.

She wriggled over to make space. The warm pressure of her body rinsed the fatigue from his limbs. He nuzzled her neck and ran his hand over her hip. "I'm so glad you're here."

He rolled toward her so that he almost covered her entire body as she sunk into the pillows.

She pushed her palm gently against his chest, looking into his face. "In your sister's house?"

"She's not here." He kissed her lips. "And we've got some unfinished business."

Emma grinned as his mouth landed on hers. Her lips parted immediately. His hand crossed over her belly and rose to stroke her ribs. He stopped at her breast, reigniting the heat that had smoldered at the beach.

"Are you sure they're not coming back any time soon?"

"Certain."

She guided his free hand to her shorts and undid the buttons. "Touch me," she whispered.

His fingers danced around her waistband, moving down to trace to hollow of her of her hip. She pulsed for him, eager. "Please…"

"Not so fast," he whispered into her hair. His hand ran up under her shirt, exposing her breasts. In one swift move, he unhooked her bra and shifted the cotton out of the way. His mouth landed on her, sucking hard. She swallowed a moan. She ached for him, needed to feel him move inside her. "Jordan…"

"Nope."

He raised her arms over her head and moved his mouth down her body, his tongue swirling around her navel. She grabbed for his face, pulling him up and kissing him hard. His palm slid down over her skin and under her panties. Emma gasped as his index finger found the spot between her legs. Concentric circles of pleasure engulfed her. A sweet, warm feeling raced to her throat. She moaned quietly into his neck. "Don't stop."

"I won't," he whispered. "You feel so good."

Their tongues swirled around each other, hurried and hunting. She felt his hardness press against the inside of her thigh. She went to grasp it, but he pulled away. His fingers slid inside her and kept moving, taking her higher and higher. Pleasure circled through her, spiraling her mind to the ceiling.

"You can tell me to stop," he murmured into her ear, "and I will. But until that moment, I'm going to do everything I can think of to convince you I'm for real."

His stroke quickened. Her breath rasped. She could barely make sense of what he was saying.

"Jordan…" She wanted to feel him, the weight of him on her, pounding and hard. "Jordan…"

He seemed to understand. "Not this time, baby."

While his finger kept stroking her inside, his thumb circled.

"Jordan…" she whispered against his chest as a deep sweep of delight rushed her to a peak, held her there until she couldn't take it anymore and she released, rippling into him, panting. Her mouth found his. She held onto him, breathing him in, throbbing against him.

Emma stirred at the sound of Beth and Jordan talking in the kitchen. She startled, remembering how he'd removed her clothes. She pulled on her cutoffs and t-shirt under the blanket, feeling like the rebellious teenager she never was in her aunt's house.

Her phone said it was six-thirty. She sat up and ran her tongue around her teeth, remembering the taste of him, the swirl in her tummy as he touched her, the feeling that swept through her entire body as he stroked her to a climax. The memory would live in her for a while. She already knew that.

"Coffee?" Beth, in a pink terry robe, turned with the glass jug in her hand.

"You're home." Emma spoke to Beth but glanced at Jordan, already showered and dressed. He grinned.

"They gave Mom some heavy sedation. At her age, with her MS, even a cold can be dangerous, but she's in excellent hands."

Her mind raced. "When did you arrive?" Had they heard them when they came in? She ran her fingers slowly through her knotted hair.

"Around five."

They were in the clear.

Beth was obviously exhausted; worry circled in her eyes. "Listen, thanks for watching the girls."

"No problem."

Beth sipped her coffee. "I don't know what's going on with our family. Everyone is getting sick."

Jordan reached for his keys. "The consultant is doing his rounds at seven, so I've got to shoot." He looked at Emma. "Beth will give you a ride home. Is that OK?" He held her gaze, checking.

"Sure."

As he left, he touched her on the shoulder, lighting a tingle across her skin.

Emma climbed into Beth's SUV, eager to get home, shower, and get to the office. Beth, with her mascara and lipstick applied and hands on the steering wheel, seemed to be willing herself to conquer the world. "It's just such a responsibility, y'know, to know what to do for the best," she said as she eased the car out of the driveway.

"I'm sure." Emma nodded.

"Mom's so fragile. Mason too." Beth shook her head.

Elegant clapboard houses painted cotton candy colors slid by the window surrounded by well-watered lawns and maple trees with thick trunks.

"How long has Abigail been ill?"

"She was diagnosed just after Dad passed. That would be twelve years ago. But she'd had symptoms for years. Everyone thought she was just depressed because of Dad's issues. We were all focused on him, didn't think there was anything really to worry about with her."

It was tragic for Beth and Jordan that one parent would die of long-term addiction, and the other would receive a life sentence shortly after. "You've been through a lot."

"Yeah." Beth turned the corner. "But we're strong."

They were a solid family that pulled together. For the first time in a very long time, Emma felt an impulse that she would like to be part of something like that; that her independence and freedom from family drama might not be the precious jewel that needed as much protecting as she thought.

Beth glanced at her, talking fast. "And, oh gosh, the cottage, I'm so sorry. I meant to tell you. There's been a development."

"We don't have to do this now."

"No. I should tell you. Yes. The paperwork is all filed. I just need one signature from you, and it can officially go on the market."

"Great." Emma should have felt elated; things were moving. But the lift didn't come.

With the paperwork lined up, she could leave at any moment. The desire to pack up and get going as soon as she possibly could failed to spark. Suddenly, she was in no rush. The realization surprised then unsettled her. Who was she if she wasn't on the move, about to leave and arrive somewhere?

Jordan's cedar scent hung around her as the SUV sped through town. She was sure Beth must have been able to smell it on her, but she said nothing. Was he a reason to stay, or a reason to move on?

Beth sighed as she pushed on the brake, slowing behind a trash collector as it trundled along the curb. A teenage girl on her bike flew past, maybe on her way to her summer job.

Emma had been the same at high school, always rushing from here to there, brimming with purpose, ready to seize the day, working hard. Until the office banished her on mandatory sick leave, she'd always tried to keep up the same pace at work and play. It occurred to her that perhaps it was time to grow up a little and accept the slower one forced upon her.

Beth stopped at the signal by The Siren. Emma peered up at

the building, wishing she had a change of clothes and she could hop out. The car drove on. She would be back as fast as she could.

Chapter Forty

Mason beamed at Emma as she walked into the newsroom, carrying Tallulah under her arm.

"Did you hear me on the radio?" he bellowed.

"You were great, Mason." She didn't know he had it in him. As she drove in, the old man had talked fluently and with passion about their fishing permit story. As its local proprietor, he was the rightful voice of the paper, and she was glad he was thrilled.

"Nice plug for The Siren too."

She placed the cat on the floor. Tallulah had stowed way in the car again and by the time Emma had noticed, she was too far into town, and it was too late to turn back. The team got in early, and she hated being the last. She guessed the cat had gotten fed up spending so much time in the cottage alone.

Han sneezed. "Allergies."

"Cat's too?"

He nodded.

Tallulah jumped into Mason's arms and began purring, her eyes squeezed shut. She looked like she was in heaven. Perhaps something invisible emanating from Mason, his pheromones, reminded her of Ben.

"I just joined Facebook." Mason brimmed with excitement. "Whole new world. Got fifty friends already! I'll take her upstairs."

Riley leaned toward Emma's desk. "I don't know what this means or if it's important. But, I made a few calls before you all got here—I gotta leave at lunch for the café. One of our new advertisers asked me if I knew anything about a new land use code the city is proposing? She said there's been a lot of talk about it since the mayor announced it last year, and a lot of the local business owners are worried it'll attract unwanted newcomers, competition." She looked down at her pad. "Her exact words were, 'if it goes through, letting in those megastores will kill us mom and pop outfits'."

Kirsty croaked: "If they want to build a casino up there, that'll sure clear the way."

Dave shook his head in dismay. "What is going on in this town? This used to be a quiet little place with good fishing and hiking."

It was great intell.

"Amazing. Thanks Riley. Nice reporting." Emma smiled at their new sales rep, who, if Emma was correct, might have even blushed under all that foundation. She was a sweet girl, under-used at the cafe and probably underestimated her whole life, a teenage mom who barely finished high school. She was a quick-study, and excellent on the phone. She had the necessary instinct to know who to call and how to lead them down the path to a sale. Like Han, Emma felt a twang of responsibility for her. She hoped that whatever happened at The Siren, that Riley would take this experience and run with it into a better future than life currently had in store for her.

"Anymore tips like that, we need to hear them. Dave, you look into the zoning issue?"

"Sure thing. This story is sprouting tentacles." Dave rolled his eyes and grinned.

Yes, and they didn't want to get distracted. She'd keep Mason on Senator McDermott; Dave could check out gaming applications. She'd comb through the USB again.

Adrenaline and caffeine buzzed through her system. They were inching closer, stalking their exclusive. She would miss the kill if she left now. And she would miss her team. Having asked them to give their energy and time, it wouldn't be right to abandon them now. They were getting somewhere, and she was having fun. Where was Jordan in all of this? She preferred to think he stood in the background, his handsome, steady company a bonus. Although she wasn't certain. She'd decide that another day.

Emma locked The Siren's main door and walked down Bayview. She stretched, tipping her head to the moon, and took a deep breath. The sudden quiet after a day of calls and conversations surprised her. The lights strung over Maggie's twinkled. The panic she'd felt just a few nights ago sitting across the table from Jordan seemed like a long ago feeling. Her feet landed on the sidewalk like she was walking on firmer ground. She didn't know what she was getting into with him, or how long it would last, but she understood that his presence lifted a sense of doom she hadn't realized she was carrying. It gave her the courage to step out of her comfort zone and the curiosity to see where whatever this was with Jordan might lead.

She sat in the Dodge and checked her phone before she turned the ignition. A calendar notification slid into her inbox. What was that for? She tapped the screen. An event popped open. She froze, staring at the reminder. Doug's birthday. He gave her hell year on year for forgetting, so at some point after he wasn't around anymore to remonstrate with her, she'd put it into her phone. She hadn't wanted to forget. And yet she had. Doug hadn't crossed her mind all day.

Her head dropped back onto the rest as she let her cell rattle into the cup holder. She closed her eyes as tears leaked down her cheeks. It was an impossible notion: Doug would never, ever again tell her she was useless for forgetting, give her a kiss and insist she buy him a drink to make up for it. How could that be?

Jordan pulled up outside the cottage. His eyes scanned the familiar front door, never used, and windows. That he'd once resented her for owning it seemed ridiculous. He didn't want anyone else to live there. Ever. He strode around to the back to find Emma sitting in the porch light absorbed in her phone, still in her work clothes, her eyes rimmed red.

"Hey," he sat, lowering himself down beside her and placing an arm around her shoulder.

"What's going on? Has something happened?"

He'd come over to apologize for rushing off that morning. At least that was the rationale he'd come up with to convince himself that he wasn't being too eager to see her again. He hadn't expected to find her distressed. He glanced down at her screen. On it, a sunburnt man with red hair, Oakleys and a bandana talked to the camera. He turned and pointed to a burned-out Humvee lying on its side against a sandbank, baking in the desert heat. The guy was handsome in a rugged sort of way.

"Who's that?" Jordan asked, trying to keep the prickle out of his voice.

"Doug," Emma sniffed. The yellow diamonds buried in her irises sparkled through her tears. "It's his birthday."

Sharp unease cut through him. He felt disturbingly possessive. "Who's Doug?"

"We used to be together." She sighed and turned her phone over, face down. She didn't want him to see, it seemed. Her pain was private. She clearly still cared about the guy, but she'd never mentioned any kind of love interest at all.

"Right." Jordan nodded, trying to sound casual, not floored.

Emma must have heard the sharpness in his voice. "It's not like that. We were together on and off for years, as friends, and then friends with benefits, then lovers. We were partners. We worked together at the Informer."

They had history. They were close, clearly, and probably still were.

She wiped her finger across her eye, squashing a tear. "I miss him."

Jordan smarted. His blood heated in a way he wasn't proud of. Why hadn't she mentioned this guy Doug before? He didn't know what to say, whether to leave her with her sadness, or stay.

Eventually, he brought himself to ask, "And where is Doug now?"

Was he arriving any minute?

Emma looked at him with a grim smile. "He died."

"Oh." He relaxed in a moment of relief and immediately felt ashamed. The guy meant something to her, and she was hurting. "I'm sorry."

Her green eyes stared at the water. He hugged her close and kissed her hair. She leaned into him. He didn't want to pry, but he couldn't help himself. "When did he pass?"

She heaved a sigh and looked at him. "You want the complete story?"

"If you want to tell it." He tried to sound easy, but he wanted to know everything about Doug if it meant knowing everything about this woman.

"It's gruesome."

"I've seen plenty gruesome." He'd witnessed ripped limbs, blown-out eyeballs, third-degree burns, and men bleeding out on the battlefield.

"A bit more than a year ago, we were on assignment in Syria. He was a photographer. A good one. Brave too."

As he watched Emma talk, staring straight ahead, he reminded himself it was better to know.

"He was ready to get out of there. I promised I'd buy him dinner in Istanbul if he went on one last job with me." Her inhale rattled against a sob. She composed herself. "Job done, we were in the car waiting at the checkpoint close to the border. It was taking ages, as you know. We were next but one to cross. Doug got impatient; insisted on driving, as if that would make a difference. We were arguing—as usual—about…I can't remember what exactly. Probably where to go for dinner."

Her words formed with cool detachment, as if she was recounting the plot of a movie, not an incident in her own life. He'd heard guys describe encounters in the field in the same way. It was an attempt to distance themselves from a horrific reality, a way of protecting themselves from the trauma of reliving the entire story again. He was sure at some point he'd done the same.

Her gaze drifted. "We both saw something coming. A lorry, a truck, barreled down the road on the other side of the security barrier, heading straight for us. The guards open fire, then jump out of the way. I scream. The truck crashes through. A black cloud engulfs us." She gulped. "And then everything turns upside down."

"Jesus." Jordan whispered. "Suicide bomber?"

Emma nodded. "The driver was a kid. I saw his little face. He was smiling. I remember it exactly. I can't forget."

Jordan wrapped both arms around her and pulled her close.

"The car flipped several times, apparently," Emma continued. "Doug got tossed." She swallowed the catch in her throat. "He didn't have a seat belt on. I did. I got away with a serious concussion, some cuts and bruises, and a broken collarbone and arm. And he died."

"I'm so sorry." Jordan smoothed his hand over Emma's hair in a gesture he hoped was soothing.

She glanced up at him, sadness swimming on her face. "I got taken in a minivan to the nearest town. The Informer organized for me to be evacuated back to D.C. Doug went home in a box. It isn't fair."

Jordan understood that feeling. Guys on tour braver than himself had been taken too soon. No one should get left behind, but they did. Most days, he was glad he wasn't running for his life through hostile territory, eating MRE rations for breakfast, lunch and dinner, living in fear that he or a guy under his command would get shot or blown up. But some days he longed for the implicit brotherhood of the marines, the easy comradery of long, hard hours in the same company, fighting together for a shared cause. "Oh, Emma."

He kissed the top of her head.

"He was my partner in crime." She paused, then let out a tired laugh. "He would have made a very good criminal, actually."

"That's a lot to carry."

"I still have moments when it rushes back to me. Something happens and I freeze, and my mind tumbles back to that place, and I can't quite keep a grip on where I am or what's happening. It's getting better, being out of the city helps, I think. But loud bangs and flashes, lightning, can set me off."

His brain rewound to the day at Sharpe's Rock. She must have been terrified. He had no idea. "The storm?"

She frowned. "It's just fragments, bits and pieces of memory."

He'd dismissed her behavior as arrogance. He'd totally misunderstood. Regret pinched him.

Emma continued: "Doug would be forty today." She smiled. "Old, in his words."

"Easy, girl." Jordan tried to laugh. "Remember who you're talking to. I'm not so far off."

Emma smiled softly and lay her hand on his thigh. "I'm sorry."

"For what? For saying forty is old?"

"No, for being a downer." There was something almost childlike about the vulnerability shining through her eyes. But she was all adult woman.

"Never apologize for that. It's fine. It's human." His fingertips traced over her cheekbone. He wished she wasn't so sad. And he was ashamed he'd been so disappointed that she was so cut up about another guy.

"How's your mom?" she asked, as if she'd decided to change the subject.

"She'll be OK. She's been ill for so long. We've been through this before. It's still scary though. And she gets weaker as time goes by."

"It's so lovely the way you all look after her."

"Of course; she's our mom."

He liked this woman. She was smart. She knew her own mind. She was funny and fearless. And her body switched on a current somewhere deep inside him. He knew the cottage was ready to sell. Dread gripped him. She might decide she'd had enough of Sirens Bay and leave. She had made it clear there were no certainties or guarantees. He hoped to heaven that there was time for him to get to know her at least a little deeper. If she stayed a short while longer, and he had no reason to expect that she would choose that, and against the evidence, he wished to be a factor in her decision.

In this moment, sitting on the porch bench listening to the waves lap the shore, her palm in his, she wasn't going anywhere.

"Where's Tallulah?" he asked, suddenly noticing the absence of a purring machine looping around his ankles.

"Staying with Mason." Emma said with something like mixed

emotion.

"Seriously?"

Emma nodded. "Seems she's found a better option." She shrugged. "Cats."

Emma waved him off from the porch, heavy with a sense of aloneness, her familiar old friend. Her ambivalent relationship with solitude had its roots in being an only child. When Jordan suddenly realized he needed to rush to make visiting hours at the hospital, she hadn't wanted him to go, but she didn't dare say it.

She lifted her phone, thinking she might text, just to wish his mother well. No service.

"Dammit," she whispered to no one, awash with longing.

Walking inside, she called for the cat before she remembered Mason had her. Emma shook her head, half laughing at Tallulah's betrayal, half sad. She hadn't ever wanted a pet and now she missed her.

Smothered with melancholy, she pulled the comforter up to her chin and closed her eyes, listening to the ocean whispering hello and goodbye to the beach. Her thoughts shifted to the team.

Han was a lonely kid. You could see it in his face, in his grateful friendship. High school was harsh. He was the kid who would come into his own at college; his peers were too immature now to recognize his qualities. He and Riley were a match. She, too, was a square peg in a round hole. They needed each other.

When she was Han's age, she hadn't lacked for friends. She'd been captain of the school netball team and performed in the end-of-year play. She always had someone to sit with at lunch. By the end of her twenties, her pool of friends had shrunk to colleagues or people she met through work. It was her life. At some point she'd lost the skill of being a normal person able to talk about normal things: spouses, kids, schools, mortgages. Few people outside of the office were interested in discussing the impact of the oil price on the chances for democracy in the Gulf, or where to find the cheapest hire a car on the Turkish-Syrian border.

Emma tossed onto her side. She missed Doug. He got it. With her eyes still closed, she smiled. God, he was eye watering-ly rude to her. He saved his worst put downs for the ones he loved best. It was his way of being intimate, and it had made her laugh. Still did.

Jordan was so far from the oafish redneck she thought he was when they first met. That night, she was literally in the dark about where she was and what she'd find. Then, she could never have known that there would come a time when she wished he was lying next to her, his body comfortably substantial alongside hers. She should have invited him to come back after he'd seen his mom. Why hasn't she thought to do that?

On the porch, as she had talked, he had listened. He understood the depth of connection she and Doug had built over the years in the field—as colleagues and lovers. She couldn't speak to anyone else about her grief. Ben had been too ill to burden with her feelings, and office gossip already insinuated that she was unstable. She had folded up her loss and tried to store it neatly inside. She hadn't wanted to talk to anyone about it until Jordan asked.

Sitting outside on the bench, her hand wrapped in his long fingers, her body leaning against his, she felt closer to him then than she could have ever expected to feel. She trusted him. Something that had remained wound tight inside her for as long as she could recall, loosened.

And then she let him leave. Why did she do that?

Chapter Forty-One

Ben, relaxed in a purple velvet dressing gown, smoking a cigar, sat with one kneed crossed over the other. In his free hand, he held a teapot made from a human skull. Blood streamed from the nasal cavity into her overflowing cup. She recoiled, but he kept on pouring.

Emma jolted awake, panting, her throat paper-dry, sweat clinging to her skin. A breeze from a crack in the wooden window frame rippled through the curtain. She shivered.

Stumbling through the dark, awash with sleep, her hand landed on the kitchen faucet, and she poured herself a long glass of water. Finished, she placed the glass on the counter and closed her eyes, focusing on lengthening her breaths, in and out, in and out. She let the drafts of air rattling under the porch door pull her back into her body.

She twitched. Was that a cough? Her lids burst open. Alert for any sound, she turned, her eyes trained on the backdoor. Nothing. She let her shoulders drop. Her nightmare had set her on edge. She stood for a few seconds to let the panic drain. The porch step squeaked. She tensed. Backlit by the moon, a silhouette crossed by the backdoor. Jordan? No, he'd never turn up in the middle of the night unannounced. More heavy footsteps. Maybe two people?

She ducked behind the counter, curling into a tight little ball. Jesus, who was outside and what did they want? Glass smashed. Her head snapped up. They were trying to get in. It was pitch black outside and there was no one around for miles. Her nearest neighbor was a banker from Boston who only came up on the weekends with his buddies to fish. Her heartbeat in her throat.

On all fours, she scuttled across the floor into her bedroom to grab her phone from the nightstand. No signal. She tried dialing 911 anyway. No connection. Keeping low, fumbling around in the dim glow of the moon, and still gripping her cell, she pulled on her sweats and shoved her feet into her sneakers. She knew better than to stick around and try to put up a fight.

On her feet, she hovered behind the bedroom door. There was a crash, and the back door flew open with a bang. A gust of cold air whipped under the door. Torchlight swept the floor and up the walls. Hidden, she blinked against the beam. A thick shape held a crowbar, signaling to someone behind him to stop. Knitted ski-masks covered their faces. Her eyes widened, her skin stretching with fear. They were professionals, not kids out burglarizing for kicks. Boots stomped through the living room. They were looking for something, or maybe someone, maybe her. She glanced at the phone trembling in her hand. Still no signal.

Wi-Fi. She had Wi-Fi.

She tapped the screen: Jordan.

Then: Intruders 911.

Message sent.

She hoped to God that Jordan would see it.

Heavy male breathing. As the figure stepped across the threshold into her bedroom, she slammed the door in his face. He yelped and stumbled backward. She shoved a chair under the handle and ran to the window. Behind her, the crowbar crashed through the wood. She flung open the frame, hoisted herself onto the ledge and jumped.

Scrambling to her feet, an arm hooked her around her waist and dragged her backward. A ragged scream burst from her mouth as she thrashed against his hold with all the rage and grief she had. Fury propelled her elbow backwards into soft flesh and rammed her heel into a shinbone. She spun around, grabbed her stumbling assailant by the shoulder, jerked him forward, and kneed him in the face. He dropped to the grass, clutching his nose, gasping. She took off into the woods. Sharp pine needles crackled under her feet and slid into her sneakers. Blood drummed in her ears. Branches scratched at her face. Behind, a thick Boston North End accent thundered through the darkness. "We just wanna talk."

She dove into thick fronds at the base of a tall conifer, crouching and catching her breath. Torch light strobed the woods.

"Make it easy on yourself," the man continued. "After all, there's nowhere to run." Leaves rustled as someone pressed by. She shrank back against the trunk.

"Coming to get you!" The North End voice sang above her head. He'd rolled his balaclava into a beanie, and she could see his boxer's face. His light swung directly at her. Blinded, she leaped forward, her hands flying at his face like claws. She knocked his flashlight into the undergrowth and sprinted, adrenaline firing up her legs. She kept running, pushing the branches from her face. Then she was on the road at the top of the drive. She stopped dead, panicked, her head whipping back and forth. Which way to go?

Truck headlights trapped her in their beam. She froze.

"Emma?" Jordan shouted out the window. "Emma!" Was it him? "Emma, get in!" He hollered at her.

A spike of joy powered her forward. She grabbed for the passenger door and, panting, leaped onto the seat. "They're...at the...house," she gasped. "Two guys."

The truck wheels screech as Jordan pushed his foot on the accelerator and swerved into the drive. He slammed the brakes, stopping just short of colliding with a black SUV. The car curved around them, knocking the mailbox from its post. Jordan reached for his phone on the dash, and leaning out the window, snapped its plates.

Standing on the deck, Jordan held Emma's hand in a tight grip as she explained to Trooper Cleary with astonishing calm and detail how the men had broken in. She pointed to the porch door swinging on its hinges. Splintered wood and glass shards glimmered in the moonlight.

Trooper Cleary shook his wide head, puzzled. "And you sure nothing's missing?"

"Nothing," Emma said.

"And you're not hurt?" The trooper asked. Jordan shuddered at the thought of what they might have planned to do to her.

"No." Emma shivered in her sweatshirt. Her fingers were stone cold in his palm. Jordan wrapped his arm around her shoulder and held her close. Her arm looped around his waist. An unsettling mix of gratitude for her proximity and concern about what she'd been through swilled through him. Nothing like this ever happened in Sirens Bay. Nothing. Bricks through windows, intruders, speeding black SUVs—what the hell was going on?

"This Ben's old place?" the policeman asked. They both nodded. "Smart guy." He shook his head sadly. "You wait in your car while we secure the scene."

As Cleary stood on the porch and requested assistance on his radio, Jordan led Emma to the truck, trying to distract her with small talk about how generations of the Cleary family had served in the state police. Emma didn't seem to take in any of what he was saying. He opened the door. "Let's get you warm."

Wearing a heavy sweater he found in the cab, Emma stared straight through the windscreen. He let the silence envelop them. She had drifted off somewhere unreachable. He'd wanted to stay the night, but she hadn't offered. He hadn't wanted to push and be that guy who couldn't take a hint. If he'd been there, he could have kept her safe. None of this would have happened. He blinked away unwelcome images of her fleeing into the woods and arriving stricken on the road. They made him feel nauseous.

Eventually, they waved off the cops just as the sun rose over the bay. Emma walked up the porch steps and inside, and he followed. Charcoal black forensic powder dusted almost every surface. Jordan rubbed his eyes, suddenly exhausted. Emma sighed at the mess. He brushed aside some shards of glass with his boot.

"Take a hot shower," he urged her gently. "I'll make a start on cleaning this up." She looked at him. "Honestly, let me make a start, at least."

She was too tired, it seemed, to insist that she could take care of it herself.

He heard her turn on the water. Pushing the broom across the floor, he thought back to Emma's arrival in Sirens Bay. It seemed like only yesterday that he had surged with dislike for her, viewed her as an unwelcome intruder. The irony. He didn't know she was coming to terms with a double bereavement, and that she'd barely started on that journey.

When Soph passed, Lily was his life vest; she kept his head above water and his mood afloat. Beth was his anchor, tied his feet on the ground, reminded him to take each day as it came. Emma had few friends around and no family to support her; it was amazing she'd not gone insane. And now this. Jordan maneuvered the porch door back onto its hinges. All for a story.

The Siren, he had to admit, was buzzing. Mason was enjoying a fifth, six, seventh wind. He had as many lives as Tallulah. The paper had regained its dignity and purpose. Dave's job might be safe. Kirsty was in her element. And the kid, Han, seemed to have found his calling. Riley, God bless her, was making much-needed cash. Emma, an outsider he'd once resented so much it made him mad, brought more than he ever could to the paper. She probably didn't realize how much. Ben's legacy lived on in her. The items Emma had unearthed from years of private obscurity and brought by the shop thrilled Erik.

Jordan closed the bedroom window and tested the catch. A sour, hot taste rose in his throat. If anyone ever tried to hurt her again, he'd be there to smash them.

After he'd tidied and fixed what he could with the tools he had in the truck, he knocked gently on the bathroom door. It had been a while. "Emma, how're you doing?"

"Yup." Her voice sounded like her mouth was full. "One minute."

Was she crying? His chest tightened. Or was she brushing her teeth?

He sat on the couch, beyond tired, taking in the same old cushions and covers, the familiar wooden coffee table that his uncle must have bought in the seventies and his ancient TV stand, now emptied of magazines. And then, lit up by a beam of morning light, he noticed it. How had he not seen it before? The gently curving wooden tendrils of his flame sculpture reached up from the mantlepiece as if it had always been there. He hadn't asked Felix for a name; he hadn't wanted to know who had taken the piece he'd taken hours, days to carve, delicately scoring the wood. She liked his work enough to pay that price tag? A broad smile broke across his face. Why hadn't she said anything?

The floor was swept; the couch slid back into place. The only signs that someone uninvited had been here were a boarded-up kitchen window, a splintered backdoor frame, and the absence of a bedroom door altogether. There was also clean linen on the bed, her old sheets stuffed in the top of the laundry basket. Emma pulled on a fresh pair of sweatpants and lay down, her arms over her face, her hair still wrapped in a towel. A blanket of numbness enveloped her. She couldn't move. She heard footsteps on the porch. The catch clicked.

"It's only me." Jordan's voice. "Where are you?"

"Bedroom."

She heard the kettle boil.

"Tea?" He stood in the doorway, his face folded with concern.

They sat on the bed propped up against the headboard, a mug of chamomile tea in each of their hands. She let her head drop onto his shoulder. "You know, I've been chased before. Many times."

"Yeah?" He sounded surprised. His arm reached around the back of her head and under her neck. She shuffled into his embrace.

"More times than I can remember. For trespassing, outstaying my welcome, for not being invited in the first place, for being in the wrong place at the wrong time, for talking to the right person at the wrong time." That was the nature of her work; she couldn't wait for permission. "But no one has ever broken into my home before. Ever," she said, drained of feeling.

Jordan stroked his knuckles over her cheek. It was a soothing gesture.

"I'm sorry." She felt his lips on her head as he delivered a soft kiss. The warm skin of his neck smelled of soap. "I'm so sorry," he whispered and wrapped his arms around her.

"Thank you for coming."

"Of course."

Her brain drifted through the night's events as if she was watching a home movie. Slowly, her eyelids dropped, her head rising and falling with the rhythm of his breath, his body holding her tight.

She woke with a start. Tires shook the gravel driveway.

"Don't move." Jordan flew from the bed.

She could hear voices, a man, and then a woman, and then Jordan's.

As Emma reached the porch, Mason and Kirsty rounded the corner of the cottage. Mason shuffled up the steps, leaning on Jordan. "Police Chief called, said there'd been some trouble, so we came to check that you were alright." Mason's wrinkles quivered with worry.

His concern threw her off guard.

"It's six forty-five," she blurted.

"We're old. We get up early," Kirsty said, taking Emma's hand and pulling her in for a hug. "Are you OK, Bub?"

They both looked at her, imploring her to confirm all was well. Jordan seemed as interested in her reply.

"I'm fine," she said, as a tear leaked from one eye and then another. She couldn't stop them.

"Shock." Kirsty hustled them indoors. "Bastards."

Emma talked them through what had happened, while Jordan sat beside her on the couch, holding her hand. His grip calmed her. It was comforting to know he was just there.

From his spot on the plaid armchair, Mason, gruff with anger, banged his cane on the floor. "Goddamit. Those sons of bitches."

"I'm going to be fine." She tried to sound certain. "Jordan's been looking after me."

Sitting on the arm of the couch, Kirsty gave him an approving look. "Good."

Mason frowned. "You think the attorney sent them?"

"Maybe." She thought about it. "Probably." There was no other explanation. Who else would want to threaten her? Vinnie Whatever-his-name's visit to the gallery was reconnaissance, she was sure.

Mason sat back, his fragile frame swamped by the upholstery. She could read the expression on his pinched face. Before he could speak, Emma cut in.

"We're not spiking the story."

Mason raised his eyebrows. Kirsty looked from Emma to the old man and back.

"It's too important and we've all done too much work."

Neither Mason nor Kirsty contradicted her. Jordan shifted his grip. She continued: "These are dangerous people, clearly. They are threatening your town. We can't let them win. This could be just the beginning; they could just be getting started. There's too much at stake."

Emma's eyes swung to Kirsty, who had willingly grappled with the intricacies of the latest software to produce a layout that was both fresh and clear and which also echoed The Siren's glory years. Dave had spent days trailing officials round city hall looking for an in. He'd literally worn out one pair of shoes, which Mason said they should get framed as a tribute to real journalism. And Han, this was his future they were talking about, his chance to show what he was capable of, and Riley's, and she was smashing it. Turning away from this story just as they gathered momentum would crush them. For Mason and The Siren, it would be hard to restart the climb.

"It'll be dangerous," Kirsty said, like she felt an obligation to remind everyone about the obvious risk.

Emma shrugged. "Yes, that's certain."

But whatever short-term threat they faced, the longer-term implications of not exposing what was going on at the plant would be catastrophic for the river, the lobster beds, the tourism industry, the kids in high school who would need jobs in the very near future and deserved to live in a healthy place. "Not to report what we know would be a betrayal of our readers. Imagine what Sirens Bay will look like if that resort goes ahead?" She looked Mason directly in the face. "We have no choice."

Over the past weeks, Mason almost hummed with renewed energy. Pulling the plug on the story also risked short-circuiting his new lease on life.

He turned to his grandson. "What do you think, Jordan?"

Mason was from a generation of men who couldn't rely on a woman's opinion alone and always needed to hear it supported by a man. Emma bit her tongue. Jordan glanced at her, hesitating before he said slowly, "Pops, Emma knows what she's doing."

Right answer. As much as she appreciated him and the reassurance she drew from his warmth, care, and thoughtfulness, the decision wasn't his to make. At all.

Mason leaned forward and peered at her. "Are you sure?"

In his intensity, she could see Ben, that questioning look, the determination.

The way forward was to fight fire with fire until the blaze burned out. "I'm sure."

"Well then," he slapped his palms on his thighs. "We have work to do."

Chapter Forty-Two

Emma closed her laptop with a satisfying click. "OK, Han, you nearly done?"

"Uh-huh," he mumbled, deep in the middle of something.

To no one's surprise, Han had discovered that it was ridiculously easy to hack into The Siren's server and had spent all day with his head in his screen devising evermore complex attacks on its newly reinforced firewall.

Her phone buzzed with a text from Jordan. He'd checked in on her throughout the day. Rather than irritated by the interruption, she felt connected to someone reliable and safe. Constant. The realization surprised her.

She opened his message: Where are you?

She texted back: Office. Han here.

Lucky Han. Krav Maga later at my place?

Emma laughed out loud. But maybe he wasn't joking? She pictured his handsome face and imagined the touch of his lips on her neck, the feel of his five o'clock shadow under her fingernails.

Han looked up.

She dropped her head and tapped back: Will there be food?

At lunchtime, Lily had sent over burgers on the house. As the others shoveled food into their mouths, the idea of eating had made her feel wretched. Now she was starving.

A third message: Of course.

It really was time to call it a day. "Han, I've got to go."

He shoved his computer into his backpack. "No problem." He glanced at his watch. "My dad's waiting at home for me, anyway. He wants me to show him what I've been doing for my college classes." Han rolled his eyes. "He's worried I'm not giving them my full attention and won't get the credits. The classes cost a lot."

Emma hadn't realized he was also supposed to be attending summer school. "Are you giving them the required attention?"

The team relied on him. He was their go-to guy for all manner of tech issues, big and as miniscule as a broken charger, which she sensed he enjoyed. But she didn't want their gain to be at his academic expense.

"I'll get the credits. I keep telling him I can use my work here. My dad knows I can't wait to get back to California and I need to get into Stanford first."

Emma activated the alarm. "You notice anything weird, anyone hanging around your house. You call me right away," she instructed him as they parted ways.

"Will do!" He said as he walked toward his car.

At the lighthouse, Emma parked the Dodge and locked the doors. And then opened and locked them again.

The smell of garlic, onions, and parsley wrapped around her as she climbed the steps. She stood in the doorway to the kitchen and knocked on the frame. Jordan stood in front of the stove in a t-shirt and jeans, a dishcloth thrown over one shoulder. An enthusiastically focused look occupied his face.

He turned to smile at her as he lifted an enamel pot off the heat. "Just in time."

A small bunch of delicate white wildflowers bloomed in a ceramic jar positioned in the middle of the white tablecloth. A bottle of wine cooled in a clay flask holder and a crispy baguette lay across a wooden board. When she'd said food, she'd expected takeout and a beer. "This looks lovely."

"Take a seat."

He placed the pot on the hot plate next to the bread and took off the lid. Buttery steam wound up to the ceiling. She took a long draw. Mussels. "Smells absolutely delicious."

He bent down to kiss her on the lips. He tasted like home-cooked broth. She kept her head tilted up for more, but he moved away, busy.

"Wine?"

"I mean yes, if you don't mind?"

He shook his head. The muscles of his forearm tweaked and flexed as he poured. "Can I do anything?"

"No. Just sit."

He moved around the range, stirring, checking something inside the oven and finally raising a net of fries out of their oil. He was so confident, sure of what he was doing, enjoying himself, and she thought, enjoyed being observed. The shadow of Jordan's traps moved under his shirt as he shifted back and forth. She remembered the feel of his body under her fingers, like something you could mold.

He dropped the fries into a bowl to drain the grease and grabbed a huge salad from the refrigerator. Turning off the heat, he arrived at the table.

"Wow, this is incredible." She looked up at him.

"It's easy." He shrugged.

"That's a matter of perspective. You've gone to a lot of effort." She held his gaze, trying to convey the strength of her appreciation. His blue eyes glittered.

"Cheers." He clinked his glass of soda with hers.

The seafood melted in her mouth; the fries crunched with golden perfection, and he'd mixed everything fresh and good tasting under the sun into the salad.

"I can't remember the last time anyone cooked for me like this." Emma really couldn't, except for Beth, but that dinner felt different. He'd crafted the food just for her, in total contrast to the takeouts, one-pot meals and restaurant dinners she'd lived on since she'd had her wings clipped in D.C.

"I don't cook for just anyone," Jordan replied with a tease in his voice. "Or. Let just anyone sleep in my bed."

She paused, a fry lifted to her mouth. So, that's how he expected the evening to unfold? Not that she would mind, but his assumption was crass. Cocky. And not like him.

"What?" He seemed genuinely puzzled by her silence. "Have I said something?" His eyes widened with alarm.

Confusion glitched, then she got it. "Oh, you meant the night I spent in your bed flat-out drunk."

"Well, I wouldn't put it like that, but yeah, that night you spent here. What else could I mean?"

She shook her head as she mopped up the salty juice on her plate with a chunk of bread, chiding herself for being overly alert to any possible wrong move on his part. She wanted to trust him, and to trust herself to trust him. She wanted to let her guard down an inch.

"Nothing." She chewed and smiled.

He cleared the plates. And there was more. He'd baked a dessert and made custard from scratch. She'd never heard of anyone doing that, not even her mother when she was little.

"Abigail's cinnamon and apple pie," he said, cutting her a slice. Thick chunks of glossy apple oozed onto her plate.

She raised her glass. "To Abigail." The alcohol spiraled inside her head, down through her chest and into her stomach.

"To Abigail."

After dinner, they walked down to the water's edge, watching the lighthouse beam play across the inky ocean, rolling and retreating over the stones. She'd been insane to want to swim out from here. He put his arm around her waist, pulling her close. His strength released something in her she was holding tight. She softened and dropped her head onto his shoulder as her arms encircled him, her fingertips brushing his ridged abs. A warm breeze melted across her body, lifting her hair away from her face. It was an exquisite feeling to stand there with him; but it wasn't enough.

She turned and lifted her face. "Kiss me."

His face bent toward hers. His lips tickled hers. Her hands moved to his neck, encouraging him to reach deeper. But his mouth caressed her throat and along the skin of her neck. She shivered with pleasure. His teeth lightly nipped her lobe before arriving back at her lips. She pushed her body against his, kissing him with increasing urgency. He didn't respond to match her pace. Instead, he continued to kiss her slowly, his tongue moving around her mouth carefully, feeling every inch.

"Shall we go inside?" she whispered.

"You sure you want to do this?" he looked down at her.

She ached for him. She wanted the most delicate parts of their skin to touch, their fingers to entwine, their legs to knot together, his tongue to seek her out, and to feel him move inside her. "Certain."

He led her by the hand toward the cottage, through the doorway and into his bedroom. Emma glanced at the trunk and noticed the picture of the woman, Sophie, she guessed, had disappeared. She was glad. It seemed he didn't want an audience of past lovers, either.

When they reached the bed, Jordan stopped and lifted her t-shirt gently over her head. Then he sat down on the mattress, pulled her toward him, and undid the buttons of her jeans. She dropped her head to watch him, letting him lead. He yanked her denims to the floor and clamped his palms on either side of her hips while he kissed her tummy. Warm waves of delight rippled up into her chest. Her fingers reached for his hair.

In one swift move, he tugged off his shirt. He looked up at her, a boyish grin on his face.

"Don't stop," she whispered.

His lips returned to her skin to trace the line of her panties. Gently, he eased them down, and they fell to her feet. His tongue moved to the dip of her groin on one side, and then the other. Standing almost naked before him, she quivered. His hands ran up the inside of her legs, tickling soft skin and sending shock waves of anticipation to a spot he knew exactly where to find. She felt his tongue hot on her. She gasped and gripped his hair as he sucked and licked the softest molten area between her legs. Concentric rings of pleasure echoed through her, building, and strengthening. She thought her knees might buckle.

Just when she thought she might be close to climaxing, he pulled her onto his lap. Her hand found his hardness pushing against his zipper. She reached in and began stroking up and down. He shuddered a low moan into her ear and scooted further onto the bed, while she pulled at his pant legs and dropped his jeans to the floor, followed by his boxers. He stood large and erect. She straddled his thick thighs, moving on her knees. He unhooked her bra and threw it behind him. He mumbled something against her breast as his mouth sought her nipple.

"Sorry?" she gasped.

"I'm so hard."

"I'm ready."

Jordan stretched for the bedside table and threw a box onto the bed. She rolled the condom on, his eyes never leaving hers, his hands moving down her back to her butt. She moved to position herself and gently, he lifted her over him. She gasped as his heat cut through her. A pulse seared inside as he thrusted, his wide hands holding her steady. Pressure built in her as she rocked back and forth. Jordan's face had taken on a fixed expression, his eyes never leaving hers. He let out a low grunt through his teeth.

"God, I want you," he muttered.

"I want you too."

She dropped her head back, straining to feel everything he was giving. His thickness felt like a match igniting her over and over, each time the flame flaring brighter. She shuddered and looked down. Deep pools of desire started back at her.

"Let's do this." Holding her close, Jordan rolled her over onto her back. The mass of him spread her legs. With one hand, he clasped her wrists above her head; the other supported his weight. He pushed into her. She shook with delight, her fingers clawing the muscles of his back.

"Deeper," she whispered into his neck. "Harder."

She wanted to feel the full force of him. The power of his drive took her higher and higher. He moaned, gritting his teeth. She whimpered; any second she was going to burst.

Then his mouth was on hers, searching furiously. She wrapped her legs around him, pulling him in. In that moment, her world was just the two of them hunting sensation in each other's bodies. There was no other sight or sound except for him. He raised himself onto his palms to thrust. Her hips rose to meet him. He dipped and reared back, the muscles of his arms and chest pumping, their curves caught in the moonlight. He surged further than anyone had ever reached. She forgot where she was. She cried out, tearing at his shoulders, trying to find something steady as pleasure barreled through her.

"Oh," she gasped. "Oh." And then she held still for a moment, ecstatic, and tumbled into a river of delight. "Oh, Jordan," she panted. "Jordan."

His lips pinched, holding his breath. He drove into her faster.

His face stretched with pure joy. In a rush of release, he fell on her, still warm and pulsing inside her. "Emma, oh, God."

He held her close, his breath hot on her neck, his wet skin slipping against hers. Her whole body drifted in a pool of pleasure. She felt free.

Chapter Forty-Three

Emma's eyes fixed on the screen, frowning. Beside her, Mason leaned on his stick, wobbling slightly. Han clicked the cursor while Kirsty's face moved from scowl to delight as the new software revealed the most recent design. Emma smiled.

"Looks good!" Mason said with surprise. Kirsty shot Emma a wink. She nodded back her thanks. The updated layout looked fantastic. All they needed was to pin down Senator McDermott, and the next revelation could go to press. It turned out the tech was the easy bit. Getting anyone to second source the spreadsheet and confirm that the politician had his fingers in the till was proving impossible.

Emma got back to her desk. "Dave, what have you got?"

Dave slouched in his chair, scratching his head. "Not much."

Emma twiddled her pen between her fingers, thinking. She could still feel the weight of Jordan's thigh resting against hers. Her lips tasted like metal, raw from the brush of his stubble, and she could still smell him: the scent of clean cotton and cedar. Her entire skin prickled, alive and ready to be stroked, held and touched by him again. She swallowed and leaned forward, focusing her gaze back on her laptop screen. She read the last sentence she'd written. Words swam in the tide of oxytocin flooding her brain. She reread it: what exactly did she want to say about the corruption? The words wouldn't stick. Instead, she felt Jordan's fingers tracing a feint line across her collarbone, chased by his mouth.

She strode over to the coffee machine and took several deep breaths, watching the filter drip. It was no good, the sense of him wrapped around her, smothering her thoughts, holding her attention hostage.

Evening drew a veil of pink and blue over the mountains at the end of the drive. "You don't have to stay here, you know," Jordan said, a nail gripped between his teeth. He positioned the bracket on the bark and hammered the tack into the tree. The little black sensor box slid neatly on, mirroring another secured to a tree on the other side of the drive. "My place is more than big enough for two."

His invitation sounded more permanent than he'd intended, but he liked the thought of having her around. He wanted Emma close by, safe. The image of waking up with her lying in his bed sent a glorious thrill through his body. He loved the feel of her soft skin, her breath hot in his ear, the pull of her yearning for him. She could stay for as long as she liked.

Emma shook her head. "I can't let them chase me out of my home."

Home. Emma thought of the cottage as a place to live. She was getting attached. A little flame of hope ignited in his chest. Was she setting down roots? He kept the question to himself.

Jordan stood back and assessed his handiwork. "OK, let's test it."

Emma walked back to the house, holding the receiver in her hand. She stopped at the front door and shouted. "Ready!"

He walked through the open gate and what he hoped was an invisible beam that would set off an alarm inside.

"It beeped!" he heard her call. "Channel one."

The new system worked. He sighed with relief. If anyone came down the path, she'd know. No more unwanted visitors.

"You're all set," he said as he followed her inside.

She kissed him on the cheek. "Thank you. Want to stay for dinner? My turn."

"Mmm, what are you making?" He sounded deliberately

283

suspicious as he joined her in the kitchen. He already knew she was no chef.

She turned her head, nose crinkling. "Baked beans on toast?"

He grimaced. "What? Tinned beans? You know the Second World War is over, right?" She nodded and laughed. He shook his head. "British people are obsessed with toast."

She grinned. "It's true."

"I'll stay on condition that I cook."

"No argument from me. I've been to the store."

"Progress. I'm going to teach you to cook."

"You can try." She sounded doubtful.

With the carton of eggs, two potatoes and a few strips of bacon, he made his version of a Spanish omelet. He flipped it from the frying pan onto a large dish and brought over a salad.

"Dinner is served."

Emma lifted her fork to her mouth as she sat beside him on the couch, plates resting on their knees. "Amazing."

The growling in his stomach subsided. He'd been absolutely starving and hadn't realized. When he was with her, she drew his focus like a magnet. He forgot about everything else. He rested his empty plate on the coffee table and decided he would not be shy. He would ask. Looking at the sculpture on the mantelpiece, he inquired quietly, "Why didn't you say you'd bought one of my pieces at the exhibition?"

She placed her cutlery down, blushing. "I'm not really sure." She took a breath. He waited. "It's kind of intimate owning someone's art, I guess." He agreed with that. She looked at him with a question in her voice. "And, I wasn't sure you'd want me to?"

"Seriously?" He was delighted she did.

She was one of the most self-assured women he'd ever met, at least on the outside. Maybe he'd mistaken her independence for confidence. She was certainly reserved. What he had ascribed to polite British reticence might actually have been social unease.

"Well, yeah…" She stood up and took their plates into the kitchen. There was something in her walk, a stiffness that suggested she felt uneasy with the direction of conversation. A safe distance away, she turned. "It's like…"

"What is it like?" He was curious to know how she felt.

"… like I have a part of you almost, don't you think?"

"Kinda," he nodded. It was he who should feel exposed. It was his craft, his passion channeled into the wood, on show for all to see.

She sat back down on the sofa. "Anyway, I like the energy of it. It feels hopeful, ambitious."

He glowed. He felt exactly the same. On the ledge in Ben's old cottage, in her home, with her, was exactly where he wanted his work to be. It was weird that wasn't clear. "You hold your cards very close to your chest, Emma…" He realized he didn't know her second name.

"James," she supplied.

"Exactly my point." He rested on the seat cushion, his muscles loosening, and turned his head to her. "I might have to investigate exactly how close."

He reached for the hem of her top, ready to lift it and slide his hand under. He kissed her and felt her shiver. He caressed her jawline, then her collarbone. Her skin prickled under his touch, igniting snaps of pleasure in him. She looped her arms around his neck and straddled him. Her weight was delicious on his thighs. He kissed her mouth slowly, taking in the taste of her.

"So, dinner is your tried and tested seduction technique?" she whispered against his cheek.

"Is it working?"

"It's working." Her lips landed back on his, hungry, it seemed, to drink him in too.

Emma's fingers molded around the back of Jordan's neck, tracing his hairline. His hands ran down her spine and rested on her bum. She felt him harden. His mouth traced a line from hers to the dip at the bottom of her throat, igniting tingles around her body that earthed in her groin. All her nerve endings seemed painfully, joyously delicate. His torso pressed against hers as he held her in a tight embrace. She gasped for breath. His thigh muscles tensed underneath her as he stood up and lifted her in one fluid motion. Her legs curled around him and she pressed her cheek to his, breathing in his salty sweat scent. Her blood beat for him.

"Let's go to the bedroom," he whispered into her hair.

At the bed, he lowered her down. Before he could join her, she reached for his belt buckle, undid the clips, and unzipped his fly. He looked down at her, his hair mussed and his blue eyes deep with want. Something tumbled in the pit of her stomach. She went to touch his hardness standing upright and firm, but he caught her hand, holding it midair. "Don't."

A flicker of self-doubt must have shown on her face.

"I'm too ready. It'll be over in seconds." It was as if he was apologizing for his desire. She smiled, pleased his yearning met hers. She ached to feel him inside her again, clamoring for that place she hadn't known existed.

"Don't wait." She took his hand and drew him close.

He slowly surrendered, lowering himself onto her. His weight pinned her to the bed in a glorious hold as he nuzzled into her neck. His lips moved to her breasts, licking and sucking, teasing her nipples, stoking her longing. He lifted his head. "You are so beautiful."

She repeated, "Don't wait."

"You ready?"

"Very."

The foil wrapper ripped. He nudged slowly inside her. A quiver of pleasure tickled all the way up her spine to her throat, and she gasped. She swallowed hard. He pressed deeper. She gripped the curve of his shoulders, smooth and hard, like one of his carvings. She shuddered, pulling the length of him fully inside her. He moaned and heaved back from her, holding still for a second, as if waiting for the moment to pass, before his thrust quickened. He groaned, the vibration of his voice rippling through her. Her hands clasped his butt. Under her fingertips, his muscles pulled like steel chords. He moved faster, lifting his chin, gasping. She kept pace with him, moving with a desperate desire to reach the place where nothing else mattered. Molten pleasure pooled between her legs and kept swelling, taking up more space in her body, powering her heartbeat and emptying her lungs. Her breath came fast and shallow. He panted, hot against her skin.

"Jordan," she whispered as he plunged inside her again, needing to say his name, needing a release. "Jordan…"

Layer upon layer of desire unfurled inside her body, rippling to every fingertip. His mouth grazed hers as he whimpered her name quietly. She caught his kiss, hungry for the feel of his tongue.

"I'm close," he moaned. "Really close."

"Me…too." The words grated in her tight throat. She could barely speak.

He pushed deeper, harder, and faster. She threw back her head, her spine arched, contorted by relentless delight, and her thoughts ran away in different directions into nothing. She soared, hovered for a second, engulfed in rapture, and descended with a rush of freedom. An avalanche of joy surged through her, steeling her breath. He made one more thrust, gasped, and collapsed on top of her, hot, sticky, and surging. She wrapped her arms around him, catching her breath, never wanting to let him go, as he gulped for air.

"My God," he muttered, as much to himself as to her.

Her body felt loose, as if she had just stepped out of the most delicious warm bath. She was fluid and light. She stroked her fingers through his hair. It made no sense at all that this man could do all that to her.

The sun inched its way through the gaps around the curtain. It was as if Emma's arms and legs were laden with a gorgeously heavy weight. Jordan's warm skin pressed against her back, his arm draped over her, his fingers interlaced through hers. The passion of the night before had flushed her usual morning dread from her system. She rolled over to face him. His face was almost perfectly symmetrical, fine-boned, like a Greek statue. Jordan's lashes batted against the light as he opened his eyes. The blue of his irises glittered like frozen water.

"Hi." He stroked her face, his fingers tracing across her mouth and down to the dip at the base of her throat. Even his lightest touch sparked a current of desire that pulled her closer to him.

"I've got to go to work," she sighed.

He stared into her face and smiled a wicked grin.

She snuggled into him, feeling the stubble on his chin scratch her cheek. "Two minutes and I'll get up." It was as much a promise to herself as it was information for him.

He encased her in his arms. He was so warm. He felt like he was the place she was supposed to be.

"Stay longer." His hips pressed into her as his hand traveled over her waist and rested on the soft skin of her inner thigh.

"Just two minutes," she mumbled, basking in the warmth seeping through her body.

She was going to be late. Usually, the thought would horrify her. She strove to be professional. She had a story to chase. She never prioritized her private life over work, not even with Doug. She didn't make any movement away from him.

"Only two?" He asked as his finger glided toward her softest skin.

"Yes, two," she whispered, catching her breath.

"Really?" He kissed her lips. Her mouth parted, letting him in. Her leg wrapped around his. She could feel the heat rising between them and him harden. Her want for him throbbed. They were edging deliciously close to the point of no return.

Her phone pinged. And pinged again.

"One sec." She groaned and reluctantly reached to check her messages. A voicemail and two texts. She inched up onto her pillow, her brain slowly winding into gear. Jordan shifted and kissed her neck.

Dave: Did you get my message? McDermott. Heading up to the Senate.

Mason's text was more to the point: Leaving 0830 for Augusta. She checked the time. 8:01am.

"Oh no," she swung her legs out of bed, "I've got to go."

Jordan's face crumpled with a mix of confusion and disappointment that tugged at her. She didn't want to leave him and not in a rush, but if they were going to get that scumbag, she wanted to be there. She bent to kiss him. "Dave's got a lead. They're waiting."

Standing in his boxers in the doorway to the bedroom, Jordan watched Emma race around the cottage, gathering her laptop and purse.

"Go, go," he urged. "I'll lock up."

She pecked him on the cheek and flew out the door. He smiled to himself. His body burned with want for her, throbbed with the unrequited pleasure. And he was proud of her commitment to the job; her energy and drive, her desire to see the story through. She was not deterred—unfortunately for him at that very moment—but he admired her singular focus. Later, they could resume what they had barely begun minutes ago. The thought sent a flash of heat through him. He would look forward to that.

Chapter Forty-Four

It had been a long day, but what a day. Emma pulled up to the curb outside The Siren to let Dave and Mason get out. Stiff and tired from the drive to Augusta and back, the two men righted themselves on the sidewalk and shuffled toward the main door. She drove on to the parking lot.

Dave stood in the middle of the newsroom, Mason sat on a chair beside him; Kirsty perched on the edge of a desk, Riley beside her, and Han had stopped tapping away at his laptop. Standing behind him, at the edge of the group, was Jordan. She smiled shyly and moved next to him while Dave continued to describe their day at the State House.

"So, we take our seats in the public gallery, and there he is..." Dave said.

"What are you doing here?" she whispered.

"I got worried." Jordan glanced down at her. His fingers circled into her palm. "You didn't return my calls?"

She inched closer until their bodies were touching. She could feel his breath rise and fall. "Intense day," she said, softly.

"Anyway," Dave held the room's attention like a pro, "the session winds on. Yadda, yadda, yadda."

Kirsty interrupted. "Hold on a minute." She turned to Emma. "How did you get in without credentials?"

The Informer had taken her press card when they put her on leave. It still seemed petty to her, punitive.

"Told them I was Mason's home care," Emma said with a smile.

"I can't go anywhere without her!" Mason replayed the ham assurance he'd given the uniformed security guard, a short blonde woman with pale skin, who was too absorbed in Candy Crush to pay an elderly constituent and his nurse, too much attention.

"Beautiful building, isn't it?" Kirsty turned again to Emma, who nodded. The State House was impressive, its granite stonework and wide hallways suggesting a permanence and status that perhaps McDermott had conflated with his own.

"Built in 1832," Han noted. "Learned that in middle school."

"See! We have history too!" Kirsty added for Emma's benefit.

"Let the man speak!" Mason huffed.

Leaning ever-so-slightly against Jordan, just enough to feel the heat of him, Emma was happy to listen to Dave recount how they day had unfolded, how they'd chased McDermott down a marbled corridor, Mason hobbling as fast as his balance would allow, Emma holding his elbow and Dave jogging on ahead. How the senator's jowls had jiggled with indignation when Mason confronted him.

"And then he says, with this phony smile, what can I do for you, Mr. Allen? And I say, Maynland Chemical, what's your involvement with the plant, sir? You could have heard a pin drop." Mason slapped his thigh. "He looks affronted, says he has no idea what we're talking about, isn't that right Emma?" She nodded. "I say we have documents listing the government officials who have taken cash to obstruct the cleanup. And you're one of them!" Mason added triumphantly.

Emma felt Jordan's hand move up toward her waist and rest there. She looked around the room. No one else seemed to notice. She let it stay, relishing the easy weight of it.

"I wish I'd been there," Jordan whispered into her ear. A shiver raced down her neck.

"McDermott denies all knowledge. Asks if I have dementia!" Mason's eyes grew large with affront. "And I say, you bet your ass I don't. We've got proof of your involvement!"

In the State House, Mason had waved a printout of the

spreadsheet in the senator's face, then gripped Emma's arm as he heaved to catch his breath. As they watched the senator's eyes scan down the paper now gripped by his fingers, her focus had shifted to Mason and she wondered, with alarm, if she'd let him push himself too far.

"McDermott looks like he's gonna choke," said Dave.

"Then I say we go to print tomorrow. If you've got somethin' to say, this is your chance," added Mason. "And he says I had no choice. They threatened my family. I never wanted to be involved."

"Money grabbing liar." Dave shook his head.

"He confessed?" Kirsty looked astonished.

"We got him cornered. And he knew it," said Dave, beaming.

Mason slapped his thigh as he spelled out a headline: "Senator admits bribes in pollution scandal."

Han and Riley high-fived while Kirsty clapped.

Jordan murmured, his eyes sparkling, "This would never have happened without you."

Warm energy fizzed through her body. She blushed. Again, no one else seemed to notice.

Mason shook his head, rising to his feet: "McDermott, he smudges his cards at golf. Everyone knows it. Never liked the guy."

"Me neither," Kirsty rasped.

Emma knocked gently on Mason's office door. The old man sat at his desk rolling an unlit cigar between his fingers, apparently taking a moment before he called it a day. He seemed small in the leather armchair, surrounded by mementoes collected over the decades: a firefighter's scorched helmet, a baseball from a Little League championship, and the wooden model ship.

"Big day tomorrow," Emma said. Mason looked pale and tired, but his eyes were dancing with something like contentment.

"Press day," he nodded.

She didn't need to tell him that when their story hit the newsstands, things were going to get hectic. It would capture the attention of everyone in this town and state. If the wider regional press had any sense, they'd jump on it too and there'd be competition to keep ahead.

"You need a ride?"

Mason shook his head. "Troy's coming."

As she reversed out of the room, he spoke up. "Not so fast, young lady." He beckoned to her and when she got closer, she noticed the trace of tears on his skin. "Sit." He paused as she pulled out a chair, his blue eyes wet in the warm office light. "I want to thank you for everything you've done. Today might have been the best day of my working life."

She didn't know what to say. His gratitude surprised her. It stirred her own. She loved working with this team; their loyalty, willingness to collaborate, not compete, and their commitment to the story inspired her. "My absolute pleasure, Mason."

Mason broke into a grin. "The look on McDermott's face. I shall treasure it forever!" He chuckled, then became serious again. "You know, Ben never wanted to work on the paper. Too small for him, too parochial. That left me. I didn't have a choice. I had to takeover. But I never thought I quite had the knack."

"I beg to disagree." Emma smiled. "I think he would be proud of us, Mason."

"Yes." Mason looked her dead in the eye. "I think he would."

Chapter Forty-Five

Dusk rolled over the mountain top toward the ocean. Jordan clicked on the radio. The truck gathered speed on the highway. The Friday night local shock-jock roared with disgust over McDermott's admission he'd taken a gigantic bribe to ignore toxic runoff from the plant. He went apoplectic over their revelations of plans for a casino. They'd put the story up online before the paper hit the stands tomorrow. Keeping ahead. Smart. Jordan was thrilled for the team, but the threat level had just spiraled. He wanted to see Emma and remind them all to take due care.

The office door was locked, and the newsroom was empty when he arrived. The Claw, however, was jammed with people beginning their weekend.

"You seen Emma?" he asked Lily at the bar.

She nodded to the corner. "People have been buying them drinks since they got here."

The Siren team huddled around a table, talking animatedly among themselves.

"Congratulations, everyone." Jordan stood, breathing hard. "You're the talk of the town."

The group shifted to make space for him to sit.

"Congratulations yourself!" Dave called out. "You're a part of this."

"Ah, that's not entirely true." He shrugged it off. It was their hard work; it was their achievement. "Where's Emma?"

"Outside with your sister," Mason said with a touch of disapproval in his voice. With a glass of scotch in his hand, he was in the mood to celebrate, and Emma's presence was required.

"Take it easy, Pops," Jordan said gently as he headed out. Behind him, he heard Ed, Troy's fishing partner, say, "This is gonna change things, Mason. Things are gonna get better."

"I hope so, son, I hope so," his grandfather replied.

Jordan hoped so, too.

Beth and Emma stood on the back patio, deep in conversation.

"Hey!" Jordan pecked Beth on the cheek, and then Emma, lingering just a fraction longer to take in her scent. "What's up? Why aren't you inside celebrating?"

The air held a slight chill.

Emma spoke. "I've had an offer on the cottage."

"A very generous one," Beth said with emphasis. Her voice carried an edge of warning. Her raised brows signaled Emma would be a fool not to take it.

"Oh." His stomach dropped. Any sense of merriment fled. "From who?"

Emma looked to Beth, giving her permission, it seemed, to speak. "They're not local, you don't know 'em." A mix of apology and concern played across Beth's face. She rested her hand on his arm. "We're done. I'm going to find Troy before he gets too loaded with the guys. He's in party mood. See you inside?" She gave his bicep a comforting squeeze.

"Sure, thanks Beth." Emma smiled at his sister. "For all your hard work. It's great news."

"Thank you, and for yours."

Jordan took Beth's place in front of Emma. Her face was thrown into shadow and completely inscrutable. "Are you happy about it?"

She might not be. Maybe, after today, she'd change her mind and want to stay? The desperation coating his thoughts startled him. He could barely recognize the guy he was a few short weeks ago, the one who resented her presence with a vengeance.

"It's a lot to think about." Emma crossed her arms over her

chest, the evening breeze playing with the ends of her hair. She hadn't answered his question.

He shivered slightly. He wanted to ask what her thoughts were—was she inclined to take the money and go, or was there any chance that Sirens Bay offered more? Might she reconsider the sale? He stopped himself. Right now wasn't the time to ask. He stood a good chance of getting an answer he didn't want. Better to let the news settle.

He looped a strand of loose hair over her ear. "Big day for you."

Emma sighed and leaned her cheek against his palm for a moment.

"I haven't felt such a thrill nailing a story in a long time. Dave's been so dogged. Mason's worked all angles." She continued to list the team's attributes. "Han's amazing. Kirsty's been phenomenal, and Riley, she's on fire. I'm really proud of all of them." She paused. And what did she think of him? "And thank you for everything."

She sounded alarmingly final. Jordan's body tightened as he searched her eyes for a hint of what she really meant. Uncertain, he kept it light. "I'm just a willing tour guide, that's all." His hand stroked the cool skin of her arm and reached for her palm. "Let's go inside."

She nodded. He hesitated for a second, aware that they were stepping toward a future where he had absolutely no idea what was coming next, or if she'd even be in it. If he could have remained there, holding her close to his side, he would have. He yearned for her to stay. He wanted to tell her. He ached to say, see what we have here; give The Siren, the town, me, a chance. We could make something together. But his throat clenched shut.

He didn't want to scare her away. He put his arm around her waist. "Let's get out of here."

Emma's head spun. The news had spread like wildfire across the state. Jordan turned to her from the driver's seat. "Your place or mine?"

"Er," she couldn't think for a second. "Yours."

Congratulations poured in. She felt part of something, appreciated, useful. And then, on top of that, she had a buyer. She should have felt elated. Disposing of the cottage was what she'd come here to do. But did she still want that? There was the paper, her team, their story. She glanced over at Jordan at the wheel, driving with one hand, the other resting on her thigh. This man. Emma felt good around him. That was a surprise. But he wasn't a reason to stay. How could he be? No one in their adult right mind made a significant life choice based on their burgeoning romantic feelings for a man they hardly knew, did they? No one took that risk, or was that stupid, were they?

"What's up?" He looked at her.

Deep green forest flushed past the window. She shook her head gently. "What a day. I've never owned a place before, let alone sold one."

"Huh." They fell into silence. "Would Ben be pleased you'd found a buyer?"

His question niggled at her. "I mean, I guess so?"

She still didn't understand why her friend had bequeathed her the cottage. His handwritten note said only that there was no one else he'd rather leave it to. Was Ben hoping she'd spend time there and enjoy it? She'd feel settled and secure somehow? Or had he meant for her to scoop up the windfall and be on her way? Moving on, not outstaying her welcome, was her usual rhythm. Ben knew that. But a tug of doubt had stopped her from immediately asking Beth for the papers to sign. A thought had flashed through her mind: she could keep the cottage—for herself. The idea scared, delighted, and totally confused her. It could be her home. Of sorts. Was that what Ben intended?

Walking into Jordan's living room, it struck her: this was what a well-loved home looked like. Each piece of furniture, book, art, throw, down to the handcrafted drinks coaster, meant something to him; his tastes and desires spilled through every room. Owning the cottage would tie her to this town. How often would she actually visit? Rarely occupied, the property would become a liability, and a drain on her wallet with its upkeep expenses and winter weather repairs. It wasn't viable. She wasn't thinking straight. Beth had found someone eager to own it, who would get to enjoy the rustle of the pines and glory of the sun skimming the ocean. Ben's place deserved that.

"Wanna watch a movie?" Jordan asked, sliding onto the sofa beside her, his arm unfurling across her shoulder.

"Sure."

He reached for the remote. The screen demanded: Continue to watch? Frozen II.

She gave him a meaningful look. "I see another side to you."

Jordan rolled his eyes. "Piper and Nora. They always wanna watch Frozen II. They've seen in a million times."

"Really?" she teased. "They want to watch it?"

He shook his head with lighthearted exasperation. She snuggled against his chest as he scrolled for a movie, his body solid and warm behind her. Her eyelids drooped as images from a non-stop day buzzing around the newsroom flittered through her mind. She drifted off to sleep to the rise and fall of his breathing, his arm lying across her.

Chapter Forty-Six

Emma craned her neck through the truck's passenger window. Mobile TV units bristling with satellite dishes blocked the street. A gaggle of neat men and women in sharp-shouldered jackets stood in front of a battery of cameras set up on the curb. Around them, sound technicians wearing earphones and camera guys in army fatigues and fishing vests ducked and dived, running cables, hooking up equipment and grabbing booms. A helicopter buzzed overhead.

"I hope this town is ready for this." Emma turned to Jordan.

Under the pristine makeup and hairspray, TV reporters were a rapacious breed who hunted in packs.

"I've never seen a Saturday morning like it." Jordan looked bemused as he rammed the horn at a wagon trying to cut in. Behind it, a cop car arrived, flashing its lights and sounding its siren. Trooper Cleary sat at the wheel.

"They'll be gone as soon as they came." She tried to sound reassuring. Once they'd grabbed their slice of the story, the networks and cable channels would chase the next turn of the news cycle. But, until then, there would be no peace.

"No, it's good." Jordan nodded. "This story needs to be heard. Someone needs to do something about it."

"I've got to go." She kissed him on the lips, pulling herself away before she jumped out of the truck. It was going to be quicker on foot.

Picking her way toward The Siren's front door, she tripped over a knot of cables and stumbled into a reporter practicing his lines.

"Sorry."

Kit Renick's golden hair shone in the sun. His crisp, white button-down shirt and baby blue Ralf Lauren blazer set off his deep tan. He stood as still as a Greek statue, and as aloof, as a team of people busied around him setting up the shot. He sent her a clinical smile. "No problem," he nodded and returned to his phone.

He didn't recognize her. Not because they hadn't met a hundred times over the course of a decade, but because, in all circumstances, he was totally preoccupied with himself.

Wait till I tell Doug about this: the thought ran through her head before she could stop it. Rennick was a grandstander, eager to skim the cream off other journalists' hard graft, grab the story and the glory, and go. Doug thought Rennick was a joke.

Grief glitched in her chest.

At the sidewalk, she caught her breath. Her and Doug's private world of dusty, sweaty assignments had somehow bled into the clear blue sky of Sirens Bay, where Doug had never stepped foot. Rennick was like an echo from a far-off past, which she realized with what felt like a slap, might slip away faster than she'd realized. Her eyes fixed on him as he took up a spot a few feet from The Siren's entrance and began his piece to camera, his face concerned, his voice calm, his arm stretching down Bayview as he spoke about the threat to this quaint Maine fishing port. As the voice of the nation, he sounded convincing. She'd give him that.

Mason flung open the door and beckoned her in. "We've hit the big time!"

In the newsroom, Han looked up from his laptop, a wide smile dimpling his face. She'd never noticed the dimples before. "We've gone viral. We're everywhere."

"Fantastic job, Han." Emma sat down, wondering how they were going to keep ahead of the pack. "Fantastic job everyone!"

The room nodded. They knew that. They'd invested so much.

"It hasn't been like this since Dukakis visited in '88, remember that?" Dave chuckled, looking at Kirsty for confirmation.

"And that was a doozy."

Dave turned to Emma. "What's next boss?"

"Any further comment from McDermott?"

"Nope. He's gone to ground. I expect on legal advice."

Mason dropped onto the chair next to her. "I heard from a buddy at the club that the attorney general is about to launch an investigation."

"Brilliant, Mason. That's our next lead. Dave, you got a contact at the AG's office?"

"Already dialing," Dave shot back, his phone to his ear.

Emma opened her laptop and tried to arrange her thoughts in a logical order. Rennick was just outside the door. Was the Informer out there? They were her people.

Or were they?

She'd veered so far off course, she didn't know who she was anymore. She took a breath and tried to steady her gaze on her screen. Dave murmured into his phone. Han and Kirsty chatted quietly about site optimization strategy. This was their story. Rennick and the like were visitors. So. Was she? The cottage belonged to her. She was part of this team. She'd woken up that morning lying in Jordan's bed with his arm draped over her. She'd never felt so at home.

But. She was going to sell, wasn't she?

Chapter Forty-Seven

By mid-afternoon, the plague of reporters had dispersed, some down to the dock, others up to the plant in a fleet of giant SUVs, like a convoy advancing into battle. Some of the more enterprising lobster guys, Jordan's brother-in-law included, had taken bunches of them out on the water for a considerable fee. The regular charters also hiked their prices, while perplexed tourists watched the commotion from the shore. Lily said the Claw was clean out of oat milk and coffee beans.

Emma was probably used to the drama. She probably thrived on it. She probably missed it. She might even jump aboard and leave with them, sucked in by the adrenaline rush and the attention. If she did, Jordan wouldn't blame her. This was her world.

But he didn't want that to happen.

He pulled up on the sidewalk opposite The Siren with the dinghy trailer hitched to the back. Emma and the team had lifted the lid on something literally toxic that was poisoning this town. It had taken an outsider to notice. Not notice; to listen. And it was Emma. They needed her. He might need her. He had no idea what was going through her mind. They had spent last evening cuddled on the sofa, watching a movie. Emma seemed exhausted, and he hadn't known what to say.

They'd gone to bed and lain side by side, as chaste as junior high school sweethearts on their first date. He felt like he was standing at the door waiting to be let in and it might slam in his face at any minute. His gut twisted. He needed to know if there was the slimmest chance she might stay.

Emma appeared on the sidewalk, spotted him, waved, and crossed the road. The sunlight streaked through her hair. She walked with purpose, her long arms swinging by her side. He swelled with what felt like joy. It was a faintly familiar feeling, lost somewhere to a time when he would simply stand there watching Sophie doing something as ordinary as folding the laundry or working on her laptop. He'd observe, unobserved, marveling that she was with him. Emma didn't belong to him in that way at all. They didn't live in each other's lives like he and Soph. But they could. If they wanted to. Did he want to? Did she?

Emma passed in front of the truck and smiled at him. The knot in his stomach loosened. "Hop in."

"Where are we going?" she asked, looking back at the dinghy.

"I thought I'd take you away from all of this for a couple of hours. Let you enjoy the weekend."

"Really?" He hoped she wouldn't freak at the thought of going out on the water. "That would be wonderful," she sighed, dropping her head against the rest and closed her eyes for a moment. It was exactly what he wanted to hear.

"How's your day been?" He could guess.

"Nuts."

Jordan turned on the radio and let the drive-time playlist roll over them. There was time to talk later.

A few miles out of town, at the end of a track through the woods, he parked in a dirt lot and unhitched the dinghy. Together, they carried it down a shingle path toward the beach.

The sand was deserted. The ocean stretched out for miles, gleaming like glass.

"Bliss." She stretched her arms high and wide. He resisted the urge to grab her round the waist and pull her to him. All in good time.

"See that strip of green?" He pointed toward the horizon. She nodded. "That's Cornwell Island. No one lives there. There's no internet or TV. Cell coverage is terrible. It's the perfect place to chill for a few hours."

A hint of alarm twitched on her face, before she said: "Sounds lovely."

"You sure?" He didn't want to make her do anything she didn't want to.

"I'm sure. I trust you," Emma said, helping him push the vessel into the shallows.

They skimmed over the surface. She looked regal, the wind in her hair, her eyes fixed forward. He was grateful for the chance to spend some more time with her. That was all he was asking.

They hauled the boat onto the soft sand. Moments later, he'd pulled out his pack from the seat locker, laid out the blanket, and beckoned to her to sit down. His eyes lifted to the sky. "I love it here."

Emma's shoulder brushed against his. "It's so beautiful. And strange to see Sirens Bay from here."

"I know. It feels like another planet."

As the sun dropped behind Bald Eagle Peak, he curled his arm around her and gave her a gentle squeeze. She was a tall woman, but somehow delicate in his embrace. He wished this moment could stretch into tomorrow and the next day and the next. He wanted to know her, what she was feeling right now; what she thought about things, and what she might think about things in the future. But there was something about her quietness that he didn't want to disturb. It stopped the words in his mouth.

She shivered slightly as a chill bit the air.

"Help me build a fire? I brought hotdogs."

"Of course you did!" she laughed.

"Always prepared. Once a Marine, always a Marine."

"Fair." She kissed him on the cheek.

Emma's silhouette moved across the beach as she searched for driftwood. Longing for her bubbled in his chest.

"Nothing too big," he called out as he arranged a heap of rocks into a ring to make a fire pit.

Emma dumped her haul of driftwood on to his kindling, and he struck a match. The dry leaves at the bottom of the hollow flared, lighting up their faces.

The hotdogs sizzled in the pan. He offered her the last one, but she declined. He ate it in three bites and wiped his mouth. "Delicious. Nothing like eating outdoors."

"Nothing like hotdogs you hunted yourself." She raised an eyebrow.

He smiled at her joke, relieved she appeared to be finally unwinding.

A pale moon shimmered in the sky. Jordan dropped onto his side, stretching out along the blanket, inching closer to her. He ran the tip of his index finger up her arm. "This is the best way to spend a Saturday night."

She smiled down at him, apparently appreciating his contentment, but didn't speak. "You're being awful quiet for a woman who's just exposed the biggest corruption scandal the state has seen in decades."

"I'm sorry." Her eyes fixed on the flames.

He nudged her gently with his head. "Tell me. What is it?" He had promised himself that he wouldn't pry, but he needed to know. "Is it the cottage? Are you going to sell?"

She looked into his face with an uncertain smile. "I don't know. I guess. Maybe. I know it sounds silly because I've been hanging around waiting to put the cottage on the market for ages, but suddenly it's… actually real. And…"

"And what?" Hanging out didn't sound remotely committed, but her confusion gave him hope. It wasn't a done deal. There was a fraction of a possibility that she would stay.

"I…I," she stuttered.

He could almost hear Lily telling him: be straight, tell her how you feel, nothing to lose. Instead, he hedged: "The paper needs you."

"The paper would be fine without me." She dropped a twig into the fire, and they watched it catch. "At least I hope it will. I never intended to take over."

"No, really, they need you." His voice was insistent.

The Siren drew from her energy, her focus, and her experience. She was the glue that held the team together. She'd given them purpose and a way to follow through on it. She'd been a gift. She hadn't struck him as a woman who underestimated her impact on people around her, but perhaps she did. But that wasn't what he wanted to tell her. He wanted to say that he needed her; he wanted her to stay. He chewed his lip, readying to speak.

"What?" She turned to him, seeming to sense his urgency. The firelight danced over her face and glittered in her eyes.

Fear tightened his chest. As long as he didn't know her answer, he hadn't lost her. "I'm totally stuffed."

Emma and Jordan took turns feeding strips of bark into the pit. He sat behind her, his legs either side of her, as she lay back against him. A man, one simply willing to be with her, had never held like her like this. She glanced up at Jordan's face. He was smiling, his lips set in a handsome curve.

"What?" He gave her a little squeeze with his knees.

"You're so gorgeous." She watched his eyes twinkle. "I'm not sure if I told you that before."

"You can say it again." He dipped his chin to kiss her on the head.

She said it louder this time. "Jordan Allen. You are a gorgeous man."

"You're not so bad looking yourself." He let the compliment land, then said: "You wanna head back?"

"Oh." His changing the topic surprised her. "You need to?"

"No, I just thought you might. It's getting dark. We should leave now, or we camp."

"Let's stay?" she suggested softly. She didn't want to move from this spot just yet.

The sea lapped gently on the beach. The fire crackled. And apart from their breathing, there were no other sounds. No talking, phones ringing, alerts popping up on her news feed.

The delight on his face confirmed her decision.

Jordan stood in front of a makeshift bivouac of tarpaulin he'd secured against a fallen tree trunk. "Done."

Emma yawned and crawled inside. He followed behind her. He'd set out the blanket as a groundsheet. "Which side do you..."

Before he could finish, she turned and pulled his face toward her. She kissed his mouth, flaring with desire. His lips opened immediately, and their tongues wrapped around each other. Urgent for his weight on her to pin down the thoughts whizzing through her head, she wrapped her arms around his torso. With one arm around her waist, he yanked her close.

She gasped as his mouth moved down her neck and let out a long, yearning sigh as the craziness of the day slid off her. Delight tickled its way across her skin. Her hands laced together behind his back. She placed her mouth on his, kissing hard. She wanted to melt into him. He lifted her sweatshirt over her head as she tugged at his sweater. Their legs tangled as they kicked off their jeans. His breath quickened in tune with hers. Her hands sought his face as her mouth searched for his. He unclipped her bra and ran his hands around her ribs. She moaned as his palms found her breasts. Then his mouth was on one and then the other. Pleasure rippled up into her throat and circled down to between her legs. She grabbed his butt, her hand reaching around into his shorts to feel his hardness. Jordan gasped as she ran her thumb over its tip.

"I want you now," she said.

Bare-chested, he rubbed against her. "No." He kissed her furiously on the mouth, pushing against her groin, thick and strong. "You're going to have to wait."

His fingers gently pulled at her underwear and skimmed down between her thighs.

She moaned as he slipped one inside her. His touch bewitched her. She couldn't think.

He kissed her cheek and neck, and whispered, "All good things…"

She barely heard him. While his fingers moved back and forth, his thumb stroked exactly the right spot, amplifying the pulse rocking her body. She shivered with desire. She reached to touch him, but he moved her hand away, securing it to her side. His tongue circled across her collarbone, spiraling down to one nipple, which he nipped between his teeth, and then the other. A surge of electricity lit her inside, and she groaned gently. He slowly slid his fingers out from inside her. She sighed with reprieve.

In one swift move, she was on her back and his mouth was on her, circling and sucking at her want for him. She was so full of craving for him, she forgot to breathe for a second. Her hands reached into his hair, gripping and pulling as his tongue worked her soft skin. The pleasure kept building, strokes and licks stacking up on each other, lifting her out of her mind. She yearned to feel him inside her. She tried to speak, to tell him she couldn't take anymore, but all she could manage was, "I…I…"

It was too late; she couldn't hold back the wave of heat gushing through her. She gasped as it seemed her body flew an inch higher, and then swooped low on a rush of delight, convulsing with pleasure. With her eyes still closed, she panted, trying to catch her breath. Night air tickled her bare skin. Glee rang through her. But he wasn't done. His thighs resting on either side of hers, she felt his hardness about to enter.

"Okay?" he asked as she heard him snap on a condom.

She opened her eyes to see his face, gripped by raw want.

She nodded, eager again to feel him. He pushed inside gently at first, bringing her up again. This time, her body locked into his rhythm immediately.

"Oh my God," she whimpered, grabbing his shoulders, bringing him to her, hungry for his mouth. Every drive ignited a shiver of joy. Her focus contracted to one pulsing beat as he gathered speed, thrusting in and withdrawing, ready to dive again. She quivered as he reached deeper. She soared, intense throbs of pleasure zeroing her attention onto the feel of him, sliding fast, wanting, plunging, bringing her up with him, sweat slipping between their bodies. He threw his head back with delight and dropped it again, panting.

"I…I'm close…" He murmured, grimacing. He slowed, each shove reaching for her further than she had ever been touched before.

"Don't stop," she begged. "Stop. No. Don't…"

She grabbed his back, her fingertips whitening, trying to hold on to the force of rapture swamping her. An irresistible pulse flashed through his body into hers. She reached there with him, whispering his name, before streaming down the other side, cascading with utter satisfaction.

"Emma," his voice wavered as he released in a violent shudder. "Emma…" He collapsed onto her, spent and gasping.

Her arms clutched him close. Her entire body washed with joy.

Chapter Forty-Eight

The space where she expected to find him was cold. She pulled on her shorts and crawled out of the shelter, yanking her sweatshirt over her head. "Jordan?"

A coffeepot hung over glowing embers, but he was nowhere to be seen. The sun inched above the horizon, strafing the indigo water with pale yellow light. In the far distance, she could make out the lighthouse as it threw its beam across the water. She stood, her arms clasped around her, watching the silky ocean swish over the sand and then retreat, wondering if the town on the other side of the water was awake yet this Sunday morning. It was so beautiful here. Her toes curled against the cool sand. At that moment, she never wanted to leave this beach. This place.

What if she kept the cottage and stayed? She shook her head at how fanciful the thought was. For more than a decade, she had never lived in one place for more than a year, bouncing between expensive New York studios the size of a shoebox, and then apartments in D.C., all empty when she left on assignment, during which any hotel room would do for a home and an office. Could she even stay still? Did she even want to? Her eyes focused on the sun bleaching the last dregs of the night from the sky. A cool breeze slipped over her skin. Her life was constant change. Who would she be if she stayed? What on earth would she do here for the rest of the summer? How many big stories could there be lurking under the surface of this cozy little town? Not many.

Jordan's shape appeared at the far end of the beach. Warmth melted through her. When they were apart, she longed for his presence more than she'd let herself admit. She watched him stride up the beach. He hadn't asked her to stay. Did he want her to? Should that matter? It shouldn't, but somehow, it did. Why hadn't he asked what her plans were? Did he care? She couldn't expect anything of him. She barely knew him, although it felt, strangely, as if he'd been a part of her life for years. He'd grown familiar. His beautiful face circled around her mind all day, every day, swinging into focus at the most random moments, his gorgeousness piercing her concentration. It annoyed her. She loved it.

"Got more wood." Jordan dropped an armful of branches onto the sand. His lips touched hers softly. Her body leaned toward him. He'd lit something in her she'd kept buried for a long time, a delicious, smoldering yearning for a particular touch, his touch, and a craving for pleasure that she couldn't ignore anymore.

As he poured the coffee into two tin cups, she shook her head gently. "You are such a boy scout. And I mean that as a compliment."

"I take it as such." He passed her a mug.

"You could come on assignment with me anytime."

"It would be my honor." His eyes dropped to the firepit and then rose to meet hers. His sapphire beam fixed on her. "Any time. Whenever and wherever you are."

His earnestness caught her off guard. She broke the awkward pause with an attempt at humor. "You could carry my bags."

His brow twitched with what seemed like confused disappointment, perhaps at her lack of sincerity. It was a lame joke. And no one ever carried her bags. She flinched with self-recrimination. She tried again. "Are you also planning to catch us breakfast?"

He jerked his head toward the boat. His voice was serious. "No, I thought you could do that." And then he smiled.

Her body softened. She met his grin with her own, raising her eyebrows. "You want to eat today, right?"

"I do." He pulled a foil packet from his pack and tossed it at her. "Do you think you could toast them without burning them?"

She hesitated as she lay the foil over the metal stand above the flames. Homemade waffles. The aroma of baked goods made her tummy rumble. This man. She smiled at his thoughtfulness.

"You know," she turned serious, "I'm really not sure."

"I'll supervise." He edged beside her.

She swatted him away. "I'll manage."

After breakfast, he led them along a path through the woods. Ahead, she could make out the slate gray roof of a single-story cabin and then another, all connected by a skinny path.

"Do people live here?"

"Not anymore." Jordan pointed to a clutch of other buildings further along the track. "This spot was home to an artist colony. People started coming here maybe in the '20s until the war. All kinds of people stayed here apparently, mainly painters. Erik loaned me a book on it. Ever heard of Edward Howell?" Emma shook her head. "Edith Frank? Sara Butler?"

"Nope. But that means nothing." His was the first piece of art she'd ever bought.

"There's more to this part of the world than lobster fishing." He walked on slowly.

As she was learning.

Her phone buzzed in her back pocket and went to voicemail. The screen showed five missed calls. They'd all tried to get her: Dave, Mason, Kirsty, Han, and Riley. Something had happened.

"Sorry..." She stopped. Holding her phone above her head, she tried to catch a signal. Being off grid had been glorious, but in that moment, she realized she had to get back into the world. They needed her.

Still no connection.

"Bloody hell," she said under her breath. Jordan looked at her, expectant. He seemed to know what she was going to say. "Listen," her voice gathered force. "I think I've got to go back."

It tugged at her to cut the sense of togetherness binding them, but she couldn't abandon the team to fend for themselves. She waited for him to say something. He nodded, disappointed, but understanding.

She turned back down the path. "How quickly can we get there?"

Chapter Forty-Nine

Jordan spun the chisel in his palm, wondering where to start. He ran his finger over the bulging contour of a knot. The piece was slowly revealing itself. The grain stretched like a sinew of a muscle. He placed the flat end of the tool on the wood. He'd let the carving decide the shape it was going to take.

He remembered the silkiness of her skin under his touch, the way her hips fit against his, their legs roped together, her lips on his, her body searing against his, his fingers clenching hers, hers gripping his. It had been a beautiful night; one he could relive a thousand times and it would never be too much.

Beth said Emma had yet to confirm the sale, but the buyer needed an answer soon or she would back out. He was going to exercise enormous patience and wait for Emma to tell him what she was going to do. It wasn't his business. In the meantime, he was determined to enjoy every second he had with her. He brushed a bead of sweat out of his eye with the back of his hand. It was hot outside and in his workshop. She said she'd come over when she was done, and it was nearly suppertime. Where was she? Whatever demanded she work on a Sunday and this late must have been urgent. Mason had canceled his golf round, too. That was unheard of.

Jordan scraped a coil of wood from the piece in his hand. Wherever it took him, it was going to be something special; something for her.

Tires crunched on the gravel. Anticipation stopped his hand mid stroke. He listened. Emma's voice sang through the house. "Hello!"

"In here!" He returned her call, beaming. He had begun to doubt she'd come.

Emma appeared in the doorframe. His heart bounced. Around her he felt strong, able, back on the path to being the man he'd always wanted to be. Sophie's death had thrown him wildly off track. With Lily and Beth's help, he'd found his way to the start again; with Emma, he was accelerating toward a new destination, although he wasn't sure what it was, or whether, in a very short while, he might fund himself a solo traveler again.

She smiled, taking in the room. "So, this is where the magic happens."

He stood up, wiped his grit-stained fingertips on his jeans, and kissed her. "Let me wash up and I'll be with you. Make yourself at home. Look around."

Emma ran her finger over his workbench as she took in the shelves stacked with old tobacco tins and mason jars crammed with nails and blades, and piles of sketchbooks. She lifted one from the top, curious to see how he worked. Her eyes skimmed the thick pages of delicate pencil drawings depicting rocky beaches, proud mountain ranges, angry waves, veined tree leaves, and people—the slant of a shoulder, the length of a calf, a face in profile. Whatever or whoever, it seemed, caught his eye. Not a measurement or calculation in sight.

She turned the page. Her breath caught. Outlined in graphite, her face stared back at her. Her head turned slightly to one side, her eyes looking directly at her. He'd captured something in her look, a hint of defiance mixed with apprehension. He'd recognized a feeling she thought she'd kept well hidden. He seemed to have understood something about her she didn't even like to admit to herself, a sense of vulnerability underneath her veneer of capability. Touched and a little unnerved, she carefully closed the cover and laid the book back on the pile.

There was a rough beauty to the unfinished piece lying on the table. She cradled it in her hands, following the stripes of grain before she realized maybe she shouldn't touch his work. She placed it down, hoping she hadn't disturbed anything.

A cell phone rang somewhere in the cottage. She heard Jordan's friendly pitch and then his laugh. She closed the studio door carefully behind her and walked into the kitchen.

Through the other door, she could hear him moving around the sitting room.

"Sure, yeah," she heard him say. "No, buddy, it's only a casual thing, super-flexible." The other person spoke. Emma stood in the doorway, watching Jordan standing in a towel, his back to her and his hair still wet. He plumped a pillow and tossed it back onto the sofa. He laughed, a little coy maybe. "Nah dude. She's here now." Without turning, he walked into his bedroom. "Yup, zero commitment. Easy-peasy," she heard him say. "Just fun."

A chill swamped her. Had he meant what she thought he meant? Was she a casual thing, super-flexible? Of course she was. When she said she couldn't promise anything, that's what he'd heard. He'd taken her at her word. Her eyes stung.

Jordan appeared in the kitchen dressed in a t-shirt and sweats, hair mussed and a huge grin on his face. She stared at him, cold with humiliation. He'd been so blunt, so nonchalant about revealing the apparently loose terms of their relationship, sufficiently unabashed to boast about it to a friend, to talk about her as if she was a Tinder hook up. Who was this guy? What guy under sixty talked about women like that? She ached raw with hurt. She shook her head. Why was she even contemplating something more with him? What a stupid, stupid daydream.

"What's wrong?" He pulled a can of soda from the refrigerator and offered it to her.

She didn't know what to say. She'd set the trap and fallen into it. She flushed with embarrassment.

"What's wrong?" he repeated, stepping toward her.

She stood up with a sudden rush of energy and pushed past him toward the door. "I've got to go. I'm sorry." Heat gathered behind her eyes. "They need me at the office."

He looked bewildered. "Now, at this time? You just came from there. It's Sunday."

Dejection clogged her throat. She had to leave. She squeezed the words out: "Yeah, I've got to go."

She landed in the Dodge, threw it into reverse and hit drive before he could see her cry. Leaving him behind, she sobbed over the wheel at her mistake. She'd told him she couldn't promise anything, she'd been adamant, and then she'd gone and broken her own rule and let her guard down. She'd let him in, let herself feel more for someone who spoke about her like she was a high school crush.

The forest darkness rushed past her window. He'd kept his end of the deal and was keeping things super loose. He was doing what she said. She was nothing to him. She had been deluding herself that he felt more. In her grief, she'd lost her judgement. She should have known that would be the case. She'd been an idiot.

Chapter Fifty

Lily leaned against the bar, rubbing the deep circles around her eyes. "Tell me what happened."

Jordan rolled a bottle of Coke between his fingers, trying to keep his voice low but loud enough for her to hear. The last of the TV reporters had finally left town, and the bar was heaving with tourists.

"She came over. I took a quick shower. Troy called. I invited them over for a little dinner party in her honor. Thought it'd be nice. A bit of cooking, some chatting around the table. I was gonna ask you and Erik." Lily nodded, approving. "And then, I finished the call, walked into the kitchen to find her and ... she kinda flipped. She fled, like she'd received the worst news. She said she had some work stuff to do, which I don't believe. She literally couldn't get out of the house quick enough." He ran his hands through his hair. "I really feel like I'm missing something."

What had he done wrong?

Lily frowned. "She said nothing else?"

"Nothing." He continued: "You know she's had an offer for the place?"

Lily nodded. There was not much she didn't know.

Had Emma sensed his eagerness and felt smothered? Perhaps this was her way of saying goodbye? God, he hoped not. If that was the case, after all the time they'd spent together, she wouldn't be the woman he thought she was. But she'd said no promises. He shook his head, ready to walk over the road and demand to know what was wrong. "I'm gonna go over there."

"If I was you," Lily said slowly, "Let her come to you. She owes you that."

Jordan dropped his forehead onto arms. "I don't enjoy waiting."

Lily patted his shoulder. "Nobody does."

──────────── **Chapter Fifty-One** ────────────

McDermott's lawyers were on the warpath threatening to sue for libel. Mason's attorney friend said he didn't stand a chance. There were witnesses to his confession. It wasn't a concern, but it was interference.

At the State House, the Attorney General was about to start a press conference announcing an investigation into the failed cleanup. Dave was there furiously texting background to Emma at her desk, which she was typing up ready to insert into his story. Apparently, cops had surrounded the plant, and it was about to be declared a major crime scene.

Beth had called a second time. Her buyer required an immediate response. Thoughts clattered around Emma's head like a dozen balls on a spinning a roulette. They kept landing on the same number: Jordan.

Riley clasped a huge bunch of pink and orange flowers in front of her face.

For a second, Emma's heart leaped. "Who are they for?" she asked.

Riley read the card. "Thank you to The Siren team for all your hard work! From, Everyone at Sandy Beach Processing." She clarified, "Fish processing dudes on East Shore Drive." She turned on her heel. A note of pride lit her voice. "I'm tellin' ya, this town is grateful. I'll put them in water."

Of course, they weren't from him. Emma despaired of herself.

The A.G. walked onto Emma's laptop screen. She rested her palms on the wooden podium and announced to a packed room of reporters the launch of a two-pronged criminal investigation into the embezzlement of public funds intended for the cleanup, and, deliberate environmental damage.

The back of a balding head appeared in the frame. "Dave Ouellette. The Siren." The A.G. nodded in recognition. "What does the state expect to find?"

"I don't know, Dave," the attorney general raised her palms, "you tell me."

The room laughed. "But seriously, what consequences are we looking at when—if—you find any wrongdoing?"

"Long jail sentences for serious crimes. But apart from that, we'll have to wait and see."

Emma glanced at Han, also watching on his laptop. She smiled. These guys were her people: honest, tenacious, and enthusiastic, committed to the story. They were still just about ahead of the pack and the state. They had the Lorenzos to investigate.

Mason appeared beside her desk. "I'm headed to the club."

Emma understood he wasn't leaving to play golf. The club lounge overlooking the cliff had become one of his principal hunting grounds, Bloody Mary in hand.

"Keep me up to speed."

"Yes, ma'am."

The press conference continued on mute on her screen, subtitles running. She couldn't help herself, she glanced at her phone, pretending only to herself that she was checking if Dave called. Nothing. Did Jordan know what she'd heard? Did he understand she was offended? Rushing out like that wasn't polite. But if he cared, he'd have called, right?

Despite her utmost wish to be a grownup and accept that he didn't feel as much for her as she did for him, an irritating voice in her head couldn't and kept insisting that she might be wrong. It kept reminding her of their time together camping on the beach, the way he'd held her, the want that magnetized her to him. She shook her head. It was like living with a thirteen-year-old life coach who'd read too many romance novels. Of course, he was only going to see her as a bit of fun, a notch on the bedpost. That is what she told him he was to her.

Emma chewed her lip. Had she lied about what she wanted? Her head whirred again. Should she call him? What would she say? She could apologize for leaving so quickly. But why should she? She cringed at her need to hear his voice; was embarrassed by her desperate desire to hear that she'd made a mistake and misunderstood. Why was she being so needy? She'd wait to hear from him. If he wanted to get in touch, he would.

Her phone sprang to life.

"Hey Emma, it's Beth."

Her stomach dropped. "You need an answer."

"If you want to sell, you won't get a better price. They need to know by this evening, otherwise you'll lose them."

With the money from the cottage, she could do what she wanted. She could take a year off work, or two, discover places she'd never visited: see the cherry blossoms in Kyoto, walk the Great Wall of China, cruise the islands of Indonesia and swim at the Great Barrier Reef. She would be free to roam without responsibilities or deadlines. Moving was what she was good at. Picking a destination and traveling toward it held a comforting clarity. Staying still and letting life, people, come and go, was way more confusing.

"Emma?"

"Thanks, Beth, for all your work on this." She hesitated. "I'll get back to you."

She could leave anytime, she reminded herself. Just go. No ties. Usually, the idea of a new adventure kick-started her curiosity and lifted her spirits. Instead, she felt flat. She glanced at Riley chatting to Kirsty, the older woman explaining something about how to arrange flowers in the vase, Riley nodding. She liked working with them. They were generous women who looked to her and trusted her. It was a totally unexpected and delicious feeling to be part of a tight-knit group of professionals. At the Informer, she had colleagues, but she worked alone. Even when Doug accompanied her on assignment, any story she wrote was entirely hers, and her responsibility to get right: she found it, she stood it up, worked its angles, and decided when she would file. If she was wrong, it came back to her. Her editors wouldn't back her if she messed up; they were severe about holding reporters accountable. The paper's reputation rested on it.

She watched Riley place the flowers beside the coffee machine. At the Informer, she never knew who read her pieces or what impact they had. She imagined a young state department professional at her desk in D.C. sipping her morning coffee while skimming the paper online for overseas news. With the chemical plant, the impact of their story was immediate and clear. It felt good.

But. Was it enough that she'd made friends and loved the weeks spent working at The Siren? Wasn't it time to call it a day while things were going well and return to the city?

Her phone buzzed. Emma's eyebrows flew up. As if she'd summoned her, Louise's name appeared.

"Hey Louise, how are you?"

"How are you? Nice work up there. Who knew such a little place could generate such a big news story? Even if it is only one. Ever."

Emma ignored her condescension. Louise always knew how to put grit in the oyster of a compliment. "Thanks."

"Listen, I'll get straight to it. We've got an assignment. We need someone. Baghdad. We think the elections are going to blow up any minute and we need eyes on the ground, like yesterday. Can we count on you?"

"Oh." Emma held the phone to her ear. They wanted her. The urgency in Louise's voice lit her up. It was the answer to her question. "Of course."

Chapter Fifty-Two

Jordan looked across the bar at his grandfather beaming like the cat that had just got the cream.

"Jordan!" Mason called out, raising a glass.

Emma turned her head. Her cheeks pinked as she caught his eye. She looked tired, but beautiful. His chest clenched.

His grandfather beckoned him over. Emma looked away, sipping her drink. What were they celebrating on a Tuesday night? Another scoop, he guessed. They were on a roll.

"Hi Jordan," Riley smiled.

"What's up?" His eyes cast around the group.

Emma didn't look at him. It was as if someone had flicked a switch and suddenly, she had rewound to the Emma who arrived at the beginning of summer: aloof and inscrutable and not interested at all in having him around. She had said no promises. He still couldn't work out what he'd done. He glanced at Lily, who threw him a meaningful look. Give her space.

"Didn't you see it?" Kirsty slapped Mason on the back with her thin hand. The old man coughed.

"What?"

"Your old Grandpa here," she continued, "was on ABC News." Mason's eyes twinkled with delight. "He's a natural. This cantankerous old-timer is the voice of our community."

"It did go well." Mason's face flushed with pride.

Emma spoke. "He was great."

"Wow, Pops, way to go! I wish I'd seen it." Why hadn't anyone told him to watch?

"The clip is on our website," Han informed him.

"Sit, sit, Bub." Kirsty scooted along the bench, forcing Han and Riley to edge around. "The missing team member!"

His face seared with embarrassment. He wouldn't presume to be part of the gang. He hadn't earned it. "Oh, I won't stay."

"Don't be silly," she ordered, patting the seat. "One more, Lily, please!"

Lily arrived with a tray of beers and a coke for Jordan and Han. "From the guys," she jerked her head at a table of lobstermen sat near the bar.

"Tell 'em thanks," said Dave, reaching for a bottle. "I could get used to this."

"Now look who it is!" Mason boomed. Jordan turned his head to see Beth and Troy enter the bar. Beth was wearing a neat white cotton shirt and pressed chinos. Troy looked gruff; his face burned by a weekend in the sun, touring reporters along the coast. They were an odd pair, but they worked, their contrasts complemented each other. Their differences welded them together. The realization should have fed him with hope. He and Emma were from different worlds, but they could build something strong and lasting if they tried. His heart was loaded with disappointment. The opportunity seemed lost far down the river. And he couldn't pinpoint why.

Troy split off to talk to the guys. Beth whispered in her grandfather's ear.

Mason waved his empty whiskey glass in the air. "Your sister insists it is time for me to go home, but I think there's room for one more."

"Maybe she's right Pops," Jordan said, softly. He hated to throw cold water on the old man's fun, but his heart was fragile.

Emma stood up. "Beth, before you take Mason home, could I have a word?" Her voice was taut, urgent.

"Sure."

The two women walked out to the yard. Emma had decided, he was sure of it. Beth had said the buyers for the cottage were city types who couldn't wait. They needed an answer. The room spun. Riley's chattering and Han's laughter caught in the whirlwind around his head. He was an island in a ripple of people all talking at once; he was entirely alone, nauseous, and about to be hit with an incoming storm of pain. He could smell the thunder.

He straightened his shoulders, coughed, and checked his watch. They'd been gone seven minutes when Beth reappeared, alone. She walked slowly back to the table. He knew what she was going to say. His chin dropped.

She gently placed her hand on his shoulder. "She's selling, Jordy, sorry."

That it was obvious how much Emma's decision would cut him made him feel worse, humiliated. Emma was leaving. Disappointment caved his chest. He thought he might vomit. The table fell silent, their faces turned to him, their expressions bent with confusion, except Mason, who didn't appear to have heard. He raised his glass and called out, "To my niece!"

No one joined him in his toast.

"What's going on?" Riley frowned.

"Emma's selling the cottage," Beth said, her voice quiet but firm.

"She's leaving?" Riley blurted.

To a person, the table recoiled, shocked.

"I don't know what her plans are," Beth hedged.

"It's none of anyone's business," Jordan chided, as he removed the glass of scotch from his grandfather's claw.

An urge to chuck it down his throat surged through him. He

tried to think of anything but the delicious, consuming burn the alcohol would provide, the promise of oblivion. He felt like he'd been slapped round the face with news he didn't want to hear and then whacked on the other cheek with an insult. She couldn't tell him herself? What had gone so wrong?

He scoured his brain for a word, an action, a moment in which he'd crossed the line. He always tried to act like a gentleman. He just didn't get it. He placed the glass down and stood up, his hands by his sides, dejected. The urge to drink fled as quick as it had come.

"Come on Pops, I'll take you home." He helped the old man to his feet.

Behind them, the Siren team sat crestfallen, speechless.

Chapter Fifty-Three

Emma thought she'd be the first one in, but they were all there at their desks. Their silence hit her like a fist. They knew. Client confidentiality was not a value Beth adhered to, clearly. She checked herself. Beth wasn't to blame. It was she, Emma, who was about to disappoint them.

"Mason here?" she asked, trying to sound bright.

"Upstairs." Kirsty continued to tap on her keyboard, peering intently over her glasses at something on her screen. Neither Han, Dave, or Riley said a word. She'd explain, but she needed to talk to Mason first.

Emma knocked gently on his door.

"Come in," he croaked.

The blinds still down, the old man reclined in his chair, loafers propped on his desk and a flannel pressed against his forehead, eyes closed.

"Morning Mason." She braced herself for his reaction. Would he be angry, disappointed, or triumphant?

He straightened up. "What a night! I haven't had that much fun since '78 when Storm Larry forced a shut-in at the Claw." He took a breath and appeared to reconsider. "Not so good for the folks that died. But what a party."

He didn't know. Her stomach dropped. This would not be an easy conversation. She already felt like she was letting him down, fleeing at the very moment the story and the paper were gaining momentum.

"I've got some news."

"McDermott's been arrested?" He leaned forward, suddenly eager.

"No." Her lips twitched in a smile at his obsession with the story. She continued, slowly. "I'm returning to D.C. I've got a buyer for the cottage. The Informer has called me back for an assignment. I'm leaving tonight." There. She'd said it. It wasn't so hard.

The blood drained from Mason's face. "Wh…wh…what?!"

"I know it's sudden and I hate to spring it on you, but they need me. I've got to go."

Mason gawped. "We need you! You can't go."

His vehemence surprised her.

"You're all set here." She looked around the room, avoiding his gaze.

He shook his head. "The cottage is gone."

"I'm sorry." She hadn't meant to surprise him with that bit of news. "But it's the right time for me to go."

He lifted the latest copy of The Siren from his desk. "We've only just got started. I'll put you on the payroll. We should have done that from the beginning."

It wasn't about money. Before sending her on leave, the Informer confirmed her health insurance and kept her on salary. In their eagerness to get her out of the newsroom, they'd been generous. She squashed a rising sense of familiar work-related cynicism. Louise needed her now and she would go back.

Mason sat gob smacked, disappointment spread across his face. Guilt pinned her to the spot. "You'll find another editor. One with local sources, someone more familiar with the area."

He shot her a look that said, don't patronize me, young lady. "Well, we'd better tell the team!" he barked, his dismay turned to anger.

She didn't have the heart to tell him they already knew.

Emma hovered uncomfortably beside Mason as he stood in the doorway to the newsroom.

"Let's get to it. Emma is leaving us and heading back to D.C." He shot her a stern look. "Today."

Dave's head whizzed round. "Today?"

"Today?" Kirsty repeated.

She was momentarily lost for words at the surprise in their voices. She thought it would be obvious that she would leave immediately. "Yes, the Informer needs me for an assignment. It's last minute. I've got to go now, well this evening. To the Middle East, Baghdad." She sounded banal, practical.

Confusion swamped Han's face. "Right now?"

"Yes, I'm sorry. It can't wait."

"What about the Lorenzos? Our story can't wait," Han pleaded. "We're a team."

The look on his face almost broke her heart. He needed them. They were his friends.

"Will you be coming back?" Dave asked tentatively.

The trace of hope in his voice tugged at her. She took a breath. "No. I don't think so. I'm sorry, guys."

The hurt filling the room wrong-footed her. She hadn't expected them to take the news so personally. Mason looked delicate, leaning against the doorframe. Kirsty's mouth pinched, her eyes brimming with what looked like wounded betrayal.

"It's work," Emma tried to explain. She sounded lame to her own ears. After everything she'd asked them to do, all the hours invested, the commitment and hope, they would feel crossed by her departure. She got it. But her presence here was only ever going to be temporary. They knew that.

At the Informer, home from assignment, on the rare occasions she visited the newsroom, she always spotted a face she'd never seen before. Apart from Ben, Editor Emeritus, and Debbie the super-sub who had literally written the style book, both of whom had worked at the paper so long that they were part of the furniture, apart from them, the news floor seemed to be in constant flux. Things changed. People came and went. The industry was in free-fall, with freelancers commissioned to fill gaps where staff had been let go. People moved on. The disgruntled left. The idealistic or ambitious took their place. It was a merry-go-round. That was life at a paper. But in an instant, she realized, not here at The Siren. Local papers were a different animal; they required a different, more permanent commitment.

Riley broke the stony hush. "That's a new one. Bummer." She paused. "We'll miss you, Emma. We really will."

Her open expression of sadness pricked tears behind Emma's eyes. "I'll miss you too," she replied quietly.

At one o'clock, when usually they'd be debating where to get takeout and whose turn it was to order it, no one, it seemed, had anything to say. The air in the office was icy.

Emma wondered if it was wise to stick around. Her presence wasn't welcome, and she had other goodbyes to say.

The Claw was humming with lunchtime diners. Emma took a seat at the bar and waited to catch Lily's attention. She'd been so welcoming, and she didn't want to leave without saying farewell.

Lily walked over slowly.

"I just wanted to come by and say thank you for your hospitality." Emma sounded awkwardly formal.

Lily placed her hands on the counter. "So, the rumors are true."

The hint of judgment in Lily's voice pricked her with irritation. Did they think she would stay forever? She came to sell a house, and she had sold it. She was moving on. She'd decided.

"Yes."

Lily peered into her face with a look that said, don't mess with me. "Why?"

"Work." She tried to sound light. "The Informer called." "Work," Lily repeated slowly. It was like she was carefully considering the veracity of Emma's answer and determining whether it was enough.

"Yes," Emma's tone was firm.

"But you work here, at The Siren."

"Not really, well, not anymore." She shifted in her seat, suddenly unbalanced by a bolt of sadness through her stomach.

Emma willed herself to think of something else to say to fill the silence.

Lily broke the spell. "Does Jordan know?"

"Probably. Maybe. I don't know." Everyone seemed to have heard her news. He'd have called if it meant something to him.

Lily frowned. "You don't think it might be the right thing to do to tell him?"

"I don't think he'll be bothered," Emma said, a flush of humiliation staining her cheeks. She'd let herself feel for him; she'd broken her own rule and guess what, it had ended badly. Never mind, she thought for the umpteenth time. Onwards and upwards. Away to better things. New Horizons. She sighed quietly. Repeating these platitudes drained her.

"Is that right?" Lily said each word deliberately, as if Emma needed to rethink her assumption. But there was nothing to reconsider. Theirs was a casual thing, super-flexible. Emma nodded. She would not discuss it. She would lick her wounds in private.

"You are a smart woman," Lily began, looking her right in the eye, "but you are also really dumb."

Emma recoiled as if Lily had punched her in the chest. Underneath the steadiness of her tone, Lily seemed furious. Before Emma could rebut, Lily added, shaking her head, "You don't see a good thing right in front of you."

"And what's that?" Emma bristled, heat rising from the pit of her stomach. She didn't need a lecture. She'd just come by to say goodbye.

"The man is in love with you and you're going to skip out of town without saying goodbye?"

Emma heard the last part of that sentence before the first. In love? "I...I..."

"What?" Lily stood back, her arms folded and her eyes glaring. "This is news?"

"I...I don't...It is... I don't...think he is."

Lily shook her head slowly. "You seem confused. Let's think about it. Who took you on the boat? Up the mountain? Out to dinner?" She paused. Emma was speechless, astonished. "Who fixed your security? Who did all those things, and more? He's been telling you he loves you, and you can't see it!" Her voice spiraled. Emma winced. "What do you want him to do, write it on a poster and stick it up around town? Wake up!" Exasperation rinsed through her voice.

Emma blinked as her brain collected together the puzzle pieces of their relationship. Had she got it so wrong? He had said those words, after all.

"He...he...he said it was zero commitment." The words tumbled from her mouth.

"Did he say that to your face? Or did you say that to him?"

She'd said it to him. In the beginning. But he'd said it too, just not directly. "I overheard him," Emma said, softly.

"Really?" Lily lifted her chin. "Because that's not what I see." The woman's certainty about Jordan and the good man that he was unsettled Emma. Maybe Emma had got it wrong?

"I don't know what he was talking about, but I know Jordan, and he wasn't talking about you." She stared at Emma long and hard, as if she was stamping the words into her skull. Lily was a loyal friend and fierce when she wanted to be. She wouldn't waste her friendship on someone who didn't deserve it.

Had Jordan been talking so offhandedly about her? Why had she assumed he was? The pieces clicked into place. Because she felt vulnerable, exposed by her want for him, scared. Her gaze traveled across the dark wood bar, solid and long-lasting. Life in this bar was dependable, grounded, consistent. Like Jordan. There were no bomb blasts or sniper fire to run from, wiping all other thoughts from your head except the quickest route to safety. Decisions weren't life or death, all else be damned. Interactions weren't fleeting; they were ongoing, lasting. In fact, tracing your heritage far, far back in this town was a badge of honor. The depth of connection the people of Sirens Bay had to the town bonded them together. The permanency was so foreign and frightening. Yet somehow, it magnetized something buried so deep she hadn't recognized it at first when it slowly surfaced. A yearning to settle. It was terrifying.

"Why didn't you just talk to him?" Lily's voice was gentler.

"Why hasn't he been in touch with me?" Emma countered. She sounded petulant even to her own ears.

Lily spoke slowly, as if she was trying to explain something to a five-year-old. "You can always call him first." She sighed. "How do you feel about Jordan? Answer honestly. Do you even like him?"

"Yes. Very much." Her skin burned. She ached for him. She reveled in that feeling of being ever-so-slightly lifted her off her feet whenever he was around, the trace of his fingers over her skin, the touch of his lips on hers, the ease with which they fitted together, like puzzle pieces.

Lily peered at her. "Then talk to him." Perhaps she noted the panic flitter across Emma's face. Her tone softened. "I know it's comfortable in that shell of yours, all cozy and closed off. But you're all grown now. An adult. Take responsibility for your feelings, stop trying to second guess someone else's. Speak your truth!" Lily held her gaze. "I've said the same thing to Jordan before, by the way," she added. "Now go," she flapped her hand at Emma, "or you'll need to order."

Chapter Fifty-Four

Emma flew out of The Claw, scrabbling in her bag for her phone. Jordan's cell went straight to voicemail.

She hesitated for a second, wondering what to say. "Hey. It's me. Emma." In case that wasn't clear. "I just, err, wanted to talk to you." Should she tell him now? No. She didn't know what else to say. "Bye."

She redialed. "Er, me again…" Her eyes swung left and right, searching for the Dodge. "Can we…" The voicemail beeped and timed out. "Damn."

Her car tires squealed as she gunned out of the parking lot. After a drive that seemed to take hours but was probably a fifteen-minute dash, she pulled up to the lighthouse. His truck wasn't there. "Shit."

She tried his cell again. No room in his mailbox. The wind whipped in her hair. An iron-gray bank of cloud gathered on the horizon. This was stupid. He could be anywhere, at a job, out in the boat, visiting Abigail.

She put her phone to her ear. "Hey Beth, it's Emma."

"Oh, hey, is everything OK? You sound a bit…rushed."

"Do you know where Jordan is?"

"Oh, umm." She sounded like she was reluctant to say. She and Lily were like lionesses protecting their pride and joy.

Emma sounded apologetic. "I just need to tell him something." It was true, but she had yet to form those feelings into words. She couldn't leave without seeing him.

"Oh, well, he's out in the boat with Ramon. I don't think they'll be back for a couple of hours. Not unless the weather changes."

Emma grimaced with disappointment. "OK. Thanks."

Emma paced over the gravel, her gaze scanning the water. Her flight to D.C. left at seven thirty. Tallulah had settled with Mason, so that was one less thing to think about. She had to pack. Except for the sofa and the old TV stand she could donate to good-will, the only items of Ben's left in the cottage were ones she wanted to keep. She would ship them with the sculpture. She'd have to talk to Beth about that. It was an hour to Bangor, where she'd leave the Dodge at the airport and leg it to the gate. If she was going to make her flight—she couldn't miss her flight—she had to be on the road by five. Home in D.C. by ten. Up by six. Pack again. Get cash. Be in the visa queue at the Iraqi embassy by eight. No visa; no travel. Her head spun with details. But she had to see him first.

The ocean surged against the beach with an angry swell. Where was he? She pictured his face, the intensity of his cobalt eyes watching her with something close to wonder. It had taken her all this time to recognize that look, but now she had, she realized it had been there for a while. She had been so stupid, wasted time. She couldn't leave without setting the record straight. He deserved at least that.

On the porch, a towel hung over the rail. She touched its seam, crusty with salt. He must have gone for a swim earlier. This tiny insight into his day sent a shiver up her spine. How satisfying it was to know someone, to understand the rhythm of their day, to be curious about who they met and what they said and how they felt about it.

She sat and waited. There was nothing else she could do.

In just over twenty-four hours, she'd be boarding an overnight flight to the Middle East, headed for heat, dust, concrete and diesel fumes. She'd made the journey so many times before: call a cab at three, arrive at Dulles at four, hand luggage only, take off at five-thirty. As she waited in Doha for her connecting flight to Baghdad, she'd text their Iraqi driver Samir with a rough ETA. He'd be there standing in arrivals ready to collect her and take her to the Rotana.

Instead of sparking an expected flare of anticipation, she felt a pang of sadness, as if she'd already lost what she'd found here. And a little dread. She'd be heading far, far away from the cool sea air, the velvet green forest, the gulls and gannets swooping through an ever-changing pallet of blue sky. And Jordan.

The truck screeched to a halt. The door slammed and Jordan stood there. Emma got to her feet, pressed her palms against her thighs, and readied herself to speak.

"What are you doing here?" he said, his voice frosty as he marched toward her.

She stepped toward him. Everything she wanted to tell him charged to the front of her brain in a scramble to be the first thing she said. Her mouth opened and closed, but the jumble of words choked her throat.

"If you are not going to answer my question, then you can at least get out of my way. My day's been disappointing enough already."

As he brushed past her, she reached for his arm. He glanced at her with such hurt, she almost withdrew her grip. "Jordan, please give me just a minute of your time. I've come to apologize."

He shook her off and folded his arms across his chest, as if to say, go on then, his irises deep indigo.

"Right, I'll, umm." She should have rehearsed. "Your trip got canceled because of the storm?"

"You want to talk about the weather?"

"No, of course not." She shook her head.

This was her opportunity. It needed to be perfect. She had

everything to lose: his respect, his love, and her chance to set things right. "I just wanted to say…" Her hands twisted around each other. "I'll just start…"

"Please do."

"I overheard you on the phone…"

"What?" He looked confused.

"When I was inside the other day, I heard your phone conversation."

"You were eavesdropping?"

"No, no, I was just there. You were walking around talking, getting dressed. I thought I heard you say something, but it turns out I didn't." She couldn't seem to string her thoughts into an intelligible sentence. "But I got confused and thought you were being flippant. At that precise moment, I realized how much I liked you, but you didn't like me back. Anyway, I blew it before it even started by saying I couldn't give you anything. Why would you care about me or anyone who said something like that?"

She could hear herself prattling and she couldn't stop. "I was surprised. And sad…" He raised his eyebrows, apparently baffled. "…when I realized—sorry, assumed—you were talking about me." She wasn't sure if he was following along. She wasn't making much sense to herself. "I should never have said it." She shook her head. "Or walked out."

She wanted to start again, but it was too late. She'd been less nervous interviewing notoriously violent militia leaders brandishing assault rifles. She drew in a deep breath and tried to focus on what she really wanted Jordan to know. She brushed the heel over her palm over her eye. She would not cry. That would be ridiculous. "What I am trying to say is, I'm so sorry. I didn't mean to hurt you."

"I had to hear it from Beth that you were leaving." A shard of pain glinted in his eyes. "One minute you're at my place, and then you're gone without a word. No call or text. And then, when I was there, at The Claw, we had an opportunity to talk, and you just left. And then, oh, I hear from my sister, 'she's going'." His voice wavered with upset.

Emma swallowed. "I'm sorry. I thought…it doesn't matter." He watched her expectantly, a question forming on his face. She continued: "I just wanted you to know I think you are great. You are kind and generous and beautiful, and I never intended to suggest anything different. I'm glad I met you, Jordan Allen." The words tumbled out sounding more final than she intended. But perhaps this was the end. When would she be back? She willed him to say something. He glanced away, breaking their gaze. She stepped forward to touch his cheek with her fingertips. He jerked his face away.

"Jordan." She gently reached for his jaw and turned his face until she could look him in the eye. He stared at her; his lips fixed in a line. She waited for the words to come that would put this right. Instead, a thought tugged at her attention like a fishing hook: say something to make me stay.

Jordan frowned. His voice left his mouth in a low rumble. "This is your way of saying goodbye?"

Emma reached again. He jolted his head away from her touch.

"Let me get this straight," he growled. "You're leaving in a matter of hours and this is the time you choose to tell me I'm a great guy?"

"I'm not good at this." She raised her palms in a gesture of surrender and shook her head. "It's no excuse, I know. But I wanted to see you, to tell you how much you meant, mean, to me and apologize for disappearing the other night. For not being honest. For hiding."

He nodded. She'd done that. "And that's all?"

"What do you mean?" The last of the sun lit up her hair. She still didn't get it. "You're still going to catch your flight?"

"Well, yes, I guess."

He strode up the steps. "I gotta go."

Despite her warnings that she was not relationship material, he'd inched closer, softly, thirsting for more, hopeful, careful not to scare her away. He thought she was relenting, reciprocating. Well, any illusion he held she might value the magical energy buzzing between them, that they could build something together, shattered right then. She was leaving. He'd heard it direct. No ambiguity or space for fantasy. It was clear where he ranked on her priority list.

A sudden pain moved across his chest, tripping his breathing. He slammed open the kitchen door and stormed through into his studio. He'd been naïve. He spun, dragging his hands down his face, fury and distress battering his insides. Through the window, a shaft of lightning ripped through the sky. Why come to find him if she was going? Why poke the wound? What did she want from him?

——————————— **Chapter Fifty-Five** ———————————

Emma slammed the Dodge into reverse as a downpour hammered the windscreen. He either didn't believe her, or it was too late. The damage had been done. She roared out of the drive just as tears spilled down her face. She couldn't stop them. Blinded by the rain and sobbing, she pulled over. Did he not hear her? Her candor had meant nothing. She blew her nose and dabbed a Kleenex against her face. Her overseas assignment suddenly seemed like a gift. She was going to put as much distance between herself and Jordan as she could. Leave. Relief coursed through her.

Wind whipped through the conifers packed close on either side of the road, pushing and pulling at their heavy branches, trunks swaying. The windscreen wipers thumped back and forth, fighting back the downpour. Clouds rushed over the mountain peaks ahead, apparently urgent to get somewhere.

She pressed her foot on the accelerator. This was such a beautiful part of the world, even in a rainstorm. She'd always be grateful to Ben for sharing it with her.

In bold red letters she could see through the rain, a large sign pinned to the gatepost announced "SOLD". The finality hit her in the chest. As she parked up by the cottage, tears welled again. Ben's gift to her. Leaving would sever their last tie. He would become a memory captured in pictures on her phone and messages in her inbox that she couldn't bring herself to delete. She would miss this little place; its quiet, its beauty, the porch, its feeling of Ben. She would miss the guys in the office too: Han's eagerness to learn, Dave's excitement at being part of a team again, Kirsty's down-to-earth busy-ness, Riley's ambition, and Mason's cantankerous chuckle. An unexpected ache clenched her insides. She loved them, their camaraderie, and their friendship.

At the back porch, she stopped and let the last of the storm drizzle over her. She would miss this view, the way the water stretched out until it met the huge blue of the sky, the twinkling of the town lights. She stood, drinking in as much as she could, hoping to carry the picture with her.

Unlocking the backdoor, she remembered the night she arrived, exhausted and befuddled, every limb aching from the drive, and how furious she was with Tallulah for escaping; how she'd slammed into Jordan and how he'd clearly disliked her on sight. She smiled sadly. She could not have known then how much her feelings about him would change.

Underneath her hurt, she let herself feel a swell of gratitude toward him for following her into the storm and pulling her from the boat, for hiking up to the plant, their morning on Bald Eagle Peak, for coming when she needed him, and being so gentle, for cooking for her, for making her feel comfortable in her skin, for bringing her back into her body. For being a good friend. Her lover. Her first after Doug. And somehow more than him.

There wasn't much to pack. She collected her toiletries from the bathroom and shoved them into her soap bag, tossing the little Demerol bottle into the trash. That stupid fight seemed an age ago. As she rolled her clothes and shoved them into her duffel bag, she fended off a wave of regret. She'd done too little, too late. Why couldn't she recognize a good thing in the moment and reciprocate? She had thought he was the one who was going to get hurt; she thought she was shielding him. She scoffed at her arrogance.

A voice hit her ears. "Mate, you were just shit-scared." Doug's tone was so clear that she snapped around, looking for him. The porch door slammed in the breeze. She jumped. "Fucking terrified," he said. "Happens to the best of us."

She froze, her eyes searching around the room. There was no one. Doug. She shook her head in recognition. He wasn't wrong. She spasmed with grief. Had she lost everyone?

In the living room, The Flame stood proudly on the mantel. She pulled open the sideboard cupboard, hunting for bubble wrap. She couldn't leave it there unprotected. Leaving, she realized, would not be like closing the hotel door and wishing the guys still drinking at the bar a safe trip home, see you at the next one. There were people here she didn't want to lose, and she would.

Everything packed, sculpture wrapped in old newspaper, car loaded, she walked through the cottage one last time, casting her eyes across every surface. She retrieved her phone charger from the kitchen counter and slipped it into her bag. She needed to go if she was going to make her flight.

"Goodbye house," she called out, and immediately felt silly, but she added: "Thank you. Thank you so much." Gratitude rose through her chest and hit the back of her eyes. She tried not to cry as she turned the key in the porch door and slipped it under the mat.

The ocean had turned a deep indigo that matched her mood. She took a long drag of the late afternoon air, still damp with rain. Her heart sank at the sound of an engine in the drive. She thought she'd get away unseen. It must be Beth come to collect the key. She wasn't in the mood for small talk. A car door slammed, and feet hit the gravel in a jog. Troy?

She put on a polite smile, ready to receive her unwanted guest. It dropped off immediately when she saw him.

He stood before her, breathless. He held out his hand, gesturing for her to stop and wait while he prepared to speak.

"Don't go," he gasped. "Don't leave."

Her thoughts crashed into each other. Why was he here? She was glad he was. But he hated her; she'd hurt him. She was leaving, but she didn't want to.

Arms hanging down by her sides, she blurted, "Everything's packed."

"Emma?" His blue eyes looked at her earnestly.

He wanted something from her, and she wanted to give it, but the words wouldn't keep still in her head long enough for her to set them in a comprehensible order. She nodded.

He placed his palms on her arms. A slow melting passed through her. "Emma." She nodded again, waiting. His blue eyes stared into hers. "I love you."

Half-panicked, half-gleeful surprise swirled through her. She blinked. He'd just said he loved her. Her heart inflated; her head swam with fragments of thoughts: so many questions, her flight time, his hand holding hers on Bald Eagle Peak, Louise, morning light pouring into the newsroom, McDermott's grimacing face, the warmth of his body next to hers.

He took a deep breath. "Do you love me?"

A smile spread across her face, unbidden. Ben's voice boomed in her head: "You gotta be brave to get the best story. There's no easy way." She was going to be brave. And honest. "Yes," she whispered. And then louder and with sudden conviction, "Yes, of course I do."

Jordan beamed and wrapped his arms around in a hug so tight it squeezed the breath out of her for a second. She rested her cheek against his chest and closed her eyes. He loved her. Her arms reached around him, clutching his solid, strong body. She loved him. There was no other place to be.

Jordan stepped back, his face earnest. "What about your flight?"

It took her a second to remember check-in was scheduled for about an hour from now. Did she need this assignment? Did she still hanker for the thrill of filing first from a bombed-out town somewhere deep in the desert? Did her self-esteem need to know she could be terrified and put herself in the line of fire in a foreign war for the sake of a good story? Did she still need to be that person to feel worthy in the world? Did she need Louise? Or the Informer? She lifted her chin and looked him directly in the face. Her head and voice were crystal clear. "I'm not going."

A grin opened across his face. He scooped her up into his arms as if she was as light as a doll and spun her around, laughing. His joy was infectious. She clung to his neck, dizzy and high on her decision. He placed her back on her feet and kissed her lightly on the lips.

Once they'd stopped laughing, he asked, "What happens now?"

Emma shrugged. "I guess I unpack. But first things first."

She yanked her phone from her back pocket. Louise's number went straight to voicemail. "Hey Louise, it's Emma. I can't do Baghdad. I'm not ready. I hope you find someone else."

She'd never turned an editor down before. She was never too exhausted, too overworked, or too burned out to say no. She prided herself on saying yes. But this time, she didn't care. There were always ambitious, fresh faces jockeying to grab an opportunity. Someone else could go. A weight lifted from her shoulders. She was free of the responsibility. She realized in that moment that she hadn't ever wanted the assignment, the long flight, the jetlag, to be in the Middle East, in the summer heat, chasing self-righteous politicians for a quote. Her loyalty to the Informer had expired when Ben died. She didn't owe Louise anything. Being a reporter on-staff there did not define her. She was done.

Emma's phone buzzed. A text from Louise. Emma straightened, ready for a dressing down. All it said was, "Fine."

No concern or questions. Louise was already onto the next thing. Emma's final, thin tether to the Informer snapped.

She turned to Jordan. "Let's go inside."

Chapter Fifty-Six

Jordan wrapped the plaid blanket tightly around them as they lay together on the old couch. Her bare skin was warm against his. With her arms hugging his naked waist, Emma buried her face in the crook of his neck. Their legs intertwined, her thigh over his, their feet poking out the end of the throw, he could spend the rest of his life like this. He kissed the top of her head. She had stayed. Her flight would be in the air by now. He could barely believe it. Any lingering anger at her lack of communication had dissolved in a shower of relief.

He had one niggling question. "What was it you thought you overheard?"

She sighed with what sounded like self-recrimination. "At your place, when I came over after work, you said something on the phone about zero commitment, being casual. I thought you were talking about me."

He shook his head, bemused. That made no sense. "I was organizing a dinner party for you."

She looked up, embarrassment clouding her green eyes. "I freaked out. I felt unsure, scared, I guess. I'm so sorry."

"To be clear. I'm in for the long haul." He held her gaze. "It's not casual. I am making a promise. This is a commitment." He waited a beat. "And you?"

"Long haul?" She visibly shuddered.

He stiffened, suddenly unsure. It seemed like she was deflecting.

She rolled on top of him, her skin warm on his, and looked him directly in the face, apparently aware there'd been a misunderstanding. "I just thought of flights, long-haul flights, and how I don't want to take one for a very long time."

She lowered her lips to his and kissed him. His lips parted as their fingers interlaced. He was ready for her again. She sat up, her knees on either side of his waist. Her weight on him sent his blood rushing. His hands moved down to her hips. Her green eyes glowed. She looked exhausted and elated, make-up-less and raw in a way he'd never seen her before, and that made him want to touch every inch of her with his mouth.

"For the avoidance of any doubt," she said. "I want you Jordan Allen. I'm being very serious," she smiled. "And I'm making a promise."

He pulled himself to sitting and started at her neck. She tasted of silk. She dropped her head back, and he moved to her throat, drinking her in. Without his tongue leaving her skin, he inched his way across her collarbones. She sighed, her breath rasping at the back of her throat. He wanted this woman over and over. Her fingers grabbed his hair as his mouth worked one nipple and then the other. She let out a low moan. He was so hard it was almost painful.

Gently, he lifted her onto him. Currents of delight ricocheted around his body. She gasped as she moved against him. He knew he was going to enjoy every minute of what was to come, and he was going to make damn sure she felt the same. With one tug, he pulled her down and thrust up into her. They cried out together. They were skin against skin as their mouths locked, searching, and finding, and hunting for more.

"You are so beautiful," he whispered in awe. He barely got the words out as she rocked against him, gathering pace. "I don't think you realize how beautiful you are."

Absorbed in the feeling of him deep inside her, her mind emptied. There was nowhere else she wanted to be. Ever. His hands moved over her like he was sculpting her body. His lips were on her breasts again, his teeth lightly tugging at the pink skin of her nipples, echoing pleasure around her body. She tipped her hips forward and back to feel the breadth of him pulse against her. They should stop and take precautions, but she couldn't. She sucked on the skin of his neck, a vampire searching for the source. She licked the sweat trickling over his jaw.

"Baby," he pulled away from her gently. "Let's get off this couch."

Slowly, she lifted herself off him, leaving a hollow that needed to be filled. He led her by the hand into the bedroom and laid her on the bare mattress. He hovered over her, kissing her face, her throat. His mouth traveled into the valley between her breasts and landed on her belly button, circling. She was wet for him, aching. He kissed her tummy and skimmed his way to her inner thighs. He nibbled at the dip of her groin and shifted to the other side. His stubble tickled. Her body was growing impatient for him. She needed to feel him again.

"Come here." She grasped his head gently between her hands and pulled him toward her face.

He lay on top of her, their mouths sealed together. In her palm, he was solid. He groaned and threw his head back as she moved her hand up and down. She pushed him onto his back and slid down his ridged torso to caress his tip with her lips, moving his velvet skin with her hand. He almost squealed with pleasure. Her ache for him turned into a gaping yearning.

Again, she sat across him. Before she could mount him, he held her still with one palm on her stomach. He slid his finger inside her, sending a shaft of pleasure deep within. His thumb found her clitoris, circling and stroking. Heavy delight swamped her. Pleasure flowed in all directions, lapping over itself. She dropped her head back, basking in the feeling. She let out a long breath and withdrew his finger. "In my bag…"

She watched the muscles of his chest and arms tweak and stretch as he ripped open the little foil square and then he was on top of her, pushing in hard. His thrust jolted through her body. She kissed him with all her strength, drinking him in, luxuriating in his taste. Her fingertips dug into his back, urging him deeper. He was thick and hot. Her body heaved as a surge of joy cascaded through her veins. Blood rushed to her groin. She throbbed as he plunged faster, whispering something she couldn't understand into her hair, kissing her ear and cheek.

Her head dropped to one side; her lips parted. She couldn't speak. He kept going as a whirlpool of delight accelerated. "More," she moaned. She wanted all of him all at once. "More…"

He rocked with vehemence, gasping. She groaned with the feel of his pounding inside her. Whatever he was reaching for, there was so much space for him. He grabbed her buttocks, pulling her to meet him. His skin slipped against hers. She wrapped her legs around his waist, shuddering with delight. Wave upon wave of feeling piled up inside her as he stoked pleasure so intense she had to remember to breathe.

"Baby…" he murmured into her cheek.

"…Uh-huh…" she managed, wanting him to know she was with him, rising. Delight pulsed at the center of her being, filling up and leaking all over her body. She was almost choking on it. She murmured a string of sounds into his chest as he thrust faster and stronger. The power of him almost overwhelmed her. She clasped his fingers, trying to anchor to him so she didn't disappear. He kept receding and coming in for more. The presence of his body above her wiped her thoughts. She hovered higher and higher, rapture tickling her edges. She panted, unsure if she could take any more. When he responded by jolting his pelvis, she arched her back, ready to explode. "Jordan...I can't..."

"Hold on," he whispered, his face bent with passion. He plunged, withdrew and entered again, holding still inside her.

"I can't..."

"One more..." He pulled back again, paused, and surged forward. An eruption of pleasure tipped her over the edge. She was falling in a pulsating, hot lava of delight that rolled and tumbled. He slid back one last time, dropped his head, and pounded in again, letting out a loud, indeterminate battle cry and fell on her, sweating dripping from his forehead.

Her arms clutched him as she lay catching her breath. His body was deliciously heavy with muscle. She didn't want him to move. He was still inside her; they were still connected. She ran her fingers through his hair and kissed the salty skin of his neck.

How had she found this man? And in such a tiny place on the edge of the United States.

"I love you, Jordan Allen," she said quietly and swallowed, as he panted against her neck. "I really do."

Chapter Fifty-Seven

Jordan felt so light on his feet it was as if he could walk right off the dock and stride across the ocean glittering in the morning sunlight. At Maggie's, he spotted Lily and Beth at a table for two, sipping coffee. Beth waved. "Where are you headed so early?"

"Gallery." He nodded up the street, beaming. "To collect my paycheck."

Lily beckoned him to join them. "Well, don't you look like you won the Powerball," she said as he arrived and pulled out a chair. Both women scrutinized his face. "I believe this megawatt smile is not just about any old payday."

Jordan rolled his eyes. They could read him like a book.

Beth spoke pointedly to Lily. "Here," she raised her sunglasses, her eyes swiveling to look directly at Jordan and back to Lily, "is the reason I lost my wicked commission."

"I'm not the only reason she's staying," Jordan smiled.

Lily sat back in her chair, clasping her cup in her hands. "I'm so happy for you."

It didn't seem possible, but his mood inched a notch higher.

"Me too."

As he said it, an image of Sophie dancing on the deck, the moon rising high behind her, lights twinkling in her hair, shot into his head.

"What is it?" Beth asked.

He knew he was going to sound stupid, childish even, but he needed their confirmation. "Soph would be OK with it, wouldn't she?"

He would never wish to betray her memory or suggest that he was leaving her behind. He would always love her. She would always be a precious part of his life; she could never be replaced or forgotten.

"Are you kidding me?" Lily grasped his hand, her face flickering with sadness and something like encouragement. "She'd be so proud of you. She'd be overjoyed for you."

Lily was right. Sophie wasn't a selfish or resentful person. She didn't have a bitter bone in her body. He had always admired her for that.

"She loved you so much and she would want you to find love and be loved," Beth added. "You deserve this."

He wasn't sure he deserved Emma, her beauty, intelligence, and fire, but he wanted her close for as long as she wanted to be with him, and he hoped that would be for a very long time.

At the cottage that morning, he'd stirred in his sleep, unsure where he was until he felt her body curved into his, her breath rising and falling against his chest. They'd fallen asleep on her unmade mattress, their lips raw from kissing, their bodies spent. Her bag leaned against the wall, still packed. He'd almost lost her. If he'd waited any longer to tell her how he felt, she'd be gone. He shuddered at the thought. But she hadn't gone. He'd kissed the top of her head and ran his fingertips down her arm and clasped her fingers in his.

"Hello," he'd whispered as he pulled her even closer.

"Hello," she snuggled into him.

They'd drifted back into sleep for a while before her alarm dragged them into the morning. They'd got up slowly and showered together. He couldn't get enough of this woman. He knew her well enough to know that there was so much more to get to know about her and he was going to love doing it. He would never let her leave without a fight.

Chapter Fifty-Eight

Emma pushed the buzzer and waited. Kirsty's face appeared behind the glass pane.

"Hi."

"Mornin'" Kirsty's voice was stiff.

Emma had broken their trust, and she was willing to do whatever it took to repair it. If they'd let her. "Mason here?"

"Inside," Kirsty jerked her head.

Dave and Mason fell silent as Emma entered the newsroom. Han looked up from his laptop. Riley put her phone down.

"Left something behind?" Mason barked.

His hostility stung.

Emma addressed the room. "First, I wanted to apologize for announcing my departure so abruptly. You didn't deserve that." She took a deep breath. She felt like the burning skin of her cheeks was about to peel off. "And second, if the editor's position is still open, I'd like to reapply for it."

The team stared at her. The gurgle of coffee percolating through the filter broke the silence. If Mason said no, she was prepared to argue to bring him round. It might take time. But she would fight to be part of this team. "I made a huge mistake by quitting. I'd like to come back."

Mason's eyes glinted just like Ben's did when he was examining all angles of a story. Dave and Kirsty exchanged glances. Would they forgive her for, as Kirsty said, dumping them like a hot potato when she got a better offer? Han tipped his head, making his own calculations. After a minute, Riley piped up, "C'mon guys. Give her a break."

Emma gently smiled her appreciation at the young woman. With Riley's sales skills and appetite to make money, the paper had the glimmer of a commercial future. It could really be something.

"OK," Mason croaked.

"OK?" She wasn't sure that she'd heard correctly.

"I said OK. Here's your desk." He tapped a gnarled finger on her old spot.

Emma closed her eyes with relief. "Thank you, Mason."

She walked over and gave the old man a careful hug. He was as frail as a bird, his thin bones tied together by tough sinew.

"Easy now," he cautioned.

"Thank you," she whispered in his ear, and turned to the group. "I've been an idiot."

"Happens to the best of us, Bub." Kirsty arrived beside her and opened her arms. Emma dropped into her embrace.

Dave held out his hand, grinning. "Welcome back."

"Thank you." she said, as she shook it.

He continued without missing a beat: "I've got a lead on the Lorenzos."

"Nice. And I got an email last night from the guys at the lab. The nitrate levels in the Sharpe's Rock water samples are through the roof. They've sent them off to FEMA."

"At last!" Kirsty exclaimed. "A federal agency needs to get involved!"

The team nodded. They were back on the story.

"Did you have your morning meeting?" Emma asked.

"Nope," Mason answered.

"Shall we do it?"

As they finished updating each other, a deep sense of satisfaction swept through her. These were her guys, the only people she wanted to work with.

Mason turned to her. "I suppose now you'll be asking for a

raise?" He cocked an eyebrow. She'd missed his wry humor.

She smiled. "I mean, to be paid would be nice."

At noon, Mason stood up. "Lunch! At The Claw. On me!"

"Let's go." Kirsty grabbed her bag. "He might never offer again."

The mid-day sun pounded down as they crossed the street.

"Good afternoon, Sirens Bay's favorite news hounds," Lily greeted them. Emma smiled at her. As they walked by the bar toward their regular table, Lily caught her gaze. "So, you figured it out." A ripple of affection crossed her face. "Smart girl."

"Took me a little while." Emma flushed, sheepish about how far off track her fears had taken her. She'd been so dumb; let herself be led by her insecurities. "I've learned my lesson."

"Always communicate."

"Always communicate," Emma repeated in agreement.

Lily was wise, generous, and sincere. She was Jordan's best-buddy and Emma would never encroach on that, but she hoped they could become good friends over time. She was grateful for the chance.

While they waited for their order, Riley ribbed Han about some girl in his class. Kirsty argued with Mason about the benefits of digitizing the archive. "You need to get with the program, old man," she chided him.

He threw her a warning look.

Dave continued a call, turning away from the table with his finger stuck in one ear. The air filled with a sense of celebration, new beginnings. It was like she'd never said she was leaving.

"Ayuh, yeah, I'll be there." Dave placed his cell down.

He had Emma's attention. "What?"

"Well, I'll be damned." The conversation around the table quietened. "McDermott's been arrested. The arraignment's at two."

My source says he's planning to squeal." Dave lifted his palm and Emma smacked it with a high-five. "Yes!"

Mason banged his cane on the wooden floor. "The chicks are coming home to roost!"

"Great job, Dave!" Emma paused. "Great job team."

"If he goes for immunity, he could blow this thing wide open," Dave nodded.

Ben would be so proud of this small but powerful crew of committed local news journalists. She blinked back tears before anyone could notice.

After a rushed lunch of burgers and fries, the team dispersed, Dave to the arraignment, the others back to the office to prepare for his story. Emma sat alone at the table, taking a minute to absorb everything that had happened in the last twenty-four hours. She felt as if she'd shrugged off a heavy coat of grief that she'd been wearing for a year. It had protected her from outside elements, people, opinions, interruptions, and it was comfortable, and familiar, if a little battered, but it was also a dead weight to haul around. Without that layer, she felt lighter, a little exposed, but steady, at ease in her own skin, and dare she admit it, a little saner.

Chapter Fifty-Nine

The last of the evening sun rippled over the ocean. Sitting on the porch bench, Emma could never get bored with this view. Far in the distance, a speck of red told her that lighthouse was there, warning boats away from the rocky shoreline. The town lights twinkled, petering out into deep green forest rising toward the sky. A breeze tickled her face, wafting the scent of pine and salt over her skin. She loved this place. She dropped her head back, feeling the last of the day's warmth press on her.

Was this the life Ben wanted for her? She had a thought that maybe this was exactly his plan.

The team had wrapped her back into the fold. Dave had ferreted out an old source in Boston P.D. who ran a snitch in the Lorenzo crime family. He was going to call her in the morning. The story was gathering speed, and she was riding along with it. She let out a long breath.

Heavy tires grumbled on the gravel behind the cottage. She smiled. Familiar footsteps hit the path, and then there he was. Her whole body surged with joy at seeing him.

"Hello stranger," Jordan's voice sang out. Her heart heaved with pleasure at the sight of his smile. The handsome, artistic, adventurous man making his way up the porch steps wanted to be with her, and she wanted him. If she'd taken that flight, she'd be running around her apartment in D.C. right now, gathering her kit together, checking batteries for the satellite phone, and searching for her sunscreen. It would be just her, alone, with only her wits and experience to rely on, heading out. The thought sent a chill through her.

"Fancy meeting you here." He slid onto the bench, one arm reaching across the back of the seat.

"Well, I did text you." She kissed him on the cheek. Overnight, she'd become addicted to this man's presence.

"How did it go?"

"Great," she shook her head, still amazed at how quickly they let bygones be bygones. "I've had a really great day. Did Mason say anything on the ride home?"

"He's delighted you changed your mind, as you can probably tell." He let out a little relieved breath. "And he's now claiming that he always knew you would never abandon such a fabulous scoop."

"Of course I couldn't!" She clasped his hand and gave it a squeeze. That wasn't the only reason she'd chosen to stay.

"And I dropped by the bookshop on my way back from his place. Erik says to say hi and to tell you he's found a library in Portland who's interested in purchasing all of Ben's stuff for an archive dedicated to his work."

"Really? That is incredible news!" Such a collection would rightly honor Ben and his career. "It's what he deserves."

"It is."

"Erik is such a great guy."

"But not too great, right?" Jordan gave her a gentle nudge.

"Not as great as you." She nudged him back. His vulnerability melted something in her. "No one is."

His blue eyes stared into hers, searching. "You happy?"

No one ever asked her that question. It was not something Doug would have thought to. Their relationship was built on companionship, being mates, work, getting the job done, not deep inquiry about feelings. Neither would any of her bosses. Her editors, all of them except Ben, had only cared if she was able and up to the task. Her emotional health had not been their priority. But it was for Jordan. It took her a moment to file through her feelings and check her answer. She took his strong jaw in her hands. Her lips lingered on his before she tipped her head back so she could see his eyes.

"Yes, I am very happy." She smiled. "I love you. I love it here."

He cocked his head to one side in mock consideration of her statement. "Yes, I think I see that." He embraced her, his whole body clasping hers. "I love you too."

A bang and something smashed inside. Emma startled. Jordan stood up, motioning for her to stay seated. He slowly opened the porch screen. A bundle of brown and ginger fur flashed by.

"Tallulah?" Emma watched her race across the yard. "Did you bring her from Mason's?"

Jordan shook his head. "She must have jumped in the truck." He disappeared inside for a moment. "She got in through the bathroom window. She's knocked a glass off the sink."

"That bloody cat." Emma grinned, watching Tallulah sit on the small patch of lawn licking her fur. "She's come home, after all."

Acknowledgements

I have many people to thank for this book. It took two years to write, but it's been in the works for a very, very long time. It's the product of a lot of support and encouragement from generous friends and acquaintances, as well as input and advice from other writers.

If I know you or have met you and you've asked about my writing, thank you!

I am enormously grateful to James, who asked, "Why don't you write a romance?" Writing this book has been an absolute blast. Thank you.

Anna, your willingness to share your expertise and experience is beyond generous. It's priceless. Thank you.

To my other beta readers Loveday, Rohays, and Zoe, your feedback helped me hone the plot, fill the gaps, and add some oomph. I'm so grateful to you for the time and enthusiasm you invested in my book.

Other supporters of my work are my long-term creative collaborator Dawn, my partner in crime (not literally) Cindy, and Real Writers Circle members. I am enormously appreciative for all your feedback, your inspiration, and your unwavering conviction that I can do this.

And thank you Orly, who when I typed the first lines of fiction on my laptop more than a decade ago, reminded me that sitting down to write a novel counted as work, and not just play.

Finally, Bruce. My pal. You offer limitless support from your spot on the sofa, and you don't even mind the book stars a cat and not a dog. You're the best.

About the Author

Cassie Bruce is a British author and journalist who lives on the south coast of England.

During her journalism career, she reported business news from the Middle East for many years, having got her start as a newbie reporter in Washington, D.C.

Sirens Bay is the first book in the Sirens Bay Series and her first romance novel.

Keep in touch and join her mailing list at: www.cassiebruceauthor.com.

Milton Keynes UK
Ingram Content Group UK Ltd.
UKHW021607060824
446608UK00005BA/90

9 781738 564101